Adam Hamdy is an author and sc̲... ...ducers and studios on both sides of the Atlantic. Prior to becom...g . writer, Adam was a strategy consultant and advised global businesses operating in a wide range of industries. Adam lives in Shropshire with his wife and three children.

Follow Adam on Twitter @adamhamdy.

Praise for the *Pendulum* series:

'I read *Pendulum* in one gloriously suspenseful weekend. Definitely one of the best thrillers of the year' James Patterson

'Adam Hamdy's *Pendulum* is something new . . . kinetic, cinematic and bracingly original' Barry Forshaw, *Crime Time*

'A heart-pounding hit' *Peterborough Telegraph*

'Adam Hamdy's thriller definitely justifies its previous hype' *Vavel*

'A fabulous thriller, with a very contemporary spin . . . Excitement guaranteed' *Northern Crime* blog

'I loved *Pendulum*. I loved the characters, the way the story plays out, the interwoven threads . . . so subtle, yet so brilliant and unexpected' *Bibliophile Book Club* blog

'*Pendulum* is well worth the hype and attention' *A Thirst For Words* blog

'Adam Hamdy . . . puts you bang into the heart of the action . . . an absolute joy to read' *Love Books* blog

'Hamdy is authentic and well researched. This book hooked me like a fish on a line' *Bookaholic's Refuge* blog

By Adam Hamdy

FREEFALL

ADAM HAMDY

HEADLINE

First published in 2017 by
HEADLINE PUBLISHING GROUP

First published in paperback in 2018 by
HEADLINE PUBLISHING GROUP

3

Cataloguing in Publication Data is available from the British Library

ISBN 978 1 4722 3351 6

Typeset in Aldine 401BT by Avon DataSet Ltd, Bidford-on-Avon,
Warwickshire

Printed and bound in Great Britain by Clays Ltd, St Ives plc

MIX
Paper from
responsible sources
FSC
www.fsc.org   FSC® C104740

Headline's policy is to use papers that are natural, renewable and recyclable
products and made from wood grown in sustainable forests. The logging and
manufacturing processes are expected to conform to the environmental
regulations of the country of origin.

HEADLINE PUBLISHING GROUP
An Hachette UK Company
Carmelite House
50 Victoria Embankment
London EC4Y 0DZ

www.headline.co.uk
www.hachette.co.uk

For all the broken people who have found
the strength to carry on

PART ONE

PART ONE

1

Sylvia Greene longed to accept her fate. Knowing what was coming, she had tried to prepare herself, but all rational thought was lost to instinct as she faced death. There were no words, no conscious thought, nothing she could articulate, just an overwhelming urge to fight the noose that crushed her neck. It didn't matter that she wanted to be there, hanging at the end of the rope, that she knew it was the only way to protect her family. The darkest, most primitive regions of her mind rebelled and sent her fingers flying up, setting them to work on the thick rope. Her nails clawed at the rough fibres, and her bare legs kicked the air, desperately searching for something solid.

She could see her chair, lying on its side, beneath her flailing feet. The pain of the noose biting into her neck was unbearable, and her struggle was only adding to the misery. Her manicured nails were being shredded by the ferocity of her efforts, sending shards of agony shooting along her fingers. She tried to comfort herself with the knowledge that it would all be over soon.

Research had been her business and she'd gone into this situation armed with as much knowledge as possible. She knew she had to endure less than five minutes of suffering before her brain died. Once that happened the pain would stop. Her heart would keep beating for another fifteen minutes, but like an orchestra robbed of its conductor, would eventually lose its rhythm and cease. Then she'd grow still and cold, and the ugly business of death would begin, the rigor mortis, the decomposition. Sylvia hoped that Connor found her. Not the boys, she prayed. Not the boys. She hated to think of them seeing her dangling at the end of a rope, naked but for her underwear. Blue. Lace. She'd chosen a matching set in her favourite colour, knowing what was coming.

Sylvia wished she hadn't thought of the boys. Pictures of their faces filled her mind, and the urge to survive became unbearably strong. She saw them staring up at her as unsteady toddlers, holding her hand, their moon cheeks pushed back by broad smiles, basking in her unstinting love for them. Bigger, older, the puppy fat lost, laughing manically as the rollercoaster hurled them around Thorpe Park. Crying over a grazed knee. Arms cradling a boy lost in awe of a Star Wars film. A startled face suddenly exposed from beneath a duvet, discovered reading Harry Potter way beyond bedtime. Then, her husband Connor, watching her undress, his desire palpable, his love enduring. Sadness, smiles, fear, anger, hope and joy, rich moments, all shared together. She and Connor steering the boys through the storm of life, trying to help them chart the most favourable course. Her heart ached and tears streamed as she thought of the three of them making the rest of the journey alone, but this was the only way.

She'd known she'd cry. The scale of loss made it inevitable. She was healthy, smart, just the wrong side of forty, and she had a family she adored and a job she cherished. Everything was being cut short and it was the theft of her unlived life that saddened her most.

In the days leading to this moment, Sylvia had often found herself wondering whether it truly was inevitable. Perhaps if she'd handled things another way? If she had been a different person? If she'd sought help sooner? But there was no more to be gained from lamenting what had happened than there was from mourning her unlived future.

She wondered if this was how schizophrenics felt. Her rational mind was calm and reflective, but there was part of her that was determined to fight the inevitable. It felt feral in its angry efforts to try to breathe, to tear the rope, to lash out. Her whole body shuddered with the sheer force of this beast, while her brain registered what was happening as it might note the behaviour of a stranger, as though her death was happening to someone else.

Bright lights suddenly flared in her vision. Colours so vivid she could taste them. They exploded wherever she looked, filling her eyes with beauty. Sylvia had read about this, the last furious firing of the brain before it began to shut down. Her body writhed violently as though the primitive regions of her mind sensed they had very little time left. It was hard to see through her tears and the crackling colours, and now Sylvia had a sense of the world growing distant. Then there was a sudden pinprick of white which burned brighter than anything she'd ever seen. It grew bigger, consuming everything until her eyes saw nothing but the blazing heart of a sun.

Freefall. The reason she was dying. The unwelcome word violated her mind, burning through it, leaving nothing in its wake. Her very last thought: *Freefall.*

Sylvia's body fell still, and the primal resistance died, the instinctive and the rational uniting in emptiness as the last embers of her life were extinguished. Her heart kept beating after her body fell still. After a while it stopped and the blood began to cool in her veins.

2

The stars didn't judge him. Seated beneath the sweeping canopy of distant suns, for a moment John Wallace shed his burden in contemplation of the eternal fires that blazed in countless distant galaxies. They were unmoved by the guilt he'd carried ever since the woman he loved had died in his arms, and they, like the jagged mountains that surrounded him, would stand undiminished when Wallace and everyone who might remember him were long dead. Considering the eternal gave Wallace momentary respite, but he did not live in the endless heavens and was bound to the earth, caught in the tangle of emotions life had woven for him. Guilt dragged him back, and the majesty of his surroundings faded as he remembered that he did not deserve to be free. He pictured her distraught face looking up at him, and the looming peaks of the Hindu Kush Mountains were lost to maudlin grief.

'I miss you,' he said softly. 'I miss you so much.'

The heavy ache that had filled his chest ever since her death intensified, spreading from his heart until it pulled at his entire body, as though trying to force it to collapse from within. It was a familiar sensation, one that Wallace knew he needed. This painful burden was the only remaining connection he had to the woman he loved. He couldn't let it go.

'I thought I knew what I was doing,' he continued. 'I don't . . .'

The peace of the forest was broken by the crunch of

6

approaching footsteps, and Wallace fell silent immediately.

'*Tr'ok Si'ol.*' The boy's voice came from behind Wallace, and he turned to see Kurik, his host's youngest son, approaching, his olive complexion lit by starlight.

For all his months in Kamdesh, Wallace had been unable to learn the meaning of *Tr'ok Si'ol*, the name his host, Vosuruk, had given him. Whenever he asked, people smiled sympathetically, but would simply repeat Vosuruk's pronouncement that it was his Kom name.

'*Oasa mes I'a*,' Kurik continued as he stepped closer. '*T'ot gij'a ku t'u z'otr.*'

'English, please,' Wallace replied, having only recognised a single word; *z'otr*, which meant kinsman. He could speak passable Pashtun, and a little Arabic, but was still struggling with Kamviri, a dialect that was spoken by fewer than ten thousand people.

'Father say come.' Kurik was mildly embarrassed and hesitated over each poorly formed word.

'I don't want to intrude.' Wallace raised his hands and took a step back, but it was clear that his words and gesture were lost on the teenager. He wasn't ready to leave; his memorial had just begun.

'Come,' Kurik responded emphatically, before turning away.

Wallace took a last look at the stars and tried to imagine his love up there with them, free. But he knew that the only place she existed was in the hearts of those who'd known her. It was with some resentment that he turned to follow the boy. Wallace's nightly conversations were a way of bringing her back to life and tonight she would remain buried.

Kurik looked back and smiled when he saw Wallace had started to follow.

Wallace had spent a great deal of time in Afghanistan and still didn't fully understand the country's complex culture. Forced together as a single nation by the British, Afghanistan was in fact a patchwork of provinces whose people often had more in common with their tribal cousins in Pakistan or Tajikistan than they did with those who shared their nationality. Wallace had travelled to Nuristan because all the reports he'd heard suggested it was still riven by conflict. The Nuristani tribes that had spent hundreds of years fighting each other had banded together to resist the resurgent Taliban. Western media presented the conflict as a simplistic struggle between government forces and Islamic militants, but the fight was far more nuanced. For decades, Nuristan had been known as Kafiristan, which, roughly translated, meant Land of the Infidels, so called because the locals had long resisted conversion to Islam. Pockets of the ancient Kalash faith still flourished in Nuristan, and even Muslim converts still observed the rites and practices of their ancestors' religion. The Nuristani tribes were doing what they'd done for decades, resisting the imposition of an alien authority, be it British, Islamic, Soviet, Taliban, American or Pashtun. Right now, the Kom were engaged in a battle to prevent Taliban forces taking control of their homeland, and Wallace had chosen them because he knew they were an open people with a social hierarchy based on wealth, which meant he could buy his way in.

After some delicate negotiations in the capital which almost ran aground in misunderstanding, Wallace was smuggled out of Kabul, up the Bashgal Valley to Kamdesh, the ancestral home of the Kom. The town consisted of simple, two-roomed homes, arranged in terraces on the steep slopes. The room on the ground floor was usually a livestock stable, and goats were the most common residents due to their ability to thrive on the mountains and survive the bitterly cold winters.

Wallace offered Vosuruk, the town's magistrate, two hundred dollars a week for lodging. Vosuruk was a middle-aged landowner, who looked young for his fifty-something years. He had a warm, approachable face, but his eyes could not conceal a sharpness that helped keep the remote mountain town in order. Three wives and nine children stood testament to Vosuruk's wealth, but even a high-ranking magistrate could not turn down two hundred dollars a week in a country where the average annual salary was only double that figure.

Vosuruk partitioned the stable that took up the lower floor of his house to create a room for Wallace, where he could sleep next to the goats and horses. Vosuruk's family were fascinated by the wealthy stranger who lodged with their livestock, but Wallace wasn't interested in fostering a reputation as a curiosity. He asked Vosuruk to introduce him to local warriors fighting the Taliban. Normally Vosuruk spoke passable English, but whenever Wallace raised the subject of war he would feign sudden incomprehension. All he could ever manage was, 'O'c n'a san'oa san'i', which Wallace came to understand translated roughly as, 'I don't know any soldiers.'

Wallace understood enough Kom social custom to know that militia could not operate in the region without the blessing, and probably the assistance, of the magistrate. A bed and safety could be purchased, but he knew that Vosuruk's trust would only be gained by time. So he had spent his days getting to know Vosuruk's family and photographing them and the other towns-folk. Vosuruk had five sons and four daughters. The eldest son, Guktec, was a rugged man in his late thirties, who had two wives and five children of his own. At fourteen, Kurik was Vosuruk's youngest son, and was the child of his most recent wife, Zana, a slight, introverted woman who did not look more than thirty. Kurik had inherited his mother's wide eyes and gentle demeanour.

On his third day in the town, trailed by Kurik and some of his younger friends, Wallace had gone exploring and found a rocky outcrop deep in the cedar forest that covered the surrounding mountains. The first visit had been marred by the sniggers and giggles of his young coterie, but the following week, after the children had lost interest in him, Wallace had returned in an attempt to find a private place where he could be alone with his grief. Vosuruk had jokingly referred to the outcrop as *V'ot Tr'ok Si'ol*. Wallace had been able to discover that *V'ot* meant rock, but, since his efforts to translate his Kom name had floundered, all he knew was that the townspeople now identified the place as his and seemed to take some amusement from the fact that he would go to such lengths to find solitude.

Wallace's Rock was located fifteen minutes' walk from the edge of town, and was accessible by a difficult trail which had been cut through the thick forest for some long-forgotten reason. Now, as they pushed through the brush, Wallace began to see flickering lights dotting the mountainside, and then the sharp-edged silhouette of the town started to come into view. As he and Kurik emerged from the shelter of the trees and crested the lip of the dirt track, Wallace felt a blast of the April wind and pulled his Deerhunter jacket tight around his neck. There had been no snowfall since the week he'd arrived and the bitter weather had started to ease into summer, but the nights still offered a chill reminder of some of the desperate cold he'd felt when he first came to the town in February.

The arduous conditions didn't just demand hardy livestock, they fashioned rugged people. Living at altitude, coping with the rigors of the terrain, the Kom were slightly built, but strong and fit. It had taken three days to get Vosuruk's permission for him to use his camera, for which there had been a hundred-dollar surcharge, but in chronicling the people of the town, Wallace had not seen a single case of obesity. The mountains simply wouldn't allow it, and would sweep aside any who became unable to deal with life on their unforgiving slopes.

It had taken a month of quiet persuasion for Vosuruk to finally understand that the strange westerner did not pose a threat to his people. Wallace had shown Vosuruk photographs and accompanying articles from his previous stints in Afghanistan, and his work in Iraq, Somalia and other troubled regions around the world. He'd explained that he wanted to document the life of a people for whom war never seemed to end. Like the other tribes of Nuristan, the Kom had been fighting almost ceaselessly for more than forty years, ever since leading an uprising against the Afghan Communist Government in the seventies. Children had been born and died knowing nothing but conflict, and Wallace wanted to show the world what life was like for a people who lived with ceaseless war, where the insignia on the enemy's uniform was the only thing that ever changed.

Wallace's impassioned rationale had affected Vosuruk and finally, in early March, he and his eldest son, Guktec, had taken Wallace into 'c'er to' – the high country. Wallace hadn't ridden for years, but his confidence soon returned and he was able to avoid disgracing himself as he'd followed the expert horsemen into the mountains. With ancestors who'd resisted Islamification in the late nineteenth century, decades of tribal warfare, and almost half a century of foreign interventionist conflict, the Kom had learned how to conduct military operations in a way that minimised their impact on daily life. Wallace was not surprised when, during their ride up to the snow-capped peaks, Vosuruk had revealed that he played a key role in organising the militia and that Guktec was one of its leading lieutenants.

Wallace had been led to a *gurk'ata vo* – a large cavern – two days' ride from Kamdesh, where twenty-five warriors lived when they weren't engaged in operations against the Taliban. Vosuruk explained that his people had been instrumental in the Northern Alliance and had led the struggle against the Taliban government. They had no desire to see a return to those dark days, so now they worked within a loosely organised Nuristani force to fight the largely foreign insurgents who operated from bases in

Northern Pakistan. Some of the men spoke rudimentary English and Vosuruk translated for the rest. After overcoming their initial suspicion and reticence, Wallace had spent three days getting to know the men, who were all from Kamdesh and ranged in age from sixteen to forty-five. Winter closed many of the passes to Pakistan, limiting the opportunity for action, but with the advent of spring, all of them had been expecting to see combat very soon.

The older warriors had fought many enemies. The eldest, Malik, remembered running ammunition up to his father during the war against the Soviets. The men had spoken of friends who'd died, the enemies they'd killed, and the dishonourable '*dillik*', which Wallace gathered meant 'rats', who sold them weapons. Most of all, they had talked about their families, and the toll taken by their absence in the mountains. Living in a perpetual state of war for four decades necessitated sacrifice, and every able Kom man spent six months of the year in the high country, fighting. Service was carried out in two-month rotations so that the men could have time with their families and attend to their land and livestock. Like the British and American soldiers Wallace had known, these men missed their wives and children and longed for an end to conflict. When they finally trusted Wallace enough to let him photograph them, he'd seen that their eyes were haunted by a painful longing for something none of them could remember: peace.

Wallace had watched Vosuruk and the men consulting old maps and knew that they were preparing for an operation, but his host had refused to discuss it and said that it would be inhospitable to place his guest in danger. Wallace knew this was simply a polite way for Vosuruk to say that he still didn't trust the strange Englishman and his camera. The Kom did not have many positive experiences of westerners. The British had handed Nuristan to the Afghans, the Soviets had tried to overrun their country, and the Americans had come in anger, to avenge the deaths of thousands of innocents.

After three days and over fifty saleable photographs, Wallace and Vosuruk had returned to Kamdesh. Guktec had stayed with the fighters to begin his rotation, and, as they'd ridden back through the mountains, Vosuruk had spoken of his hopes for his children and his people. He longed for the comforts of a Western life, for education and for a time when Nuristan was no longer touched by war. Wallace listened sympathetically. He knew the pain of longing for something that was beyond reach, but had said nothing of his own dark experiences.

On their first night back in Kamdesh, Wallace had shown Vosuruk his laptop and the satellite uplink that enabled him to transmit the photographs to Getty, where they would be sold to any interested buyers. When Vosuruk saw them uploaded, and finally understood that Wallace was genuine in his desire to portray the truth of their struggle, he'd quietly assured his guest that he would soon have the opportunity to document one of their operations. Vosuruk had said no more about the subject, and, after almost four weeks of diligent patience, Wallace wondered whether his host had changed his mind.

'Pam'o gu Soa,' Kurik said, pointing at his father's brightly lit house.

Wallace smiled, guessing that Kurik's remark had something to do with the celebration that he'd purposefully tried to avoid. Vosuruk's second son, Druni, a quiet, thoughtful man in his late twenties, was taking his third wife, Arani.

The forest thinned as Wallace and Kurik reached the edge of town and the fragrant smell of cedar was replaced by the ripe scent of livestock and the aroma of food. Kurik led Wallace along the narrow track that ran up to his father's house, and, when Wallace hesitated by the door to the ground-floor stable, he insisted, 'No. Come.'

Reluctantly, Wallace followed him up the ladder that rested against the stable wall, climbing on to a balcony that was built on the roof of the adjacent house. Kurik ushered him through the open doors into the main room, which was packed with happy friends and family, dressed in their most colourful clothes, all talking excitedly about Druni and Arani and their life together. Wallace could not help but notice that Somol and Bozor, Druni's first and second wives, sat slightly apart from the rest of the group and he wondered how they felt about the union.

The wedding party stood on a huge, intricately woven coloured rug that covered most of the floor. In prime position in the centre of the room, a roasted goat was proudly displayed, surrounded by a rich banquet.

'Welcome, *Tr'ok Si'ol*,' Vosuruk boomed from across the room.

Most of his guests hadn't noticed Wallace enter and now they turned to look at the reluctant westerner. Hearty cheers rang out, echoing their host's sentiments, and Wallace shrank back slightly.

'I didn't want to intrude,' he explained.

'*T'chah!*' Vosuruk waved dismissively, as if to indicate that Wallace had been guilty of great foolishness. 'Now we can eat.' He signalled to his guests, who needed no further encouragement and set about the feast with enthusiasm. 'Camera,' Vosuruk shouted above the hubbub, and it suddenly occurred to Wallace that his attendance wasn't purely social.

'Of course.' Wallace nodded, and he hurried from the room, clambered down the ladder and opened the stable door carefully, so as not to allow any of Vosuruk's goats to escape.

Three bridled horses pulled at their tethers in an effort to nuzzle Wallace as he crossed the room, making for the small partitioned space that had been his home for over two months. He drew back a hanging drape and placed his large camera bag on the low but surprisingly comfortable straw cot, then selected the 750, which would give him better performance in low light than the D4, and opted for the 50mm f/1.4 lens. Just as he was replacing the Peli lens case in his camera bag, he heard an unfamiliar sound outside. Hurrying from the stable, he climbed the ladder to find Vosuruk and Druni standing on the balcony peering up at the sky, their faces suddenly solemn.

'What is it?' Wallace asked as his ears tried to identify the low throbbing that was growing louder with each passing moment.

Vosuruk looked at Wallace, his eyes uncharacteristically fearful, his voice alive with apprehension. 'Helicopters.'

3

They'd started burrowing the moment he'd come out of the coma, and the depressions they dug deepened every day. Physically, the bullets were long gone and scars covered the places where they'd torn into his body, but their psychological damage haunted him. Patrick Bailey wore a convincing mask of professionalism, and he doubted whether Superintendent Cross had noticed any change. His colleagues might have caught him drifting during a conversation, but it was only his family and old friends, like Salamander, who recognised the lingering effects of his shooting. His life was smaller, darker, and Bailey felt vulnerable, fearful – mortal. He'd noticed it in hospital, where he'd found himself jumping at unexpected noises and treating passing strangers with suspicion. Even after his doctor had given him the all-clear and he'd started his physical therapy, Bailey worried that they'd missed one or more of the bullet fragments – that deadly metal was lodged somewhere in his veins and would one day be dislodged to flow to his brain or heart, killing him instantly.

Once this fear had taken root, Bailey found it impossible to shake. And the ghostly bullets, like burrowing insects, kept digging into his insecure mind and throwing up new filth. A residual blood clot lingered near his lungs; the stress and strain on his heart had weakened it; the coma had changed his sinus rhythm, making him prone to stroke. As their burrows grew bigger, the parasites became stronger, adding new fears, which compounded Bailey's stress. The Met's resident psychotherapist, Jean Davis, a thoughtful woman with a dark little office off Edgware Road, tried to talk Bailey through the aftermath of trauma, and explained that anxiety would manifest itself in physical symptoms. She tried to teach him techniques to cope with his fears and Bailey smiled and pretended to learn, so that by the end of his mandated six weekly sessions, Jean would declare him fit for duty and the force would have no hint of the damage being done by the terrors conjured by his paranoid mind.

During calmer moments, Bailey told himself he was being irrational and knew that Jean was right: he was just as fit, healthy and capable as he'd been before Pendulum shot him, and his fears were unfounded. But whenever rationality threatened to take hold, the evil parasites burrowed deeper and revealed some new horror to unbalance him and push him into the grip of panic. Bailey had sacrificed so much of himself, saving John Wallace from Pendulum, and it had taken months of intense physical therapy for him to recover from the shooting. He'd been commended for his bravery, but he didn't think there was anything brave about his actions. He'd simply done what was necessary, and had paid a heavy price. His body was better, but he feared that his mind might never recover.

So Bailey spent his days pretending to be the detective he once was, wearing a smile like an ill-fitting mask, feigning competence like an actor in a TV cop show. At night he became reclusive and withdrew from those who knew him best, so that they would not question him about the changes they'd seen, and, through voicing their concerns, give his anxiety even more power. He set his intellect against his fear and tried to solve the problem, spending lonely evenings in his flat researching ways to combat anxiety. But every new fact only seemed to give the parasites greater power and each new revelation only seemed to stimulate a new fear. Finally, he realised that logic was no match for primal irrationality. He'd come close to seeing his doctor, but didn't want anxiety or mental health issues flagged on his record, so he'd resigned himself to the hope that time would heal him, and forced his way through each day trying to ignore the growing feeling that death waited for him at the end of every step.

A uniformed officer walked in front of his car and Bailey slammed on the brake. The seatbelt snapped tight as he jerked forward, and he felt his heart start to race as he realised that he'd almost run the man over. The young officer moved to the driver's window and knocked on the glass.

'Sorry, sir, the street's closed,' the officer said.

'DI Bailey,' Bailey replied, fumbling for his warrant card.

'Park anywhere on the left,' the PC instructed, stepping away to move the barricade that blocked the road.

Bailey waved his thanks as he drove on, shaken by the manner of his arrival. His efforts to combat his anxiety so consumed him that he often found himself retreating into his mind, becoming oblivious to the outside world. He relied on autopilot to keep him functioning, but now and again it was starting to fail. He would miss entire sections of the daily briefing, or set out for a location and end up somewhere else. This time his autopilot had succeeded in bringing him to the right place; Ufton Grove, a short residential street that was either in South Dalston or North Islington, depending on whether you were buying or selling one of the four-storey Georgian terrace properties. But he was unnerved that he'd nearly collided with the uniform and concerned at his inability to recall most of his journey through London's busy streets.

Bailey pulled into a space marked by police cones, behind one of the two liveried police cars that were on the scene. The forensics truck was parked directly outside number 112, an end-of-terrace located on the south-eastern corner of the street.

He turned away from the low afternoon sun slanting through the branches of the budding blossom trees, and hurried across the street, into a tiny garden. As he walked up a stone path set between patches of brushed gravel that swept like a frozen sea around a handful of pot plants, Bailey willed himself to focus. He challenged himself to rise above his anxiety and to allow his keen eye and incisive mind to truly connect with the world. A detective cut off by fear was no use to anyone.

A shabby-looking man waited for Bailey on the threshold. Greasy black curly hair fell around a lard-white, puffy face.

'DI Bailey?' the man asked as he offered his hand. 'DS Murrall. Call me Jack. Thanks for coming.'

Bailey shook Murrall's clammy hand, and wondered whether the sheen of perspiration that covered his face was a sign of nerves or ill health. Murrall's poorly fitting, cheap suit was speckled with patchy stains – he looked more like a deadbeat travelling salesman than a cop.

'Happy to help,' Bailey replied with a smile. 'What you got?'

'Upstairs,' Murrall said as he headed inside.

Bailey felt an arrhythmical thump in his chest, and fear instantly shrank the world to nothing. He paused by the front door, aware that he was incapable of doing his job until the wave of panic had subsided. His mind turned inward, studying his body for further signs of imminent death. He longed to take his pulse, but knew he was being watched.

'You OK?' Murrall asked.

'Sure. Just getting my bearings,' Bailey lied.

As suddenly as it had arrived, Bailey was through the tunnel of panic and the sensory world burst into life all around him. He became aware of his own reflection in a large, gilt-framed mirror that hung in the white hallway. *You've aged*, he thought, looking at his haunted eyes. The rest of his body hadn't markedly changed since the shooting, but he knew he was carrying a few more pounds on his previously athletic frame, and a close observer would notice that his dark skin was blemished by traces of stress-induced acne.

He followed Murrall up a narrow staircase. The thick green carpet reminded Bailey of a stately home, and the red runner, complete with brass fixings, suggested old-fashioned class combined with easy access to money. Family photographs lined the stairs. An attractive couple, both lean, both exuding confidence, smiled with two handsome young boys.

'Sylvia Greene,' Murrall noted as they climbed the first flight of stairs. 'Editor of the *London Record*.'

'I thought I recognised the name,' Bailey observed.

'Husband is Connor Greene. He's a graphic designer,' Murrall continued. 'The two boys are Hector and Joseph. They're at their cousins'.'

'The mother?' Bailey asked, studying a portrait photograph of Sylvia. He saw it now, a familiar look in her eyes that lay well concealed beneath the confident ease – a haunting.

Murrall nodded. 'She's upstairs,' he said, indicating another flight of steps.

Bailey followed the rotund detective, who was already slightly out of breath. He glanced into the family's bedrooms as they crossed the landing and saw that even the boys' were immaculately well ordered. The furniture was an eclectic mix of antiques that looked as though it had been cobbled together at numerous estate sales. Creating this casually beautiful family home had taken a great deal of careful effort. Bailey noted more silver-framed family portraits on an occasional table that stood at the foot of the next flight of stairs. He followed Murrall up to a tiny landing set in the eaves of the roof. Two doors led off the small space. Bailey sensed activity in the room that lay to the right and followed Murrall inside.

Sylvia Greene's body was hanging from an exposed rafter. A

couple of forensics officers working in their white overalls acknowledged Murrall as he and Bailey entered.

'They haven't finished,' Murrall said, 'but I wanted you to see her. See why we called you.'

Bailey noticed the similarities immediately. The rope around Sylvia Greene's neck was the same gauge as the one found in John Wallace's flat, and, like Wallace, Sylvia was in her underwear.

'Is that blood?' Bailey asked, noting deep red droplets on the green carpet.

'We think so,' Murrall answered. 'She isn't wounded, so we think she might have cut an assailant.'

'May I?' Bailey said, stepping forward.

'Sure.' Murrall nodded, and Bailey continued towards the body.

'Who found her?' Bailey asked as he studied the scene.

'The husband, Connor Greene.'

Bailey concentrated on his surroundings and tried not to think about the man's profound horror as he discovered his dead wife. A large leather-topped desk stood beneath a Velux window which was cut into the sloped roof. The desktop was neatly presented: a laptop, ordered piles of paper, more family photographs, a pot of pens and pencils – nothing looked out of place apart from the captain's chair that lay on its side directly beneath the body. Bailey drew close to Sylvia and studied her fingers, which hung at head height. Her nails were ragged and broken and had a great deal of dirt and material pressed beneath them. He looked up, and felt himself go light-headed as he gazed at death. Bodies never used to bother him, but now he had to fight the urge to run, to get as far away as possible. He forced back his fear and concentrated on Sylvia's neck, which was raw with scratch marks, where she'd tried to rip away the noose. The abrasions were bright red and her skin wasn't yet showing the blueish tinge of the long dead – the body hadn't been hanging for more than a few hours. Bailey looked beyond her lank blond hair to the rafter, where the heavy rope pressed tightly against the hard wood.

'What do you think?' Murrall asked.

Bailey hesitated, forcing himself to look directly at Sylvia Greene's face. *You're not haunted any more*, he thought darkly as he peered at her glassy, bulging eyes. 'You find a note?'

Murrall shook his head. 'This is going to be a hot one, sir. I don't know if you read the *Record*, but she really turned it around. Broke a lot of big stories. Pissed off a lot of powerful people.'

'Where's the husband?' Bailey asked.

'Downstairs with victim support,' Murrall replied.

'He said anything?'

'No. He kept it together until his sister collected the boys, but then he lost it.'

'We should see if he's ready to talk,' Bailey suggested as he headed for the door, relieved at his growing distance from grim death.

Bailey didn't answer any of Murrall's questions but instead considered what he'd seen as he followed the wheezing detective downstairs. Apart from the bloodstains on the carpet, there was nothing to suggest murder, and the beam that supported Sylvia Greene's body showed no signs of abrasion, suggesting that she had not been hoisted up there by someone else. Subject to the results of the forensic report on the blood, Bailey had been inclined to view Sylvia Greene's death as suicide, but that changed the moment he caught sight of her husband, Connor. The distraught widower was seated at a pine-topped table near the high windows of his basement kitchen, and, while there was no doubting the authenticity of his grief, Bailey saw the man glance over at him and Murrall as they entered and recognised a familiar expression, one he'd seen on the faces of countless criminals: the discomfort of deceit.

'Mr Greene?' Bailey crossed the expensive white kitchen, the heels of his shoes clicking against the hard stone tiles. 'How are you feeling?'

Connor looked at the uniformed victim liaison officer, a young constable with an earnest face, no doubt in the vain hope she could answer on his behalf. The young constable caught Bailey's eye and shook her head slowly. Connor's chin dropped and he kept his eyes fixed on the delicate natural patterns embossed on the stone beneath his feet.

'Do you think you can talk?' Bailey continued, leaning against the butcher's block that stood at the heart of the kitchen. Ignoring Murrall's concerned looks, he took off his suit jacket and rolled up his sleeves while he waited for Connor to answer. 'It's humid down here.'

Bailey tried to read Connor's eyes as the bereaved man glanced up at him: grief, anger, hostility – all the usual emotions he'd expect to see, but there was also discomfort, which manifested itself in Connor's inability to hold his gaze. Bailey crouched down and forced himself into Connor's eyeline. 'What do you think, Mr Greene?'

'We can do this later, right . . .' Murrall began, but he stopped talking when Bailey shot him a disapproving look.

'Saturday morning,' Connor began quietly. 'Saturday morning. Give the boys their breakfast, get them in their kit, take them to football. Vee came every now and again, but Saturday mornings are mine. Me and the boys. She said she was going to catch up on some work.'

Bailey watched Connor as he choked back his tears. The grieving husband looked hot and uncomfortable, perspiration clearly visible on his brow. Connor was wearing a thick woollen submariner's jumper, complete with tight roll neck. His right hand was holding his left forearm, his fingers teasing a loose strand of wool. Thick jeans and heavy boots completed the husband's outfit, clothes that might have been sensible for the touchline, but were bound to stifle in this well-insulated, hot kitchen.

'Would you like me to open a window?' Bailey asked.

Connor shook his head. 'What would you like to know?' – his voice rising, searching for a name.

'Detective Inspector Bailey. Just tell us about your day. Exactly what happened.'

The kitchen fell still. Bailey could hear Murrall's laboured breathing and the muffled sounds of distant traffic. Someone outside the house dropped something that clattered to the pavement and made Murrall jump. Bailey was studying Connor too intently to react.

'I take the boys to football practice every Saturday,' Connor began. 'Out at the Hackney Marshes. Vee, Sylvia, my wife . . . she uses the time to work. She likes the house quiet so she can concentrate. Me and the boys stop for food on the way home, McDonald's normally. She was fine when we left, maybe a little preoccupied, but she's always like that when she's got a lot on at work. When we came home . . . I . . . I found her upstairs. I tried to get her down . . .' Connor crumbled, his voice failing utterly as he recalled his efforts.

'And the blood?' Bailey pressed.

Connor took a moment to compose himself and then stared directly at Bailey, holding his gaze with unnatural intensity. 'I cut myself,' he responded flatly, rolling up the sleeve of his thick jumper to reveal a nasty gash on his left forearm. The bloody wound was still weeping.

Bailey gave Murrall a dismayed look; that was not the sort of thing he should have missed. 'We need to have that looked at, Mr Greene,' he advised, before telling the scruffy detective beside him, 'See if you can get someone in here.'

Murrall nodded at the victim support officer, who quickly left the room, and Bailey turned back to Connor. 'How did you cut yourself, Mr Greene?' he continued.

Connor didn't answer, but instead looked sheepishly at the floor.

'Mr Greene, what did you cut yourself on?' Bailey insisted, and the atmosphere changed.

'The chair,' Connor responded at last. 'I caught myself on the mechanism when I tried to lift my wife down.'

Bailey looked to Murrall for confirmation, and the pale detective shook his head emphatically.

'There was no blood on the chair, Mr Greene,' Bailey countered. 'How did you cut yourself?'

Connor was unresponsive, his attention held by the patterns on the floor tiles.

'People go into shock in these situations, do strange things, things they might struggle to remember,' Bailey added. 'You need to tell us how you cut yourself, Mr Greene.'

Connor's mouth twisted into a half-smile as he shook his head. 'Why would I call the police?'

Exasperated, Bailey turned to Murrall. 'I think we're going to have to continue this at the station,' he said. 'Once we've got his arm seen to.'

Connor's smile fell away and he stared past Bailey, towards some distant point far beyond the walls of the kitchen. 'Why would I call the police if I'd had anything to do with my wife's death, Detective Inspector Bailey?'

4

The first gunshots echoed around the valley and Wallace looked down the mountainside to see flashes of fire erupting in the darkness. He heard distant cries, followed by urgent shouts, and peered into the night to see silhouetted figures running up the valley, holding long-barrelled weapons that sprayed death. He knew he should have been afraid, but life's calluses had robbed him of the sense to be scared.

'Afghan Army,' Vosuruk announced urgently. '*Satr'ama*, Druni,' he said, turning to his shocked son. '*S'u pre le'ea moc h' u-kum bu kal' a ku*. I send him to wake people. They must escape,' he explained to Wallace.

Druni nodded, then ran to the edge of the balcony and slid down the ladder. Wallace heard him shouting, '*Kal' a ku*,' as he sprinted down the street banging on doors. Within moments the cry had been taken up by countless voices around the town.

Arani, Druni's beautiful young wife, stepped on to the balcony, thoughts of her wedding celebrations killed by gunfire. '*T'ot*, Vosuruk?' she asked hesitantly. Wallace could see the rest of the family crowded around her, eager to learn the cause of the commotion.

'*San'oa s'ea dor in'rama zan'or!*' Vosuruk commanded as he stared out at the gunfire that was drawing ever closer. 'We must all go to the mountains.'

Arani and the rest of the family immediately withdrew, and

there was hurried chatter as some of them rushed to gather their belongings, while others simply fled the building. The sound of the approaching helicopters grew louder, and, as Wallace saw the first dark shadow crest a distant ridge, the valley below them crackled with gunfire. This time Wallace could see the tracers blazing downhill.

'My men will hold them,' Vosuruk told him. 'They made a bad mistake. The helicopters should have come first.'

Wallace was not about to argue with the veteran of so many wars. He watched bursts of light illuminate the valley below as fire spat in both directions.

'*In'rama zan'or!*' Vosuruk yelled and his cry was echoed by other voices. 'We must run to the high country,' he told Wallace. 'Take only what you can carry. Go!'

Wallace looked inside the house and saw that Vosuruk's immediate family had almost finished preparing their packs. He ran for the ladder. As he stepped on the first rung, he saw a spark of flame shoot across the sky. Moments later there was a massive explosion where it hit the earth. The sound of distant screams froze Wallace's blood; he was sure he heard a child's voice. More fire from the sky as the approaching helicopters rained missiles on Kamdesh, concentrating their fury on any pocket of resistance.

'Go!' Vosuruk commanded.

Wallace slid down the ladder, landing on the hard dirt with a thud. He scrambled into the stable, where he found Kurik preparing the horses. Outside, the valley was alive with the sound of battle. Explosions shook the building and the rattle of automatic gunfire had become incessant, as had the cries of the townspeople. Wallace hurried into his quarters and grabbed his camera bag. He thought about taking his other backpack, which contained clothes and medical supplies, but had no idea where they were going or how long they'd need to travel, so decided against the extra weight.

'*Tr'ok Si'ol!*' Kurik shouted.

Wallace slung his camera bag over his shoulders, pulled back the drape and stepped into the stable where Vosuruk's youngest stood holding the reins of all three horses. Vosuruk entered, clasping an AK-47.

'We must go!' he said urgently.

Kurik handed Wallace the reins of a white gelding, before mounting a tan mare. Vosuruk jumped on to the grey and dug his heels into the horse's body, spurring it forward. Wallace struggled to stay in his saddle as his horse galloped after Vosuruk and Kurik, and he felt his heavy camera bag accentuating the effect of every twist and turn, threatening to throw his balance, as the horses bolted up the mountain along the narrow, winding streets of Kamdesh. Bullets sliced the air and clouds of dust burst all around them as the slugs studded the mud-walled buildings.

A piercing whistle cut through the sky above them, and Vosuruk suddenly turned his horse, shouting, 'This way!'

Kurik and Wallace followed Vosuruk along a narrow alleyway, as a missile hit a house further up the mountain. Black night was banished by a powerful explosion. The force of the blast threw Wallace against his horse's neck, and he felt his forearm scream with pain as he clasped the reins and willed himself not to fall. He righted himself, and, as the horse thundered on, he caught sight of figures lit by the burning building to his rear. Men, women and children fleeing their homes, running for the safety of the surrounding forest, as those able to fight tried to repel the highly organised invaders.

A light flared further up the mountain and Wallace saw fire streak into the sky. The deadly flame headed directly towards the nearest helicopter, its heavy silhouette looming in the heavens like a fearsome god. The pilot must have registered the threat, but acted too late, and the surface-to-air missile hit the belly of the chopper as it tried to bank away. Wallace turned from the blast and saw Kurik and Vosuruk riding on to a dirt track that led towards the thick forest above Kamdesh. He looked back at the helicopter, which burned brightly as it fell to earth, and saw that the valley was being torn apart. Afghan soldiers pressed through the town, exchanging fire with outnumbered locals, while the remaining helicopters targeted the surface-to-air launcher. Missiles streaked through the sky and destroyed a collection of houses on the upper slopes. The force of the blasts threw Wallace sideways, and he felt the heat of the explosions as he tumbled out of his saddle and hit the ground hard enough to knock the wind from his lungs.

Dazed, he tried to get to his feet but stumbled and fell forward. His rebellious legs no longer obeyed his commands, and he looked around anxiously, acutely aware that he was alone. There was no sign of Vosuruk, Kurik or his horse. The ground shook with the force of another explosion, and bullets hit the walls of nearby buildings. The treeline was no more than a hundred yards away, but Wallace doubted his legs would carry him to the nearest building, let alone the safety of the forest. Further down the street, which flanked the eastern edge of town, he saw the first Afghan soldiers approaching. There were two of them, and they were working cover-and-clear as they made their way up the mountain, one sweeping the abandoned homes, while the other ran ahead and took position to give cover for the move to the next building. They saw Wallace at roughly the same time and exchanged urgent looks, before breaking into a run.

The nearest man spoke urgently into his radio. '*Sahib, mung laral paida el-khareji.*' He trained his gun on Wallace. '*Khateez sarak, mujawar el-zanggal.*'

Wallace recognised the Pashto words for foreigner, east and road. They were radioing their location and telling someone that they had found the foreigner. Something about the way they phrased the word bothered Wallace, but his thoughts were interrupted by the painfully loud rattle of gunfire. Both soldiers fell dead, yards from where he lay. Wallace looked up the mountain and saw Vosuruk holding his weathered AK-47. Behind him, Kurik rode down the track, clasping the reins of Vosuruk's grey and Wallace's own white horse.

'Thank you,' Wallace said as Vosuruk approached, but his host didn't stop and instead ran past him towards the fallen soldiers.

Kurik gave Wallace the reins of his horse. As he hoisted himself into the saddle, Wallace looked round to see Vosuruk concealing something beneath the nearest soldier.

'Hurry! Quick!' Vosuruk yelled urgently, as he ran back towards his horse.

Kurik spurred his mount towards the treeline and Wallace's white gelding needed no further encouragement, following at speed, while Vosuruk brought up the rear. Wallace heard barked commands as they raced towards the safety of the dark trees. He looked over his shoulder to see more soldiers come into view, their muzzles flashing as they opened fire. Bullets whipped around Wallace, and he gripped the reins tightly and clamped his thighs around his galloping horse. He looked back and saw a soldier approach one of the men Vosuruk had shot. As the man checked his fallen comrade, a massive explosion tore him apart and set the street aflame; Vosuruk's booby trap threw the detachment into chaos, as those not caught in the blast sought to extinguish their screaming, burning companions. Wallace glanced at Vosuruk, and the grizzled veteran smiled sourly as they crossed the treeline and rode into the cold embrace of the dark forest.

5

Christine Ash shifted position in a vain attempt to make the tiny stool more comfortable. The atmosphere in the van had moved from close to oppressive and she was aware that she was covered in nervous perspiration. Her colleague, Deon Reeves, a slim black man, was also glistening. He was so tall that he couldn't really sit on his stool; it looked more like he'd been folded up and precariously balanced on top. He watched the bank of monitors, his eyes darting from one to the other with the intense diligence that Ash had come to expect of him. A New Year promotion to Senior Special Agent had put Ash in charge of the team investigating a serial killer known as Babylon. Profiling had pegged him as an intelligent white male, possibly a professional, almost certainly college educated, with a deep-rooted but warped belief in one of the Abrahamic faiths. The moniker, Babylon, had come from a series of emails sent to the *New York Post* shortly after each murder. The correspondence provided rambling justifications, and details of the killings that only the murderer would know. Inspired by Pendulum, Babylon said he had made it his mission to rid the world of those who were helping the evils of technology overrun society. Like the unholy tower that was destroyed by God, Babylon would tear down the evil edifice that was technology, and return humanity to a simpler way of living. He had murdered Tim Smith, a systems programmer at a small app development company; Robert

31

Cornish, an account manager who worked at Dell; Sally Lonner, a website developer; Molineaux Lund, a YouTube technology reviewer; and Andie Fong, a Wall Street fund manager who specialised in technology stocks. Babylon's chosen method of murder, beheading, had the tabloids in a frenzy. What the media didn't know was that the Bureau was struggling to identify the murder weapon. The victims were decapitated by something that cauterised the massive wound, removing the head with minimal blood loss.

Babylon claimed to have been inspired by Pendulum, but he lacked the same level of sophistication, and once they'd been made aware of the *Post* correspondence, Ash had tasked Reeves with tracing the source of the emails. She found it ironic that someone on an anti-tech crusade would use email to boast about his crimes, but she knew from bitter experience that most righteous zealots were terrible hypocrites.

Working with the Bureau's cybercrime team who were able to circumvent the proxy servers Babylon used, Reeves had traced all the emails to Network Connections, an internet café in a Brooklyn mini-mall. Babylon usually sent them within forty-eight hours of a murder, always between midday and two p.m., and the manager of Network Connections, Jeff Sandos, an overworked middle-aged man who looked like he didn't see enough daylight, said there was a guy who might fit the profile who came in every couple of weeks or so.

Andie Fong's girlfriend had found her body at nine the previous evening, and forensics estimated she'd been dead for no more than two hours, so Ash had assembled the team and ordered a stake-out. She and Reeves were in the van with monitors that were hooked up to five remote cameras watching the entrance to the mini-mall, the parking lot, the interior of the internet café, the main entrance and the emergency exit.

Parker was inside the café. 'Because you look the nerdiest,'

Ash had joked, adding, 'and because you get to make the arrest,' in an effort to mollify his ego.

Miller and Price were posing as employees of Bull Burger, a fast-food joint opposite Network Connections that garishly proclaimed it was the home of Brooklyn's best quarter pounder. Miller was a tough, stocky agent, three years out of Quantico, and reminded Ash of a wild boar, someone who'd incessantly sniff around a case and charge down any trouble. Price was right at home in Bull Burger, joking with the staff and customers. Four years from the Academy, Price had an effervescent personality and a broad smile that could charm snakes.

The last member of the team, Valentina Romero, sat in a beat-up Sebring in the mini-mall parking lot, playing the part of a homeless person living in her car. The tragedy was the car actually belonged to Romero, as did all the personal possessions piled on the back seat, which she'd hurriedly collected from home. Ash got the impression that Romero modelled herself on Al Pacino's Serpico, grunting through life with anti-establishment belligerence. She seemed far more comfortable in army surplus and heavy boots than she did in the Bureau's standard business casual. Most in Federal Plaza viewed her as an oddball, but Ash knew Romero was a diligent, dedicated agent.

The mini-mall was located on the corner of Linden and Rockaway, a couple of blocks from Brookdale Hospital. It was a squat complex of buildings arranged around the north, east and west sides of a small parking lot. Potash red, the low structure was covered by years of ground-in pollution and was home to an assortment of struggling independent businesses – a dry cleaner, a mailbox provider, a nail salon – places that survived on the margins.

'You should get some sleep,' Reeves advised, as Ash rubbed her eyes.

'I'm OK,' she replied, forcing herself to sit upright. They'd been in the van since midnight, and it was now approaching noon. Apart from a couple of bathroom breaks and a short period when she thought she'd fallen asleep, Ash had spent the night staring at the screens, watching the comings and goings of a handful of people who still needed access to a public computer. The remote camera inside Network Connections showed Parker sizing up every new entrant before returning his attention to his computer, one of a dozen arranged in rows on either side of the café.

The stake-out wasn't the real reason for Ash's tiredness. She'd been pushing herself too hard, leading the Babylon investigation for the Bureau while spending every free moment trying to tie up the Pendulum case. As far as the world was concerned, the killer had been caught, but despite SAIC Harrell's concerted efforts to convince her otherwise, Ash was certain at least one other person had been involved and she was determined to prove it.

Ash wasn't the only one struggling with the aftermath of the Pendulum killings. The death of so many innocent victims had generated real anger and there was a growing consensus that people should be prevented from exploiting the anonymity afforded by the internet. The older generation, people who remembered a time before technology connected every home to a world of potentially dangerous strangers, was particularly vocal in demanding some sort of protection, and it looked as though lawmakers were finally responding to their call. Two senators, Joe Castillo, a sharp Republican from Florida, and Polly Blake, an Arizona Democrat, had tabled the Blake-Castillo Bill, otherwise known as the International Online Security Act, which they claimed would reshape the internet. Among a number of other changes, the bill would end anonymity through the issuance of biometric digital passports. Officially, the Bureau supported the bill, but Ash had reservations, viewing it as a knee-jerk reaction to a deranged killer.

The Bureau had embarked on a massive investment pro-gramme to bolster its capabilities to deal with cyber-threats and had adapted its profiling to take account of the potentially random connections the digital world could facilitate between victims and criminals. But for all the money and resources being thrown at ensuring a future Pendulum would be caught, Ash couldn't help but resent the fact that no one believed her testimony that someone had been helping the killer, and she was angry that she was being forced to build a case alone.

Despite this, Ash considered herself luckier than John Wallace. He'd retreated to Afghanistan, claiming to be on a mission to remind the world of the plight of the Afghan people. But Ash knew the truth; he was out there chasing death. He'd been unable to come to terms with his role in the Pendulum killings and Ash could sense him almost drowning in the deep guilt he felt.

They'd spoken a couple of times since he'd left New York, and exchanged a handful of emails. Ash had used each communication to try to convince Wallace not to return to Afghanistan, but to find some other way of doing something meaningful with his life. She even offered to help him get work in New York, but Wallace hadn't listened, and eventually their communication had become more sporadic, as if he was trying to avoid her. Even though he was in some godforsaken part of the world, Ash knew he still had access to the Web because a Google Alert had informed her that he'd uploaded new photographs to Getty, pictures of Afghan fighters in the Hindu Kush Mountains. Haunted consciences were writ large on the craggy faces of the hardy warriors, and Ash wondered whether they and Wallace had bonded over their common experiences of grief. She had emailed Wallace a short note of congratulations when she'd seen the pictures, but had not received a reply. She knew there was every possibility that she'd wake up one day and see a Google Alert drawing her attention to Wallace's short obituary in a photography magazine. Whenever she had such dark imaginings, she regretted not telling him the real reason she didn't want him to go to Afghanistan: she missed him. Forced together for a few frantic weeks, Wallace had been closer to Ash than she'd allowed anyone since she was a child in California, and his absence had made her much more aware of the lonely, detached life she'd created to protect herself.

When they'd first met, Ash had thought Wallace a vulnerable child who needed to be protected, but their ordeal had demonstrated how resilient he was. He'd overcome the confines of his lesser self to save her life, and for that Ash owed him a profound debt. He'd come into her life seeking nothing more than protection and had trusted no one but her to give it to him. Despite herself, Ash had responded in kind, and the damaged Englishman had become the closest thing she'd ever had to a true friend. She recalled how Wallace had looked at her in the motel room they'd shared, and wondered whether his feelings had run deeper.

'That's him,' she said suddenly, indicating a man walking across the parking lot.

She and Reeves peered at the screen, which showed an overweight Caucasian male with cropped black hair heading towards the café. He wore jeans and a cream sweater and had a black backpack slung over his shoulder. The guy cast the occasional glance around the parking lot, but Ash saw no evidence of nerves; he was like a bobcat checking its surroundings for other predators. The interior camera showed five people: Parker; Jeff, the bored café manager; a young mother with a toddler asleep in a buggy; and an old guy who sat at one of the terminals with a thick sheaf of papers and an expression of constant annoyance.

Ash spoke into her lapel mic. 'I think this is our man. I want everyone sharp.'

On screen, she saw Parker shift in his seat as the target entered the café.

'Over here?' the man asked Jeff, pointing at one of the available computers. Ash noted that it was in the far corner, away from the other customers. Jeff nodded, and the target settled into a cheap plastic chair opposite the machine. Ash guessed he was about six-one and well over a couple of hundred pounds.

She checked an iPad which displayed a mirror of the *Post*'s news desk email account, and waited. She watched the target's chubby fingers dance around the keyboard. Then they suddenly stopped and the man looked over his shoulder towards the counter and caught Parker watching him.

'Hey, dude,' the target said, getting to his feet. 'I forgot to pay.'

'He knows something's wrong,' Ash said.

'You always ask me to pay before I use a machine,' the heavy man said, indicating a notice hanging next to the counter which read 'All time to be paid for in advance'. 'It's policy. It says so right there.'

Ash saw Jeff choke with nervous tension. His mouth opened and closed repeatedly, making him look like a suffocating fish. He glanced at Parker, who was watching the exchange, and finally said, 'You're right. Boy, did I have a late night.'

'He's reaching,' Ash told her team as the target put his hand inside his backpack. 'Everybody move!'

She saw Parker draw his pistol as he got to his feet, but he wasn't fast enough.

'Sit down!' the target yelled, smacking Parker across the face with a heavy revolver – it looked like an old .357.

Parker fell back, unconscious, and the killer reached down and picked up his gun.

'Come on,' Reeves cried, opening the rear doors and jumping out of the vehicle. Ash rushed after him, adrenalin surging with the sudden shift from stake-out to crisis.

She ran across the parking lot and crouched over the hood of a blue Ford, her Glock trained on the glass-panelled door. The target had acted quickly, locking the front door to prevent Miller and Price from entering. He'd pulled the slatted window blinds, leaving the door as the only way to see into the café.

Realising they weren't going to be able to storm the building, Reeves returned to the surveillance van to inform command of the hostage situation, and to relay information on what was happening inside. It seemed the target didn't know about their cameras. Miller and Price had taken up positions either side of the café, and Romero was stationed by the emergency exit at the rear of the building. Ash could see Parker's legs through the door, and caught intermittent glimpses of the other hostages' limbs, but the killer was very careful not to expose himself and stayed behind the protective cover of the blinds.

They were now facing a hostage situation and Ash knew that she'd quickly lose control to the Bureau's negotiator and NYPD SWAT, who were on their way. Reeves had told her the target had attached devices to the hostages' necks, and she'd asked him to instruct local PD to establish a blast cordon when they arrived, even though she harboured a dark fear that the devices were not explosives, but something far more terrifying.

She finally saw the devices Reeves had been talking about when the mother approached and unlocked the door. A taut black wire ran around the woman's neck, pressing tight against her windpipe. The woman looked behind her, and then pulled the door open.

'He's gone!' she shouted.

Ash was surprised that the suspect had given up the advantage of hostages.

'I've got movement at the fire exit,' Reeves said, as Ash ran towards the café. 'He's trying to escape through the back.'

'Copy that,' Romero replied. 'Freeze!' Ash heard Romero's

shout over the roof of the building, a millisecond before the radio transmitted it into her ear, creating a strange echo effect.

Two gunshots rang out, and Romero exhaled violently as the wind was knocked from her.

'Romero's hit, she's down,' Reeves said urgently. 'Target's running.'

Ash spoke into her lapel. 'Get after him!' She turned to Miller and Price, who'd taken up position by the door. 'Go with him.'

Miller and Price nodded and set off towards the rear of the building at a sprint, while Ash entered the darkened café. Behind her she heard the sound of the van's engine roaring to life and the squeal of tyres as Reeves accelerated away from the parking lot.

Parker was on his feet but looked unsteady and was bleeding from a long gash across his face. The mother was checking her child, who had managed to sleep through the incident, and Jeff was helping the old guy to his feet. Ash approached Parker, whose hands were bound by a cable tie.

'I screwed up,' Parker said apologetically. 'I'm sorry.'

Ash froze as she noticed a device attached to the wire at the back of his neck: a black box about four inches square and two inches thick. The wire ran through two eyelets and vanished into the device's innards. The only visible marking on the box was an LED, which had just illuminated.

'Ash,' Parker cried nervously, drawing her attention to the other hostages.

She saw red lights on the devices that were fixed to the back of their necks. She could hear a whirring coming from all four of them, and noticed that the black wire was starting to change colour as it dug into Parker's neck.

'It's hot,' Parker said as he tried to pull at the wire, which was getting tighter and tighter.

The mother cried out in pain, and the old man yelped, as the wires bit into their necks.

'Get it off me, get it off me!' Jeff shouted.

'Reeves, Price, Miller, I need you back here now!' Ash said into her radio as she cast around the café for something that could help.

'You want us to abandon pursuit?' Reeves asked incredulously.

'Yes, get back here,' Ash responded urgently.

'I don't want to die,' Parker croaked as the wire started to glow red with heat. It had dug so deep that it was almost lost between two massy folds of flesh. 'Help me.'

Ash tried not to think about the victims she'd seen killed by this man, their heads separated from their bodies, but, confronted with four people about to die, she could not avoid imagining the trauma of their deaths, trauma that was now being played out in front of her. The old man was struggling to breathe and collapsed to the floor. Ash knew it would not be long before the wires started slicing through their necks.

'I'm going to try something,' she told Parker, and she raised her pistol as she approached him. The thin cable looked tough enough to resist anything but wire cutters, so her only hope was to go for the mechanism. 'Cover your ears.'

Parker did not have the strength to comply, and he fell to his knees as the first blood started to flow. Ash pressed the barrel of her gun against the device on the back of his neck and pulled the trigger. Whatever was in the box was under high tension, and the device burst open with a mini explosion that sent tiny pieces of razor-sharp shrapnel searing into Ash's arm. But she didn't care; the wire around Parker's neck stopped contracting and cut no further. Elation quickly turned to horror as she noticed a shard of plastic embedded deep in Parker's neck. Blood started to ooze around it in steady, rhythmic pulses and Ash knew that the shrapnel had hit an artery.

'I don't . . .' Parker managed before passing out.

The other hostages were struggling to breathe as the devices tightened around their necks, and Ash felt rising panic; she knew that she'd have to risk causing similar injury in order to save them. As she moved across the room, she saw Miller and Price enter.

'Get an ambulance,' she cried.

Miller radioed for assistance as he and Price hurried over. Ash could hear the sound of sirens approaching – local police department.

'Help him,' she commanded, indicating Parker. 'But be careful, I think it's hit an artery.' She moved to the young mother, praying this bullet would chart a better course as she held her pistol against the device and squeezed the trigger.

6

Wallace feared the thunderous pounding of hooves would betray their location. His white gelding bucked and twisted as it galloped through the forest, chasing the other horses. He clung to the reins and rode low, close to the neck, to avoid being unseated by stray branches. He could hear the horse snorting and panting, and felt its muscles straining as fragrant cedar trees flashed past. High above them a helicopter purred, a tiny tell-tale green light indicating that someone was using night-vision goggles to scour the landscape. Vosuruk spurred his horse forward, urging them on with a cry, claiming there was safe haven less than a mile away, and so Wallace and Kurik pursued the Kom magistrate through the forest, pressing their horses, desperately hoping they would not be spotted.

Wallace caught sight of a solid shadow through the blur of trees. Lying ahead of them, slightly to their left, he could make out the jagged edges of a rock formation protruding from the mountainside. Vosuruk threaded his horse between the trees and pulled up within feet of the base of the rocks. He leapt out of the saddle and took his grey forward at a run. Kurik followed, but Wallace stumbled when he dismounted and realised that his whole body was trembling. He held the reins to stop himself falling, and forced himself up the rocks in pursuit of Vosuruk.

'Come on,' his host urged, looking nervously towards the chopper, which was sweeping the forest in their direction.

Wallace pulled his horse into a narrow gap between two high rocks and followed Kurik along the damp earth that covered the bottom of the ravine. Looking back towards the approaching helicopter, he felt a momentary stab of panic when the luminescent green pointed directly towards him. He redoubled his efforts, moving even faster, but when he turned his attention to the ravine, he was dismayed to find it empty; Vosuruk and Kurik were nowhere to be seen. He looked back at the insectile silhouette of the helicopter, which was coming directly towards him.

'In here,' Vosuruk commanded.

Wallace felt someone tug the other side of his horse's bridle, and he and the creature were pulled into the darkness of a shallow cave. Kurik was pressed against the back wall, holding the other mounts, and Vosuruk led the white gelding towards them. The excited horses pawed the soft ground and snorted steaming breath into the cold air. Wallace, Kurik and Vosuruk exchanged nervous glances as the sound of the helicopter pulsed around the ravine and thrummed off the walls. The vibrations were so powerful that Wallace was convinced the huge machine had landed on the rocks above them, but after a few agonising moments, the noise diminished and the machine buzzed on. No one said anything until the sound of its engines had died away completely.

'It's gone,' Vosuruk said finally, before turning to Kurik and speaking in rapid-fire Kamviri.

Wallace slumped to the floor and leaned against the moist cave wall. His body was signalling pain, but he was too pumped with adrenalin to notice. The fall from his horse and the chase through the forest would take their toll, but Wallace wasn't interested in his injuries; he was fixated on the fact that, right before Vosuruk shot them, the Afghan soldiers had referred to him as 'the' foreigner, as though they knew him.

'What just happened?' he asked, interrupting Vosuruk.

'I don't know,' his host replied. He crouched beside Wallace. 'The Kabul government does not like us, but we have not had this trouble for many years. I do not know what made them come. They hate Taliban like we do, they know we fight the enemy.'

Wallace considered Vosuruk's response, wondering whether to share the nagging suspicion that he'd been the target of the operation. When he strung the thought together, he was instantly struck by how much Pendulum had changed him: he'd become intensely paranoid. In a region noted for its violent sectarian conflict, would the Afghan Army really mount a major operation against an entire town in order to capture a single westerner? Much more plausible was the idea that he'd misunderstood what the soldier had said. He looked at Vosuruk. 'What now?'

'We had this before, many years ago. We know what to do. The women, the children, the old people, they take the mountain to Pakistan. Stay with our people on the other side of the border until it is safe to return,' Vosuruk explained. 'The men, we go to the high place, with Guktec and the others. We find out why Kabul did this, and if they want war, we give it.'

'And your family?' Wallace asked.

'My wives go to Pakistan with daughters. The men will find us in the mountain.'

'And Kurik?' Wallace nodded towards the young man who seemed to be sulking by the horses.

'I tell him to go with the women. Help keep them safe, but he thinks he is a man,' Vosuruk said with a wry smile. 'He wants to die. Like you.'

Wallace froze, unsure how to respond.

'I see many men fight. Seen them afraid, angry,' Vosuruk continued. 'When those soldiers come, your face show nothing. You not afraid to die. Maybe you want it?'

Wallace shook his head, but found himself wondering why he hadn't got up to run, why he hadn't called for help.

'You come with us, it's possible the mountains they give you what you want,' Vosuruk added darkly.

Wallace tried to read the Kom elder, but the darkness meant he could only see the shadows of the man's eyes.

'You go to Kabul. Go home,' Vosuruk suggested. 'We are not your people. This is not your war.'

'The world needs to know what's happening here,' Wallace argued. 'I want to help stop it.'

'You are both crazy people.' Vosuruk gestured dismissively at Wallace and Kurik.

The boy replied with a rapid volley of Kamviri.

'He says he's only as crazy as his father,' Vosuruk translated.

Wallace smiled and nodded. The motion triggered a stab of pain that shot up his back into the base of his neck, forcing a wince.

'You are hurt?' Vosuruk asked.

'I'm OK,' Wallace lied. 'Just the fall.'

'You stand,' Vosuruk instructed. 'Hurt man no good in mountains.'

Wallace realised the adrenalin had dissipated as he tried to stand. His legs resisted his commands, seeming to ache all over, and his back added its own sharp signals. He couldn't stop himself from groaning, and Vosuruk sighed with disapproval. Wallace forced himself to walk a few paces, and the pain eased off slightly.

'I'm OK. It's just a few knocks,' he reassured his host.

'You stubborn man,' Vosuruk told him. 'But Kom are stubborn people. The mountains make us that way. Come here.'

Vosuruk rummaged beneath his budzun cloak, and, as Wallace lowered himself into a seated position with a suppressed moan, produced a small, foil-wrapped package. Wallace rested his head against the cave wall and watched Vosuruk unwrap the foil to reveal a dark lump a couple of inches long. His host produced a short hunting knife and cut a slice off the lump and handed it to him. Wallace looked at the sliver of clammy matter.

'What is it?' he asked, but he had already made a guess.

'*Janat p'is*,' Vosuruk replied. 'It take away pain. Make you feel good. Just eat.'

Wallace sensed pain swelling all over his body as he considered what was undoubtedly an opiate. He watched Vosuruk cut two slices off the lump and hand one to Kurik, before popping the other in his mouth.

'Good for sleeping,' Vosuruk explained.

Unwilling to return to Kabul, Wallace knew that whatever lay ahead would be arduous enough without the added burden of pain-induced sleepless nights, so he popped his slice into his mouth. The soft substance reminded him of jelly, but any similarities ended there as his taste buds recoiled and his mouth puckered at the bitterness that followed.

'Don't chew, swallow,' Vosuruk advised, and Wallace hurriedly complied. 'Crazy,' Vosuruk added with a chuckle.

Wallace watched Vosuruk and Kurik unroll their packs and prepare makeshift cots, aware that a gentle warmth was slowly infusing his body and that he was becoming mesmerised by the intricacy of movement, the gentle beauty of limbs spurred to action by directed thought. *Man, I'm high*, he thought as he rolled into the cot Vosuruk had prepared for him.

'Thanks,' he said, covering himself with the softest, warmest blanket he'd ever felt, but his host and saviour didn't reply, and instead looked blankly back.

Wallace laid his head against something soft and closed his eyes. He could hear the sound of water dripping somewhere in the cave, the impact of each chiming drop magnified by the sensory effects of the bitter jelly, until they sounded like crashing waves. He imagined himself lying on a tropical beach, the domed night sky glittering above him. A soft hand reached out and touched his arm and he turned to see Connie smiling down at him. A lump formed in his throat, some small part of him aware that he was lost in a drug-induced hallucination, the sweetness of the moment mixed with bitter sadness that it wasn't real. He took Connie's hand and she leaned her head on his shoulder, pressing so close that he could smell her sweet fragrance. He lay frozen, unwilling to say or do anything that might shatter the beautiful illusion. He fought the heavy draw of sleep for as long as he could, desperate to cling to this happy moment, but in the end he succumbed and his eyes closed, rolling him into soft, colourful dreams of what might have been.

7

Interview Room C smelled of disinfectant, but other odours lurked beneath the institutional cleanliness: musty decay, acrid urine and a hint of vomit. Bailey sat opposite Connor Greene, whose arm had been bandaged by a paramedic at his house. He'd removed his thick submariner's jumper and wore a formal blue shirt that was rolled up at the elbows, the left sleeve marbled with drying blood. Connor had declined Bailey's offer to call a solicitor and looked impatiently from Bailey to Murrall, who sat on the neighbouring cracked plastic chair.

Bailey pressed the record button and saw the red indicator light illuminate, signalling that their exchange was now being documented. He stated their names and the date, and noted that this was a taped interview agreed to by Connor Greene, who had declined the offer of counsel.

'You worked the Pendulum case, didn't you?' Connor asked before Bailey could say anything else. 'I recognise your name. Vee wrote a big piece on it.'

Bailey nodded. 'Mr Greene, could you—'

'That's why you're here,' Connor interrupted. 'Someone might have murdered Sylvia.' He eyed Murrall with an intensity that bordered on aggression. 'If the world wasn't so fucked up, we could all do the right thing, but . . .' Connor trailed off, his eyes drifting away from the detectives.

'What would the right thing be?' Bailey asked.

'You did the right thing, didn't you, Detective Bailey? My wife's a . . . was a journalist, it was all she talked about last summer. If you hadn't believed that guy, Wallace, well . . .' Connor drifted for a moment, before suddenly asking, 'What made you believe him?'

Bailey looked at Murrall uncomfortably; they'd barely started and he'd already lost control of the interview. 'Mr Greene, we're not here to talk about me. We need to find out what happened to your wife.'

'You and my wife are connected, Detective,' Connor countered. 'She told me to find someone I could trust. How can I trust you, without first knowing you?'

'When did she tell you this, Mr Greene?' Bailey tried.

'What made you believe him?' Connor repeated.

Bailey sat back, exasperated. He'd seen grief make people behave strangely, but this wasn't random distress. Connor Greene's erratic behaviour had a sense of method. He was weaving around, which would normally suggest guilt, but Bailey got the feeling there was something else going on. 'I don't know,' he said at last. 'Something about John Wallace's story struck me as genuine. I've been doing this job long enough to know that lies ring hollow. The truth has a sound all of its very own, like it's alive.'

'And you were prepared to die for this truth,' Connor observed.

'I didn't know that going in,' Bailey responded, trying to ignore the sudden pounding in his chest. His heart felt as though it might burst out of his body, and he wondered whether Greene or Murrall would notice the forceful rhythm. He looked down at his chest and let out a deep sigh of relief when he saw nothing abnormal.

'Would you do it again? Knowing you could die?' Connor asked.

Bailey glanced at Murrall.

'How did I get put on the spot here?' He turned to Connor. 'My past isn't at issue, Mr Greene, but your wife's death is. We need to stick to the subject. When did your wife tell you to find someone you could trust?'

'Do you think my wife . . . do you think she did it?' Connor asked quietly, the words wounding him as they left his mouth.

'That's what I'm trying to find out, but I can't do that without your help, Mr Greene. Look at me.' When Connor glanced across the table, Bailey held his gaze and said, 'I can't imagine what you've been through, but I'm here to help. You can trust me.'

Connor studied him for an age, and Bailey finally felt as though he'd made a breakthrough.

'Can you tell us how you cut your arm?'

Connor sat back and pursed his lips as he considered the question. 'I'd like a lawyer,' he said finally, each word knocking Bailey's self-confidence – he'd been convinced he'd reached the man.

Bailey turned to Murrall and shrugged.

'I have one I use; Tim Tomkins at Vale and Co.,' Connor added. 'They're in the book.'

'Interview terminated at four forty-six,' Bailey noted, checking the clock before he stopped recording. 'We'll get you your lawyer, Mr Greene, but then we're going to need you to answer some questions.'

Connor nodded, but Bailey had no reason to believe he'd be any more cooperative in the presence of a solicitor; usually the reverse was true.

'You want me to make the call?' Murrall asked, loitering in the open doorway.

'I'm just here on a consult,' Bailey pointed out, and started to follow Murrall.

'Detective,' Connor began. 'How long will I be in custody?'

'You go ahead,' Bailey advised Murrall, who nodded and shuffled off. Bailey allowed the door to swing shut and turned to Connor. 'You don't have to be here at all, Mr Greene, but I suspect as a journalist's husband you already know that.'

Connor's demeanour shifted suddenly and he leaned forward conspiratorially. 'Sit down, detective. He may come back.'

'Who? Murrall?' Bailey asked in disbelief. He didn't comply with Connor's instruction, but instead leaned over the edge of the table. 'What are you trying to do, Mr Greene?'

'I'm honouring my wife's last request,' Connor revealed. 'I cut my arm on one of three sharpened pieces of metal that were left on her desk.'

'What metal?' Bailey asked. 'There was nothing like that on the desk.'

'I did it deliberately,' Connor continued, ignoring the interruption. 'Hector was the one who found her; he panicked and tried to use one of the metal pieces to cut her down. He sliced his hand open. I cut myself to explain the blood on the carpet. I don't want him being drawn into anything.'

'What metal?' Bailey pressed. 'What are you hiding, Mr Greene?'

'Have you got any idea what it feels like to think someone you loved was miserable enough to commit suicide? To know that they kept such sadness secret? Vee didn't kill herself. She was murdered, and I want you to find the killer. Just like you did with Pendulum.'

'Why didn't you say anything before? Why ask for a lawyer?'

'Because there was a note,' Connor said emphatically.

'There was a note?' Bailey couldn't believe what he was hearing. 'Why doesn't Murrall know about it?'

'Vee's job,' Connor replied. 'We both knew it was dangerous. There's a strongbox in her office. It's disguised as a plug socket. It was supposed to be full of work files that I was meant to give to the newspaper if anything ever happened to her. I checked it to make sure nothing had been stolen, but it was empty, apart from a note addressed to me. It told me to ask for you.'

'What? Was it typed?' Bailey asked.

'Apologised, said love . . . would . . . love would . . .' Connor broke down.

'Was the note in your wife's handwriting?' Bailey pressed.

Connor tried to respond, but the words wouldn't come. 'The kids,' he said finally. 'It talked about the kids.'

'Did your wife write the note?' Bailey pushed.

'It was in her handwriting!' Connor admitted at last, his enraged voice echoing around the tiny room. 'But that can be faked,' he added quietly. 'Or she might have been forced to write it.'

'If your wife was mixed up in something, we can protect you and your family,' Bailey said.

'Vee pissed off a lot of powerful people. She was so cavalier about putting herself in danger, but she was always so protective of the boys. The note . . . there was a warning . . .' Connor's voice broke again.

Bailey nodded sympathetically. 'Where is it?'

Connor stared up at him with glistening eyes. 'Will you find the person that did this?'

'I'll find the truth,' Bailey replied honestly.

'Joseph has it,' Connor said. 'My youngest. He's got the metal pieces too. One-four-six Chalcot Crescent.' He grabbed Bailey's arm, squeezing it tight. 'The note said our lives would be in danger if the wrong people found out. You have to promise not to tell anyone.'

Bailey nodded.

'Promise,' Connor demanded.

'I promise,' Bailey agreed, and the bargain was memorialised by a moment's silence.

'I'm going to recommend we let you go,' Bailey said at last. 'But I'd suggest you don't leave London for now.'

Connor nodded.

'Do you still want your solicitor?' Bailey asked, and Connor shook his head.

'He's fake,' he confessed. 'It was the only way I could get you alone. Vee was right. I think I can trust you. After what you went through for Wallace, well, you seem like a good man.'

'Thanks,' Bailey said, but he wasn't so sure. He couldn't shake the feeling that the man he once was had been destroyed by Pendulum's bullets.

'Find whoever did this to us,' Connor implored. 'Find them for me, for my boys.'

The raw power of the man's distress cut through Bailey's self-doubt. 'I will,' he assured Connor.

8

Their proximity to Brookdale probably saved Parker's life. The ambulance took less than two minutes to reach them. Ash travelled with Parker, who was the most badly injured. Jeff had flinched just before Ash pulled the trigger, but she'd been able to hold fire and press the hot barrel into his neck, making the point that she needed him to be utterly still if he wanted to live. Apart from that unnerving moment, Ash was able to free the other hostages from their guillotines with no more than some superficial gashes. They all needed medical attention, but none were as severely wounded as Parker, who was still unresponsive when the paramedics arrived. Ash had watched a dedicated medic hold her gloved hand over Parker's neck during the short ride to the Brookdale Emergency Room. She'd told Ash that she believed the shard was actually preventing massive blood loss, and was trying to make sure it stayed in.

Their arrival reminded Ash of a similar journey she'd had to make with Valerie Templeton, who'd been shot during the Bureau raid on the Hopeland Family. Ash had taken down Hopeland leader Marcel Washington, but his followers had responded with fiery vengeance, shooting Templeton. Ash had accompanied her to hospital, reassuring her, holding her hand, lying that she was going to be OK, even though the look on the frantic medic's face made it clear that the battle was already over. Ash had seen Templeton lose consciousness as they'd arrived at

Sharon Hospital, and wondered whether that was the moment her brave colleague had died, or whether she'd passed away after the paramedics had taken her inside. Whatever the precise moment of Templeton's death, the experience haunted Ash, and she prayed to non-existent gods that Parker's journey would not end the same way.

She was pushed into the background as medics mobbed Parker, checking his vitals and hurriedly trying to assess the best course of action. Ash heard people mention 'carotid artery' a lot followed by 'ligation'. A young ER doctor said it wouldn't be enough, and recommended a graft. His words were followed by a flurry of activity, and Parker was rushed from the ER into surgery, steered by a team of medics that included a nurse whose only job was to ensure that the shard of plastic didn't come out.

As she watched Parker roll out of sight, a nagging vibration alerted Ash to an incoming call. When she pulled the phone from her pocket, she saw that it was Reeves.

'Romero was hit by a brace, but her vest caught it,' Reeves said. 'Couple of ripe bruises, but she's gonna be OK. How's Parker?'

'They're taking him into surgery.'

'We had local PD canvas the area and got an ID,' Reeves revealed. 'Charles Haig, age thirty-eight. He's an engineer for a tech company on Ditmas. Hidyne Systems. They build drones.'

'Put out an APB,' Ash instructed.

'Already did,' Reeves replied. 'Miller and Price are on their way to Haig's apartment on Blake. How are the hostages?'

Ash looked across the ER and caught sight of the young mother, whose wounded neck was being checked by a doctor, while a nurse amused her toddler. The grateful young woman looked back at Ash and nodded her thanks. Further along the ER, Jeff was trying to resist treatment, claiming he had a pathological fear of needles, while the old guy sat quietly as a nurse tended the cuts on his neck. Local uniforms milled around nearby, waiting for the opportunity to talk to the victims. 'They're going to be fine,' Ash told Reeves.

'What about you?'

'Ask me that when Parker comes out of surgery. Let me know when you get anything on Haig.'

'Will do,' Reeves agreed before hanging up.

The first hour passed quickly. Ash got her arm seen to and then liaised with Reeves and local PD, coordinating the search for Babylon, now identified as Charles Haig. Miller and Price hadn't found anything unusual at Haig's apartment. The place hardly looked lived in, which suggested it was a decoy, a clean residence to give Haig a veneer of respectability while his real life was lived elsewhere. The guillotines that almost killed four people were not off-the-shelf. Haig, or someone he knew, had manufactured them, a specialist task that would require a well-equipped work-shop. Reeves said that Hidyne Systems was full of industrial machining tools, but Ash doubted that Haig would have risked discovery at work. He'd have somewhere private, somewhere secret.

She called SAIC Harrell and briefed him on the situation. He was already aware of the broad strokes, but Ash gave him the details and let him know what was happening with Parker. Harrell sent Parker his best, congratulated Ash on her initiative and asked her to keep him informed, before turning his attention to whatever was next on the list of myriad problems that kept the special agent in charge of the New York Field Office awake at night.

Shortly after Ash had spoken to Harrell, the young mother came over, accompanied by a well-built man with a shaved head. He wore jeans and a grease-stained shirt, had rough, dry hands, and looked a little like Eli Manning's grizzled cousin.

The round-faced toddler squirmed in the man's muscular arms.

'They're letting me go,' the grateful woman told Ash, her tearful eyes brimming with relief. 'I just wanted to say thanks.'

'You did good, officer,' the man chimed in. 'Is there someone we can write to? I want people to know what you did.'

'You don't have to write to anyone,' Ash assured them. 'Just give the officers your contact details,' she added, nodding towards the uniformed police gathered by the entrance.

'You saved my life,' the woman protested. 'We'd like to do this.'

'Special Agent in Charge David Harrell, New York Field Office, Federal Bureau of Investigation,' Ash relented.

'Thank you,' the woman reiterated, as the family backed away.

Ash watched the man put his arm around the mother of his child and pull her close, and they both looked back gratefully as they walked towards the exit. The dark-haired child clasped his father's neck and stared at Ash, and she was surprised to feel a sudden pang of jealousy. She envied the love the little boy's parents had for each other and wondered what it would be like to be raised in such a loving family.

The little boy waved at Ash, and, as she watched the family disappear from view, she was suddenly struck by the thought that she might never know such love. Her childhood had been rotten and devoid of any happiness, and now her life was dominated by work that isolated her from any normal human contact. Would she ever find comfort in a man's arms, or cradle a child of her own? Fearful of the answer, Ash pushed the question from her mind.

Over the next half-hour, the other two hostages were discharged. No one came for Jeff or the old guy, and so they shuffled over to Ash alone and expressed their thanks before leaving. The ranking uniform asked Ash whether she wanted an officer to wait with her, but she instructed him to devote everyone to the search for Charles Haig while the trail was still fresh.

The young ER doctor emerged from wherever they'd taken Parker and confirmed that the shard of plastic had sliced a carotid artery. He told Ash that they were trying to repair the damage using a vein graft, but the surgeon was only midway through the delicate procedure. The young doctor withdrew, promising to keep Ash posted as soon as he heard anything.

As Ash watched the ER staff deal with the steady stream of patients that walked, staggered or were rolled into the Emergency Room, she began to replay the afternoon's events, wondering whether she could have handled things differently. She could have acted on her hunch and jumped Haig before he even got inside the café, but that would have risked blowing the case. Except they would have found the guillotine devices in his backpack, which would have been enough to tie him to the murders.

Her self-doubt was cut short by a phone call.

'NYPD got a tip.' Reeves's voice was serious and urgent. 'Willard Brest, says he manages a bunch of properties in the neighbourhood. He recognised Haig's photo from the news, says the guy leased an old warehouse on Bristol—'

Ash was on her feet before Reeves finished. 'That's right around the corner,' she said, interrupting him.

'NYPD are gonna check it out,' Reeves advised.

'No. Call them off,' Ash commanded, jogging towards the exit. 'I don't want them spooking the guy. What's the address?'

'Chris,' Reeves began.

'The address,' Ash repeated.

'Two-one-six Bristol,' Reeves said at last. 'Miller and Price are on their way. We'll meet you there.'

'OK,' Ash replied, hanging up. She ran into the bright April sunshine and picked up pace as she crossed a small parking lot.

The sudden sound of a siren startled her, and she narrowly avoided being hit by an ambulance as it roared out of the lot. She reached the wide, four-lane Linden Boulevard and danced her way across the road, dodging oncoming traffic. Drivers pounded their horns and some swore at the crazy woman, but Ash ignored them and kept running, glad that she'd opted to wear trainers and jeans for the stake-out.

She raced across 98th Street, pounding the hood of a van to force it to a shuddering, tyre-screaming halt. The shocked driver didn't have time to react to the fleet figure, who vanished up Linden, sprinting past the red-brick row houses that lined the busy road. Ash dodged a gleaming yellow school bus as she cut across Thomas Boyland Street, and ran past the Brooklands Family Care Center, a squat brown building with a sloped roof, which sat on the corner of Linden and Bristol. Her legs cried out for her to slow down and her lungs screamed for mercy, but Ash ran on, desperate to reach the warehouse before Reeves and the others. She'd almost watched Parker die, and was not going to be responsible for losing another member of her team.

She tore down Bristol Street, her feet hammering the sidewalk as they carried her past rows of neatly kept two-storey red bricks. As she neared the intersection with Ditmas, Ash realised that she had not been quick enough. She slowed to a walk when she saw Reeves, Miller and Price exit their vehicles, which were parked opposite a low, windowless brick warehouse that was ringed by barbed wire.

'We were closer than I thought,' Reeves said, and Ash knew that he hadn't called her until they were already on their way. *What happened to good old-fashioned trust?* she mused as she caught her breath. Reeves handed her an earpiece and microphone, which she fitted as they walked towards the solid metal gates obscuring the building's parking lot.

'What do we know about the place?' she asked.

'According to Brest, it's pretty much derelict,' Reeves told her. 'The owner is holding out for an offer from a housing developer, so he lets people have the place on a short-term lease. Brest leaves tenants to themselves. Last guy was a pornographer and discouraged visitors.' Reeves indicated the metal gates and barbed wire.

'We got a warrant?' Ash inquired as she produced her pistol and checked her clip.

'Working on it,' Miller replied.

'Brest is concerned that someone might have recognised Haig on the news and broken into the place,' Reeves revealed with a wry smile. 'He wants it checked out.'

'Good. Get it open,' Ash instructed Price, who pulled some delicate tools from his pocket as he approached the metal gates. Ash, Reeves and Miller checked their surroundings while Price picked the lock.

'Done,' he said. The mechanism clicked and the gate swung open.

As Ash led Miller and Price towards the red-brick warehouse, Reeves swung the gate closed, careful to ensure that the lock did not snap shut.

Two shuttered windows flanked a narrow porch that led to a solid steel door with a single lock. Ash and Miller stood either side of the porch and waited while Price picked the lock. Reeves scanned the parking lot, which was littered with garbage. The place reeked of abandonment, and like anything in New York that wasn't used properly, it had become a magnet for the city's detritus.

Price pushed the door open and silently signalled for them to follow. He went first, with Ash behind, Miller third and Reeves taking the rear. Ash hadn't wanted the responsibility of a team, but realised that she almost certainly wouldn't have been able to gain entry without Price.

They stepped into a dank corridor that led into darkness. Price produced a flashlight and Reeves did likewise, throwing pools of illumination around the narrow, decrepit space. Ash caught sight of a DVD slipcase and the rotted cover of a porno lying in a pool of filthy water on the bubbled linoleum floor.

They pressed on, until the corridor widened into what might have once been a reception space. The broken remains of a counter lay near one wall, and a doorway with no door stood directly ahead. The ceiling tiles had been removed, exposing pipes and electrical circuits. Price walked into the corridor beyond the open doorway, which formed a T-junction that led left and right. Ash signalled Price and Miller to go left, and she and Reeves went right.

The corridor stank of damp, and she could feel sodden carpet beneath every step. Reeves led, his flashlight illuminating their way.

'Stop,' Ash whispered, noticing something stuck to the wall. 'Give me some light.'

Reeves threw the beam in Ash's direction and revealed an old front page of the *New York Times* that Ash recognised; the lead story was the Pendulum killings. She looked along the corridor and saw that the walls were covered with newspaper clippings, screenshots of internet stories, bulletin board messages and photographs – all about Pendulum.

'I think he's a fan,' Reeves noted darkly, before moving on.

About twenty-five feet from the open doorway, the corridor dog-legged left, and, as they crept round the corner, pistols at the ready, Ash noticed a row of familiar silhouettes ahead of her. Hanging from exposed girders high above them, a dozen evenly spaced nooses formed a line down the middle of the corridor. Reeves reached out to touch the nearest, which was slightly above his head, and it swung slowly in the silent corridor. Reeves looked at Ash in disbelief, before moving on. Ahead of them stood a door in the left wall, perhaps sixty feet away, a thin line of light bleeding through the narrow gap beneath it.

'We've got light,' Ash whispered into her mic.

'Nothing on this side,' Miller replied. 'Just a load of nooses. There's an open door ahead, but it's dark.'

'We'll go in first,' Ash advised, nodding at Reeves, who moved on.

Ash ignored the nooses hanging above her head, and tried not to look at the Pendulum cuttings that lined their way as she and Reeves crept towards the door. She could feel her pulse rising and each breath becoming shorter as nervous tension built. *Forty feet.* She caught sight of the now infamous photograph of a body swinging beneath Malibu Pier and wondered how anyone could lionise such brutality. *Thirty feet.* Reeves glanced back and nodded; Ash returned the gesture. She flicked the Glock's safety, her every sense alert for—

The scream savaged Ash's ear and was loud enough to echo around the entire building. Ahead of her, Reeves cradled his head, an instinctive attempt to counteract the effects of the shrill noise coming from his earpiece.

'Miller? Price? What's happening?' Ash asked urgently as the screams continued. She ran back the way they had come. Reeves followed, his flashlight bouncing its beam around the decaying building. The screams became a cry.

'Help me!' a voice called, but it was so horribly distorted and guttural that Ash couldn't tell whether it belonged to Price or Miller.

She rounded the corner and sprinted towards the open doorway that led to the exit. The anguished cries were close now, just beyond the corner that turned right about thirty-five feet ahead. Ash was almost level with the open doorway when her heart juddered at the sight of the figure that stepped through it. She tried to level her pistol, but didn't have time. The figure cracked her in the face with a metal bar and she went down, hard. Ash's senses struggled for purchase as the world swam, and the last thing she saw before blacking out was Reeves getting off a single shot before he was disarmed and then brutally knocked out by a man in the familiar mask and body armour of Pendulum.

9

Chalcot Crescent was an upmarket narrow road in Primrose Hill. It was lined by a mix of single- and double-fronted three-storey Georgian terraces which had been painted in pastel colours, making the street look like some pricey offshoot of a beachfront promenade. Bailey pulled to a halt in the residents' bay outside number 146, a large, green, double-fronted house on the crescent's bend. He walked up the short run of stone steps between the two Doric columns supporting the lintel above the front door and rang the doorbell. A quiet chime sounded somewhere inside. After a few moments, a flurry of hurried footsteps ended when the door opened and a quizzical young face peered up at him.

'Who are you?' the boy asked.

'Arthur, I've told you not to open the door,' a woman's voice admonished the boy, who shrugged and quite deliberately closed the door on Bailey.

When it reopened moments later, a tall, slim woman in her mid-forties stood in the doorway. She wore tight jeans and a roll-neck and had Connor's pronounced cheekbones. Her wide eyes were red raw.

'Sorry about that,' she said. 'What can I do for you?'

'DI Bailey. I'm here to talk to Hector and Joseph,' Bailey replied, flashing his warrant card.

'Oh. Is there any news?' the woman asked.

'Can I come in?'

'Of course. Sorry,' she said, standing aside. 'I'm Marcella, Connor's sister.'

Bailey stepped into a large, open hallway. *This is money*, he thought as Marcella shut the door. A double-width winding staircase rose through the centre of the house, climbing to the upper floors, and tasteful contemporary art hung from the walls, somehow managing not to jar with the traditional Georgian fittings.

'The other officer said they wouldn't be bothered,' Marcella observed.

'Ordinarily they wouldn't,' Bailey replied. 'But we believe they might have important information that could help the investigation.'

'Investigation? So you don't think she . . .' Marcella trailed off.

'That's what I'm trying to find out,' Bailey explained, ending with a pause that quickly became an awkward silence.

'I'm sorry,' Marcella said, sensing his impatience. 'They're through here.'

Bailey followed her through a doorway beneath the staircase and found himself in a huge kitchen. Marcella crossed the marble floor and opened a door on the other side that led to a cosy family room. An L-shaped couch was pressed into one corner, opposite a large television. Four boys crowded round the machine, each holding a console controller. The TV almost shook with the ultra-realistic mayhem of a combat game. The boys didn't even look round when Marcella and Bailey entered.

'Boys!' Marcella exclaimed above the staccato machine-gun fire, but there was still no response, so she picked her way over the prone bodies and switched off the TV, provoking disapproval from two of the group. 'That's enough,' Marcella said firmly. 'Arthur, Crispin, go to your rooms.'

'But, Mum,' Arthur protested. 'We can't leave Hec and Joe.'

He gestured towards the other two boys, who Bailey recognised from the Greene family photos. Hector, the eldest, had maybe two or three years on his younger brother. They'd both inherited their father's high cheekbones but had their mother's almond eyes, which looked blankly at him from deep pits of sorrow.

'They'll be fine,' Marcella assured Arthur. 'This gentleman wants to talk to them. He's from the police.'

Bailey noticed the words register with Hector and Joe, and saw them both stiffen. Arthur and Crispin got to their feet and trudged from the room in a huff.

'I'm sorry to trouble you,' Bailey told the boys as gently as possible. 'I know this is a really difficult time. Your father sent me.'

'Is he OK?' Marcella asked.

Bailey nodded. 'As well as anyone could be.' He turned his attention back to Hector and Joseph, who watched him silently. 'He told me what happened.'

The boys looked at Bailey with growing indignation. He could imagine what was going through their minds. Connor had sworn them to secrecy and here was this stranger trying to get them to betray the only parent they had left.

'I wish I could . . .' Bailey began, but he was cut off by a violent coughing fit. 'Could you get me a glass of water?' he asked Marcella when he was able.

'Of course,' she replied, hurrying from the room.

Once she was gone, Bailey crouched beside the boys.

'I know about the cut on your arm, Hector,' he told them. 'I know you did it on one of three metal spikes arranged on your mother's desk. And your father told me about the note he gave you, Joseph. He wants me to take a look at it.'

The brothers exchanged uncertain looks.

'How would I know about all this if your father hadn't told me?' Bailey challenged them. 'He sent me to help.'

Hector nodded at his younger brother. 'Give it to him,' he said flatly.

Joseph leaned around the side of the couch and grabbed a cloth backpack that was concealed under a veneer coffee table. He handed the bag to Bailey, who unzipped the main compartment and reached inside. Bailey recoiled immediately, and when he pulled his arm out, he saw a deep gash along the palm of his hand.

'Here you go,' Marcella said as she entered, carrying a glass of water. 'Oh my goodness, what happened?' she cried when she saw the blood running down Bailey's wrist.

'I nicked myself,' he replied. 'Could you get me a cloth or something?'

Marcella hurried out of the room and Bailey wiped his hand on his suit trousers before carefully reaching into the backpack. He gingerly removed three long, curved pieces of metal which looked like stakes that might be used to dispatch a vampire, and three dense metal balls about four inches in diameter. Bailey placed them on the thick carpet, but Hector shook his head.

'They weren't like that,' the boy said, leaning forward and carefully rearranging the metal artefacts to form a pattern. The three balls lay in a row, with the pointed ends of the metal stakes almost touching them, their thick ends fanning out to form the edges and centre of a trapezoid. Bailey recognised this wasn't a random pattern but some kind of symbol, and he hurriedly produced his phone and took a picture.

'Thanks,' he said, rooting around the backpack until he found what he was looking for: a white envelope addressed to 'My Darling Connor'.

He carefully replaced the metal objects in the backpack and shoved the envelope in his jacket pocket.

'You can't take—' Hector began, but cut himself off as Marcella entered with a first-aid kit.

'How did you do that?' she asked Bailey, handing him an antiseptic wipe.

'Thanks,' he acknowledged, cleaning the wound. 'I caught it on my pen.' He reached into his jacket pocket and produced an innocuous-looking ballpoint.

Marcella eyed the pen, Bailey and the boys with suspicion, but said nothing.

'Well, I think I'm done here,' Bailey announced, getting to his feet. 'Hector and Joseph have been most helpful. I'm very sorry to have troubled you.'

Hector brimmed with indignation, but remained silent. Joseph looked as though he couldn't care what the world might throw at him – he'd endured its worst.

'I'll make sure your father knows how good you've been,' Bailey assured them. 'Thank you so much, Ms Greene.'

'It's Ambrose, actually. I'm married,' Marcella explained.

'Thank you so much,' Bailey repeated. 'I'm sorry for your loss.'

He backed out of the room, leaving the grieving boys to face their bemused aunt's futile questions, then hurried through the kitchen. He had reached the front door when a voice called out behind him.

'Detective!' Bailey turned to see Marcella approaching. 'What happened in there?'

'The boys were very helpful,' he replied. 'I got what I needed,' he added as he opened the door. 'I won't trouble you any more.'

Marcella shook her head in puzzled disapproval as he shut the door. He walked to his car, aware that she'd moved to one of the large picture windows, where she was eyeing him with suspicion. Ignoring the blood that was still flowing from his wounded palm, he started the engine and pulled away.

Bailey drove a couple of blocks and stopped beside the park. Grabbing some tissues from the glove compartment, he wiped his hand before reaching into his pocket for the envelope, then opened it and pulled out the single sheet of paper that was folded within. He unfurled the letter and saw a handwritten message above a large block of typed numbers. The message read:

My dearest darling Con,

Do you remember the conversation we had on our wedding night? How we agreed to go on a journey together, come what may? I'm afraid my journey has ended. Words cannot express my sorrow, but if you're reading this, I've had to take the next stage of the journey alone. Know that this was not my choice. Others did this to me. One day you'll understand that it was the only way. Until then, I need you to ask the police to involve Detective Inspector Patrick Bailey. What's written below is for him. It hurts me to keep secrets from you of all people, but I know that if I didn't, you might put yourself in harm's way. Truth can be more dangerous than any weapon, and whatever happens, I want to leave knowing that you and the boys will always be safe.

My infinite love

Vee

Detective Inspector Bailey, I followed your work on the Pendulum case. Unless my instincts fail me, you're a good man. What follows is meant only for you. Don't make my death meaningless, and be very careful.

There followed ten lines of seemingly random numbers with no breaks. Bailey considered the message, which was unlike any suicide note he'd ever seen. He wasn't sure it even was a suicide note. There was no claim of responsibility, and it was so balanced, so rational, as though death was just research for another article. But if it wasn't a suicide note, it was clearly written by a woman who knew death was coming for her. Bailey wondered at the steel of a woman who could write such a compassionate note in the face of her own demise, and felt ashamed of his own paranoid fears. He studied the block of numbers beneath the handwritten message but could make no sense of the rows of digits. Carefully folding the letter, he replaced it in the envelope and put it on the passenger seat. Whether Sylvia Greene died by her own hand or that of another wasn't what was important. *The real question is why she died*, Bailey decided as he followed Regent's Park Road back towards the bustling city. He suspected that the numbers held the answer.

10

The smell of fresh blood was overpowering. Ash came round to find herself seated in the centre of a large room, her arms tied over the back of the chair. A jolt of pain shot down her neck into her spine as she lifted her head and looked around. Ahead of her, the man in the Pendulum suit sat at a workbench in front of a bank of computers. He was lost in concentration and didn't notice Ash stir. Nervous excitement mingled with pain as she considered the possibility that this might have been the second man she saw at the Twin Lakes facility, the man Harrell refused to believe existed.

The excitement died the instant she saw Price. He was lying on the bare concrete floor, his face a mashed mess, his arms and legs so bloody that they looked as though they'd been flayed. Dark liquid pooled around him, and Ash realised he was the source of the bloody stench. She couldn't bear to look at him, and as she turned her head away, she caught sight of Reeves, bound to a chair on her left. His head hung limp and his eyes were closed; he was still out. His arms were stretched over the back of the chair, his wrists bound by a heavy duty cable tie. The most worrying aspect was the black box fixed to his neck. Ash recognised it immediately and saw the dark wire running around Reeves's throat. Ignoring the pulsing pain, she moved her head to confirm that she too was wearing a guillotine. She could feel the wire pressing against her neck. She heard a groan and turned to see Miller trussed up on a chair to her right, his wrists cable-tied behind his back, his neck adorned with one of the horrific wire chokers.

'You're awake.' The man in the Pendulum mask was drawn by Miller's moan.

'Who are you?' Ash demanded.

'Great men never die,' the menacing figure growled. 'Their legacy echoes throughout history.'

The man's voice was unfamiliar, but his mannerisms almost convinced her that Pendulum had returned to wreak terrible revenge.

'Pendulum tried to change the world,' the man continued, drawing near. 'To make it a better place. My work will honour him.'

Ash knew then that the man in the mask wasn't the second person she'd seen at Twin Lakes. There was too much reverence in his voice, too much worship in his words. This man had never met his twisted hero.

'You know how these work,' the masked man observed, holding up one of the guillotines. 'It's your time,' he added, raising his other hand to reveal a remote.

He flipped the solitary switch and Ash suddenly felt the wire tighten around her neck, pressing deep into her flesh. Heat began to radiate off the taut metal and the box at the back of her neck started to shudder as powerful gears hauled the wire inwards. Ash knew she didn't have long, and prayed that the masked man had bound her tightly. She propelled her arms as high as they would go, forcing them to rise until they were almost popping out of their sockets, and then she slammed them hard against the chair back. The cable tie held, and the masked man, realising what Ash was trying to do, ran to the workbench and reached for a length of metal pipe as she repeated the motion. She slammed her arms against the chair with all her strength and the cable ties snapped.

Ash rolled clear of the chair as the masked man swung for her. She felt the pipe slice the air inches above her head, and quickly turned, jabbing her assailant in the left kidney, between the front and rear plates of body armour. He lashed out with the pipe, but Ash dodged it and picked up the chair, thrusting its back into the man's chin. The blow dazed him and he dropped the pipe, which Ash snatched before it had stopped clattering. He tried to step away, but Ash was as relentless as the scorching wire slicing its way into her neck. Pain urged her on. The masked man tried to lash out, but Ash ducked the punch and came up with the pipe, driving it into his face, sending him sprawling. Breathing was getting difficult, and she could feel the wire gathering momentum and knew that it would not be long before it severed her windpipe. She leapt on the prone man and cracked him over the head with the pipe, knocking him out.

She was starting to feel faint as the wire cut deeper, and she didn't want to think about the fact that blood had started running down her neck.

Don't be afraid, baby.

Her mother's final words rose unbidden, but she ignored the morbid memory and staggered to the workbench, the edges of her vision growing black as she tried to choke down tiny breaths of air. Alive with panic, Ash scoured the workbench but could not see the remote. Frantic, she turned towards her assailant and saw it still in his hand. She tried to run, but the wire forced her to her knees. She pulled herself across the rough, cold floor, willing herself to stay conscious. Reaching for the remote with trembling fingers, she flicked the switch. The pressure ceased but it didn't ease, and Ash knew that she'd pass out if she didn't get the guillotine off soon. She patted the familiar body armour, searching for a weapon, but found none. Forcing herself to her feet, she surveyed the room. Apart from the workbench which was covered by monitors, there were three machining benches laid around the edges of the room and a row of lockers. Ash staggered over to the lockers and opened them in sequence until she found one that contained their weapons. She grabbed her Glock and held it to her neck, then pushed it back a couple of inches.

She was about to take the shot when she suddenly felt searing pain and the wire resumed its terrifying journey inwards. Ash turned to see her attacker awake, holding the remote. She repositioned the pistol and took the shot. Her neck burned with scorching agony, but the wire flew free of her neck and she could breathe again. She longed to crumble to the ground, but she knew her assailant was almost upon her and turned.

'Stop!' she croaked, waving the gun, but he ignored the command, so she opened fire, hitting him square in the chest and knocking him off his feet.

He rolled around on his back, clutching his chest, and she knew that even though the body armour had stopped the round, at such close range the bullet would have probably cracked a rib or two. She walked over to him and stamped on his solar plexus, driving her heel down as hard as she could. He cried in pain, and, satisfied he was incapacitated, she leaned down to remove his mask and revealed the face of Charles Haig – Babylon.

Ash staggered back, relieved to be alive, but certain that she needed urgent medical attention. She had to free the others in case she blacked out, but, as she made her way over to Miller, something stopped her cold. With her senses finally able to focus on more than pure survival, she noticed that the walls were covered with more Pendulum memorabilia – photographs, clippings and internet postings – but one picture particularly unnerved her. Pinned above the computer workbench was a photograph of John Wallace, taken on a long lens through the windows of a converted church, which Ash guessed was his London apartment. The picture had been taken before Pendulum had tried to kill him. She lurched over to the workbench to take a closer look, then heard movement behind her. Haig was dragging himself towards the lockers.

'Freeze!' Ash gasped, but the word wouldn't travel, so she staggered over to the injured man and knocked him across the back of the head with the butt of her pistol. He fell forward, cracking his nose on the concrete beneath, stunning him.

Ash hurried to the nearest machining bench, where she found a putty knife which she used to cut Miller and Reeves loose. She was trying to rouse Miller when she noticed Haig had pulled himself to his knees, his hands inside the locker that contained their guns.

'Get away from there,' Ash ordered, her voice wet with blood.

Haig froze, but didn't acknowledge her as she approached.

'Show me your hands,' she commanded, trying to peer into the darkness of the locker to see what Haig was holding.

The dazed man turned to look at Ash, his cold eyes flecked with blood from a broken nose that had erupted across his face. He was grinning like a fool who'd heard his first joke.

'Where did you get this picture?' she asked, holding up the image of John Wallace. 'Where did you get that armour?'

'I'm a true believer,' Haig replied. 'I've been somewhere you can only dream of.'

The shot came without warning, the muzzle flash flaring from inside the locker as Haig put the gun in his mouth and pulled the trigger. His head snapped back as a bullet tore through his chin and erupted out of the back of his skull. He died instantly, and, as his body fell limp, Ash collapsed to the ground, tears of relief welling in her eyes.

11

Wallace woke to the sweet smell of millet porridge. Kurik hunched over a small pot that hung above a fire near the cave mouth. He smiled at Wallace when he caught the Englishman's eye. Vosuruk was nowhere to be seen, but his horse was still tied to a stone near the back wall. When Wallace sat up, he realised that his comfortable cot was nothing of the sort. He'd been sleeping between two rough blankets on a bed of damp stone, and was now stiff and sore. His head felt as though it was at the centre of a huge ball of elastic bands, and was tight with the intense, grimy pressure of an opiate comedown. But Wallace didn't care. At that moment he felt like he'd endure a lifetime sleeping in a dank cave if it meant he could end each day with Connie in his arms. He sighed sadly, but quickly rallied when he noticed Kurik looking at him.

'I slept too long,' he told the boy, getting to his feet. He pressed his palms together and placed his hands beside his head, closing his eyes to mimic sleep.

'Yes, yes, big,' Kurik smiled. He snorted a few snores and laughed as Wallace walked off his aches. '*Tchina?*' he added, pointing at the contents of the pot.

Wallace approached the fire, his nostrils filling with the rich aroma of honeyed millet and goat's milk, his stomach growling emptiness. 'Please,' he said.

Kurik reached into his pack and produced a pockmarked

stainless steel canteen. He handed it to Wallace, who turned it over to see Cyrillic writing on the base – a souvenir of the Soviet invasion.

'Ruskie,' Kurik nodded as he offered a ladle of porridge, which Wallace gratefully accepted.

He sat on a large rock near the fire and started to eat the thick mixture with his hand. It was stove-hot and burned his fingers and mouth, but he was so hungover and hungry that he didn't care.

'Good,' he told Kurik, who smiled and gave a thumbs up.

After a few mouthfuls, with the worst of his hunger sated, Wallace took a break and asked, 'Where's Vosuruk?'

Kurik considered the question, and Wallace thought he hadn't understood, so he added, 'Father, t'ot.'

Kurik nodded impatiently, suggesting that he'd understood the initial question but was struggling to think of a way to answer. He pointed at his eyes, 'Vosuruk look,' he replied, and then lowered his fingers to the ground and walked them up a rock. 'Look way.'

'Teach him English and I will give you a hundred goats,' Vosuruk said in a voice that boomed around the cave.

Wallace turned to see the Kom magistrate leaning a hand against the cave entrance as he rested, his forehead glistening with a thin sheen of perspiration.

'The mountain very hard today,' Vosuruk told Wallace, who could only guess how far the hardy veteran had walked. 'I'u pik i'a gac,' Vosuruk instructed his son, and Wallace guessed he was asking for food.

Kurik pulled another canteen from his pack, filled it with sweet porridge and handed it to his father, who sat next to Wallace and began to eat.

'No army,' Vosuruk announced between mouthfuls. 'Not this valley or next. The way is safe.'

'When do we leave?' Wallace asked as he finished his meal.

'Soon,' Vosuruk responded. 'After food and cigarette.'

After they'd eaten, Kurik led Wallace into the forest beyond the southern end of the ravine, until they came to a narrow winding stream. Kurik retreated to the cave, giving Wallace the privacy he needed for his ablutions. As he walked back towards the ravine, Wallace looked down into the valley, but they were too far from the town to see anything but cedar forest. The scent of the fragrant trees filled the cool air and the crisp, clean aroma made it almost impossible to imagine the violence of the previous night. Above him, snow clung to the high peaks, stubbornly resisting the strong sunshine that beat on Wallace's back whenever he emerged from the protective shade of the trees. By the time he returned to the cave, Vosuruk and Kurik had broken camp and were astride their horses, waiting for him.

'You are too slow, *Tr'ok Si'ol*,' Vosuruk commented. 'The mountain does not like slow.'

Wallace climbed into the saddle, his inner thighs protesting at being stretched across a horse's back yet again. Vosuruk urged his mount forward with a cry and Wallace and Kurik followed him south towards the forest. Once out of the ravine, they turned east and started a hard climb that slowed the horses to a walk. They rode in silence, and Wallace mimicked his hosts by scanning his surroundings and staying alert for any sign of danger.

They reached the edge of the forest by late afternoon and moved into terrain that was too high, rocky and arid for even the hardiest trees. Wallace recognised the pass from when he'd ridden out with Vosuruk and Guktec, but it had lost a little more snow, which made the going easier. Vosuruk and Kurik occasionally exchanged whispered words and nervously scanned the high peaks that flanked them. Wallace guessed they were worried about an ambush, but none came, and, as the sun sank lower, they emerged on the other side of the mountain. The cavern that acted as base of operations for Guktec and the other warriors was about two hours' ride, and, with the light quickly fading, Vosuruk suggested that they complete the remainder of their journey in the morning.

He led Wallace and Kurik down a steep gorge to a long, dark cave that seemed to have no end.

'It goes under the mountain, to Hell,' Vosuruk told Wallace as they tied the horses and made camp. 'At night you hear the screams of evil men. If you call back, they say the Devil will come for you.'

Looking into the void, Wallace thought he could hear voices, but told himself it was just the sound of the wind blowing cold air into the darkness.

They spoke little as Kurik prepared them cold porridge left over from earlier. Vosuruk explained that they could not risk setting a fire as the exposed cave mouth meant the flames would be seen for miles. The sun was quickly lost behind the high peaks, and its warmth vanished just as swiftly, so Wallace, Vosuruk and Kurik prepared their blankets in the dying light. Wallace chose a spot near the cave mouth, tucked against the east wall, while Vosuruk and Kurik opted for spaces on the other side. No one wanted to venture into the deep darkness, and even the horses moved as far away from the innards of the cave as their fettered reins would allow.

Wallace left the cave to take a leak, and walked no more than fifty feet in the grey light. He looked out over the magical Hindu Kush mountains, their peaks given a golden hue by the last fingers of light. When he turned back, he realised how easy it would be to get lost: the cave mouth was hidden in a jagged pattern of gullies and rocks. He retraced his steps and eventually found the entrance when he was no more than ten feet away.

Inside, his companions were seated on a rock near their blankets. The wind was starting to pick up and as it whistled down into the darkness, Wallace began to realise the truth of the legend: it did sound like the tormented screams of the damned. Vosuruk had the little lump of jelly in his hand and cut a piece for Kurik.

'You want?' he asked.

Wallace didn't hesitate. The prospect of seeing Connie was simply too strong to resist.

'Thanks,' he said, as the Kom elder handed him a slice.

Wallace crossed the cave to his blankets and swallowed the bitter jelly as he lay down. He could hear Vosuruk and Kurik talking quietly from across the cave, their voices becoming even lower and more distant as comforting warmth spread all over his body. He willed Connie to come to him, but the bliss of the previous night was not to be repeated. He could see the silhouettes of distant peaks from the cave mouth and above them the dotted heavens, where the spectral light cast by the stars seemed to be brighter than normal, illuminating the bright colours of distant galaxies.

He focused on two stars, a distant binary system, and as he watched them they became eyes. His heart leapt as a face formed around them, but he was confused and disappointed to discover that it wasn't Connie, but Christine Ash. Perhaps his subconscious need for protection had summoned his guardian angel? Or maybe he missed the only other person who could truly understand his ordeal? Whatever the reason, Wallace felt a pang of guilt at having pictured another woman. He tried to visualise Connie, but his mind was no longer his to command, and the soporific drug oozing through his system kept Ash firmly in place. Lost in his own tragedy, weighed down by an intense sadness that Connie wasn't with him, Wallace's body eventually grew heavy and still, and sleep took him away from his misery.

★

Noise. Movement. Wallace's disordered, sluggish senses struggled to comprehend what was happening. The first thing that hit him was the stench of old sweat, then the realisation that a rough hand was clamped over his mouth. He looked up, and, as his eyes focused, saw the outline of a masked face in the faint starlight. It was only then that Wallace realised that the cold, hard object against his temple was the barrel of a gun.

12

'*V*ona!' the masked man said sternly, gesturing with the gun.
Wallace guessed that he was being told to stand and got to his feet, his opiate-addled mind muddling the world, making him confused and unsteady. He could hear indistinct snatches of conversation and saw other masked figures in the darkness, clustered around Vosuruk and Kurik.

'*Pr'ec!*' Vosuruk's voice boomed across the cave, and Wallace saw him push through the crowd and storm over. He grabbed the man threatening Wallace and forced him against the wall. Wallace struggled to comprehend what was happening, until he saw one of the men lower his mask and recognised Guktec's face in the faint starlight.

'My son thinks he's clever to stop my heart in the night,' Vosuruk told Wallace before shaking his head at Guktec.

The man who'd woken Wallace lowered his mask. He hadn't been with the group when Wallace had gone up to the mountains with Guktec and Vosuruk, but as the other men in the cavern removed their scarves, Wallace saw a number of faces he recognised.

'They are on the move. Kabul Army is in the mountains,' Vosuruk explained. 'They find our high place and attack, but they lose. These mountains belong to us.'

Guktec said something so quickly that Wallace hardly registered that he'd spoken.

'Guktec says he and his men kill thirty soldiers. They hunt the mountains for soldiers who escape,' Vosuruk explained. 'Maybe six, seven still alive. Tomorrow we find them.'

Vosuruk issued a command in Kamviri and the men, fifteen of them, proceeded to bed down for the night, dropping their packs, unfurling blankets and stowing their weapons and ammunition within easy reach. Wallace suddenly found his rough cot surrounded by four other men who all stank of toil and battle, but the smell didn't bother him, and, as he lay down and pulled up his blanket, he took comfort in their increased numbers. The soporific effect of the bitter jelly soon overpowered any residual adrenalin, and Wallace listened to the swelling rumble of snores for a short while before falling asleep.

Low conversation woke Wallace, who was one of the last to rise. Most of Guktec's men were up, their breath clouding the air as they packed their gear or crammed down cold porridge. Wallace rose, nodded at Malik and some of the other men he recognised, and wandered outside, where he found Guktec and Vosuruk surveying the range.

'*Tr'ok Si'ol*,' Guktec greeted Wallace warmly. 'You lazy man.'

Wallace smiled sheepishly.

'Guktec says the soldiers try to get to main army,' Vosuruk told Wallace. 'The men who attacked Kamdesh. They were stupid. They know never to come up here. The mountains protect us. One Kom man kill a hundred of them, no problem. We track these men, pick up trail and . . .' Vosuruk's fingers formed a pistol and pulled the trigger.

'Why would they come here?' Wallace asked, remembering how the soldiers had referred to him in Kamdesh. He couldn't shake the paranoid feeling they were here for him, but how could he even begin to explain his concerns?

'Who knows?' Vosuruk shrugged. 'Kabul is crazy. Maybe a

new minister wants to have big name? Or maybe all these soldiers hate their lives and want to die in such a beautiful place?' He gestured towards the ruffled surface of the earth, its peaks reaching thousands of feet into the sky.

Guktec lit a cigarette and smiled at Wallace while Vosuruk moved into the cave and barked staccato commands in Kamviri. Wallace drifted away from Guktec, past a couple of other craggy-faced warriors, and found somewhere secluded to take a leak. By the time he returned to the cave, the men were ready to leave. Kurik had gathered Wallace's belongings and strapped his pack and camera bag to the white gelding's saddle. The boy's face was clouded with anger and his movements were sharp and hostile. Wallace smiled at him, and was trying to figure out the cause of Kurik's sudden change of mood when he noticed the reins of Vosuruk's horse tied to Kurik's.

'Kurik will take you over the mountains to Pakistan,' Vosuruk told Wallace. 'He wants to be man, but he is good boy so he will do what father tells him. He will take my horse. I travel with my men, on foot.'

'I want to come with you,' Wallace protested.

'I know,' Vosuruk smiled. 'But this is not your fight. When you get to Pakistan you take bus, get to Islamabad. Go home.'

'I want to tell the world . . .' Wallace began.

'Your people don't care,' Vosuruk interrupted. 'This is not your fight. It is not their fight. It is *our* fight.' He embraced Wallace. 'You a good man, *Tr'ok Si'ol.*'

Wallace struggled to accept the truth of Vosuruk's statement. He did not believe himself to be a good man.

'You don't understand, Vosuruk,' he pleaded. 'I have to do this.'

'Die in your own bed, *Tr'ok Si'ol.* Die an old man. Not here,' Vosuruk said firmly. 'Goodbye.'

Wallace watched impotently as Vosuruk yelled at his men and

they marched from the cave. Malik, Guktec and a few others smiled and nodded their farewells, but for the most part, the combat-hardened warriors ignored Wallace and focused on the task at hand: tracking down the few surviving soldiers who had been sent into the mountains to kill them.

Kurik took Wallace east, the boy's mood and the language barrier leaving them little choice but to ride in silence. They traversed the high ridge that led off from the cave, and then they turned into a ravine that ran down to the wide valley below. After two hours, bare rock was replaced by thick forest and they reached the shade of the tall cedars at the edge of the valley. Wallace guessed it must have been about five miles from side to side and they were about halfway across when they came to a narrow stream. Kurik dismounted and allowed his two horses to drink, and Wallace did likewise.

Wallace watched his horse drink, the pink and black of its lips particularly striking against its white muzzle. The first shots came without warning, and bullets tore into the flank of Vosuruk's grey horse. Kurik dived for cover behind the thick trunk of a tree, and Wallace stumbled down into the stream and hid by the rocky bank. Vosuruk's horse whinnied in anguish as it fell. Kurik's mare tried to bolt but was still tied to Vosuruk's wounded mount and could only buck violently, until the reins snapped, freeing it to gallop away. Wallace's horse bolted through the forest as gunfire tore through the air around it. Wallace peered over the bank to see Kurik throw himself in front of his mare. Convinced that he was acting out a death wish, Wallace only realised Kurik's true intention when he saw the horse slow just enough for the boy to whip round it and grab the Kalashnikov that was stuffed in his saddle. As his horse raced on, Kurik returned fire, spraying bullets that cut into the forest near whoever was shooting at them.

Smart and brave, Wallace thought as the manoeuvre bought Kurik enough time to cover the ground to the stream and dive down the bank. The boy scrambled through the water until he reached Wallace. The two of them would have to work together if they were to survive. Kurik pressed himself against the rocks and studied the forest. Wallace wondered how many teenagers could handle a Kalashnikov with the same expert ease as his young neighbour. Kurik ducked and looked at Wallace, his eyes alive with nervous energy.

'Two,' he said, holding up a pair of fingers. He reached beneath his budzun cloak and produced a heavy pistol. Wallace recognised it as a Makarov, a popular trophy from the Soviet invasion.

'Go,' Kurik whispered, pointing downstream.

Wallace understood the plan immediately – he was to use the stream to get behind their assailants, while Kurik did the dangerous job of keeping them occupied. Two unknown attackers against a teenager and a photojournalist. Wallace didn't like the odds, but they'd have a better chance taking the initiative than if they waited for death to come to them.

He nodded at Kurik before starting downstream, his waterproof hiking boots saving him from the worst of the freezing cold. He looked over his shoulder and saw Kurik watch him for a moment before scrambling up the bank. There was an immediate burst of machine-gun fire but Wallace stayed crouched as he moved, not wanting to risk giving away his location to see whether Kurik had survived. His question was answered moments later when bullets spat from somewhere nearby, Kurik's angry response to their would-be killers. More gunfire as Wallace pressed along the stream. The Makarov felt heavy, and as he looked down, Wallace was suddenly struck by the realisation that he had no idea how to use the barrel-mounted safety. The markings next to the switch were Cyrillic and therefore incomprehensible. The Kom had such a martial culture that Kurik had simply assumed that every man of age would know how to handle a weapon. Wallace could not test the safety without running the risk of giving away his position and, if he was fortunate enough to get within striking distance, faced the prospect of being unable to get his first shot away. He tried to remember whether Kurik had touched the switch when he'd handed him the weapon, and convinced himself that the teenager hadn't, so, if he assumed that not even the battle-hungry Kom would ride around with the safety off, the firing position would be to turn the switch from horizontal to vertical. He flipped it down as he moved on, trying to ignore the loud bursts of gunfire that were now above and behind him.

Wallace stumbled and fell into the stream, smacking his knee against a skull-sized rock. He swallowed a yelp and rolled on to his backside, clutching his leg. A combination of pressure and ice-cold water numbed the stabbing pain, and he got to his feet and peered over the bank. His eyes took a moment to acclimatise to the subtle shades of brown and green and the shadows and highlights that dappled the world between the trees. A sudden flash of light alerted him to the presence of a man, no more than thirty feet away. He was crouching behind a tree and poking his machine gun round the trunk, not really aiming when he fired. The point-and-hope shooter had salt-and-pepper hair and was wearing an Afghan Army uniform, meaning he was probably one of the survivors of the attempted assault on Guktec and his men. Wallace couldn't see any sign of a second shooter, and wondered how Kurik could be so sure there was someone else. Moving without knowing the location of the second man would have been suicidal, and Wallace was struck by the idea that if he'd been alone, he might have walked straight up the bank and welcomed their bullets. But he wasn't alone, and he owed it to Vosuruk to ensure that his son survived.

The sudden burst of gunfire was so loud that it pounded Wallace's ears and left them ringing. He looked up and saw a short, chubby man peering round the far side of a tree that was ten feet away. The man hadn't seen him and was aiming in Kurik's direction, but, unlike his colleague, he was directing his shots carefully, pinpointing each burst. Epaulettes on his shoulder suggested he was an officer, which meant he'd be better trained and potentially more dangerous than point-and-hope. Both men ducked for cover when Kurik returned fire, his bullets shredding bark and branch. Wallace could see the teenager's muzzle spitting flame from behind a tree, and he crouched down behind the bank and considered his next move. Kurik's life depended on Wallace's ability to climb out of the wet trench without being noticed and dispatch two men who doubtless had families and friends who loved them. Men who had been ordered to be there, commanded to kill strangers, and who probably didn't want to be in that forest facing death any more than he did.

The teenager stopped shooting and the forest fell into numb silence for a moment before Wallace's ears attuned to the sound of birds tweeting, their song unbroken by the violence around them. The beautiful choir was suddenly lost beneath the rattle of guns as the officer and point-and-hope opened fire. Wallace hauled himself over the lip of the bank and, crouching as he ran, swept counter clockwise, moving in an arc to come up behind the officer, who was focused on trying to kill Kurik. Wallace felt that he was creating a din as he moved, but knew that any noise would be buried beneath the thunderous gunfire. And then the shooting stopped.

The officer heard Wallace's crashing progress and turned quickly, yelling at his comrade. Wallace leaped, forcing himself towards the rising gun. He swung wildly, his arm coming round quickly and heavily, driving the pistol into the officer's temple.

The man fell instantly, but Wallace had no time to marvel at what he'd done. Point-and-hope sprayed the area with bullets, and Wallace dived behind the thick trunk for cover. He could hear the gunfire getting closer, and peered round the shredded trunk to see the soldier picking his way across the forest, using trees for cover to avoid being shot by Kurik. The boy was running towards Wallace, but the soldier was moving faster, urged on by the thought that it was now two against one, and Wallace couldn't rely on Kurik hitting this wild gunman. He inhaled and counted to three, praying he was right about the safety, then rolled out from behind the tree. He ignored the hot lead that sliced the air around him – better one accurate shot than hundreds of wild ones – and took aim. He squeezed the trigger and felt relief as the pistol recoiled and spat, first one, then two more bullets. Point-and-hope was hit in the leg and fell to one knee. Wallace was shocked when bullets burst through the man's abdomen and looked beyond the bewildered soldier to see Kurik finishing what he'd started. Point-and-hope yelped and turned, firing his gun wildly as he died. Wallace watched aghast as the barrel of the gun tracked towards Kurik, who tried to move, but he was too slow and his body bucked with the force of the multiple impacts. A look of horror crossed Kurik's face as he fell forward and hit the ground.

Tuneful birdsong replaced the terrible thunder of death and Wallace lay prone for what seemed like an age. When he finally got to his feet, his legs trembled as he forced himself over to the motionless teenager. He found himself choking on the lump that was building in his throat. He passed point-and-hope, his pockmarked corpse still bleeding on to the moist forest floor. When he reached Kurik, Wallace knelt down and pushed his hands under the boy's body to turn him over. Kurik's vacant eyes stared back at him, and he confirmed the worst by touching his fingers to the boy's still neck. Dark blood stained Kurik's tunic, oozing from half a dozen wounds. Wallace was almost over-whelmed by the wave of sadness that swept over him, the thought of so many wrongs that could never be undone, of all the lives cut short by violence. As he stared at the peaceful, unblinking face of death, he realised that part of him longed to trade places with the brave boy.

He was startled by the sound of something moving nearby and turned to see the two horses tracking back through the forest. Wallace tried to suppress a rising sense of anger. He'd failed to protect this boy. His frustration grew worse when he saw that his pack and camera bag were no longer bound to the saddle. His cell and satellite phones were gone. He had no means of communication and was lost, deep in the mountains, hundreds of miles from the nearest city, with one of the men who'd tried to kill him lying a few yards away. There was little doubt in his mind that the officer would soon regain consciousness, and if he was to have any chance of delivering Kurik's body and one of the killers to Vosuruk, Wallace knew that he'd have to act fast.

13

The *London Record* occupied three floors of a low-rise building tucked between Park Street and the Thames. Bailey gazed through the office window down at a crowd of tourists gathered around a guide who was doubtless explaining the historical significance of the Globe Theatre, which stood almost directly opposite. Four floors up, Bailey was above the thatched roof and had a partial view of the upper tier of the circular structure. For all his years living in London, he had never been to a production and told himself to find time, and someone to go with. Watching the clusters of tourists as they shuffled along Bankside admiring London's sights took his mind off the tightness in his chest.

He'd spent Sunday at home, puzzling over the code in Sylvia Greene's note, the block of numbers tormenting him with their silent refusal to reveal anything. He tried online code-crackers, puzzle solvers and even a few specialist chatrooms for maths students, but was told that without a key, or a way to break the block down into its component elements, he could spend years trying to crack it. His mind, confined to such a dry, logical, intense task, started to turn on itself, unleashing flushes of acrid panic. As his heart started to race and he became convinced of skipped beats, Bailey imagined himself dying alone in his small flat. Would anyone miss him? Today, perhaps a few would, but in ten years, he'd be nothing more than a faded memory, a ghost people would scarcely recollect. And in fifty more, they too would be gone, and there would be no trace of his ever having existed.

Bailey had tried to shake off such bleak thoughts and by evening, he'd medicated himself with rum and co-codamol. His anxiety blunted, his mind liberated and free from fear, he had resolved to ask for help breaking the code and devised a way to maintain Connor Greene's confidence. He'd transcribed the first three lines of the twelve-line block of code and emailed them to Derek Lowe, a guy he knew on the Met's computer crime taskforce. If Lowe could decipher the code, he'd only have part of the message, but he would be able to give Bailey the key to figure out the rest. Stewed in rum and mild opiates, Bailey had passed out on his tatty old couch and slept until four in the morning, when he'd woken, hung-over with what felt like a tight band pulling around his chest. He'd been to the hospital with false alarms three times in as many months, and recognised the symptoms of an impending panic attack, so he'd forced himself into his rarely used sports kit and gone for an early morning run.

The band had loosened for the duration of his run, but had returned as he'd driven south of the river to the *London Record*. He had been referred to Francis Albright, who had, until Saturday, been the paper's deputy editor. Trapped in the first meeting of what was sure to be a relentless day, Francis had instructed his assistant Abbie to show Bailey into his office. From what Bailey could see, Francis was not editor material. His desk was covered with untidy piles of paper that spilled into each other, and the large office was strewn with folders, clothes, magazines and half-drunk cups of coffee.

'I'm sorry to have kept you waiting.' The voice sounded like honey-coated gravel and startled Bailey, who'd been mesmerised by the tourists below.

He turned to see an overweight man who was probably in his

`early sixties stride across the room and toss a folder full of papers on the desk.

'Francis Albright,' the man said, offering Bailey a hand. 'Melissa Rathlin is going to join us.'

Bailey looked towards the door and saw a tall, slim brunette in jeans and a sheer floral blouse, her long hair tied in a ponytail. She was holding on to the door frame, yelling at someone across the open-plan office that lay beyond Albright's room.

'Don't fuck me around, Ollie, just do it!'

'Melissa is one of our news reporters,' Albright explained.

'Sorry about the language,' she said, crossing the room and extending her hand. 'I'm Melissa Rathlin.'

'Patrick Bailey,' Bailey replied, shaking her hand.

'Take a seat,' Albright offered, indicating a chair that was covered with books. 'Just toss that stuff.'

Bailey carefully lifted the stack of books and found space for them on the cluttered floor. The chaotic man in front of him was now in charge of one of London's leading newspapers. A mass of curly blond hair sprouted from Albright's head, and the face beneath it looked as though it had seen many hard years. Ruddy cheeks protruded from a landscape of crags and folds that made Bailey think of a pug. His grey polyester trousers were a couple of inches too short and revealed a pair of battered and scuffed shoes.

'You can imagine we're all devastated by what's happened,' Albright said. 'Sylvia was an amazing woman. She was much loved.'

'I still can't believe it,' Melissa interjected. 'I can't believe she's gone.'

Bailey saw her face grow heavy with emotion, the brash, vulgar journalist momentarily lost to sadness.

'What can we do for you, Detective Inspector?' Albright asked.

'I'm investigating the circumstances of Mrs Greene's death—' Bailey began.

'Really?' Melissa interrupted. 'I thought the case was being handled by a Detective Murrall.'

Bailey was surprised to be challenged.

'The *Sunday Record* broke the news yesterday,' Melissa explained. 'It's our job to know what's going on.'

'I've been asked to consult,' Bailey revealed.

'Because it was a hanging?' Melissa asked. 'Because you broke the Pendulum case?'

'Now I know what a grilling feels like,' Bailey observed.

'You have no idea,' Melissa countered, and Bailey found himself warming to her.

'How was Mrs Greene recently?' he asked. 'Did you have any reason to think she was troubled? Depressed?'

'No,' Albright replied. 'Sylvia was a workaholic, she lived for this job. She was always intense, but these last few weeks I got the feeling she was working on something, something big. She was alive with it.'

'Any idea what it was?'

'No. I couldn't even say there was anything for sure, it was just a feeling. She always had a glint in her eye when she was chasing down a story and the last few weeks her eyes were shining very brightly.'

'Do you think you could give me the names of any people who might have reason to want to hurt Mrs Greene?'

'It's a long list,' Albright responded with a wistful shake of his head. 'We piss people off. It's what we do. Sylvia never knew when to stop. She made a lot of enemies over the years. Powerful ones.'

'I'd appreciate anything you can give me,' Bailey persisted.

'Mel?' Albright suggested.

Melissa pursed her lips and shook her head. 'I've got a lot on. I'm leaving for Geneva.'

'I'll give you my email,' Bailey tried. 'You can send it over when you get a chance.'

Melissa shot him a beleaguered look. 'OK.' She sounded reluctant.

Bailey handed her his card. 'And if there's anything you can think of, anything that's happened in the last few weeks, or if you find out what she was working on, just give me a call. We'll need access to Mrs Greene's computer.'

'Not going to happen,' Albright responded quickly. 'Not without a court order. There's a world of sensitive information on it, sources, high-level contacts. No way.'

Bailey shrugged. 'Don't make this difficult. We both know I'll get that court order.'

'Maybe. But how's it going to look to our sources if we don't put up a fight?'

'OK, we'll do it the hard way.' Bailey stood up and moved towards the door. 'I'll expect that list.'

As he left the room, he felt his heart start pounding and sensed the familiar dread panic rising within him. He fought the urge to run and kept a measured pace, telling himself that there was no escaping the true source of his fears.

14

The Piuma Road tracing the contours of the mountain was like a thirsty grey snake reaching for the vast expanse of water that lay beyond the golden beach, Alice thought. She had lived in the Monte Nido compound within sight of that beach for as long as she could remember, but had never felt the sand beneath her feet. Nicholas believed that indulging one's desires cultivated decadence, which made a soul vulnerable to evil.

'Alice?' Nicholas called out from the main house.

She lowered her eyes. If he caught her looking at the ocean, he would get angry, and having only just been released from three days in the punishment block, she had no desire to return. She focused on her small fingers, which held a trowel that she was using to turn over the soil in the citrus bed.

'Have you learned your lesson?' Nicholas asked as he approached.

'Yes, Father,' Alice replied without looking up. Even his shadow terrified her, and she felt her mouth go dry and her stomach churn. She imagined his eyes peering into her heart, judging her for every bad thought they found there.

'Good,' Nicholas said. 'You're not like other children. Your mother and I knew that from the day you were born. The world out there is polluted. You will help cleanse it.'

'Master!' a voice called from the doorway of the devotion hall, a wide, low hut that lay at the edge of the plateau. Alice looked round and saw that it was Beau, one of Nicholas's mistresses. 'The congregation is ready for you.'

'The Almighty loves you, Alice,' Nicholas said as he turned.

Alice watched her father cross the patchy lawn, his white kaftan bleaching out in the bright California sunlight to reveal his lean, sinewy body. Her heart didn't slow until he'd entered the devotion hall and she knew that she was no longer in danger of being caught by his capricious eyes.

'Ow!' Suddenly, pain shot up her right arm. She looked down to see that she'd cut her palm on a shard of twisted metal which had been buried in the soft soil. Her father had often preached about the power of nature, and as Alice watched the blood flow she was struck by an idea. She moved beneath the nearest orange tree and held her right hand over one of its roots so that her blood dripped on to the exposed rough bark and ran into the soil beneath it.

'Mother Earth,' she whispered, 'I sacrifice my essence to you. I pray to you to keep my brethren safe.' She looked round to check that no one was nearby. 'And might I one day, please, go to the beach?'

Feeling tremendous guilt at her selfish request, Alice stood and hurried inside the main house to wash the blood from her hands and erase any trace of her treacherous sacrifice.

Ash retched as she woke. She hadn't dreamed of Nicholas for years, but the passage of time had done nothing to blunt the sharp nausea he evoked. Her mother had been alive then – it was before . . . Ash's eyes adjusted to the low light and she noticed the silhouette of a man seated in the armchair opposite her bed. Nausea swirled, until she realised fear had corrupted her senses. It couldn't be her father, could it?

'I owe you one,' Parker said as he stood and approached the

bed, his face illuminated by sunlight that prodded its way between the slatted blinds. His voice was rough and low.

Ash saw a thick bandage coiled around Parker's neck and suddenly remembered the stake-out, the raid and her narrow escape.

'How long . . .' she began, but the sound of her hoarse voice shocked her into silence. She put her fingers to her neck and felt a fabric bandage.

'Almost two days,' Parker told her. 'They stitched you up and knocked you out. Apparently movement would've aggravated the wound.' He looked pointedly at Ash, who had sat up unsteadily while he spoke, her feet dangling close to the floor.

'I wouldn't be awake if they still didn't want me to move,' she croaked, looking down at her painted red toenails, the bright colour garish against her unusually pale skin and the bleached white of her hospital gown.

She eased herself upright and tottered towards a closet that occupied the corner behind the armchair.

'I don't think you should be doing this,' Parker said, moving out of her way. He hurried over to the bed and pressed the call button.

Ash ignored him and opened the closet to find it empty. 'Where are my . . .' she began, but then she caught her reflection in a mirror that hung on the inside of the closet door. Her skin was so pale that it almost matched the white bandage choker. She felt the back of her neck and found a vertical length of tape securing the bandage. She ripped it away and unwound the bandage, quickly at first, but slowing as she neared the bottom layer.

'You can't do that,' Parker cautioned her. 'You'll open your stitches.'

Ash carried on until she reached the final layer, which involved removing the bandage and the gauze that was in direct contact with the wound. She ignored the pain as she pulled. She had to see what Haig had done to her. The gauze clung to clotted blood, which came away as Ash ripped it clear. Tears welled in her eyes before she'd properly registered the thick black line around her neck, which was criss-crossed by stitches.

'Mine isn't as bad, but it's not far off,' Parker told her, and Ash hated him for it. 'The doctors say with time and surgery, people will hardly be able to notice it.'

She couldn't tell whether Parker was just trying to make her feel better, or whether he truly believed that the deep wound that circumscribed her neck would one day miraculously vanish.

'What have you done?' a nurse cried, entering the room and rushing over. 'You can't remove your dressing for at least three days. Come along.'

She ushered Ash back to the bed and pushed her into a seated position before rifling through a chest of drawers that stood beneath the window.

'You're going to be OK,' Parker assured Ash. 'That's the important thing.'

'What about Reeves and Miller?' she asked as the nurse approached the bed with an armful of medical supplies.

'They're both fine. Haig didn't activate their devices. You saved their lives. Price too.'

Ash's heart soared at Parker's words. 'Price? I thought he was . . .'

'No,' Parker smiled. 'I mean, he's messed up. But he's going to make it.'

'What do we know about Haig? What's—' Ash began.

'You can't talk,' the nurse told her. 'Not while I'm fixing this.' The large woman held a strip of gauze to Ash's neck and started winding the bandage.

'Get me Reeves,' Ash instructed Parker, ignoring the dirty looks the nurse threw at her.

'I don't think . . .' Parker tried.

'When can I get out of here?' Ash asked the increasingly frustrated nurse.

'If it were up to me, honey, you'd be leaving right now. I'll have the doctor come by. You can ask her,' the nurse replied, her tone softening. 'Now, can I please fix your bandage?'

'Just one minute,' Ash told her. 'Parker, what the hell are you waiting for? I said, get me Reeves.'

Parker shook his head and shuffled out of the room.

'And tell him to pick me up some clothes,' Ash yelled after him.

'And I thought I was a ball breaker,' the nurse observed with a wry smile as she resumed winding the bandage around Ash's lacerated neck.

Doctor Hernandez was on her way out of the room when Reeves arrived. She had spent ten minutes with Ash explaining the nature of her injuries. As bad as it looked, Ash was lucky to have only suffered surface tissue damage. The wire had not cut into her windpipe or any of her arteries or tendons. As Hernandez's calm words soothed her, Ash had fought the urge to cry with relief, the memory of how close she'd come to death threatening to overwhelm her. Feeling her head being slowly severed had truly terrified her. Hernandez had told Ash that she was free to leave as long as she promised not to do anything strenuous and to return in three days to have her wound checked and her dressing changed. The doctor had concluded by echoing Parker, telling Ash that over time, and with some cosmetic work, the scar would not be very noticeable.

Ash brightened as Reeves strode into the room. She swung her legs over the edge of the bed and tried to stand.

'You did good,' he said. 'Real good. Thank you.'

She fought the urge to cry with relief at the thought that all four of them had escaped with their lives.

'How are you feeling?' he asked. 'You look better than

yesterday. Me, Miller, Romero, even Harrell came by. But you were out cold.'

'Feel pretty good,' Ash replied, her hoarse voice rattling around her throat. 'Sound terrible.'

'I got you some clothes.' Reeves held up a Gap bag. 'Miller took the stuff you were wearing.'

'How is he?' Ash asked, taking the bag.

'OK. Cuts, bruises, wounded pride, nothing more,' Reeves replied. 'Here.' He produced Ash's cell phone from his jacket pocket.

'Thanks.'

'Your piece has been taken into evidence,' Reeves told her.

'What about Price?'

'He's pretty bad, but he'll live,' Reeves replied. 'None of us would be here if you hadn't—'

'Don't go getting all soft on me, Deon,' Ash interrupted jokingly. 'Not right now,' she added earnestly. 'I don't think I could take it.'

There was an awkward silence for a moment.

'What do we know?' Ash asked, finally suppressing the lump in her throat.

'Charles Haig, engineer for Hidyne Systems. They manufacture state-of-the-art camera drones and stabiliser gimbals. Forensics have started analysing his devices. He was using the same high-powered servo motors they use in the drones to pull the wire. Connected it to a heat coil. We found a bunch of tools and equipment from Hidyne at his warehouse. I'm guessing he wanted somewhere near his work to make it easy to transfer stuff to and fro.'

'What about the suit?'

'Exact replica of Pendulum's,' Reeves replied. 'We haven't found a link yet. Harrell wants us working on the theory that Haig was a copycat and a fan.'

'I think he might be right,' Ash revealed, aware that her response surprised Reeves. He knew all about her theory that there was at least one other conspirator. 'Haig revered Pendulum, the kind of reverence you have when you're not part of something. He was also loud and attention-grabbing. Pendulum would never have been found out if it hadn't been for John Wallace, and if I'm right, and there is another conspirator, he or she is too smart to get involved with someone as unhinged as Haig.'

Reeves nodded.

'If Haig didn't know Pendulum,' Ash continued, 'we have to figure out how he got hold of that suit. Did he have it made, or did he find it? And there was a photo, a picture of Wallace in his apartment that must have been taken before the attempt on his life. Haig might not have known Pendulum, but he's had access to things we haven't been able to find.'

'His base?' Reeves asked.

Ash nodded. Her conspiracy theory was easily refuted, but even Harrell was troubled by the fact that they'd never located Pendulum's base of operations.

'I think Haig found it.'

Ash stood beside Price's bed. His head was bandaged, his right forearm in a cast. His other injuries were hidden beneath a sheet that was suspended over a frame to prevent direct contact with his body. His head injuries had resulted in a brain haemorrhage and he'd been placed in an induced coma until the swelling came down. After she'd put on the jeans, black T-shirt and trainers that Reeves had bought her, Ash had insisted on seeing Price on their way out of the hospital. Reeves had detailed his injuries – it seemed that Haig had used some new contraption to flay the skin off Price's limbs. The wounded man was going to need multiple grafts.

Guilt washed down Ash's face, each tear provoking yet more

remorse. If she'd called for back-up, if she'd gone with Miller, if they'd played it any other way then Price would not be facing months of difficult and painful recovery and the almost inevitable end of his career with the Bureau. Once again, she'd made the wrong call. She'd tried to control things that were beyond her. She cursed her father for robbing her of the ability to trust others.

Reeves had been in to see Price the previous evening so he waited outside and gave Ash privacy during her visit. She could tell from his expression that Reeves had been deeply moved by the sight of his colleague, and she was glad he wasn't in the room. Together, the two of them would only have fed each other's sorrow.

She took a moment to compose herself and wiped away her tears. She wanted to say something to Price, but the words wouldn't come. She knew he couldn't hear her, so she simply nodded her sympathy and turned for the door. Reeves was leaning against the wall opposite Price's room. He stood when he saw Ash stagger out, but said nothing as he fell in beside her, and they headed towards the elevators in silence.

Word had spread. Ash could tell by the way the cop looked at her as she and Reeves approached the warehouse. Bored with guarding the entrance, the NYPD uniform was mooching around, kicking his heels until he saw them pull into the parking lot. He stood straight and Ash could see him eyeing the bandage around her neck as she got out of the car, its presence clearly confirming the rumours he'd heard. If the on-site uniform knew what had happened, then the story would be all over New York City.

Reeves swung by the Bureau forensics truck which was parked beside two unmarked vehicles at the far end of the lot. He opened the door and reached inside, before emerging a moment later with a folded newspaper. 'We made the *Post*,' he explained, handing the tabloid to Ash.

She unfurled the well-read paper and saw a photo of Charles Haig under the headline 'Babylon Falls!'

'Details?' she asked.

'Harrell persuaded them to keep it pretty vague. Said the investigation was ongoing,' Reeves replied. 'But sooner or later, the city is going to learn the truth about its heroine.'

Ash groaned and slapped the newspaper into Reeves's arm, and he grabbed it and handed it to the uniform guarding the door.

'Tobin still inside?' he asked.

'Yeah, she told me it was going to be a long night,' the cop replied with a sigh.

Ash shuddered as she followed Reeves into the warehouse. She knew returning to the scene so soon was pushing it, but the Pendulum case had been her private obsession and she was determined to prove she was right, that she had seen someone else in the Facebook facility in Twin Lakes.

'Harrell wants to see you first thing tomorrow,' Reeves informed her as they pressed on. 'I think he's considering compassionate leave.'

'Why? Is he ill?' Ash countered quickly, and Reeves smiled.

A pair of bright field lights illuminated the lobby, leaving nowhere for the decay to hide. Anyone willing to lease this dump had to have something to conceal. The harsh glare of the lights revealed more than just damp; there were rodent droppings, broken glass, discarded hypodermics, and massed wet garbage that was impossible to identify. Ash followed Reeves to the corridor beyond, where they turned right. A unit light in the corner illuminated their way, and its twin pointed left, lighting the dog-leg where the nooses hung. Ash shivered and skipped a couple of steps to catch up with Reeves.

'Tobin says it's gonna take at least a week to go over this place properly,' Reeves said.

Ash could see why. Pendulum articles, photos and printouts surrounded them and each one would have to be checked, catalogued and tested for prints and DNA.

When they reached the end of the corridor, Reeves pushed the door to their left, which was slightly ajar, and led Ash into the room where they'd been held captive and almost killed.

Four HMI lights lit up every nook. Ash felt her stomach turn as she looked around and saw that the place was almost exactly as she remembered it, except for Haig's body, which had been removed. Three forensics agents in white suits made it feel more like an ordinary crime scene, rather than the place where she and her team had come within moments of meeting their death.

'Tobin!' one of the forensics agents called. Ash vaguely recognised him. His name was something like Blake or Blaine.

Linda Tobin was a well-respected agent in her early fifties. She hadn't chased flashy ambition. Instead, she'd found something she loved and she'd stuck with it for thirty years, building an enviable reputation as a forensic specialist, both within the Bureau and outside it. She'd consulted on a number of books, and advised movie and television producers, all with the blessing of a Bureau that was keen to showcase a world leader. Tobin had short blond hair, narrow eyes, and a lined face that wasn't carrying a spare ounce of fat.

'Should you be here?' she asked Ash.

'Probably not,' Ash replied. 'But my head isn't going to fall off, if that's what you're worried about. Least, not today.'

Tobin smiled. 'In case you hadn't noticed, this place is a mess. We've got machining tools, specialist motors, components, motherboards, circuit boards, firearms, tools – shit, it's like a pharaoh's tomb. Each and every item has to be tracked and traced, printed and typed. I'm guessing he stole most of it from Hidyne, but we have to check everything, make sure he didn't have any outside help.'

'There was a photo,' Ash said.

'If you saw it, it's still here,' Tobin interrupted.

'And the suit?' Ash asked.

'That's a puzzler, ain't it?' Tobin replied. 'It wasn't just a copy. It was an exact replica. The breastplate is a modified Survival Armor X50 unit and the limb protection uses similar nanotech to the Surefire Institute. The mask is modelled on a carbon fibre face-piece used by Taiwanese special forces. Pendulum spent a lot of time researching the best tactical combat gear and then adapted it. It's state-of-the-art, not something you buy off the shelf.'

'I think it was one of Pendulum's spares,' Ash told Tobin, and pretended not to see her and Reeves exchange a cynical glance.

'Really?'

'I think Haig found his base,' Ash responded. 'Look around. I think he was Pendulum's biggest fan.'

'We'll run the suit for prints and DNA,' Tobin assured her. 'See if we can link it to Pendulum.'

Ash scanned the room. 'Mind if we browse?'

'Sure, but you know the rules. Be careful and don't touch anything.'

Tobin returned to what she was doing; dusting the machining workbench for prints.

'You really think he found it?' Reeves asked Ash sceptically.

She nodded.

'I'm guessing you didn't take Harrell at his word. Maybe you've been moonlighting?' Reeves suggested. Ash was impassive, but he pressed on. 'So how could this nut find something that eluded one of the Bureau's best and brightest?'

Ash ignored the question and sidled over to the computer workbench, where the screens cycled through indecipherable code. 'What are they doing?' she asked.

'DDOS attack on Facebook,' Reeves replied. 'Tobin doesn't

want the machines turned off until cyber has had a chance to take a proper look.'

Ash focused on the photo of Wallace that was pinned to the wall. She noticed the corners of a number of other photos beneath it, and glancing round to check that the boiler-suited agents were otherwise occupied, took hold of the pictures and pulled out the pin that fastened them. Reeves signalled his disagreement with a shake of his head, but stood behind her, making it difficult for anyone to see what she was doing. Ash spread the photos out on the workbench. There were seven of them. Six were of people she recognised: Pendulum's victims. All six photographs were clearly surveillance images taken of the subjects in or around their homes.

The seventh photograph was different. It was a hand-held selfie taken by Haig and it showed him standing beside a dirt track, tall green trees crowding either side of it. In the photo, Haig was smiling broadly, like a tourist on vacation. *Or a big game hunter standing beside a trophy*, Ash thought to herself. She placed the photo on the workbench and used her phone to take a picture of it, before replacing the sheaf of images on the wall and fixing them in place with the original pin. She scanned the surrounding memorabilia – stock photos of Pendulum, his victims, reports, newspaper articles, bulletin board messages – and then she froze. There, pinned to the wall beneath a bus ticket, was a picture unlike any other. It looked as though it was an internet printout and it showed an unknown family standing in front of a diner, posing for what was undoubtedly a holiday snap. Seated inside the diner, at a table by the window, like a ghost almost lost to the background, was Max Byrne, the man otherwise known as Pendulum.

15

The first stars were visible in the grey sky. Wallace tried not to think about oncoming night and told himself that he recognised landmarks as he urged his horse on. The clatter of its hooves echoed across the mountainside, breaking the stillness of the vast landscape. He did not want to look over his shoulder, but he had to check on his captive, the short Afghan officer, whom he'd gagged and forced on to Kurik's horse at gunpoint, before binding the man's hands to the saddle-horn. But the resentful, brooding man was not the source of Wallace's discomfort. It was the sight of Kurik laid across the horse's withers, the boy's lifeless eyes staring at the rocky ground. Wallace checked the reins of Kurik's horse, which were fastened to an eyelet in his saddle's cantle, and, satisfied that they were secure, turned his gaze forward.

They'd been riding for six hours, and were heading back up the mountain towards the endless cavern. Whenever Wallace couldn't recall the route, he'd let his horse choose their way, hoping that the animal's innate sense of direction would lead it home. The desperate strategy had paid off, and they'd reached the deep cave late in the afternoon, but there was no sign of Vosuruk or his men, just the haunting sound of the wind screaming its way down to Hell. Wallace had pressed on, trying to remember the route to the narrow ravine and the shallow cave that had given them sanctuary the night they'd escaped the attack on Kamdesh.

He hoped to reach the shallow cave before nightfall, but hadn't made allowances for the distance they needed to travel or the speed with which the sun dropped behind the mountains, and after another two hours' ride, during which Kurik's horse slowed with fatigue, it became clear that they weren't going to make it to the ravine and would have to camp in the open. They were high above the treeline, and wherever Wallace looked he saw nothing but jagged rock and unyielding stone. As light faded and darkness swept over the mountain, Wallace's mind played scenarios in which they were ambushed by the remnants of the Afghan Army patrol that had attacked Guktec and his men, or were discovered and murdered by bandits or Taliban fighters. Neither prospect scared him. If he hadn't felt a sense of obligation towards Vosuruk, he might have released his captive and handed him a gun.

They finally passed through the shadow of a high outcrop, which Wallace recognised as being at least two hours' ride from the ravine.

'Tr'ok Si'ol,' a voice called from above, startling Wallace, who looked up and recognised Guktec's face poking over the edge of the high rocks.

'My brother is not a good guide. We see you across the mountain,' Guktec teased.

Wallace saw the smile fall from Guktec's face when he registered that the second rider wasn't Kurik. When he finally realised what was on the trailing horse, there was a moment of horrified disbelief.

'N'a Kurik!' he yelled, his cry so loud and pained that it seemed to shake the mountain.

Wallace heard the sound of hurried footsteps, the rattle of scree shifting and the crack of stone rolling against rock. He saw fear animate the Afghan officer's face, and watched him tug ineffectually at his restraints. Wallace turned to see the first of

Vosuruk's men round the outcrop and approach hesitantly.

'Kurik!'

Wallace recognised Vosuruk's voice and saw the Kom magistrate coming from the other side of the rocks. Vosuruk ignored the terrified officer and ran straight to his youngest son, embracing his head, clasping it to his chest.

'*N'a, n'a, n'a! I p'utr, Kurik, I p'utr,*' Vosuruk wailed, stroking his son's hair, as his men stood around him in mournful silence.

Maddened by grief, Vosuruk turned on Wallace, his eyes burning.

'What did you do?' he demanded, grabbing Wallace and hauling him out of his saddle. 'My boy!'

'I'm sorry, Vosuruk,' Wallace said. 'We were ambushed.'

Vosuruk pushed Wallace back, as though he was afraid of what he might do to the foreigner. He looked at his son's body and gave a low, guttural moan before rushing at the terrified Afghan officer. He grabbed the smaller man and hurled him to the ground.

Wallace watched as Vosuruk set about the man with his fists, pummelling his head and body with mighty blows. Guktec joined the fray, kicking the officer in the ribs, and Wallace was forced to look away as more of Vosuruk's men joined the beating. He stared at the high peaks and tried to ignore the groans that came from the officer as he was assailed by men who would beat him to death.

One of the blows must have knocked the officer's gag loose, and Wallace heard him cry, 'Help me, English!'

Wallace turned to see him lost in a maelstrom of violence.

'Help me, and I will say who sent us to kill you,' the man screamed.

The revelation confirmed Wallace's fears. Sickened, he moved towards the violent swarm and tried to pull the enraged men away.

'Help me, English, I will tell you!' The officer's feeble cries suggested he would not last much longer.

Wallace rushed to his horse, took Kurik's Kalashnikov from the saddle and fired a volley of shots into the air.

Vosoruk, Guktec and the rest of the men froze and turned to see Wallace holding the gun. Vosuruk's eyes flashed with murderous intent and Wallace knew he only had moments, so he threw down the gun and ran over to the grieving father.

'Vosuruk, listen to what he's saying,' he pleaded. 'Someone sent him here to kill me.' He looked down at the Afghan officer, whose face was a bloody mess.

'He's lying!' Vosuruk kicked the officer in the gut, and looked set to deliver further violence before Wallace pulled him back. Vosuruk looked down at Wallace's restraining hand with raw fury.

'No,' Wallace implored his host. 'You said you couldn't understand why Kabul would trouble your people after so long. And the soldiers you killed in Kamdesh, they called me *the* foreigner. I didn't want to believe it, but I think they were looking for me.'

'Why you?' Vosuruk asked, wavering. 'You take pictures,' he added indignantly. 'Why someone send army for you?'

'I don't know,' Wallace lied. There was one man with the means and motivation to have him killed in this way. 'But that's why we need him alive. If he's telling the truth, the person responsible for Kurik's death is the one who sent him.'

Vosuruk looked down at the groaning officer, his eyes flashing hatred.

'Please, we need to know why,' Wallace pressed.

Vosuruk turned away from the man. '*N'acoa!*' he told his men, who hesitated for a moment, before withdrawing. Vosuruk produced a hunting knife from beneath his cloak. 'If he lies, I will slit his throat,' he said emphatically.

Wallace dragged the Afghan officer to a nearby rock and

pulled him upright, resting his back against the rough stone. 'What's your name?' he asked.

The officer coughed up a gob of blood, his breathing shallow and uneven. 'Colonel Ghulan Ahmadi,' he replied weakly.

'Who sent you?' Wallace asked.

'An American,' Ghulan answered. 'I don't know his name. I never saw him. We deal through a broker, a middleman. He offered me two hundred and fifty thousand dollars to find you. Half before, half after I bring back your body.'

'To where?'

'Kabul,' Ghulan croaked, as blood rattled around his throat.

'You raided an entire town for one man?' Wallace's voice betrayed his disbelief.

'This is Afghanistan. Life is cheap,' Ghulan responded darkly. 'The man who paid me wanted a big noise. And this way, we also remove some local troublemakers.'

Propelled by anger, Vosuruk surged forward, but Wallace held him back. When he saw that the Kom tribal leader had calmed, he returned to the officer.

'Can you take us to this man? The broker?' he asked.

Ghulan watched Vosuruk fearfully as he nodded.

Vosuruk grabbed Wallace and led him away from the injured colonel. When he was certain Ghulan could no longer hear them, he pulled Wallace close. 'This man must die,' he whispered. 'And I must kill him,' he added emphatically.

'I need to find out who sent him,' Wallace countered. 'We both do.'

Vosuruk turned towards the prone man, conflicting emotions clouding his face. 'We take him to Kabul,' he conceded eventually. 'But when he show us man, I kill them both.'

Wallace paused to consider the dark bargain he was being offered. He looked from Ghulan's fearful face to Kurik's lifeless body and finally nodded.

Vosuruk offered his hand and Wallace shook it, before pulling his host into an embrace. 'I'm sorry about Kurik,' he said. 'I truly am.'

Vosuruk's body shook, and when he withdrew, there were fresh tears in his eyes. He retreated towards his men, who rallied around him with warm embraces and sympathetic words.

Tradition dictated burial within twenty-four hours but the rocky landscape made interment impossible, so they trekked through the night, Wallace on his horse and Vosuruk on Kurik's, his son's body laid in front of him. As they rode side by side, Wallace told the grieving father how his son had died, fighting bravely, honouring the spirits of his ancestors, standing against an invading enemy. Wallace was moved by Vosuruk's quiet grief. This man, who had seen so many die, who had lost so many friends, sobbed without shame for his fallen son. A veteran of decades of war, he was still only human, and despite a life of violence, death had not lost its bitter edge. All around them, Guktec and the men marched in solemn silence, while Ghulan was bound to Vosuruk's saddle and forced to trudge behind his captor.

The moon had set by the time they reached the ravine and the small cave where Wallace, Vosuruk and Kurik had taken shelter the night of the assault on Kamdesh. Torches were lit, and with their shadows dancing in time to the flickering lights, Guktec led the small group of men that dug his brother's grave in the cave's moist earth.

An outsider, Wallace stayed back, while Vosuruk, Guktec and the men who were a mix of friends, comrades and family lamented the passing of one so young and so very dear. As they lowered Kurik's body into the shallow grave, he saw that Ghulan, who was bound to a rock near the cave mouth, had turned away. Wallace knew the pain of living with guilt and was content to see the assassin who had brought so much misery into so many people's lives struggling with the consequences of what he had done.

He noticed Vosuruk staring at him, and replied with a respectful nod. The tribal chief's mournful gaze shifted past him, towards the cave mouth, and, as Vosuruk looked upon the Afghan officer, grief was replaced by fierce hatred. Wallace knew it was only a matter of time before Vosuruk exacted revenge. He only hoped he could keep the ill-fated colonel alive long enough to learn the truth.

16

Bailey woke to the sound of gunfire. He felt tremendous pressure deep in his chest, and panic surged inside him. Convinced that he was having a heart attack, he started to reach for the phone, but the pressure passed and he flushed with embarrassment when he realised that it was probably trapped wind. Overcome by rum, he'd fallen asleep on the sofa after a large pepperoni pizza. The television had been keeping him company as he obsessed over Sylvia Greene's code, and Bruce Willis was currently shooting some Eurotrash robbers in the Nakatomi building.

A car raced along Old Ford Road, the roar of its modified engine shaking the windows. Bailey heaved himself to his feet and staggered across the room. His curtains weren't drawn, but he wasn't worried about privacy. His neighbours were all London paranoid and kept their drapes and blinds firmly closed. Only the pigeons and squirrels could see into his flat and they wouldn't care about the self-pitying drunkard who lived within. Bailey told himself to get a grip. He was slipping along the road towards dependence, but part of him didn't care and welcomed the comforting haze of alcohol. He looked down the street and saw the receding tail lights of a souped-up car, its driver ensuring that everyone in the neighbourhood felt the throb of his engine. Bailey staggered to the sofa and checked the time on his phone: 11:23 p.m. The previous incarnation of Bailey, untroubled by a near-fatal wounding, would have logged the licence and called it in, but the battered man sitting on the sofa simply reached for the three-quarter empty bottle of Sailor Jerry and poured himself another drink.

He touched his laptop and the machine lit up. After fleeing Francis Albright's office, he'd driven across London and made his way to his desk on the fourth floor of the Paddington Green tower, where he'd dug into both Albright and Melissa Rathlin. There wasn't a huge amount on Albright, who hadn't written for the paper since his promotion to deputy editor six years ago. A search of Melissa's name returned page after Google page of *London Record* articles, each one alive with a passionate point of view. Melissa didn't go as far as an activist blogger with a political agenda, but it was clear to Bailey that she was someone with strong feelings about certain subjects and she had clearly made it her mission to expose social inequality. Her latest articles were on the proposed International Online Security Act, which was big news the world over. The Americans were pressing ahead with controls on the internet, including an end to anonymity and a centralised financial transaction system. Melissa viewed it as an attempt by the Americans to bend the internet to their will and restore their global supremacy. According to her most recent article, she was going to Geneva to cover the upcoming UN Digital Security summit, where the US was expected to push for the IOSA to be adopted as a global standard.

Murrall had tried phoning a couple of times, but when he saw the detective's number flash up Bailey had ignored it. He had promised to keep Sylvia's note secret and since he and Murrall had nothing else to talk about, he wanted to avoid the guy and minimise any potential for breaking Connor's confidence. His plan had hit a bump: Superintendent Cross had found him after lunch and asked whether there was a problem. He'd had Murrall on the phone to him complaining. Bailey had assured his stern superior there was nothing wrong, but he hadn't returned Murrall's call until five-thirty, when he'd suspected the rotund detective would be on his way home. Bailey's instincts had paid off; he'd gone straight to voicemail and had left a friendly message apologising for the delayed response and inviting Murrall to call him any time.

Bailey had left the office shortly afterwards, and ignored three calls from Murrall as he joined the long line of traffic snaking east along the Marylebone Road. He ignored a fourth when he pulled up a hundred yards east of his four-storey Victorian conversion, and he found himself wondering whether he was really trying to keep Sylvia Greene's secret or whether this was further evidence of his desire to isolate himself.

Inside his top-floor flat, Bailey had tossed his keys on the table in the hallway, which was piled high with unopened post. He'd ignored it for yet another day, and instead settled in the living room with his laptop, where he continued to obsess over the code. He'd had his first drink ten minutes after getting home and had phoned for a pizza soon afterwards. Food would make each splash of rum seem civilised, but Bailey hadn't been able to wait, and the delivery guy had finally arrived when he was five drinks in and beyond caring about the pretence of a meal. He had picked at the pizza as he knocked back more of the richly flavoured rum and couldn't recall having fallen asleep. *Passing out*, his treacherous mind suggested, but he corrected himself: he'd fallen asleep after a long day at work.

Now, two hours later, he inhabited the uncomfortable nether-world between intoxication and sobriety and sought to remedy this by downing his glass. His bright computer taunted him with a photograph of the code, and Bailey was suddenly struck by heady inspiration. He'd read Ash's report into the Pendulum investigation and remembered her referring to the assistance of an FBI contractor who'd helped her and Wallace while they were on the run. Some kind of computer whizz, but Bailey couldn't remember the guy's name. He poured himself another drink, which he necked quickly before delving into his iPhone contacts and dialling a number.

The trees in Washington Square Park were heavy with blossom, but Ash wasn't interested in their pastel beauty. She stood by her window trying to catch the bright sunlight that shone over the buildings on the other side of the park. She was looking at an enlarged print of the photo she'd found in Charles Haig's warehouse, and Max Byrne's ghostly face stared back at her from the window of the diner. Ash had been studying the image for a couple of hours, trying to figure out what had made it so important to Haig, but there were no identifying markers in the picture. The diner's name was missing, there were no posters in the window, and the business cards pinned to a cork board on the inside wall were illegible. There were no vehicles in shot, so Ash couldn't even run licence plates, and the family that was the subject of the photo looked disconcertingly average, their broad, homely smiles taunting her. How had Haig got the picture? When had it been taken?

The sound of ringing intruded on Ash's frustration and she moved away from the window and grabbed her phone from the table near the hallway. Bailey's name flashed above a FaceTime Audio notification, and Ash dropped the photograph on to the table and answered.

'Patrick Bailey,' she said, trying to make her hoarse voice sound as normal as possible.

'You OK?' Bailey asked. 'You sound like you've got the flu.'

His words flowed into each other with an ease that was on its way to incoherence. He was drunk.

'Rough couple of days,' she replied, unwilling to revisit her ordeal. Maybe she'd tell Bailey about it one day. 'How are you? You sound tired.'

'I'm OK,' Bailey responded in a wavering voice that broadcast the lie. 'You know, I've been better, but so what? That's life.'

'They still got you seeing that therapist?' Ash asked hopefully.

'Nah,' Bailey said proudly. 'Can't keep a good man down.'

'Listen, Pat,' Ash began, 'I'm kinda in the middle of something, so maybe we could speak tomorr—'

'Too big for your old friends?' Bailey interrupted. 'I'm just kidding. I know you and me are tight. That's why I'm calling. I'm working a case. Top secret stuff. I need a favour. That guy you know. The computer nerd. Helped you and Wallace . . .'

'Pavel? Pavel Kosinsky?' Ash guessed.

'Pavel Kosinsky!' Bailey yelled, his drunken enthusiasm all too clear. 'I'm gonna send you something to run by him. It's a code. A message from a dead woman,' he slurred. 'Can you help me out, Chris?'

'I can ask.'

'That's my girl!'

'Listen, Pat,' Ash hesitated.

'I'm all ears,' his uneven voice boomed down the line.

'I know a lot of cops who've had PTSD . . .'

'PTSD?' Bailey snorted derisively. 'Who's got PTSD?'

'This isn't like you,' Ash said quietly, but she wasn't sure how to continue and all she could hear was Bailey's breathing and the sound of a movie playing in the background.

'I know,' Bailey admitted sadly, his words initiating a long, awkward silence. 'I appreciate your concern. I'll email you the code. Let me know if your man finds anything.'

Bailey hung up before Ash could say anything more. She thought about calling him back, but the conversation they needed to have was one for when he was sober. Ash sympathised with her old friend. She was all too familiar with the aftermath of a shooting, but she'd thrown herself into her work, rather than succumb to the enchanting lure of drugs or alcohol. Her only vice was a nightly Ambien, which she took in an effort to deaden her past.

She glanced down again at the photograph, which had landed on her iPad. The illuminated tablet shone through the image, changing it, revealing new details, and Ash saw something that made her heart jump. She picked up the photo and went into her home office, which was uncomfortably similar to Charles Haig's warehouse. The pictures and articles pinned to the walls evidenced a shared obsession: the Pendulum killings. She crossed the room to a large desk and placed the photograph on a light box positioned beneath an arm-mounted magnifying glass. She switched on the lamp and waited for it to warm to full brightness before examining the photo. In the top right corner of the image, above the smiling family, was the faint and partial reflection of a word: 'immy's'. Ash realised that the text was part of a larger sign in the shape of a cloud – no – an ice cream. She used her phone to Google Timmy's Ice Cream, which drew a blank. She tried Jimmy's Ice Cream, which gave her four hits, all within three hours' drive of New York City. She checked each one on Google Street View and felt a stab of excitement when she saw the third: a single-storey, stone-clad building with a red tile roof. The Mountainhome Diner was less than two hours from the city. She looked at the photo on her light box and double-checked that she'd found the right place. The proximity to Jimmy's Ice Cream Parlour, the diner's cream walls, the stone inlays, the brown window frames and the Stars and Stripes hanging by the entrance left no doubt that it was the same place. She looked at Byrne's wraith-like face, almost lost behind the window, and finally felt she was getting close to him. She had no idea how Charles Haig had found the image – whether it was chance, hard hours or a computer program – but she was convinced that it had been instrumental in helping him locate Pendulum's base.

17

Vosuruk did not linger at his son's grave. He issued Guktec with a series of firm commands and then told Wallace to get ready to leave. Malik and one of the other men led Ghulan into the ravine and forced him into the saddle of Wallace's horse, binding the Afghan colonel's hands to the horn. Shoulders slumped, head lolling, Ghulan cut a sorry silhouette in the mouth of the cave.

'You ride with him,' Vosuruk said.

Wallace looked around the cave at the shadowed faces of the sombre men, and slowly nodded a farewell, before awkwardly clambering into the saddle behind Ghulan. Vosuruk mounted Kurik's tan mare.

'*Su'e je!*' Vosuruk called to his men, before spurring his horse along the ravine.

Wallace kicked his heels and the white gelding followed him, cantering between the rocks.

Vosuruk's eagerness for vengeance was ill-disguised and he set a brutal pace that Wallace struggled to match. His progress was hindered by Ghulan, who soon lost consciousness and went limp, so Wallace not only had to try to match Vosuruk's pace, but also had to keep the lolling Afghan colonel in the saddle.

He assumed they were heading for Kamdesh, but as they neared the ruined, deserted town, Vosuruk led them on to a narrow dirt track that turned east. Freed from the treacherous

121

mountainside, the grieving father pushed his horse ever faster, until they were galloping.

Black night turned aubergine as the first hint of dawn brightened the sky ahead of them. After another half an hour riding at pace, Vosuruk slowed to a trot, and Wallace could sense his caution as they approached the tarmacked main road that ran between Kamdesh and the rest of the country. Vosuruk checked the potholed highway in both directions before they crossed it. They continued on a dirt track that wound down the mountainside and led to a small cluster of houses set in the forest a few hundred feet below.

When they reached the outskirts of the hamlet, Vosuruk dismounted and tied his horse to a tree.

'Wait,' he instructed Wallace, who pulled his mount to a halt.

Vosuruk disappeared into a dark, crooked alleyway that ran between two of the wooden houses, and Wallace suddenly became aware of how exposed he was. He dismounted and led his horse beneath the cover of the surrounding trees, moving slowly so as not to topple the oblivious Ghulan. Wallace stood in the shadows for what seemed like an age, listening to the sounds of the forest: the birds chirping, the gentle breeze, the creak of branches and the crackle of small creatures scurrying over dry twigs.

He tensed when he heard movement, but was relieved to see Vosuruk emerge from the alleyway with two men.

'This my cousin, Anto,' Vosuruk said, gesturing at a spry, grey-haired old man with a crinkled face. 'And this his son, Bodur,' he added, pointing at a younger version of Anto. 'Bodur has truck,' Vosuruk added. 'Bring him,' he instructed, pointing at Ghulan.

Wallace untied the thongs and the colonel groaned as he and Bodur pulled him down. They dragged him by the arms, following Vosuruk and Anto into the alleyway.

'Anto says army has gone,' Vosuruk whispered. 'No commander, they don't want be here. They know they will die in mountains, so they go home.' He spat, reinforcing his disdain.

The alleyway opened on to a small courtyard at the centre of the cluster of houses. An old Toyota pick-up was parked next to a cart, and Vosuruk headed straight for it. Wallace followed Bodur's lead and helped him hoist Ghulan on to the flatbed where he lay among the scattered wood chippings, oil-soaked straw and cut lengths of twine. Vosuruk leaned into the cab and produced a pair of woollen trousers, a brown budzun cloak and a Chitrali hat.

'Put these on,' he said, handing the clothes to Wallace. 'If this dog tells the truth, they may look for you at checkpoints,' he added.

As he changed, Wallace glanced over to see Bodur crouching in the flatbed, stripping the colonel out of his uniform and replacing it with traditional Kom clothing.

'If people ask, he is sick man we take to hospital in Kabul,' Vosuruk told Wallace.

Minutes later, Vosuruk and Bodur embraced Anto, who muttered words of caution and farewell. Wallace followed them into the cab of the Toyota, sitting alone on the rear row of seats while Vosuruk and Bodur occupied the front of the double cab. Vosuruk leaned into the footwell and then passed Wallace a long grey scarf.

'For your face,' he said. 'In case we are stopped.'

Bodur started the engine and the truck rolled out of the courtyard and joined the steep, narrow highway that snaked down the mountain.

By the time they reached the valley floor, the landscape had changed dramatically, shifting from thick forest to parched earth which had been divided into terraced fields, some irrigated, some left fallow and bone dry. Those with water were green with a lush crop, but the uncultivated terraces were a dusty brown. The road wound around the Earth's creases, taking the Toyota through a wild, uninhabited landscape that was only blighted by a couple of abandoned industrial sites. An hour later, they were forced to stop at a police checkpoint, but after a cursory glance inside, the duty officer, a man jaded by boredom and heat, waved them on. A few miles past the checkpoint the road ran alongside a high-wire fence, beyond which lay a vast military base. If Bodur or Vosuruk were nervous neither man showed it, and their young driver kept to a steady forty-five miles per hour.

They drove south-west for three hours, until they reached another checkpoint just outside Kuz Kunar, a town that lay on the edge of Laghman Province. The police officers were slightly more vigilant and asked about Ghulan, before accepting Vosuruk's cover story that the man had injured himself in the mountains and required specialist medical care that only Kabul could provide. Waved on once more, they resumed their steady progress, passing through Kuz Kunar, until they reached the edge of the harsh desert that separated the last of the cultivated land from Kabul. Bodur turned right to join the Kabul-Jalalabad Highway, heading west. Even at ten a.m., with the windows wide open, the dry desert heat was stifling, and as he sweated under his woollen cloak Wallace longed for the truck's broken air conditioning to heal itself. They passed a parcel of green fields near a vast dam, but then drove on to mile after unrelenting mile of arid, mountainous desert. Even the river, which ran alongside the road for parts of the journey, seemed lifeless, and, stewed by the heat, slowly congealed around outcrops of dry rock.

After another hour, Vosuruk produced an old cell phone from the cluttered glove compartment and turned it on. A few minutes later, the device chimed with the notification of a signal, and Vosuruk muttered something to Bodur and indicated a turning about half a mile ahead; a dusty track that wound between the foothills of a dry mountain. Bodur took the trail and drove up, until they could no longer be seen from the quiet highway.

Vosuruk clambered out of the cab and Wallace hurriedly followed, fearful of what the veteran had planned. Ghulan was a mess. Blood and dirt caked his face and hair. Only the palms of his hands and the tops of his feet weren't covered in the gloopy mixture, but they had been sunburned instead, and his flesh looked painfully raw. Bodur slapped Ghulan until he woke, groaning and wincing with every move.

'Tell him to call the man,' Vosuruk said to Wallace, handing him the cell phone.

Ghulan squinted up at Wallace as he approached, his narrow eyes almost lost beneath the crusted blood.

'How were you going to get the other half of your money?' Wallace asked.

Ghulan looked at the phone and then reached out a feeble hand.

'Don't try anything,' Wallace cautioned as he passed the soldier the cell. 'They'll kill you,' he added, indicating Vosuruk and Bodur.

Ghulan nodded almost imperceptibly as he dialled a number. After a moment's pause, he surprised Wallace by talking in English. 'It's Ghulan,' he said. 'The operation was a success. Yes. Yes, I have him. Tell the American to bring my money to Ka Faroushi. Tonight.'

Bodur held up six fingers.

'Six o'clock,' Ghulan relayed, before hanging up.

'The broker's English?' Wallace asked as the colonel handed back the phone.

'American,' Ghulan replied. 'Was CIA, now he's a business-man.'

There was little doubt in Wallace's mind that Ash had been

right; someone else had been working with Pendulum. He returned the cell phone to Vosuruk, who stood behind him, brooding. Bodur smacked Ghulan across the head before dragging him out of the flatbed and forcing him into one of the rear passenger seats. Bodur reached into the flatbed and poked around beneath some straw until he found an old rag and a half-empty bottle of water. He wet the rag and passed it through the window to Ghulan, with a barked instruction to clean his face.

Bodur climbed into the driver's seat and once Vosuruk and Wallace had joined him in the cab, pulled a U-turn and drove back down the track to rejoin the highway.

Sunlight baked the hard mountains and as the miles rolled on, Wallace thought about Connie, about the other night when she'd come to him and they'd lain together on the beach, hand in hand. As he recalled the blissful moment, Wallace realised that Ash and Bailey were right: he'd come to Afghanistan in search of a way to escape the pain, to be free of his guilt. As the truck moved slowly towards the horizon, Wallace came to a decision. Vosuruk was taking him to a man who wanted him dead. Before Vosuruk exacted his revenge, Wallace would give his would-be killer exactly what he wanted.

'Not long, Connie,' Wallace muttered. 'I'm ready.'

18

They reached the outskirts of Kabul a little after four, and the streets were alive with the chaos of people, animals and vehicles. Motorcycles laden with two or three passengers, boxes of goods, or in one instance, an entire family, weaved between cars, minibuses and trucks, throwing clouds of dust into the faces of men on donkeys, who were often led by their wives, carrying laundry or shopping on their heads. The low buildings were a mix of old and new, but nearly all were made of cheap, functional concrete with simple block designs that could be thrown up quickly. Despite more than forty years of near-constant war, and unimaginable hardship endured by its people, Kabul somehow managed to continue to function as a capital city.

Ghulan had cleaned his face with the bloody rag that now lay in the footwell, and robbed of caked blood, the true extent of his swollen injuries became apparent. As they drove further into Kabul, the colonel slept, his head lolling as they rolled through the residential neighbourhood of Hoth Khel, past a heavily fortified military base. Wallace knew Kabul well, having spent two months there during his previous assignment in the country. Ka Faroushi was the famous Bird Market, located in the heart of the city in the shadow of the Pul-e Khisti Mosque. Afghan homes and places of business might be simple and functional, but their places of worship commanded attention, and the large, blue-domed mosque with its single minaret could be seen from a dozen blocks away, towering above the surrounding buildings.

The thick smell of the city filled the cab as the Toyota crossed the Kabul River and drove south on the Nadir Pashtun Road. Almost an hour after reaching the suburbs, they joined the long queue of vehicles trying to circle the bottleneck roundabout that connected Nadir Pashtun with Maiwand Road. Horns sang in a constant chorus, joined by the optimistic cries of hawkers, the frustrated yells of impatient drivers and the general clamour of people, children and animals. Wallace took in the sights, smells and sounds of the city with a sense of detachment. He might still exist in it, but this was no longer his world and he willed the truck towards the Bird Market.

The dashboard clock read 5:13 when Bodur reversed into a space opposite the Olympia Business Centre, a four-storey oblong building with mirrored windows that reflected the red rays of the dying sun. A lone tree, its crooked branches showing their first buds, stood at the far end of the building, an isolated reminder of the natural world in the heart of the paved city.

'We wait,' Vosuruk said, turning to look at Wallace.

The veteran's gaze shifted to the unconscious colonel, and he stared at the man as though he was trying to kill him with hate. Eventually, he turned around and kept his eyes fixed on the road ahead.

While they waited for time to catch up with their desires, Wallace watched the city ebb and flow around them, its chaotic rhythm doing little to subdue his impatience. The man they were going to meet had made an assassin of an army colonel, and, if Ghulan was to be believed, was clearly prepared to go to extreme lengths to see him dead. Wallace planned to embrace his fate like an old friend.

At 5:50, Vosuruk nodded at Bodur and the two men stepped out of the pick-up. Bodur opened the rear passenger door on his side and allowed Ghulan to topple out of the vehicle on to the hard tarmac. The colonel moaned as he hit the deck and came round as Bodur hoisted him to his feet.

'Come,' Vosuruk said to Wallace, opening the nearside rear door. 'Cover your face.'

'It's OK,' Wallace replied, ignoring the suggestion. He registered Vosuruk's disapproving look, but the old magistrate said nothing.

Wallace climbed out of the Toyota and followed Vosuruk, weaving through the heavy traffic to cross the street. Neither Vosuruk nor his nephew seemed concerned by the thought that Ghulan would break free and try to run for help, and when they reached the other side of the street, Wallace saw why. As he stepped on to the high kerb, Bodur's cloak gaped to reveal a pistol pressed tightly against the dazed colonel's ribs.

Before they'd even reached the market, Wallace could hear the squawks and caws of hundreds of birds, intermingled with the cries and catcalls of the hawkers, and the undulating back-and-forth of traders and buyers haggling. As they pressed through the crowd, he scanned the passing faces, searching for a glint of recognition that would identify his killer, but no one registered him. He was just a pale Nuristani mountain man lost in the big city.

'*Halta*,' he heard Ghulan say, recognising the word for 'there'.

The colonel pointed towards a café on the corner of the market, opposite the north-eastern corner of the Olympia Business Centre. The alleyway that separated it from the rear of the concrete office block was jammed with people, and Wallace was pushed and jostled as they forced their way towards the crowded coffee house.

Three men vacated a table as they approached, and Bodur pushed the battered man into one of the empty chairs. He whispered something in Ghulan's ear and showed him the barrel of his pistol before backing away, his face full of menace, then entered the café and took a table by the window.

Vosuruk grabbed Wallace's arm. 'Inside,' he said, pushing Wallace on.

Wallace took a seat at Bodur's table, and Vosuruk leaned against the wall of the café near the entrance, within a few strides of Ghulan. He watched the colonel intently.

Wallace looked around, scrutinising the faces of the patrons, the last people he'd see. All men, they huddled in small groups of two or three and were engaged in animated conversations. Waiters scurried between the tables serving tiny cups of thick black liquid potent enough to jolt a dying man to life. Wallace sensed Bodur stiffen and followed his gaze to see a tanned man approach. He was taller than the surrounding crowd, maybe six-two, and had straight, neatly cropped brown hair. Light slacks and a short-sleeved shirt completed the list of characteristics that marked him out as a westerner, and Wallace watched as he took the chair next to Ghulan.

A waiter obscured the view for a moment, until Bodur sent him away with an order for two coffees. When he retreated, Wallace saw Ghulan and the stranger locked in an intense exchange. He had no doubt this was the broker who'd arranged the assassination.

Wallace didn't even hear the first gunshot. A man behind him screamed and Wallace turned to see that the screamer's companion had been hit in the chest, a fast-growing crimson stain spreading across his tunic. He did register the second shot, a high-pressured hiss, followed by a crack as the bullet snapped through the window before striking Bodur in the temple, killing him instantly.

The crowded alleyway became a tempest of screams and confusion as terrified people tried to flee. Bodur fell out of his chair. Wallace's head went light and the world became distant, his body alien as though it belonged to someone else. He found himself rising, staring out of the window towards the rooftop at the end of the alleyway, where a muzzle flashed as another volley of shots was unleashed. The café window shattered, but Wallace didn't flinch and waited for the shooter to find his mark.

Patrons cried as they were hit, and those that were able to move fled towards the back of the café. Wallace felt heavy hands upon him and turned to see Vosuruk propelling him across the room. He wanted to resist, to explain that he'd made a choice, but the veteran gave him no chance, and pushed him behind the protective cover of the wall beside the entrance.

Outside, the alleyway was a sea of racing bodies, and between the waves, Wallace saw Ghulan and the tall man wrestling. He was startled when the tall man's head suddenly jerked back, propelled by the impact of a bullet that tore through the top of his skull. Ghulan stood up, the tall man's smoking pistol in his hand. He noticed Wallace and Vosuruk and started to raise the gun in their direction, but he never completed the manoeuvre. Vosuruk drew a pistol and shot him in the neck. The second bullet hit him just above the ear, and he fell, dead.

'The roof,' Vosuruk said, indicating the eastern end of the alleyway.

Wallace peered through the doorway and saw something that jolted him out of his daze. Lying prone at the edge of the flat roof at the end of the alley, peering down the scope of a high-powered rifle, was a figure clad in the unmistakable mask and black body armour of Pendulum. Wallace reeled at the impossibility of the situation.

Vosuruk yanked him back a split second before bullets cracked the plaster where his head had been.

'It can't be,' Wallace told Vosuruk in disbelief. 'He's dead.'

19

Vosuruk did not pretend to understand the confused westerner, and looked at the crowd racing past the shattered window.

'Come,' he said, stepping into the alleyway.

Hard reality dispelled the last vestiges of disbelief. Wallace had proof positive that Ash had been right; Pendulum hadn't been working alone. The man shooting from the roof might have had a hand in what happened to Connie. Pressed by guilt over his role in her death, Wallace ran outside and followed Vosuruk across the crowded alleyway.

Pendulum rained fire, and bodies fell around them as the shooter tried to single out Wallace. Vosuruk pushed on, and Wallace travelled in his wake, following the veteran's lead by ducking and weaving through the crowd to avoid giving the sniper an easy target. As they neared the middle of the alleyway, Vosuruk produced a Kalashnikov from beneath the folds of his cloak and unleashed a fearsome volley at the rooftop. Through the exploding brickwork and clouds of dust, Wallace saw the unmistakable shudder of someone who'd been hit, and Pendulum rolled away from the edge of the roof, dragging his rifle with him.

Vosuruk forced himself against the tide of fleeing people. Wallace didn't hesitate: he had to know who was under the mask. He followed the veteran through the crowd, towards the building, a ramshackle office block. They got swept into a stream of people flowing into the building's back door, but unlike the rest of the crowd, which was turning left into the lobby and using the front entrance as an escape route, the veteran lurched right and led Wallace up the tiled fire stairs, towards the roof.

They'd rounded the first floor, when Wallace saw Pendulum limping down the flight above them, his right arm clasped to his side. The man reacted frighteningly quickly and drew a pistol. He managed to get off two shots before Vosuruk's AK-47 spat fire and a hail of bullets hit him in the face and chest. Pendulum tumbled down the stairs and fell prone on the landing, midway between the first and second floors. Wallace was about to run to the man when he noticed Vosuruk leaning against the wall, unable to continue. Vosuruk collapsed to his knees and Wallace saw dark red blood running between his fingers, which were pressed against his belly.

Wallace caught Vosuruk and gently lowered the man's head to the cold marble floor. His heart pounding, his throat thick with bile, Wallace tried not to think about Connie, but it was impossible. He looked at Vosuruk and recognised the signs; the dismay, the disbelief, the hungry desire that would give anything for a few more moments of life.

'English,' Vosuruk said, his eyes staring through Wallace, his voice uneven and thick. 'You know what mean *Tr'ok Si'ol?*'

Wallace shook his head, struggling to maintain his composure.

'Sad wolf,' the veteran told him. 'You are too sad. Be happy.'

Wallace held the man's hand as he suddenly spasmed, his body shuddering violently as he gasped for breath. And then he was gone, his eyes blank, his body still.

The weight of grief pressed down on Wallace, preventing him from moving. It wasn't just the death of his warm-hearted host; Wallace was haunted by the memory of all the people who had died because of him.

Lost in mourning, he longed for the relief a bullet would bring. But none came, and the sound of pandemonium outside barged its way into his private grief, echoing from the street and bouncing around the stairwell, gradually increasing in volume until Wallace's senses returned. He heard metal scraping across something hard and turned to see Pendulum trying to point the pistol in his direction.

Fuelled by anger, Wallace got to his feet, raced up the stairs and kicked the gun away from the prone man. He stamped on the man's ribs and felt a satisfying crack beneath the Kevlar body armour. Then he knelt beside him and pounded on the black combat mask that covered the man's face. He didn't stop until his knuckles hurt, and when he did, it was with the sudden realisation that Pendulum was completely still.

Wallace hesitated for a moment, before reaching for the clasps that held the mask in place. He unclipped and loosened them and removed the fearsome veil. Lying there, taking his final breaths, was the man who'd impersonated Pendulum in the Cromwell Center: Mike Rosen.

20

A jumble of questions filled Wallace's mind. Why had Rosen tried to kill him? Was he trying to avenge Pendulum? Or was he finishing his work? Had they been working together from the outset?

'Why?' Wallace asked, but he never received a reply. Rosen stared up at him blankly until his gaze shifted beyond this world.

Wallace heard voices above him and looked up to see puzzled, fearful men peering down from the second-floor landing. One of the men yelled something in Pashtun, his voice raw with hostility, and Wallace started moving. He bounded down the steps, spurred by the pounding of shoes on the hard stairs above, then retraced his route through the back entrance, into the alleyway where the panicked crowd had started to thin. He sprinted past the injured and dead and reached the café, where he hurried in through the shattered window and rooted around Bodur's tunic until he found the keys to the pick-up.

Ignoring the cries of a group of men who'd emerged from the building at the end of the alleyway, he leaped through the broken window and sprinted towards Maiwand Road. Wallace couldn't decipher the exact meaning of the clamour that followed him, but understood enough to know that some of the pursuing crowd believed he'd been one of the shooters. With so many dead, passions would be high, and he knew that if the police didn't arrive soon, the mob would seek to exact instant vengeance.

His only advantage was the general disorder and panicked state of the crowd.

'*Hasilawal!*' a voice yelled, and Wallace saw the fear in the surrounding faces turn to bewilderment as he raced past them, pursued by a growing mob.

By the time he reached the corner of Maiwand Road, there must have been twenty angry men after him, and Wallace started to feel the first attempts to grab him. He ran faster, resisting the fingers of passers-by who reacted to the cries of the pursuing mob and tried to hold him. He raced into the road, which was choked with vehicles belonging to people who had stopped to help the victims of the attack, and he could hear the sound of sirens approaching. Seeing the Toyota parked where they'd left it, he leaped over the bonnet of an old Fiat and sprinted to the pick-up. As he fumbled with the keys, someone grabbed him and Wallace reacted instinctively, throwing an angry punch square into the man's face. He felt the crunch of bone as the man's nose shattered, and saw him stumble away in agony. The mob was halfway across the road when Wallace got the key to work. He pulled the door open, jumped inside and gunned the engine. With the street blocked in both directions, Wallace put the truck in gear, stepped on the accelerator and forced the Toyota on to the sidewalk, as the first members of the mob pounded on the chassis. The Toyota roared as it tore along the crowded pavement, leaving the frustrated mob behind. Wallace hit the horn and tried to control the powerful truck as people leaped from its path. He looked to his right and saw that he'd passed the blockage of traffic. There was a gap in the line of parked vehicles and he swung the Toyota through it. The flatbed collided with the rearmost car, and the fishtailing truck threatened to spin wildly, but Wallace rode the skid, regained control and turned left, speeding along Maiwand Road.

As the truck roared west and the scene of carnage rapidly

shrank in the rear-view mirror, Wallace tried to calm his trembling nerves. He took his foot off the accelerator, allowing the Toyota to slow, aware that he could not afford to crash or be caught. Right now, he was the only person in the world who could prove Ash right. Pendulum had not been working alone.

21

A rapid pulse hammered Bailey's ears, and he opened his heavy eyes, which were immediately blinded by bright sunlight. He raised an aching arm to his forehead and shielded his face until his pupils contracted and he could face the world. The pulse was coming from his phone, which was vibrating against his coffee table. He reached out, answered the call and switched off his TV.

'Bailey,' he croaked.

'It's Murrall,' the East End detective said, his tone abrupt. 'I've been trying to reach you.'

'Sorry, I got tied up with a couple of things,' Bailey responded. He sat up and tried to ignore the burning indigestion that seared his chest.

'I went down to the *Record* yesterday afternoon,' Murrall continued with undisguised hostility. 'They said you'd already spoken to them.'

'Yeah, I—' Bailey began.

'I don't know what you think is going on here, but I'm leading this investigation,' Murrall interrupted. 'I didn't even want you on the case. The husband insisted I brought you in. You were invited to consult as a professional courtesy, but so far I haven't seen anything professional about you.'

'I—' Bailey tried.

'Your boss said I should make allowances for you, but you

disappear, leave me searching for a brief who doesn't exist, you harass the victim's kids – yeah, I know about that – you don't return my calls, and then you interrogate the victim's colleagues without notifying me,' Murrall rattled off the charge list, his voice rich with ire.

Bailey's hungover mind searched for a response, but wasn't quick enough.

'You're drowning,' Murrall cut him off again. 'Why do you think Cross can spare you? What have you been doing since Pendulum? You think people can't see what's happened? You've lost your bottle. Cross told me to go easy, but I'm not having some big-name, past-his-prime hotshot fucking up my case. Either do your job, or fuck off.'

Murrall hung up, and, as the line went dead, the hollowness of despair grabbed Bailey and yanked him down. As he tumbled, his mind spinning, his body burning with raw shame, he tried to hold on to a single thought, but there were too many, all of them too consequential for him to face. Cross knew. Superintendent Cross had been babying him. Murrall, that fat, greasy, boorish cop had only met him once and had already seen through the facade. Bailey spun on, questioning everything that had happened over the previous few months, trying to recall his sessions with the shrink, reconsidering every raised eyebrow, every sceptical look. Had she known he was lying, concealing his true state of mind?

'Shit!' he exclaimed, forcing himself to his feet.

He looked down at the detritus on his coffee table and swept it all on to the floor. The bottle bounced, colliding with the glass, which smashed.

Bailey slumped on to the sofa and put his head in his hands. A stranger had given him confirmation that his problems were beyond him, but he had no idea what to do next. He'd isolated himself from his friends and family, and . . . a hazy memory flickered to life, a phone call, a conversation about work. He carefully brushed away the shards of glass, picked his phone off the floor and checked the call log to find a listing for Christine Ash. The sight of her name triggered flashbacks, snatches of conversation, a request, something to do with the Greene case. He checked his email sent folder and found one addressed to Christine Ash.

Hey Chris
   You sound goooood! Let me no if yr man findz anything.
Luv
Haybale

Bailey flushed with humiliation. The terrible spelling and inappropriate informality were hallmarks of someone who was more than half-cut. He scrolled down to the attachments to see a couple of photographs of the numeric code, and was relieved to discover that even in his inebriated haze, he'd only sent partials. Then he saw a third image, one that he'd almost forgotten he'd taken: three balls laid in a row, with the pointed ends of metal stakes almost touching them, their thick ends fanning out to form the edges and centre of a trapezoid. It was what the kid, the older one, Hector or Joseph, said he'd found on his mum's desk. The photograph was the final sign that something had to change. Prior to his shooting, there was no way that Bailey would have forgotten about a piece of evidence.

Whiners aren't winners.

Bailey recalled his grandmother's mantra as he heaved himself to his feet and headed for the shower, knowing that it would take more than water to wash away the filth of failure and the pungent aroma of self-pity.

22

Ash had spent the night checking her files, looking for a link between Max Byrne and Mountainhome, the town where the diner was located, but found nothing. Finally, frustrated and exhausted, she had taken a couple of Ambien and collapsed on her bed fully clothed.

Waking to the sound of Kisnou's 'Falling Deeper', her preferred alarm tone, Ash rolled on to her back, her dazed eyes coming to life. She lay for a moment, listening to the sentimental music, trying to ignore the painful throbbing that encircled her neck. The pain intensified when she pushed herself upright, and she moved gingerly as she slipped off the T-shirt and jeans Reeves had given her. She swallowed a couple of extra strength Advil and showered, taking care to follow the doctor's instruction to not let her bandage get wet. The warm water and soft soap soothed and she stepped out of the shower free of pain and aglow with a sheen of positivity, which wavered when she caught sight of herself in the bathroom mirror. The wide bandage that encircled her neck was starting to look grey and dirty, but it was another two days before she had to return to Brookdale to have it changed. Her sandy brown hair banded together in lank tresses and drooped over her face, which was paler than usual. She made a mental note to find time to visit the salon, where Aubrey would be able to wash her hair properly without getting her neck wet. Now she picked up her wire brush and ran it over her head.

Neat, but greasy, Ash thought, and she grabbed a band and tied her hair in a tight ponytail.

The prospect of a meeting with Harrell on her mind, Ash opted for a plain white blouse, a dark blue trouser suit and a pair of wheat-coloured Matt Bernson Camden heels. She hurriedly ran through her minimalist make-up routine: eyeliner, mascara and lipstick, first applying a rare preparatory layer of liquid foundation to conceal her pallor. Satisfied that she exceeded the Bureau's professional dress code, Ash was about to leave when her gaze lingered on the dirty bandage. Struck by inspiration, she opened her dresser drawer and grabbed a cherry blossom printed silk scarf that she'd bought from the indoor market in the Village. She folded it neatly and tied it round her neck, creating a fetching choker. *You can't change the past*, she remembered her mother once saying, *you can only make the best of it*. Content with how she looked, Ash grabbed her purse and left the apartment.

Ash drove her Ford Taurus up the ramp of her building's underground parking garage at 7:23 a.m. and turned right on to Washington Square North, before looping round the park and crossing on to Fourth Street. The traffic kept a slow and steady pace, the warm, idling vehicles leaching misty fumes into the spring air. Ash switched on the radio and caught a couple of light tunes before the news. The familiar, gravelly voice of WCBD News, Perry Castle, told tales of trouble in the Mid-East, before turning to domestic turbulence that was building over the Blake-Castillo Bill, as campaigners fought to resist regulation of the internet. When Ash reached the intersection of Broadway and Canal Street, Perry moved on to the sensational capture of the serial killer known as Babylon, and she could not help but turn up the volume.

'. . . with the FBI refusing to give further details and Bureau sources remaining tight-lipped, the media can only speculate on how Charles Haig was identified as a suspect and how his arrest went so very, very wrong. And now for sports news . . .'

Ash switched off the radio, annoyed at the tone of the reporting. The media had savaged the Bureau after Pendulum and had kept a keen eye out for any other perceived failings. She knew that Harrell would be under pressure to release details to celebrate the identification, if not the death, of Charles Haig as a Bureau success. The gruesome method adopted by Babylon had made the murders a media sensation and Ash loathed the prospect that she might achieve any notoriety as the FBI agent who almost had her head sliced off by a serial killer.

She nodded to the gate guards who matched her licence plate to their on-screen photo ID database. Satisfied she wasn't a threat, one of the guards lowered the wedge barrier and allowed her to drive into the parking garage. She slid the Taurus into her bay beneath Federal Plaza and five minutes later was at her desk, in her office on the twenty-eighth floor. Small as it was, Ash had a private place to work and a view of Broadway and the majestic city beyond. A framed photograph of a California beach sunset took up most of one wall and the other was covered with notes, paperwork, photographs and documents pinned to cork tiles that ran the length of the room. Ash liked to see her work laid out the old-fashioned way, and her eyes would often dance around the board looking for connections. As she sat at her desk, she realised she'd be due a clear-out – everything on the wall related to Babylon would need to be filed with the official report. While she waited for her computer to start, she looked at the framed photograph of her with her mother, both smiling in the sunshine, hugging each other high in the Santa Monica Mountains, Los Angeles sprawled below them beneath a smoky haze. Ash picked up the picture and touched her mother's face, recalling the dream she'd had about Nicholas, and wondering how such a beautiful, kind woman could have fallen for such an evil man.

When she checked her Bureau emails, she saw something from Patrick Bailey and remembered their conversation of the previous evening. He'd sounded smashed, and the email only reinforced that assessment. Ash took a quick look at the three photo attachments but codes and symbols were not her thing, so she forwarded the email to Pavel at Kosinsky Data Services, taking care to delete Bailey's drunken words and asking Pavel to drop her a line if he came up with anything.

Favour done, Ash checked her watch: 7:57 a.m., which meant it would be 12:57 in London, a civilised time to call anyone, even a hungover cop. She was reaching for the phone when it rang, and she saw Cyndy Pearl's name flash on the display – Harrell's assistant.

Ash lifted the receiver. 'Morning, Cyndy,' she said.

'Good morning, Chris. How are you?' Cyndy asked, her voice heavy with concern.

'OK,' Ash replied. 'Could have been worse.'

'Well, thank God it wasn't,' Cyndy said. 'He'd like to see you if you've got a moment.'

Ash thought about clarifying whether it was God or Harrell who wanted to see her, but decided against making an irreverent remark to the devoutly Christian Cyndy. And besides, as far as the New York Field Office was concerned, Harrell *was* God.

'I'll be right up,' she said.

Cyndy's dimpled cheeks crinkled as her mouth curled into a sympathetic smile. Her wavy brown hair was immaculately set and, as she stood, Ash saw that Cyndy was wearing a floral A-line dress beneath a pastel blue bolero, looking every inch the fifties throwback.

'He said to go right in,' Cyndy advised as she stepped out from behind her desk and opened the door to Harrell's office. 'Is that . . .' She placed a hand on Ash's arm and pointed at the cherry blossom choker.

Ash nodded.

'I'm so sorry, honey,' Cyndy said, and she pulled Ash into a surprising hug. 'I hope you feel better,' she added, before stepping away.

'Thanks,' Ash responded awkwardly.

Harrell's office was in the north-east corner of the building, overlooking Lafayette and Worth, and even though he was only four storeys above Ash, the view seemed so much better. The East River and Brooklyn were laid out in one direction and the stickleback architecture of Manhattan in the other. Harrell was seated at his desk, his posture noticeable for the plumb alignment of his spine which was probably a throwback to his military days. He was tall and thin, and unfurled as Ash entered. His mop of salt-and-pepper hair danced as he crossed the room.

'I'm so glad you're OK,' he said, shaking Ash's hand warmly. 'Take a seat.'

Ash sat in one of four low-backed chairs that were arranged around a small table, and Harrell took a seat next to her.

'Reeves and Miller say you saved their lives,' he told Ash earnestly. 'Good work. But what the hell were you doing chasing down Haig without back-up?'

'It was my call,' Ash replied. 'I didn't want NYPD spooking the guy,' she added, wondering whether Harrell would sense the half-truth. She'd always had trust issues, but the Pendulum case had pushed them into overdrive.

Harrell pursed his lips and studied Ash. 'I would've brought them in, but you're right, it was your call. We're catching heat for his suicide, but from what I can see in Reeves's and Miller's reports, there wasn't anything we could've done.'

Ash nodded, shuddering as she recalled the moment Charles Haig sent a bullet through his skull.

'Whatever the press say, you stopped a killer,' Harrell assured her.

'I think Haig found Pendulum's base of operations, sir,' she told him, noticing his eyes narrow as she continued. 'I found pictures of John Wallace and the other victims that were taken before Pendulum struck, which means Haig was either involved . . .'

Harrell gave a fatigued shake of the head, and Ash knew he was about to make another rebuttal of her conspiracy theory.

'. . . which I don't believe,' she assured him. 'Haig was too sloppy, too egotistical. Pendulum didn't want people to know he existed – not until right at the end. Haig was an egotist who wrote to the papers. No, I think Haig was an obsessive fan, and I believe he stalked a trail left by Pendulum. A trail that led him to the base.'

'Can you piece it together?' Harrell asked, intrigued.

'Maybe.' Ash nodded. 'I've got a place to start. Mountainhome, Pennsylvania.'

'Take a couple of days' leave and then check it out,' Harrell suggested. 'The trail's cold anyway. It doesn't need to be done now.'

'I'd like to get started right away, if that's OK with you, sir. It won't do me any good to be sat at home. I wasn't made for downtime.'

'You can write your report on Haig. Give me something I can use to get the press on side,' Harrell told her.

'I know you're catching heat, sir, but I'd rather just do my job,' Ash responded. 'File my report when I've investigated every line of inquiry.'

Harrell gave a wry smile and nodded slowly. 'One day you're going to realise that you can't run full throttle all your life. Something will break.'

'I appreciate the concern, sir,' Ash assured him as she got to her feet.

'Let me know if you find anything,' Harrell said.

Ash arrived in Mountainhome shortly after ten a.m., having driven against the flow of traffic, following I-80 along its tree-lined route into Pennsylvania. The Mountainhome Diner was located on the southern edge of town, about ten miles off the interstate. She pulled into the parking lot that the diner shared with Jimmy's Ice Cream Parlour, a tiny kiosk with a couple of counters and a drive-through window. The ice cream parlour was closed and the diner was quiet, with only three other cars and a pick-up truck in the lot. Ash climbed out of her Taurus and walked over to the south-eastern corner of the building, where she peered into the second window, the one where Max Byrne had been sitting. She tried to imagine him alone in a booth, surrounded by families, couples, truckers, people just living their normal lives, unaware of the serial killer in their midst. She looked up and down Peterson Road, which ran north into town and south towards the interstate, and was wondering which way Byrne had travelled when she was suddenly startled by a loud knock on the window. Wheeling round, she saw a middle-aged strawberry blonde in a sky-blue polo shirt beckoning her inside.

Ash walked up the shallow ramp and made her way through the porch, which was plastered with flyers for local events.

'You look lost,' the strawberry blonde observed as Ash entered. 'Need any help?'

A denim-clad man in a baseball cap with dirty blond hair and a droopy moustache was seated by the counter, while a dark-haired young mother sat in the booth in the far corner and fed her fat toddler a slice of cake. The air was rich with the aroma of griddled meat, a deep, savoury smell that was sufficiently enticing to get Ash thinking about a very early lunch.

'Agent Christine Ash, FBI,' she said, showing the woman her ID. She followed up by producing her phone and opening a file photo of Max Byrne. 'I'm looking for this man.'

'Tammy,' the woman introduced herself. She puzzled over the image for a moment, then shook her head. 'Face rings a bell, but I couldn't say why.'

'Hey, that's the Pendulum guy,' a voice called from behind the counter, and Ash looked over to see a man in chef whites. His curly black hair was tied under a net, exposing pasty round cheeks and wide, happy eyes. 'I seen him on the news.'

Ash nodded, and Tammy shuddered. 'He ever been in here?'

'I woulda remembered him,' the cook assured her. 'I'm Frankie, by the way.'

'What about this guy?' Ash asked, swiping to a photo of Charles Haig.

'That's that Babylon,' Frankie told Tammy. 'I told you! He's been on the TV,' he continued. 'I told Tammy he was in here a few months ago. Maybe September or October. He was asking questions. Just like you.'

'About Pendulum?' Ash watched Frankie's excitement building, certain that he'd bore his friends with this story for years, his involvement growing with each retelling until he was solely responsible for apprehending both Pendulum and Babylon.

'No,' Frankie said, shaking his head. 'He wanted to know about our camera system,' he explained, indicating the security camera in the corner of the room. 'Asked if we kept our tapes. I told him I didn't know, sent him on to Arlo, the boss.'

'Is Arlo around?' Ash asked.

Frankie and Tammy exchanged sorrowful looks.

'Arlo's dead,' Tammy said at last. 'Heart attack the day after Christmas.'

'I'm sorry to hear that,' Ash offered.

'Well, you know, when it's your time, it's your time,' Tammy observed quietly.

'Chester, his son, runs the place now,' Frankie revealed. 'He might remember something.'

'Where would I find him?'

'Eight-Fourteen Spruce Cabin Road,' Tammy replied.

'Thanks, you've been very helpful,' Ash said, turning for the door. She stopped in her tracks and pivoted. 'I don't suppose you recognise this?' She swiped her photos until she reached the pictured she'd discovered in Babylon's lair: the hand-held selfie of a smiling Haig standing beside a dirt track, tall green trees crowding either side of it.

Frankie and Tammy studied the picture blankly, clueless until Ash saw inspiration flash across Frankie's eyes.

'That's out by the falls,' he said excitedly. 'Look, you can see the antenna there in the background.'

Tammy squinted at the photo and nodded. 'I think you're right.'

Frankie pointed at a tiny, thin line that was so faint that Ash had taken it to be a blemish on the image. 'That's the old radio antenna out by the falls – Spruce Cabin Falls. Right out in the woods. Tough country. Hillbilly country,' he added with phony menace.

'Frank!' Tammy elbowed him playfully.

'Can you tell me how to get there?' Ash asked, suddenly alive with the thrill of a lead.

23

They called the easy-going detective 'Bunker', and Bailey had watched the rangy blond man for the best part of three hours, diligently working at his desk, rising occasionally to query something with one of his colleagues, all smiles and back slaps. Bunker provided a window into the past and despite their physical differences, reminded Bailey of himself before the shooting: a man at ease. The comparison was emphasised by Bailey's reason for being in the building. After showering, forcing down breakfast and studiously resisting the urge to pour himself a drink or neck a couple of pills, he had driven up to Stoke Newington Police Station, where he'd been told that Murrall was out. Bailey had asked to wait and had been shown to the second-floor detectives' room, where he'd been offered a chair by the door, near the photocopier. He'd watched the detectives come and go, observed their camaraderie and grown jealous of what he saw and what had once been his.

The arched windows that filled the yellow brick building with light were small compared with the massive panes of glass at Paddington Green, but somehow the shabby East London station seemed brighter. Bailey suspected his maudlin mood was colouring his vision and returned his attention to the symbol that the Greene boy had found on his dead mother's desk. Bailey had tried a variety of searches, but asking Google to look up 'ball and rods' or 'ball and spikes' returned millions of irrelevant and unsavoury results.

He had clocked just over three hours in the detectives' room when Murrall entered.

'Mouse! You've got a visitor,' Bunker yelled over to him, and Murrall turned to see Bailey.

'Mouse?' Bailey asked as he weaved his way around the maze of cubicles and offered Murrall his hand.

'Yeah, what with me being so small,' Murrall noted dryly. He left Bailey hanging for a moment, before taking his hand.

'I just wanted to say sorry,' Bailey confessed sheepishly. 'I've been—'

'Don't worry about it,' Murrall cut him off. 'I know what happened to you. I'm surprised you came back after something like that. I'm not sure I could.'

Murrall's sympathy made Bailey feel even worse and he started to realise that he'd misjudged the paunchy detective.

'I was just with the husband. Says he can't face going back to the house, so he's staying with his sister,' Murrall revealed, and Bailey caught him watching for a reaction. 'I know you were there,' he added when none came. 'And I know the boys gave you something. They told me.'

'Greene said something in confidence,' Bailey began.

'Confidence? This is my investigation,' Murrall protested without attempting to mask his frustration.

'The last time I broke a confidence someone was almost killed,' Bailey revealed.

'Pendulum?' Murrall asked.

Bailey nodded.

'That case has really fucked you up,' Murrall observed. 'Can't you see that? You want my opinion? We're not dealing with a serial killer. This was a suicide. I'm guessing the husband was into some shady shit and it's made him crazy with guilt.

You don't need to keep his confidence, you need to keep mine.'

Bailey tried to hold Murrall's gaze as he struggled to cope with the truth of the East End detective's words. He'd attempted to slot back into a life that no longer existed. Pendulum's bullets hadn't put him in the ground, but they'd killed the man he once was and left a fearful wretch in his place.

'So are you going to tell me what those kids gave you?' Murrall pressed.

Bailey found himself nodding and produced his phone. He opened his photos and swiped to a picture. 'They found this on Mrs Greene's desk,' he said, showing Murrall the image of three balls with the pointed ends of the metal stakes almost touching them.

'Looks like some kind of symbol,' Murrall observed. 'Let me have that.'

Bailey relinquished the phone, hoping that Murrall would not swipe the image and discover the photographs of the suicide note and the code. Whatever those numbers concealed was dangerous enough to get Sylvia Greene killed, either by her own hand or someone else's, and until Bailey cracked the code, there was no way he was exposing the rest of the Greene family to any danger. Murrall knew the boys had given him something, so Bailey had to relinquish the strange symbol in order to protect the bigger secret.

'Hey!' Murrall shouted, his voice carrying across the office. 'Anyone know what this is?' he asked, holding the phone out for his colleagues.

The dozen or so detectives and administrators clustered around Murrall and peered at the photograph, most of them studying it blankly.

'Looks Celtic,' Bunker told them, and when he noticed their surprised glances, he added, 'What? I grew up in Cornwall. I'm pretty sure it's Celtic.'

'Cooperation,' Murrall said pointedly, returning the phone to Bailey.

His colleagues went back to their desks, mocking Bunker for being a 'country boy', 'yokel', and 'druid'.

Bailey didn't bother responding to Murrall's condescending remark. He searched for Celtic symbols on his phone and found a chart of common symbols in Google images. There in the bottom right-hand corner of the grid was what he was looking for.

'This is it,' he told Murrall. He clicked on the image and was sent to a page on druidism. He quickly scanned it, then explained, 'It's not Celtic. It's the Welsh symbol for *Awen*, an ancient word for "inspiration". It also means "truth".' He wondered why Sylvia Greene had chosen this particular symbol to punctuate her death.

24

The track lay to the west of Mountainhome, ten minutes' drive from the diner. It branched off Creek Road and was so overgrown that Ash passed it twice. She finally noticed the narrow corridor on her third attempt and parked in the mouth just off the deserted road. She climbed out of the Taurus and checked the photo on her phone. The trees were slightly fuller, but there was no doubt that this was where Charles Haig had taken the selfie. She returned to the car and drove on down the bumpy trail, forcing her way into the dense forest. The trees seemed determined to repel her with branches that whipped at the windshield and scored the sides of the Taurus. Rains had purged the trail of most markings, but every now and again she could see the faint impression of tyre tracks on a rise that had avoided the water's erosion. It was obvious that the trail had not been used for weeks, possibly months, and she wondered whether Charles Haig had been the last person to travel this way.

After four slow miles winding through thick forest, the trail ended in a turning circle barely large enough to accommodate a car. Trees pressed in on all sides and there were no other tracks in any direction. Ash turned the Taurus around so that it was facing Creek Road, and then got out to examine the dead end.

The turning circle was bordered by trees and beneath them lay an unbroken, thick line of grass and bushes. Ash walked the circumference, examining it with patient care, but there was no way of knowing which direction, if any, Charles Haig had gone. There were no tyre-marks, footprints, broken branches or trampled grass. She checked the edge of the turning circle again, this time crouching low to the ground. Her back started aching halfway round, so she stopped and stretched and immediately regretted doing so. Her neck burned painfully. High above her, the mid-morning sun emerged from behind a cloud and the forest came alive with dappled sunlight. Something caught Ash's eye. Six or seven yards into the forest, directly west of where she stood, the grass glittered. She pushed her way beyond the edge of the turning circle, between tightly packed trees, until she reached the sparkling grass. Tiny droplets of what looked like dew clung to the tips of the longest blades. When Ash knelt down to examine one, she realised that it was set solid, and as it caught the sunlight she could see the faintest pink hue. Each neighbouring blade of grass was home to at least one of these faint rubies. She pulled the biggest free and scratched at its hard surface, which flaked like old plastic. When she smelled the nick she'd created, Ash recognised the scent instantly, and hurried back to the Taurus. She ran to the trunk and opened the field case she kept inside, then pulled out a spare Glock and holster, which she strapped beneath her jacket, but she was looking for something far more mundane, and after a few more moments' delving in the case, stepped back with an LED flashlight in her hand.

Ash shut the trunk and hurried back to the spot where the grass sparkled in the sun. She turned on the flashlight, and the powerful bulbs emitted a directed beam of infrared light. The crystallised droplets became bright pink dots, aglow as though alive with their own bright energy. Ash swung the flashlight in an arc and saw that the forest had been blanketed with tiny droplets. She knew what they were. Charles Haig must have mixed a dye into a cyanoacrylate compound and sprayed the area until he'd found something specific. Now she saw what it was: a couple of yards up ahead, brought into relief by the coloured droplets, was a latent footprint. Without the photoreactive chemical, the print would have been lost to the natural contours of the forest floor, but with it, the slight indentations of the shoe or boot's sole were visible. The print would be preserved by the cyanoacrylate compound which had set solid and would not biodegrade for many years. As sick as he had been, Ash had to admire Haig's resourcefulness and dedication. He'd gone to great lengths to track his twisted hero.

She followed the footprints further into the forest. Every so often she'd come to a patch of ground that was covered with droplets, where Haig had sprayed widely to rediscover the trail, but by moving slowly and methodically, Ash never lost sight of the tracks. The footprints led her into an open glade next to a small, three-tiered waterfall. The marks took her over stepping stones that crossed the creek, and once on the other side, she was enveloped by the thick canopy of the forest. She walked on for another forty-five minutes until the tracks suddenly stopped in a small clearing. The flashlight revealed that the area was well sprayed with the cyanoacrylate compound but the footprints came to an abrupt end at the edge of the clearing. Ash could not imagine Haig giving up, and her instincts told her that he'd made it to Pendulum's base – the photographs proved that.

She scoured the clearing for inspiration, and when she returned to the spot where the footprints disappeared, she noticed a slight change in the sound of her own steps. They weren't deadened by the soft soil, but instead had some resonance. She crouched down and pushed her fingers into the warm topsoil, burrowing until she felt something she wasn't expecting: damp, soft material. Ash pulled, but it wouldn't budge, so she knelt down and dug until she'd exposed what it was: a tightly woven mesh that was full of mulchy soil. She worked along the mesh, digging the surface away until she'd exposed a perfect two-foot square that revealed the edges of a trapdoor, with a recessed handle. Ash pulled it and found herself lifting a thick metal door that concealed a flight of concrete steps. She dropped the door against the soft earth and started down.

There were twenty steps, leading to a narrow concrete tunnel that ended in a thick metal security door. The keypad beside the door had been tampered with and the exposed wires cut, stripped and rerouted. Ash pulled the handle, and, to her surprise, the door opened. She stepped inside what looked like a service area, complete with generators, air conditioning units and a heating system. Everything was old, maybe from the late seventies or early eighties, but the lights were on and the machines seemed to be functioning. Ash looked at the thick concrete walls and guessed that she was in a civil defence bunker, a remnant of the Cold War. She followed the mesh walkway through the plant room and came to another steel door, this one with a multi-latch pressure locking system. She turned the central handle and all the latches opened with a loud clunk.

Ash stepped through the door into a bunk room containing thirty beds stacked in columns of three. Only one of the bunks had bedclothes on it, but when Ash touched it she saw that the sheet was covered in a thick layer of dust. She opened another pressure door and moved into a canteen. Two large tables were flanked by plastic benches. A catering stove lay against one wall and next to it was a long counter that ended in an industrial sink. She noticed some unwashed metal bowls and dirty cutlery in the sink, all covered with furry mould.

Another pressure door opened on to an operations room. Pre-digital control systems and monitors lined the walls, but Ash's eyes were immediately drawn to a square of tables and chairs in the heart of the room. The tables were covered with contemporary computer terminals, but more striking than the machines was the sight of a man in a brown hooded top working at one of them. He had his back to Ash and was oblivious to her presence, thanks to the large headphones that covered his ears. Ash drew her pistol and stepped forward slowly.

'Drop it!' a voice yelled, and Ash turned to see a tall man in a pair of black jeans and a camouflage jacket pointing a gun at her. It was a nickel-plated Colt .380, a street tool, not the weapon of a professional.

Ash guessed the guy was in his early twenties and she sensed his fear and uncertainty.

'I'm a federal agent,' she informed him coolly.

The guy at the computer still hadn't noticed what was happening.

'I don't give a shit,' Colt .380 said brashly. 'I'll fuckin' drop you.'

Ash wheeled round and opened fire, winging him in the shoulder. The gunshots were loud enough to penetrate the headphones, and, as Colt .380 fell howling to the floor, the guy at the terminal caught sight of her.

'Don't move!' Ash yelled, but the shocked man was running before the words had left her mouth.

The headphones fell away, and as Ash opened fire, he ducked behind a huge, solid-state mainframe. The heavy machine shielded him from Ash's shots, but before she could think about pursuit, Colt .380 started shooting, his bullets flying inches from her head, thudding into the metal around her. She dropped to one knee and returned fire, hitting the man three times, square in the chest.

She turned and set off in pursuit of the hooded man, threading her way between the dormant old computers and the modern machines that filled the room. She came to another doorway and stepped into a long corridor. The man in the hooded top stood at the other end, his back to her as he concentrated on a terminal next to a set of mesh steps.

'Freeze!' Ash yelled, but the guy ignored her and carried on with whatever he was doing. She moved purposefully towards him, pistol raised. 'Put your hands where I can see them,' she commanded.

The man backed towards her and slowly raised his hands, but as Ash approached, he bolted forward and bounded up the steps. She opened fire but he was too quick and the shots struck metal, creating a shower of sparks. She ran to the terminal and saw the words 'Command Destruct' flashing above a timer that was cycling its way down from 00:33 . . . 00:32 . . .

Ash ran up the stairs, which led to another steel door. She tried the handle – locked. The hooded man had fled through a second exit and locked it behind him, clearly believing he'd sealed her in. She bounded down the stairs and glanced at the terminal: 00:24 . . . 00:23 . . .

She sprinted along the corridor, back to the control room, and caught sight of a board covered with photographs of John Wallace and Pendulum's other victims. Beneath it was a table loaded with folders and documents, and even at a distance Ash could see the victims' names on the papers. Behind the table stood an open locker that contained Pendulum body armour. This was Pendulum's base, and there, within her grasp, was a trove of evidence that could have proved what she now knew for certain: Max Byrne had not been working alone. But Ash did not even skip a step as she raced through the control room, trying to guess how long she had. Her lungs burned, and the wound that scored her neck seethed with pain. Ash ignored both and forced herself on, past the man she'd shot, through the canteen, and into the bunk room. She expected every pounding step she took to be her last, but she made it through the plant room and into the concrete tunnel beyond. She flew up the hard staircase and was a few steps from the open trapdoor when the shockwave of a massive explosion caught her and sent her hurtling through the gap.

Ash landed heavily on the soft forest floor and looked round to see a jet of angry fire shooting out of the trapdoor, the scorching flames licking the sky. She tried to crawl away but her body failed her, and she collapsed where she lay. She fished for her cell phone, but even that simple motion was beyond her, and, as she brought the device towards her head, she passed out.

Ash lay unconscious in the moist dirt, the forest rumbling and quaking with the force of secondary explosions. Her cell phone rang, the screen shining with the words 'New York Field Office', but the call went unanswered. Soon the device fell silent.

25

'I'm sorry,' the operator said. 'Senior Special Agent Ash is unavailable. Can I try someone else for you?'

Frustrated, Wallace hung up and scanned the departure lounge. The international terminal was only a few years old and was a far cry from the crumbling concrete Soviet-era building that was now used for domestic flights. Panoramic windows looked out over the runway, and with only two more flights scheduled to leave Kabul that night, the airport was quiet. Wallace was on edge, watching for any subtle signs of trouble. None of the other travellers took the slightest notice of him and the armed airport police shuffled around, exhibiting little emotion beyond boredom. He moved away from the payphone and returned to his seat in the far corner of the lounge, its position buying him a degree of isolation and an unrestricted view of the rest of the building.

The attack at Ka Faroushi had sent him spiralling into paranoid despair. When he'd removed Pendulum's mask and seen Mike Rosen's face, he guessed that there were others who wanted him dead. Rosen had sent Ghulan and his men into the mountains and put a quarter-of-a-million-dollar bounty on his head, which was a fortune large enough to get every man in Afghanistan after him. *Tr'ok Si'ol*, Wallace thought, recalling Vosuruk's last words. He was less a sad wolf and more a harried fox, hunted by well-resourced, savage hounds, unable to comprehend why they'd go to such lengths to see him dead. The only plausible explanation was revenge, and that put one man squarely in the frame: Max Byrne's father.

After fleeing the mob, Wallace had driven west along Maiwand Road, desperately trying to figure out what to do. He'd pulled into a parking lot off Parmir Square and reversed into a spot by the embankment, overlooking the river. No one could approach from behind and he had a clear view of any vehicles coming into the lot. He had retrieved Bodur's cell phone from the glove compartment, but despite numerous attempts, he couldn't get the device to dial an international number. He had considered phoning the British embassy, but the last time he'd been hunted, the authorities had been his worst enemy, giving Pendulum reports and records to hack. He tried to remember whether Rosen had still been in custody when they'd finally confronted Pendulum. He was pretty sure the FBI wouldn't have released him that quickly, so he couldn't have been the man Ash had seen talking to the masked killer. That meant at least two people had helped Pendulum, and Wallace feared there could be more. Harsh experience had taught him that his best chance of survival was to stay off the grid. There were only two people he really trusted in the world: Christine Ash and Patrick Bailey, both of whom had risked their lives to save him, but without an international phone both were out of reach.

Dozens of people had seen him escape in the pick-up, so he had to ditch it. He grabbed his own clothes from the back seat and quickly changed out of the Nuristani attire Vosuruk had given him. Westerners were still pretty rare in Kabul, but not as rare as one trying to pass himself off as a local. Dressed in his filthy jeans, T-shirt and his Deerhunter jacket, he emerged from the pick-up and crossed the lot to Chihil Sotun Road, where he'd hailed a battered old taxi and asked the driver to take him to the airport.

The sun had set during their journey, and Wallace had taken comfort from the encroaching darkness. Shadow was his friend; the gloom made it less likely he'd be spotted. They'd cleared the checkpoint on the road to the airport without incident, and, when they'd arrived at the international terminal, Wallace had paid the driver, expressing his gratitude for his safe passage with a twenty-dollar tip. The gnarly old man had cracked a smile as he drove away, bemused by the filthy foreigner without any luggage. Grateful for his long-standing practice of keeping his passport, cash and credit card on him at all times, once inside the terminal, Wallace had spent the best part of two hours shuttling between numerous Ariana Afghan Airlines desks until someone figured out how he could buy a ticket on the spot. His nerves had grown more tattered and frayed with every passing moment, and he'd fully expected to be accosted and arrested by armed airport police. In the end, after pleading, cajoling and outright begging, and a process that had seemed to involve the cashier consulting with every Ariana employee in the terminal, Wallace had been sold a seat on the last plane out, a six-hour trip to Istanbul, and had paid over the odds for a connecting British Airways flight from the historic Turkish city to Heathrow.

After joining the long, slow queue that wound through passport control and security, he had finally made it to the departure lounge, where he'd been given directions to the payphones and had tried to call Bailey. Without Bailey's number, which was stored in his missing phone, Wallace had to rely on the international operator who had struggled to connect him to Paddington Green Police Station. When, after a dozen attempts, Wallace had finally been put through to the information line of Paddington train station, he'd given up and tried Ash. The international operator had no trouble reaching the FBI's New York Field Office, but Ash had been unavailable.

As he sat in the airport, nervously watching everyone around him, Wallace considered calling New York again and asking to leave Ash a message. If anything happened to him, at least she'd have recorded confirmation that Pendulum had not been working alone. Paranoia prevented him from acting on the thought. If that message reached the wrong ears, it would almost certainly place Ash in danger. He knew that his best course of action was to lie low until he reached London and could contact Bailey. When the PA system crackled to life with the announcement of Ariana Flight 719, he felt his stomach churn, and as he stood and strode towards the gate, he could not help but think that fate was going to play a cruel trick on him. The plane was scheduled to depart from Gate 12, a short walk from the departure lounge.

He entered the glass-panelled corridor that led to the aircraft, and saw two uniformed police officers walking towards him. Unlike their colleagues inside the terminal, these two looked alert and scanned the faces of passing passengers. Wallace's mouth went dry and his legs began to tremble. He considered turning around, but his body was unresponsive and his feet stopped moving. He stood frozen in the corridor, unable to do anything other than gawk at the approaching policemen, his eyes inexorably drawn to the sub-machine guns clasped by their bellies. With a monumental effort of will, he forced his arm up and his head down, and pretended to check his watch. He stood there, not daring to take a breath until the two uniformed men passed him.

Burning adrenalin subsided, and Wallace carried on towards the illuminated sign that read '12'. He joined a short queue of passengers, and resisted the urge to kiss the flight attendant when she checked his boarding pass and waved him through. The flight crew didn't comment on his dishevelled appearance when he boarded the plane; he was certain they'd seen far worse in Afghanistan. He hurried along the aisle to his seat, which was two rows behind the wing of the Airbus 310. As the last of the passengers boarded, he realised the flight would be less than half full and that he had three seats to himself. He took the one nearest the window and watched impatiently as the ground crew finished loading luggage on to the plane. Even when the plane finally reversed from the terminal and taxied towards the runway, his thoughts teemed with images of police cars tearing across the tarmac, blocking the plane's path – but the engines roared and propelled the aircraft into the night sky without incident. Wallace did not relax until forty minutes into the flight, when the Airbus levelled out at 31,000 feet. With Kabul long behind him and Afghanistan no more than an occasional faint light on the shadowed landscape far below, he finally allowed himself to slump back. Overcome by exhaustion, he immediately fell into a deep sleep.

26

Sound rose and fell like waves crashing against a rocky headland. Lights winked in and out of existence and danced across her vision, and the people around her seemed to move without travelling. Ash knew she needed medical attention, but had refused anything other than a cursory examination by the ambulance crew that had been summoned to the scene. She'd regained consciousness at 5:37 p.m., registering the exact time on her phone, which lay beside her on the forest floor. The first call she'd made had been to Reeves, but the details of what she'd said to him were lost to a groggy haze. She couldn't remember whether Reeves had suggested 911, but that was her next call. The emergency operator struggled to pinpoint her exact location, so Ash wiped the blood from her eyes, got to her feet and staggered through the forest, heading in the rough direction of the underground exit that the hooded man had used to escape. After two hundred feet she'd seen scorched trees a little off to her left, and found another blown-out trapdoor. The concentration and physical effort required to stay on her feet had made Ash sweat and she'd quickly become fatigued, leaning against trees for support as she lurched on. She'd careened from one trunk to another for a hundred feet, until she'd come to a wide, dusty trail. Ash's estimate of her distance from the radio mast had enabled the emergency operator to identify the trail, and the ambulance had reached her twenty minutes later. Pocono

Mountain Police officers Gary Chaffee and Erica Haas had arrived ten minutes after that, and, when Ash explained what had happened, they'd alerted their chief, who had implemented a cordon and dispatched another two units and a fire crew to the scene.

The paramedics had cleaned her up and advised her to let them take her to an ER, but Ash was determined to stay at the scene, and had sent the frustrated men away with a promise to follow their advice if her condition deteriorated. Reeves, Miller and Romero had arrived a little over an hour later. Ash knew they'd spoken to her, but couldn't remember anything of the conversation. Every so often, Reeves would tell her that he had things under control and that she should go to hospital, but she couldn't leave. As darkness had swept over the forest and local PD had fired up field lights powered by a portable generator, she had sat down on the trunk of a fallen tree and watched the world around her skip through time. She was losing moments to intermittent blackouts.

'You look like shit,' Reeves said, suddenly beside her. 'You need to go to a hospital. Miller will take you.'

The world suddenly came into focus. Miller and Romero were on their phones, pacing around as they talked urgently, while the local police searched the area. Ash concentrated, trying to get a better handle on reality.

A five-man fire crew moved in and out of the bunker collecting the equipment they needed to make it safe. The Pocono chief, whose name Ash couldn't remember, was a gaunt, tanned man with a short black beard, who reminded her of an old-school cowboy. He stood beside his all-black SUV, directing the search and liaising with his radio dispatcher. Ash could hear him asking for the ETA of the forensics team.

'I gotta see inside,' Ash told Reeves, aware that her speech was uneven. 'See what's left.'

'Firefighters say there's severe damage,' Reeves told her. 'And whatever is in there will wait. You need a doctor, Chris.'

'And the perp?' Ash asked, as the world warped around her.

'We got nothing,' Reeves replied. 'Without a description, the cordon was window dressing. He was probably long gone by the time it went up.'

Ash hung her head. 'At least we know Pendulum wasn't working alone,' she said quietly.

Reeves slipped an arm under hers. 'Come on. I'll help you to the car.'

Ash shook her head and immediately regretted the motion. It triggered a dull throbbing that grew more pronounced and painful with each passing moment. She tried to conceal the pain from Reeves, but noticed that he wasn't watching her. His eyes were fixed on a light in the sky. It took Ash's battered mind a few beats to piece together what was happening, and by the time she did, the helicopter had swept over them and landed in a clearing a few hundred feet away. She was relieved when the chopper's rotors slowed and the throbbing died away.

Relief turned to dismay when Ash saw six silhouetted suits striding through the forest. Five of them peeled off towards the police chief and his subordinates, while the sixth stepped into the glow of the field lights, revealing the stern, unforgiving features of SAIC Harrell. Ash looked up at Reeves, who shrugged.

'I couldn't bury this,' he said apologetically. 'Not even for you.'

Ash struggled to her feet, but Reeves had to catch her when she almost fell forward.

'What the hell happened here, Chris?' Harrell began.

'I was following up that lead. Charles Haig,' Ash replied, struggling to articulate her thoughts. 'Pendulum base.'

'Alone? Again?' Even through the haze that clouded her mind,

Ash could sense Harrell's exasperation. 'Law enforcement isn't some one-woman crusade. Where was your back-up?'

'I wasn't going to find—' Ash started, before pausing for a moment to compose herself. 'I didn't expect to find this, sir,' she said, forcing a coherent sentence.

'Look at you,' Harrell noted. 'Why isn't she in hospital?' he asked Reeves, who simply shook his head.

'I—' Ash began.

'Carney's team are going to run with this,' Harrell told her.

He was giving her case to another agent. She tried to shake her head but almost lost her balance, and had to lean on Reeves for support.

'But that's not why I'm here,' Harrell continued.

'I saw another man. Two. Men,' Ash tried to protest. 'Pendulum was not alone.'

'I know what you think you saw up at Twin Lakes, but we've discussed this,' Harrell said.

'No. In there,' Ash countered.

'She says she shot a man and that another triggered an explosive charge before escaping,' Reeves explained.

Harrell studied Ash, who managed to force herself to nod. 'If there's a body in there, we'll find it,' he assured her. 'But I want to talk to you about John Wallace. When was the last time he contacted you?'

'I don't . . . maybe a month, two,' Ash replied uncertainly.

'He's just made the watch list,' Harrell revealed. 'CIA says he joined an insurgent group. He's wanted in connection with a terror attack in Kabul.'

'What?' Ash staggered back and collapsed on to the fallen tree.

'You are to let me know if Wallace so much as looks in your direction,' Harrell said emphatically. 'You hear me?'

Ash nodded, struggling to process what she'd just been told.

'Get her to a hospital,' Harrell instructed Reeves. 'And then take her home,' he added, before turning back to Ash. 'I'm signing you off sick until we figure out exactly what happened here.'

He gave Ash a pitying look before walking over to the police chief.

'Come on,' Reeves said, helping Ash to her feet. 'Let's get you patched up.'

Ash lacked the energy to resist as Reeves shepherded her towards his car. Troubling, disjointed thoughts assailed her mind, and she caught herself wondering whether Wallace's despair had thrown him so off-balance that he'd bought into a misguided cause. Suddenly she saw the face of the man she'd shot in the bunker, his flesh consumed by burning fire. She faltered as she and Reeves neared the car, and though she longed to be rid of the dark thoughts, they kept coming. Rising from the fire, she saw Nicholas, her father, his wrathful gaze directed towards her rotten soul, a smoking pistol clasped in his vile hand. She shivered as Reeves helped her into the passenger seat, and, as the soft fabric pressed against her body, she felt herself slipping away. By the time Reeves had slid into the driver's seat, Ash had been released from her torment by the sweeping shadow of unconsciousness.

27

Bailey's pounding headache was not helped by the blur of numbers that taunted him, the digits bleeding into each other, creating a senseless blob. After spending the rest of the day with Murrall, catching up on the case and rebuilding his relationship with the surprisingly perceptive man, he had gone home, his thoughts circling fruitlessly about Sylvia Greene's secret. He had her and Murrall to thank for the headache. Murrall had pierced Bailey's self-delusion, and the memory of the man telling him exactly what a mess he'd made of his life had stopped Bailey from reaching for the bottle or a handful of pills the moment he walked through the door. Sylvia's numbers gave him an obsession that drowned out the whispers of booze and drugs, and their promises of familiar relief. He had woken with the headache but hadn't even risked taking a paracetamol, and had instead tried to alleviate his suffering by drinking copious quantities of water. Now, in addition to the headache, he had the urge to urinate every twenty minutes.

He couldn't ignore the building pressure that told him he needed to go to the men's room for the fourth time since he'd arrived at Paddington Green. He stood and was about to leave his desk, when his phone rang.

'DI Bailey?' a voice asked when he'd picked up.

'Yeah.'

'It's Toby McEwan. Sergeant McEwan. We met a couple of years back.'

'Yeah, Toby,' Bailey lied. He had no idea who the man was. 'What can I do for you?'

'I shouldn't even be talking to you,' Toby said in hushed tones. 'But he's going nuts. And after the Pendulum thing. Well, when I saw his name, I couldn't just leave it.'

'Who?' Bailey probed.

'John Wallace,' Toby replied. 'Service Operation Command Unit arrested him coming in from Istanbul. There's an Interpol alert out on him. Some shoot-up in Kabul. He's been asking for a call, but they arrested him under the Terrorism Act, so he's in lockdown.'

'Where?' Bailey asked urgently.

'I've got him in the custody suite at Heathrow,' Toby responded.

'I'm on my way,' Bailey told him. 'Don't let anything happen to him.'

Wallace paced the cell in frustration, angry at himself for being so stupid, but deep down he knew that leaving Afghanistan had been his only choice. He'd managed to glean that he was the subject of an Interpol alert, and knew that if he'd been caught in Kabul, there was little doubt that he'd already be dead. Travelling under his own name had been a risk, but at least he might stand a chance in London. If anyone was working with Mike Rosen, they wouldn't be able to shoot him in a Heathrow police station. They'd have to take him elsewhere, and transportation meant the opportunity for escape.

The flight from Istanbul had passed without incident, and Wallace had slept most of the journey to London. It was only after the plane had landed that he'd noticed something was awry. The pilot had informed them in the calming monotone common to all aviators that there would be a slight delay at the gate, and that everyone must remain seated. The aisles had been clear when a dozen uniformed officers had boarded the aircraft. Wallace had known he was the target the moment he'd seen their black boots march in his direction. He hadn't resisted as two of the men grabbed him, hauled him up and cuffed his hands. He'd been frogmarched along the gangway and forced down a flight of stairs that led to an exterior door, then manhandled across the tarmac to a waiting police van. The men pushed him into the back, where two officers had positioned themselves on the bench either side of him.

They'd been joined by a short, wiry man with curly, jet-black hair, dark eyes and olive skin, who'd sat on the bench opposite. The man hadn't said a word, but had kept his intense eyes on Wallace for the duration of the journey. The man's legs had been splayed open, his confident position reminding Wallace of the little gangster Danny who'd once saved his life. The most unsettling thing about the man had been the fact that he'd kept his hands in the pockets of his black bomber jacket, and Wallace had fully expected him to produce a knife or gun at any moment. After a short drive, the van had stopped, and Wallace had been hustled inside the police station, where Bomber Jacket had exchanged harshly whispered words with the custody sergeant. The man, who'd flashed some kind of ID, clearly wanted to take Wallace somewhere else, but the custody sergeant countered in firm but hushed tones, and Wallace was able to pick out the words 'proper channels'. Frustrated, Bomber Jacket had stalked away, eyeing Wallace menacingly.

Once he'd left, Wallace had pleaded with the custody sergeant, begging him for a phone call, trying to convey the seriousness of his situation without sounding like a conspiracy nut. The sergeant had listened to Wallace's story, but quietly informed him that he'd been arrested under the Terrorism Act and that the arresting officer would take a view on what contact with the outside world, if any, was appropriate in the circumstances. Despite his best efforts at resistance, Wallace had been processed and forced into a cell, where his sense of time was lost to dark paranoia.

He expected the cell door to open at any moment, and imagined that he would be confronted by Bomber Jacket, who'd obtained the necessary official sanction to lead him to his doom. Pacing back and forth, slapping the walls, he tried to calm his rising sense of panic. His heart thundered when he heard the lock snap, and he turned to see the door swing slowly open.

Wallace almost wept with relief when he saw the face on the other side. Patrick Bailey, the man who'd saved his life at the Maybury.

'Give us a minute,' Bailey said to the skittish custody sergeant. The man nodded and withdrew, and Bailey stepped inside the cell and pulled the door closed behind him. 'How are you, John?' he asked, embracing Wallace.

'I don't know,' Wallace replied, stepping back.

'Why don't you sit down?' Bailey indicated the Melamine bunk.

Wallace nodded and lowered himself on to the hard bed, and Bailey sat next to him.

'They've arrested you on an Interpol alert issued by the Americans. According to an unnamed intelligence source, you shot up a market in Kabul and killed a number of people. We both know that's bullshit concocted to get you pinched, so why don't you tell me what really happened?' the detective suggested.

'They came for me,' Wallace replied hesitantly. 'The army attacked a village. They killed so many people to get to me. Mike Rosen, the man who'd impersonated Pendulum, paid an Afghan colonel two hundred and fifty thousand dollars to assassinate me.

Rosen tried to kill me, but the man I was staying with saved my life. His name was Vosuruk.'

Bailey shook his head, and in the quiet, Wallace heard the distant sounds of doors opening and closing, telephones ringing and people talking, as normal life echoed down the corridor and bounced into the hollow cell.

'So Ash was right,' Bailey said slowly. 'Pendulum wasn't working alone.'

Wallace nodded. 'Rosen was wearing the suit when he was killed. The FBI had him in custody the day Pendulum . . .' He trailed off, recalling the day he'd saved Ash's life. 'Rosen was a soldier. He didn't have that kind of money. Someone else financed the operation.'

'Steven Byrne?' Bailey suggested. 'He has means and motive.'

'After what's happened to his family, it wouldn't surprise me.'

'Toby, the custody officer, says there was a guy, reckons he works for the Box,' Bailey began.

'The Box?'

'MI5, security service.'

'The guy in the bomber jacket,' Wallace noted.

'Toby says he wanted you released into his custody, but that he didn't have the proper authorisations. My superior, Superintendent Cross, tried to get you transferred to us, but whoever Bomber Jacket is, he has more pull.'

'He can't be working for them,' Wallace said in disbelief.

'I'm not taking any chances. You remember what happened the last time I left you locked in a cell?' Bailey asked, a mischievous smile crossing his face. 'That isn't going to happen again. We're going to get you out of here right now.'

The door opened silently, and Bailey beckoned Wallace to follow him. They stepped into the short corridor. There were six cells on either side, and his was the only one that was open.

Bailey moved quickly and quietly towards the custody suite reception, which lay beyond a heavy security door. When they reached the door, Bailey signalled Wallace to step back and conceal himself against the inside wall, before rapping the picture window. Wallace held his breath while Bailey smiled and waved. He didn't exhale until the buzzer sounded and the latch unlocked.

'You know what to do if this doesn't work,' Bailey said, giving him a nervous glance. He took a deep breath before pushing the door open.

Toby, the custody sergeant, a squat man with a paunch, shouted, but seemed rooted to the spot, unable to react to the sight of one of the Met's own helping a prisoner escape. The other man, who stood at the counter holding a sheaf of papers, moved instantly. Bomber Jacket lunged forward, dropping the forms and reaching into his pocket as he rushed towards them.

'Sound the alarm,' he yelled at Toby, and Wallace saw the shocked sergeant's hand disappear beneath the counter.

A klaxon sounded, its ear-piercing wail echoing off the reception's hard walls.

Bomber Jacket produced a collapsible baton and extended it as he swung for Wallace's head, but Bailey surged forward, running into the wiry man, knocking him backwards. Bomber Jacket went tumbling but grabbed hold of Bailey and took him down too. Toby, who'd finally spurred himself to action, scrabbled his way out from behind the counter and ran towards Wallace.

'Go!' Bailey screamed at Wallace, as he grappled with Bomber Jacket. 'Get out of here!'

Wallace saw four uniformed officers spill into the room through an interior door. He sidestepped Toby, who attempted to grab him, and ran for the exit, accelerating with each step, his heart racing as he tried to ignore the sound of boots behind him.

He risked a quick look over his shoulder and saw two of the uniforms struggling with Bailey, trying to pull him off Bomber Jacket, while Toby and the other two officers gave chase. They were only nine or ten steps behind.

Wallace burst through the exit and collided with a police officer, who fell backwards. As he sprinted across the car park, he reached into his pocket for the car keys that Bailey had given him in the cell and pressed the fob. Indicator lights blinked on a blue car that was parked in a bay near the gate, and Wallace rushed towards it, racing a heavy-set man in a suit who'd emerged from an unmarked van. Wallace's legs rose and fell in a blur as he closed on Bailey's car. The suited man was a dozen yards away, about the same distance as Wallace, but wasn't moving as quickly.

'Stop, or I will shoot!'

Wallace heard the command echo around the car park and looked over his shoulder to see one of the uniforms crouched by the station door, Taser in hand, while his colleagues veered to the side, to give him a clear shot.

Wallace ignored the man, and swerved suddenly. He heard a loud snap and saw the barbed contacts shoot into the air beside him. He rolled across the bonnet of Bailey's car and pulled the driver's door open. He was about to jump into the vehicle, when heavy hands grabbed his arms and yanked him backwards. Recalling his Aikido instruction, Wallace used the momentum and brought his right elbow up and round, sending it smashing into his assailant's face. He turned to see the heavy-set man fall against the neighbouring vehicle, and scrambled into Bailey's car. He thrust the key into the ignition and stepped on the accelerator, ignoring the officers who hammered on the windows as the car roared towards the high blue gates. The impact tore the metal barriers from their hinges and they clattered under Bailey's car, throwing up a shower of sparks as they were dragged across the pavement. They fell away with a loud clang as Wallace swung left, tyres screeching, to join a service road that ran towards a roundabout.

The sirens started almost instantly, and Wallace saw flashing blue lights fill his rear view as two police cars burst out of the car park and gave chase. Drivers hit their horns and screeched to a halt in an attempt to avoid Wallace. He hurtled across the roundabout before turning left and driving into oncoming traffic to avoid a queue of cars that would have trapped him. As he swerved his way round shocked and terrified motorists, he noticed that the lights ahead were red. The intersecting road was a dual carriageway, and Wallace guessed it was the A4, one of the arterial roads that ran from Heathrow into Central London. He passed a woman in a red Audi, her face a contorted mask of dismay, and stepped on the accelerator.

Wallace held his breath and drove across the A4, hoping fate would smile on him. After narrowly missing a speeding truck, the car made it over the twin-lane westbound carriageway, and Wallace was halfway across the eastbound when he looked in the rear-view mirror and saw the lead police car collide with a black Mercedes, both vehicles becoming mangled masses of metal as they bounced off each other, spinning wildly. The second police car stopped, and Wallace thought he was home free until a violent impact sent him reeling, and the world became a chaotic blur of white plastic, dust and grinding metal.

Wallace didn't even bother to check himself. As soon as the car stopped moving, he popped his seatbelt, fought off the deflating airbag and opened the door. He staggered on to the road, aware of the growing pandemonium as a multi-vehicle pile-up brought one of London's busiest routes to a halt. Dazed, Wallace cast about, desperately searching for an escape. The road was blocked in both directions, and as angry drivers started to emerge from their vehicles he could hear the sound of yet more sirens.

'Stop!' a gruff voice commanded, and Wallace turned to see one of the officers from the trailing police car running towards him.

'You fucking nutter!' a man cried out, and Wallace realised that the driver of the car he'd hit, a large, red-faced man with a bloody nose, was staggering towards him, full of menace.

'Stop that man!' the sprinting police officer yelled.

Wallace ran towards the petrol station located on the northeast corner of the intersection, and sprinted on to the forecourt. Sensing danger, people gave him a wide berth and a clear run towards the motorcycle that was parked beside pump number four. The helmeted motorcyclist, who'd been about to ride off at the time of the collision, realised Wallace's intention too late.

'Hey!' he yelled, his muffled voice scarcely reaching Wallace, who jumped on to the bike and pressed the starter button, then stamped on the gear pedal and twisted the throttle as the chasing police officer got within arm's reach of him.

The bike lurched forward and almost slid out from under him, but Wallace fought the powerful machine and got control of it, before racing on to the A4 and roaring east.

28

Alice sat huddled in the corner of the disciplinary cell, clasping her knees tightly, her head bowed so as not to meet the eyes of the man standing over her.

'You will falter and you will stray,' he said, 'but eventually you'll learn to keep to the path.'

As the man crouched down and lifted her chin, forcing her eyes to meet his, Alice tried to count the number of times she'd wished him dead, but he only ever seemed to grow stronger, as though feeding on the life-force of the new members who came to the clan. When she was younger she longed to discover that she'd been snatched as a baby, and dreamed that one day her real parents would come to take her away from this cruel place.

'Your mother knows that too,' Nicholas said, holding her faltering gaze. 'That's why she has to be punished. But punishment by a righteous hand is nothing more than a blessing. A gift from the divine to keep us on the path.'

Alice tried to look down, but Nicholas held fast, applying more pressure to her chin.

'It is through our eyes that we see the truth,' he told her. 'I need to know that you understand. I am your salvation, Alice. I am your mother's salvation. I am the salvation of the world.'

Alice looked at the man she wished wasn't her father and nodded. 'I understand, Father.'

'So if you ever see me ministering to your mother in that way, you will never again lay hands upon me, nor try to stop me,' Nicholas said, his soft voice concealing bitter menace. 'You will know that her punishment has been ordained by the divine.'

'Yes, Father,' Alice nodded.

'You will have three days to consider your transgression,' Nicholas announced as he stood up.

Alice watched her father leave the cell and shut the cast-iron grille behind him. She'd been expecting seven days, so when she heard the bolt snap into place, she was buoyed by the thought that she only had to face seventy-two hours in the cramped six-by-four cell.

Watching through the bars of the grille, she saw Nicholas say something to Manny, the duty warden who was tasked with monitoring the occupants of the six disciplinary cells that had been erected in the old garage. Manny nodded and Nicholas stalked away without even giving his daughter a backward glance. Alice liked Manny's shifts, because the crafty man had somehow managed to smuggle a portable television into the compound, and he now produced it from a drawer in his rickety desk. She sidled up to the grille as Manny switched it on, and her movement caught his attention.

'You say a word about this to your father and we'll both suffer,' Manny warned her, before shifting position slightly so that Alice had a clear view of the screen.

She watched snatched images flash in rapid succession as Manny clicked through the channels, searching for a suitable show to settle on. Alice didn't care what they watched and would have happily spent three days looking at the senseless staccato snapshots of unknown programmes, if they'd been able to suppress the traumatic memories of her mother's cries. She tried to concentrate on the television but she kept reliving the moment she'd stumbled in on her parents in their bedroom, and the sight of her mother's shame-filled, tear-stained, bloody face as Nicholas savagely beat her.

The sound of her ringing cell phone yanked Ash from her childhood nightmare and she took a moment to come round. She realised she was in her bedroom and reached a shaky, heavy hand out towards her bedside table.

'Here, let me get that,' Reeves said, startling Ash by appearing in her bedroom doorway. He hurried over, picked up the phone and handed it to her.

'Ash,' she croaked.

'Agent Ash,' came a formal voice. 'You have a call from a Mr Rosen.'

'Thank you,' Ash replied, clocking that she was speaking to a Bureau operator and suddenly becoming alert to the real identity of the caller. 'Can you give me a minute?' she asked Reeves, who nodded and left the room.

'Christine?' a familiar voice asked.

'Yeah,' she replied. 'It was a great night, but I asked you not to call me at work. Let me give you my home number: 212 555 6731.'

The line went dead and Ash rolled upright, the world wavering as her spaced-out mind struggled to cope with the sudden change in position. She recalled Reeves taking her to hospital the previous evening, the doctor telling her she had mild concussion and advising a few days' rest, and Reeves brooking no argument when he said he'd spend the night on the couch to make sure she was OK. Her landline rang and Ash answered it instantly.

'It's me,' Wallace said.

'Are you OK?' Ash asked.

'No. The police arrested me, Bailey helped get me out,' Wallace replied. Ash could hear the sound of traffic racing along a busy street. 'Mike Rosen tried to kill me. He sent the army into the mountains for me.'

'Mike Rosen?' Ash asked, her voice betraying her irritation. 'We had him, and we bought his story.'

'You were right,' Wallace responded. 'Pendulum wasn't working alone. There's more of them.'

'I know,' Ash assured him. 'I found something, but we can't talk about it over the phone.'

'I'm coming to New York,' Wallace said.

'You can't. It's too risky. Find somewhere to lie low until we figure out what's going on. I'll call Bailey—'

'The police got him,' Wallace interrupted. 'He sacrificed himself so I could escape.'

'Shit,' Ash muttered.

'Hiding doesn't work,' Wallace told her. 'You're the only person I can trust. I'm not safe anywhere else. I'm coming over.'

'It's too risky,' Ash repeated.

'I have to,' Wallace countered. 'I need to find the people who did this.'

'How will you get here?' Ash asked.

'I know a man who can help,' Wallace replied. 'I'll be there in a day or two.'

He hung up before Ash could say anything else. She tried to make sense of what was going on, but rational thought was beyond her addled mind, so she forced herself to her feet and staggered out of the room.

'Toast?' Reeves asked from the kitchen, where he was buttering a slice.

'No, thanks. I'm not sure I could keep anything down,' she replied honestly.

Reeves took a big bite. 'Everything OK?' he asked between crunching mouthfuls.

'Yeah,' Ash lied. 'I think so.'

'OK,' Reeves said. 'Well, listen, I want to go home and shower before I hit the office. So . . .' He trailed off, backing towards the front door.

'Of course,' Ash responded. 'Thanks for taking care of me, Deon.'

'No problem.'

'I'll call you later. I need to know what they found in the bunker,' Ash told him.

'You're signed off,' Reeves pointed out.

'You think that's going to stop me?' she asked with a smile.

'No,' Reeves said as he opened the front door. 'No, I do not,' he reiterated before he stepped into the corridor and shut Ash in her apartment.

She slumped in one of the kitchen chairs and thought about her brief conversation with Wallace. Even in her damaged state, she couldn't deny the jolt of excitement she'd felt when she'd heard his voice, nor the sense of anticipation at the prospect of seeing him again. After a lifetime spent isolating herself, fate was sending her the only person she'd ever trusted, the only person she'd truly cared about since she'd lost her mother.

Wallace had ditched the motorbike after about three miles and had used the money Bailey had given him to jump on the tube at Hounslow West, riding the Piccadilly Line into Central London. He had got off at Leicester Square, losing himself in the lunchtime crowds, until he'd found a pair of payphones at the mouth of Bear Street where it joined Charing Cross Road. He'd made a call to the number Bailey had given him, before speaking to Ash.

The man who'd answered the first phone call sounded familiar, but Wallace knew better than to ask questions or use any names, so he'd simply listened as the man told him to stay put.

After he'd spoken to Ash, Wallace waited for twenty-five minutes, circling the block every now and again so as not to catch the attention of any lingering eyes. Finally, shortly after midday, he saw a familiar black Mercedes crawling north along Charing Cross Road. The car stopped in a loading bay directly opposite the payphones, and the nearside rear door opened.

'Still alive, eh?' Danny, the rat-faced youth who'd once saved his life, showed his yellow teeth in what Wallace thought might have been a smile. 'Climb in.'

Wallace slid on to the back seat and saw two other faces he recognised. The Scarred Man was driving, and the huge, muscular figure of Red Skull sat beside him in the passenger seat. These dangerous men had helped him once before, and he hoped they could do so again.

'Say hello to your old friends,' Danny teased. 'Come on,' he told the Scarred Man. 'Sal wants to see him.'

29

The Scarred Man turned off the Westway on to Old Oak Common Lane, heading north into the upper reaches of Acton. Danny kept up a steady stream of chatter, touching on everything from the awesome action of the latest Marvel movie and the stinking selfishness of the political classes to the tacky transfer choices made by Arsenal. Wallace tried to focus on the scrawny gangster's words, but his mind was drawn to thoughts of Bailey, and he spent most of the journey wondering what had happened to the brave policeman.

The Mercedes passed rows of post-war terraced homes until they came within sight of a blue railway bridge, and when the Scarred Man turned left on to Brunel Road, the sur-rounding architecture suddenly changed and they were in an industrial estate of modern, two-storey warehouses. A couple of hundred yards later, the Scarred Man pulled into the car park of a new-build, yellow-brick warehouse, the sign beside the building indicating that this was the home of 'Oakwood Medical Systems'.

'Come on,' Danny said, opening his door.

Wallace hesitantly followed suit, while the Scarred Man and Red Skull remained seated.

'We haven't got all fucking day,' Danny admonished.

Wallace trailed after him into the building and they entered a small reception, where a young man with a long ponytail sat behind a desk. He wore a black polo shirt that bore the Oakwood Medical Systems logo.

'Alright, Boomer?' Danny asked.

'Not bad, D,' Boomer replied, barely looking up as Danny produced his wallet and swiped it over a card reader.

'After you,' Danny said sarcastically, opening the inner security door and ushering Wallace into a short corridor. 'Straight up,' Danny added, indicating the stairs that lay directly ahead.

A powerful smell of fresh paint filled Wallace's nostrils as he walked beneath the harsh strip lights illuminating the carpeted corridor. They passed a doorway to their left, and Wallace glanced through to see a dozen men and women, all in Oakwood uniforms, working in a brand-new loading area, stacking boxes on palettes.

'Worker bees, bringing in the honey,' Danny observed as they started up the steps.

When Danny opened the door at the top of the stairs, Wallace found himself in an open-plan office. Half a dozen people sat at desks, making phone calls or working at computers. Whatever this was, it looked like a legitimate business. No one gave them a second glance as they weaved around the desks towards a corner office, its interior obscured by blinds drawn across the inner windows.

'I don't care what Haybale says, ya still owe me twenty grand,' Salamander said as Danny and Wallace entered.

The South London villain hadn't changed and was still as smooth and calm as when Wallace had first met him in the Monkey Puzzle pub.

Danny shut the door behind them.

'How'd ya like my new place?' Salamander asked. 'Take a seat.'

Wallace sat in one of two chairs directly in front of

Salamander's desk. Danny stood by the door, leaning against the wall and watching Wallace disdainfully, as though sitting was a sign of weakness. Salamander reclined behind the desk, his chair at a ninety-degree angle, his feet up on a small filing cabinet.

'Danny tells me yer in trouble,' Salamander observed. 'It seems to follow ya around like a horny dog.'

Wallace nodded. 'Someone was working with Pendulum. He tried to kill me. I got arrested and Bailey helped me escape.'

'Where is he?' Salamander asked, his good humour suddenly vanishing.

'I don't know. He stayed back so I could get away,' Wallace replied.

'Look into it,' Salamander instructed Danny, who nodded and quickly left the room. 'Ya want somewhere to hole up?'

'I need to get to New York,' Wallace responded. 'Fast.'

Salamander rubbed his face. 'Last time I helped, I came out even. Gotta do better this time. I got overheads.'

'OK,' Wallace agreed. 'How much?'

'Hundred and fifty grand,' Salamander replied. 'Got a new way of getting you there, guaranteed. And in case ya get set on haggling, that's the mates' rate.'

'OK,' Wallace conceded.

'Put it on ya tab, right?' Salamander suggested.

'No,' Wallace replied. 'I'll pay up front this time.'

The uniforms had dragged Bailey off the man Wallace had referred to as Bomber Jacket, and stripped him of his watch, wallet and phone before bundling him into Wallace's old cell, while they figured out what to do with him. Bailey guessed he'd been locked up for three or four hours and was struggling to keep a lid on the raw acid building in his chest. His breathing was shallow with panic and the tightness in his chest had him convinced a heart attack was imminent. He tried to calm himself, remembering how alive he'd felt when he'd traded punches with Bomber Jacket. Free of fear, he'd launched himself at the man and had watched with satisfaction as Wallace fled the building. There had been no panic, just a powerful rush of energy and the exhilaration of knowing that he'd done the right thing.

He tried to recapture that moment, that feeling, but the memory could not stem the flood of anxious emotions that swept over him. He heard the lock snap and tried to compose himself before the door swung open to reveal Bomber Jacket and Bailey's superior, Superintendent Cross. Behind them stood two uniforms, who were obviously present in case there was any more trouble. Tall, with broad shoulders, Cross was a formidable figure, his long face capped by greying, short spiky hair which was currently concealed under his peaked cap. Bailey didn't need to be a mind reader to know that his boss was furious. His furrowed brow and clenched jaw said it all.

'My name is Sam Mayfield,' Bomber Jacket said, stepping into the cell. 'You're going to get one chance to make this right, Detective Inspector Bailey. Where is John Wallace?'

Bailey stared at Mayfield in silence, inwardly celebrating the fact that Wallace had successfully escaped.

'There's no coming back—' Mayfield began.

'Who are you?' Bailey interrupted, before turning to Cross. 'I need to speak to you alone, sir.'

'I work for the security services, detective. That's all you need to know,' Mayfield snapped. 'Superintendent Cross has told me that you tried to get John Wallace transferred to your custody because you think he was framed by people who may have been working with Pendulum.' Mayfield leaned forward, drawing close to Bailey. 'I believe you, detective.' He gave Bailey a moment to absorb the revelation. 'My work is classified but I can tell you this: I believe you. Pendulum was a small part of something much bigger. I need to talk to John Wallace urgently.'

Bailey studied Mayfield, trying to gauge the veracity of the man's statements.

'I'm probably the only person in the world who can help John Wallace right now,' Mayfield said.

They tell you what you want to hear, Bailey thought, *that's what makes them so dangerous.* There were only two people he trusted with John Wallace's life: his old friend Salamander, and Christine Ash, whose ordeal put her beyond reproach.

'I don't know where he is or what you think happened,' he responded at last. 'John Wallace overpowered me, stole my car keys and held me hostage in order to escape.'

Mayfield shook his head in disappointment.

'He pushed me into you, and you mistook it as an attack on my part,' Bailey continued. 'So I was only defending myself against you, Mr Mayfield.'

Mayfield smiled darkly as he stood up. 'That's your line? You can try it, but I don't think it'll stick. I'm pretty sure you'll do time, and given what I know about your recent emotional issues,' – Bailey shot a concerned look at Cross, who shook his head sympathetically – 'I think you'll struggle to survive inside. So I'm going to give you one final chance to make good. Where's John Wallace?'

The panic Bailey had felt had been replaced by growing fury. 'Do your worst,' he snarled at Mayfield, who turned to Cross and nodded.

Superintendent Cross stepped forward. 'Pat, it doesn't have to be like this—'

'It does,' Bailey cut him off. 'It's the only way he'll be safe.'

'Is he really worth your freedom?' Cross asked.

'It's not about Wallace,' Bailey replied. 'This is about doing the right thing.'

Superintendent Cross looked at Bailey sadly, before turning to the nearest uniformed officer and signalling the man with a nod of his head.

'Patrick Bailey,' the uniform said as he entered the cell. 'My name is Police Constable David Edgar and I'm arresting you under Section Five of the Terrorism Act on suspicion of assisting in the preparation of an act of terrorism.'

'That's bullshit,' Bailey objected. 'Wallace isn't a terrorist. Whoever's behind this trumped up the charge to get him brought in.'

'Interpol says he's a wanted terror suspect,' Mayfield replied coolly. 'That gives us grounds to charge you with assisting terrorism.'

Bailey felt hollow despair. They could have arrested him on a charge of ABH, resisting arrest, assisting an offender, any one of about a dozen crimes, but they'd chosen one that carried the prospect of a life sentence.

'You do not have to say anything, but it may harm your defence if you do not mention when questioned something you later rely on in court,' Edgar continued. 'Anything you do say may be given in evidence. If you'll come with me, we'll book you in.'

Bailey got to his feet and directed all his anger at Mayfield. 'We both know this isn't going to stick.'

'Don't be so sure,' Mayfield replied coolly. 'You know what section five means – you'll be in Belmarsh before the day is through.'

Bailey lunged for Mayfield, but Edgar and the other uniform intervened, pulling him towards the door. Bailey fought for composure, but the moment he was in the corridor and out of sight of the MI5 man, the facade crumbled. Mayfield was right. He'd never get bail on a section five charge and he faced the prospect of being remanded in custody in London's most notorious maximum security prison. His feet leaden, Bailey allowed himself to be hauled into the custody suite and tried not to think about what lay ahead.

30

Harrell didn't return Ash's call until early evening. She had spent most of the day in her home office, feeling a little light-headed, poring over the Pendulum files and trying to figure out what she'd missed. Why would Mike Rosen try to kill John Wallace? Had he been attempting to honour his former comrade's mission, or was there another reason for him to target Wallace? Mike Rosen had served with Pendulum, which suggested a connection to their Ranger unit, but Ash had been unable to follow that line of inquiry. The unit's records had been classified and despite a volley of clearance requests had remained firmly sealed. Ash had toyed with the idea of asking Pavel Kosinsky to help her obtain unofficial access, but had baulked at asking for a favour that could send them both to jail for a very long time.

The falling sun had tinted the sky pastel red by the time Harrell phoned.

'Ash,' she said, answering almost immediately.

'What are you leaving me messages for? What don't you understand about sick leave?' Harrell asked, his voice laden with disbelief.

'I'm OK, sir,' Ash replied.

'This isn't about being OK, Ash.' Harrell's irritation was palpable. 'I was doing you a favour. You almost blew the Haig bust. Price is still in hospital. You nearly got yourself killed.

You're a good agent,' he said, his tone softening. 'But you've got to learn that obsession is dangerous.'

'Did they find anything in the bunker?'

'Cut it out,' Harrell vented his exasperation. 'I'll call you when we've got something to talk about.'

'I—' Ash began, but the line went dead. She kicked back her chair and gazed out of the window, wondering how the heck she could get Harrell to believe her . . .

THUD

Startled by a noise so loud that it reverberated through her apartment, Ash almost fell backwards.

THUD

She felt the floor vibrate. She got to her feet and raced into the hallway.

THUD

Ash saw the crossbar buckle, and the locks give. When her front door burst open, she was transfixed by the horrifying sight of a man in a Pendulum mask.

Ash didn't move for what seemed like an age. She watched with horror as the masked man threw a heavy battering ram into the apartment. Behind him stood another two heavy-set men in matching masks. There was no sign of Pendulum's terrifying body armour; the three intruders all wore dark clothes and trainers, but it didn't make them any less intimidating. They stared at Ash for a moment before they surged forward, storming into the apartment.

She ran into her office, slammed the door shut and turned the key in the lock. It wouldn't hold against the men, but it would buy her precious time. Her guns were in her bedroom, beyond her reach, and as she desperately cast about the room searching for a weapon she could use against the three big men, she realised that escape was her only option. She bounded across the room to the window and flung it open.

'Open that motherfucker!' a deep voice yelled from outside, and as Ash pulled herself on to the ledge, four storeys up, the door splintered from its frame.

The smallest of the three men crossed the room, a pistol in his gloved hand.

'Don't you fucking move!' he yelled at Ash, revealing a thick New York accent. He cast his eyes over her desk and took in the Pendulum evidence. 'Get her.'

As the other two men stepped forward, Ash jumped, clearing the three-foot gap between the window and her living-room balcony. She landed hard, her bare feet screaming pain as they collided with rough concrete.

'Get after her!' the gunman shouted, and Ash sensed hurried movement inside her apartment.

Ignoring the pain coming from her feet and neck, she clambered on to the balcony railing. She thought about trying to jump down to the balcony below, but noticed an unfamiliar black van parked in the street beneath her, and when the driver looked up she saw that his face was covered by a dark Pendulum mask. Her only choice was to go up, and she jumped for the grey stone lintel that ran the length of the building. The tips of her fingers clasped the solid surface and she heaved herself up, pushing her feet against the wall to give her leverage. She heard the sound of her balcony door opening, and her heart pounded even more violently. Propelled by coursing adrenalin and sheer bloody will, she kicked her leg free of the gloved fingertips that reached for it and pulled herself on to the lintel.

'She's going for the roof!' a voice below her exclaimed. 'Just shoot her.'

Ash glanced down to see the gunman step on to the balcony. She didn't wait to see what he would do. Instead, she jumped, grabbed the lip of the balustrade and hauled herself over it, on to the roof.

'Get up there!' the gunman yelled.

Breathless, exhausted and in pain, Ash simply wanted to collapse, but she forced her sweat-sheened body upright and started running.

The neighbouring block was a twenty-one-storey high-rise, and part of the upper floors were built over the roof of Ash's building, like a giant resting its elbow on a tiny friend. The south-facing apartments on the fifth floor had balcony doors that opened on to the roof, and Ash sprinted directly for the nearest one. She was halfway across the red, grit-covered roof when she heard a noise and, as she looked to her east, Ash saw the three masked men burst out of the stairwell. She raced towards the glass balcony door, catching the eye of the man beyond it. Overweight and wearing nothing but boxer shorts, he lay on his long couch watching television. He sat up as Ash approached, his face a mask of horror. She heard a familiar loud crack behind her and a bullet whipped past her. It struck the balcony door, shattering the glass, breaking the fearful man's face into a thousand little pieces. Another shot and the second bullet blew out the pane entirely, the glass exploding inwards, showering the apartment in sharp fragments. Ash rushed through the broken door, and her hand felt clammy flesh as she pushed the rising occupant back on to his sofa.

'Stay down,' she instructed as she ran on, ignoring the agonising shards of glass buried deep in the fleshy soles of her feet.

She had made it to the living-room door when she heard another shot, and she turned to see the gunman lift his smoking pistol away from the fat man's head. Shocked that her assailants had killed an innocent bystander, Ash raced on.

She yanked the front door open, and her pursuers scrambled

out of the living room as she ran into the corridor beyond. Glancing nervously behind her, she saw that her lacerated feet were leaving a trail of blood along the grey carpet. Ash sprinted on, ignoring the doors that lined her way, reluctant to draw any other victims into the gunman's path. The snap of another gunshot echoed along the corridor, and the bullet buried itself in the plasterwork beside Ash's head. She burst into the emergency stairwell, leaping, stumbling, barrelling down the stairs, her lungs burning, her legs screaming with fatigue, her feet alive with pain. But the sound of her three masked pursuers and the intermittent crack of the gun spurred her on.

When she spilled out of the emergency exit on to the courtyard behind the building, the fourth masked man, the one she'd seen in the van, was waiting, and tried to grab her. Ash had been expecting him, and, absolutely determined that her painful flight should not end in failure, she kicked him in the groin, her bloody heel connecting with such force that he crumpled instantly. Ash scarely missed a step as she ran on, sprinting across the courtyard and up the narrow alleyway that led on to Eighth Street. She looked behind her to see the three masked men clustered around their injured associate. He nudged one of the other men and the two of them hurried towards Ash, but she didn't linger. She ran down the sidewalk towards the intersection with Fifth Avenue and jumped in front of a cab. The vehicle shuddered to a halt, and, before the driver could react, Ash lunged on to the back seat.

'Federal Plaza,' she instructed. 'Go now.'

The cab driver, a grey-haired, Middle-Eastern man, muttered something under his breath, but the taxi started rolling south. As it pulled away, Ash looked up Eighth Street. There was no sign of the masked men who'd pursued her.

31

The cab driver wasn't happy when Ash revealed she didn't have the money to pay the fare. When they arrived at Federal Plaza, she left him to deal with the site liaison manager, who tasked a suited security guard to take Ash to the medical suite. The adrenalin of the chase had subsided, and Ash was relieved when the large man produced a wheelchair from a closet behind the reception desk. She slid into it, eager to take the weight off her bloody feet.

'Thanks,' she sighed, as the big man pushed her towards the security gates that stood in front of the elevators. 'What's your name?'

'Tevez,' the man replied. 'What happened to you?'

'I'm still trying to figure that out,' Ash said. 'You got a phone, Tevez?'

'Should you be making calls?' the big man asked.

'You got one or not?' Ash responded, wondering whether Tevez would have been more comfortable wheeling a gibbering wreck through the building. One thing she could thank her father for was a toughness other people could only dream of. The things he'd put her through, the courage it had taken to confront him, the strength it required to finally leave, Ash hadn't encountered anything in life that had come as close to breaking her.

'Sure.'

Tevez handed Ash his phone and she made a series of calls as he wheeled her through the building. The first was a 911 call to the NYPD, informing them of her neighbour's murder. The second was to Harrell but he wasn't available, so she left a message, telling him what had happened. The remaining calls were to Reeves, Miller and Romero, summoning them to the Plaza. By the time she'd finished talking to Romero, Ash was in the medical bay, trying to ignore the impatient duty nurse.

'You need a hospital,' the nurse advised, aghast at the state of Ash's feet.

'No,' Ash replied firmly. 'Call the duty doc and get him to patch me up. I'm not leaving this building.'

Tevez hovered, and the presence of the powerful man helped Ash relax. He stayed, standing silently near the door of the spotless medical suite, while the nurse helped Ash on to an emergency bed.

The duty doctor was a chubby Middle Eastern man with pockmarked cheeks, who introduced himself as Mafez. He echoed the nurse's advice that Ash needed hospital, but when she refused, he anaesthetised her feet and set about extracting the remaining shards of glass.

Reeves arrived just as the nurse was cleaning Ash's wounds. Mafez was preparing to stitch the worst of them.

'You OK?' Reeves asked. 'What happened?'

'Three guys bust into my place,' Ash answered. 'There was a fourth guy with a van. They were all wearing Pendulum masks. I think they were trying to kill me.'

Reeves looked at Ash in disbelief.

'They killed one of my neighbours – guy in the next building. I've informed NYPD,' Ash added.

'You want us to get down there?' Romero asked. She was standing in the doorway with Miller.

'Yeah,' Ash replied. 'Check traffic and security cameras in a three-block radius. See if we can get an ID on the van.'

'I'm driving,' Romero told Miller.

'I think I'll get a cab,' Miller remarked, earning himself a playful punch as they left the room.

'You think you could give a description?' Reeves asked, recoiling slightly as Mafez pushed a needle through the fleshy sole of Ash's right foot.

'It's just going to be build and clothing,' Ash replied. 'You're not squeamish, are you, Deon?'

'Does it hurt?' he asked.

'I can't feel a thing,' she responded.

'Maybe not now,' Mafez interjected. 'But once the anaesthetic wears off you will experience severe discomfort. I'm going to prescribe you a course of painkillers.'

'Agent Ash, what happened?' Harrell asked, entering the room. He looked as though he'd been harried to the point of exhaustion. 'Are you OK?'

'I'm fine, sir,' Ash replied, noticing Reeves stiffen slightly at the sight of their boss. 'Three men invaded my apartment, and there was a fourth man with them, a driver. All four were wearing Pendulum masks. Maybe they think I can identify the guy I saw at Pendulum's base, or that I know something dangerous. Either way, the timing is no coincidence, sir.'

Ash could see Harrell struggle for a moment, unsure how to deal with the final revelation. True to form, he ignored it. 'I've spoken to the NYPD unit commander. He says the fire department are on the scene dealing with a blaze in the neighbouring building. You know anything about that?'

'One of my neighbours was killed during my escape. I'd guess the assailants torched the place to conceal evidence.'

Harrell nodded. 'OK – here's what we're going to do. You're going to give Agent Reeves everything you've got on the men who attacked you, and then we're going to put you into Witness Protection. I'll speak to Jordy Wiltshire and get a Marshal team assigned to you as soon as possible. Until we've figured out what happened, you're going off grid, agreed?'

Ash was itching to lead the investigation to find the men who brazenly broke into her home and ruthlessly killed her neighbour, but she knew there was no way Harrell would allow it, so she nodded and said, 'Yes, sir.'

Bailey spent the ninety-minute journey from Heathrow to Thamesmead staving off a full-blown panic attack. Sharing the back of the unmarked van with two uniformed private security contractors, he forced himself to remain composed in the face of the bleak fate that awaited him. Belmarsh Prison was home to Britain's most notorious criminals and was used as a remand centre for those charged with acts of terrorism. Sam Mayfield knew how to apply pressure; Bailey's life would almost certainly be forfeit if the other inmates discovered he was police.

It was dark when the van pulled to a halt. Bailey was ushered through a courtyard, into a long, low, yellow-brick building. The security guards presented him to the custody officer, who booked him in and provided him with a uniform – a blue T-shirt, grey jogging bottoms and Crocs. He was then assigned to a prison officer, who led him through a number of security gates, deep into the block, before locking him in a cell. Bailey was relieved to discover he'd been placed in solitary and that he would not have to share the confined space with another inmate, but his solace was short-lived. As he sat on the narrow, metal-framed barracks bed and listened to the sounds of movement, and distant shouts echoing around the two-storey block, Bailey felt a familiar thumping in his chest, as though his heart was trying to smash its way through his ribcage. He held his left wrist with his right index finger and found his pulse, which felt fast and irregular.

Bailey was certain he'd registered a number of skipped beats, and panic surged through him, burning his body with its familiar, unnatural heat. He stood, and immediately regretted the sudden movement. The world grew blurred and distant, and his head throbbed with painful pressure. Bailey's legs felt too weak and unsteady to move, and his knees gave way, causing him to collapse back on to the cot, which wobbled violently, the frame clattering loudly against the wall.

When the panic finally subsided, he checked his pulse and found it to be steady and regular. Finally emerging from his anxious introspection, Bailey realised that the cell block was utterly silent. He rolled off the bunk and looked out of the high window to see that the moon had set, and the sky was dark with heavy clouds. He guessed it was long after midnight, but had no way of being sure. He used the toilet in the corner of the cell, washed his hands and lay down on the bunk, hoping that he would soon find sleep. As he looked at the painted white ceiling, searching for calm, Bailey heard a noise outside his cell. It sounded like a footstep against the hard floor. He held his breath, and his ears strained against the silence.

The sound of the lock rang around the cell, almost assaulting Bailey with its volume. As the noise echoed off the walls, it triggered Bailey's excitable heart, which resumed its manic rhythm. He felt his throat shrink with panic, and much as he longed to cry out, when the door opened and he saw the two figures who stood before him, all he could do was scrabble back ineffectually until his spine was pressed against the metal headboard of his rickety bed.

Two men in black, both wearing the unmistakable masks of Pendulum, stormed into the cell. Bailey's mind reeled as he tried to make sense of events. How could this be happening inside one of Britain's most secure prisons? As the two men loomed over him, he suddenly thought that he must have fallen asleep, and that he was trapped inside a vivid nightmare. He tried to lash out, kicking his feet towards the two men, but his efforts yielded nothing. The smaller of the two sidestepped the futile effort and punched the top of Bailey's skull with a gloved fist, the powerful hammer blow landing with such force that it sent Bailey reeling into darkness.

32

O nce she'd finished giving her statement to Reeves and the two of them were happy with the faceless digital likenesses of the suspects produced by the Bureau's compositor, Ash retreated to her office. Jordy Wiltshire couldn't assign a protection team until morning, and Ash declined Reeves's offer of a bed, remarking that if she wasn't safe in Federal Plaza, she wasn't safe anywhere. Reeves tried to stay but Ash sent him home, saying she wanted him fresh and at his best. Prevented from working the case herself, she was relying on Reeves and the team to find out who her attackers were. Reluctantly, Reeves complied and left shortly after midnight. Ash changed out of her grimy clothes into the spare outfit she kept in the office: a pair of jeans, grey vest top and black sweater. She found a box of Ambien in her desk and took a pill, but her mind was racing and she was unable to sleep on the tiny couch parked in the corner of her cramped office. She gave up, left her office and wandered the almost deserted building until she found herself ordering a small salad and what would hopefully be a soporific warm milk from the quiet cafeteria. Her feet were starting to ache so she took a couple of the Vicodin Dr Mafez had prescribed, and by the time she'd finished her meal, warm relief had reached the very tips of her toes, and the cork sandals the nurse had sourced for her felt like beds of cotton candy. She staggered back to her office and collapsed on the couch, drifting off to sleep so quickly that she couldn't even recall closing her eyes.

The drone of a vacuum cleaner pierced the powerful fog of painkillers and sleeping pills, and Ash's eyes rolled open only to immediately shrink at the hazy light that filled her office. It was morning, and the clock on her desk said 6:15. Ash sat up and instantly regretted the motion as needles of pain shot up her legs. She leaned over, grabbed the bottle of Vicodin from her desk and forced down two pills, then walked gingerly to her chair, using the desk to take as much weight off her feet as possible. She slumped into the seat and started her laptop, which took a moment to come to life. When she checked her mailbox, among the dozens of unread emails, one stood out: a message from Pavel Kosinsky written in reply to the email she'd forwarded from Bailey.

> Hey Chris,
>   I couldn't ID the symbol, but the code you sent me contains dates followed by a series of three coordinates. The dates are written in reverse, but the coordinates don't refer to long or lat, or any other form of map positioning. I'm not sure what they are. Hope this helps.
>   P

Ash wrote a quick reply of thanks and then tried phoning Bailey. Wallace had told her Bailey had sacrificed himself during the escape but hadn't given any details, and now she wondered whether he'd been injured, arrested or worse. When his phone rang out, she emailed him Pavel's response, with a short note saying she'd got proof Pendulum wasn't working alone. Given the ease with which Pendulum had previously compromised Bureau systems, Ash knew she couldn't risk revealing any details, but she hoped that once she was at a secure USM location she'd be able to follow up with the London detective.

Thinking about Bailey prompted her to check for updates on Wallace. She searched Interpol and wasn't surprised to learn that he'd escaped from police custody and was still on the run. If he did make it to New York, he would find it almost impossible to contact her in protective custody, so she sent him an email:

Call Deon Reeves. Bureau. You can trust him.

'Agent Ash?'

She hit send and looked up to see two men standing in the doorway. The shorter of the pair, in a light grey suit, had pale, almost translucent skin and sported a few days of neatly clipped stubble on his lean face. A taller black man stood behind him in a dark blue suit, his height concealing the burden of a few extra pounds, his moon face stern and unsmiling beneath a shaved head.

'I'm Lou Egan, and this is Taye Gatlin,' the grey-suited man said. 'We're US Marshals.' He flashed his ID. 'Jordy Wiltshire asked us to take care of you.'

Ash pulled herself to her feet.

'You want me to carry anything?' Egan asked.

Ash shrugged. 'I'm all there is.'

'We'll get you some clothes and anything else you need,' Gatlin said.

'If you're set . . .' Egan said.

Ash glanced around her office, wondering when she'd be able to return. Her eyes settled on the photograph of her with her mother. Suppressing an unbidden, irrational fear that she would never come back, she shut down her computer and followed her two guardians out of the room.

★

Ash sat in the back of the Buick Regal watching the city pass as they headed north. Egan was driving and Gatlin sat next to him.

'Where are we going?' she asked.

'To RV with your protection detail,' Egan replied, looking in the rear-view mirror.

'I thought you were my detail,' Ash probed.

Egan shook his head. 'We're just transit,' he replied. 'The service altered its protocols following the Pendulum case. We lost two marshals; it forced the brass to review how we do things.'

'I knew them,' Ash told him. 'Perez and Hill. They were good men.'

'They were,' Egan agreed. 'We believe Pendulum was able to discover the location of the safe house by hacking USM servers, so we no longer keep any electronic records of anyone in protection. And transit and protection are handled by two separate details, to reduce the number of people who know a subject's location.'

They drove for another thirty minutes, until they reached the intersection of 147th Street and Seventh Avenue. Egan pulled up behind a black Cadillac ATS parked opposite a supermarket at the foot of a high rise. As the Buick rolled to a halt, two men emerged from the Cadillac: a large, lumbering white man and a short Latino guy. Ash immediately noticed that neither man seemed comfortable in his suit.

'This is the protection detail,' Egan told her.

'Do you know them?' she asked.

Egan shook his head. 'You?' he asked Gatlin.

'No. Never seen them before,' Gatlin responded.

'I'd like you to ask for ID,' Ash said firmly.

'Agent Ash,' Egan began, but he caught her serious expression and relented. 'OK.'

He climbed out of the car and strolled over to the two men.

Ash saw him say something to the shorter of the two, and was horrified when the man reached inside his jacket and produced—

'Gun!' Ash yelled, as two rounds tore through Egan's chest. Gatlin drew his weapon, but the large Caucasian man produced a sub-machine gun and sprayed the Buick with bullets. Ash ducked into the footwell as Gatlin's body shuddered and jerked with the force of the impacts. Ash didn't stay down long. She reached for the door handle and rolled on to the asphalt, narrowly avoiding a brown van that had screeched to a halt. She looked up to see the driver staring at the Latino and the Caucasian in dismay; he hadn't even registered her presence. A loud crack sounded behind her and a bullet shattered the van's windshield. Ash turned to see the short Latino man levelling his pistol at her from the other side of the Buick.

'Don't move!' he commanded, and the moment he spoke Ash recognised his voice from her apartment: he was the man with the pistol, the shooter. Her mind raced with questions, but she ignored them and started running.

The snap of gunfire filled her ears and she heard the thump of bullets hitting the van's chassis as she sprinted round it and ran along the far side. She could feel her feet protesting, but was grateful that the worst of the agony was muted by the numbing effects of the Vicodin. When she looked over her shoulder, she saw the Caucasian had stepped into the street and was level with her, his sub-machine gun pointed in her direction. She ran behind the van as the large man opened fire, and a hail of bullets hit a white Honda that had stopped on the other side of the intersection. The driver bucked as the bullets pierced his body, killing him instantly. Ash noticed a silver BMW on the corner of 147th Street, its driver struggling to reverse his car against the tide of traffic. She skirted the rear of the brown van and poked her head round the corner, looking north to see the Latino man changing his clip as he stalked towards her.

Ash knew the large Caucasian would be coming up the other side of the van, giving her little choice. She broke cover, and the Latino man who'd led the invasion of her apartment immediately opened fire. She leaped over the hood of the silver BMW, bullets slicing the air around her, then wrenched the passenger door open and tumbled into the car.

No time for explanations. She yelled at the startled driver: 'Go! Drive!'

The driver hit the gas and the car lurched forward and picked up speed. Bullets peppered the windshield as the BMW sped alongside the brown van, towards the Latino gunman, who leaped out of its path.

A spray of machine-gun fire shattered the rear window, and the driver cried out but didn't slow down as the two assailants and the scene of their murderous violence receded. Ash checked herself for injuries but found none. The car hurtled north and she wondered what to do next. Despite their new security protocols, someone had compromised the US Marshal's office, suggesting that her assailants were at least as resourceful and determined as Pendulum. Bitter experience had taught her that nowhere was safe, and that there was only one person she could trust. Until she could figure out a way to reconnect with Wallace, Ash knew she'd have to rely on herself if she was to stay alive long enough to find out who was behind all this and why they wanted her dead.

33

Bailey's heart raced, and fear coursed through him as a screeching wail forced him back to consciousness. He tried to cover his ears but his wrists were bound, and when he opened his eyes, they saw nothing but burning white light, so he quickly shut them. The wail was joined by the discordant sound of a guitar being shredded and 160 beats per minute of violent drumming. Bailey finally recognised the savage noise as thrash metal, which assaulted his ears at a volume loud enough to make them throb. He became aware of a dull ache where his assailant had punched him, and an uncomfortable tightness around his ankles, where the bonds that restrained his legs bit into his bare skin. Another bond anchored his torso and his hands were bound above his head. He'd been stripped to his underwear and was lying on a bed or stretcher in a small cell. The music, the restraints, the removal of his clothes were all hallmarks of the kind of psy-ops used by intelligence agencies.

He yelled above the din. 'Hello!'

The music suddenly died and the room went black. Bailey opened his eyes but couldn't see anything other than deep, speckled darkness. Then suddenly the outline of a Pendulum mask above him.

'Where's John Wallace?' the masked man demanded, his voice low.

'I don't know,' Bailey said.

He was instantly rewarded with a powerful fist driven into his groin. Pain engulfed his body, making him convulse as the restraints that bound his hands above his head prevented him from curling into a ball. Blinding light forced his eyes shut and thrash metal filled his ears.

'Please,' he moaned, but there was no response, and he lay prone and vulnerable, willing away the pain emanating from his groin.

Suddenly the light and music died away, replaced by still darkness. He opened his eyes and tried to look around, but saw nothing.

'Please,' he said again, trying to sound composed. 'I don't know where he is.'

Light illuminated the space, and once his eyes had adjusted, Bailey recognised the source: his mobile phone.

'Tell me about the code,' the man in the Pendulum mask growled. 'What does it mean?'

'It's nothing to do with Wallace,' Bailey replied, his voice pathetic and fearful.

'Don't tell me what it isn't,' his assailant yelled, punching him in the gut. 'Tell me what it is!'

'I don't know,' Bailey cried.

His interrogator drove an elbow into his solar plexus. The blinding lights and deafening music returned, assaulting his senses. Bailey tried to hold on to something, anything that would keep him connected with the real world, one without the torment of pain. He focused on the question that had arisen when he'd seen his phone. How had it got here? It had been taken from him in the police station at Heathrow. How had this man infiltrated Belmarsh Prison and obtained his phone? There was only one possible answer.

'Mayfield!' Bailey yelled, recalling the name Bomber Jacket had used at the station. 'Sam Mayfield!'

The lights went out and the room fell silent.

'Mayfield?' Bailey tried, his voice booming off the walls. 'I want to help.'

The Pendulum mask drew close. 'There's no Mayfield here. And you will help. I'll make sure of that.'

Bailey sensed rapid movement and felt a heavy fist hit his solar plexus again, unleashing agony that threatened to overwhelm him.

He cried out. 'Please! Please, I want to help!'

But there was no response, and as tears of pain swept down his temples, the searing light and punishing music returned. He willed himself to be strong and tried to imagine wreaking revenge on his tormentor, but as the immediate wave of pain subsided it was replaced by despair. He didn't know how long he'd be able to resist, and once he'd given this man what he wanted, Bailey had little doubt his life would be forfeit.

The city gleamed in the April sunshine, growing larger as the Gulfstream descended. The pilot informed Wallace that they were headed for Teterboro Airport, a small airfield in New Jersey that almost exclusively served private jets.

Wallace and Salamander had been surprised by each other's resourcefulness. The previous day, Wallace had asked the Scarred Man to take him to a gold broker on St James's Street, where he had a safety deposit box containing some of the proceeds from the sale of his flat. After the Pendulum experience, and with Ash's contagious paranoia infecting his mind, Wallace had taken precautions to ensure that if he was ever threatened, he could easily access the things needed to make a swift escape. He had taken £200,000 out of the safety deposit box, most in sterling, some in dollars, along with the William Porter passport that Danny had delivered to the miserable safe house off the Old Kent Road over a year ago.

Before he'd handed over the money, Wallace had demanded to know how Salamander planned to get him out of the country.

'Private jet,' Salamander had explained. 'We use them to move stuff around. People ask less questions if they think you're rich. You'll be flying out of RAF Northolt. It's the same airport the Queen uses,' he'd added with a wry smile.

The Scarred Man had deposited Wallace at a cheap hotel near Heathrow, where he'd spent a sleepless night poring over his experiences in Afghanistan, trying to rid his mind of the memory of Vosuruk bleeding to death in the gloomy stairwell. As always, his thoughts had turned to Connie and hers was the last face he'd seen before he'd finally drifted off.

The Scarred Man had returned in the early hours, with Salamander. As they'd travelled the deserted West London streets, Salamander had told Wallace what Danny had found out about Bailey.

'He's in Belmarsh,' he revealed. 'But don't you worry about it. We'll make sure he's got a good brief. They can't hold him. They're just trying it on.'

Wallace felt a rush of guilt but didn't press the matter. There was nothing he could do to help Bailey, and he only risked being caught if he stayed in the UK. He might not be safe on the other side of the Atlantic, but he'd rather take his chances with Ash.

When they arrived at RAF Northolt, Salamander produced a duffle bag from the boot.

'Creature comforts, courtesy of ya friendly travel agent.' He handed it to Wallace, who opened it and found clothes and toiletries inside. Salamander gave him a mobile phone. 'There's one number programmed in the memory. Call it if ya get in trouble. Charger's in the bag.'

'Thanks,' Wallace said gratefully.

Salamander and the Scarred Man stayed with Wallace as he

was welcomed by the GlobalJet flight attendant, who steered him through the immigration process in the Northolt Jet Centre, a tiny terminal building located within the RAF base. Wallace appreciated the effectiveness of the Oakwood Medical Systems front. Salamander's new company regularly exported high-value medical equipment, which gave him the ability to move other things when he needed to.

The Porter passport had held up, and Wallace said his thanks and farewell to Salamander then followed the flight attendant out to the Gulfstream G650 which had been chartered to take him to New York. The pilot and co-pilot gave him a courteous welcome before continuing their pre-flight checks, and Wallace settled into one of the comfortable leather seats. He refused the flight attendant's offer of a drink and drifted off to sleep before the aircraft started its taxi. The flight attendant woke him shortly before the pilot announced their descent into Teterboro Airport, and he looked out to see New York City stretched out beneath them.

Once they'd landed, Wallace thanked the flight attendant and pilots and went through the quickest, most pleasant immigration check he'd ever experienced. Outside the small airport operations building, he caught a cab and asked to be taken to a comfortable hotel. The driver, a bearded Ukrainian who was having a tough time in America, spoke of his troubles as he drove them to the Teaneck Marriott, about fifteen minutes from the airport. The grey glass and steel structure was visible from the expressway and loomed high over the surrounding buildings. It was exactly what Wallace had been looking for, the sort of place where he'd be anonymous and forgettable. He paid the driver, tipping him well for his hotel recommendation.

The vaulted lobby was a blend of cream marble and dark wood. Brown columns supported the high ceiling, and cream

couches and chairs were artfully arranged in carefully coordin-
ated groups. The large space was packed, mainly with business
people, although there was at least one family, the chaotic
behaviour of the three children and the strained voice of their
mother standing out against the calm murmurs of the suited
professionals. Wallace walked quickly towards the elevators and
found a couple of payphones. He called Ash, but the number
rang out and went to voicemail. He tried again, and got the
same result. There was a bank of computers just off the lobby,
where people were checking emails and surfing the Net. Wallace
pulled up a chair by an unused machine and agreed to Marriott's
terms and conditions before logging into his email, where he
immediately found a message from Christine Ash, telling him to
contact Deon Reeves.

He re-read the short text, wondering whether he could trust
that the email really was from Ash. There was no identifying
marker, no signal that only they would know, and she hadn't even
signed it. Maybe she was in a rush, or in danger. It was possible
that she'd been compromised, that the Bureau had become aware
of their contact and this was a trap. He tried to find the line
between caution and paranoia. If the Bureau knew they'd spoken,
Ash would be watched. They wouldn't risk putting Wallace on
edge by suggesting he trust a complete stranger. He decided he
didn't have a choice. Alone in New York, the target of an
international manhunt, he had to call Reeves. But that didn't
mean he had to trust him, and, as Wallace logged off and returned
to the payphones, he resolved to be extremely careful.

Deon Reeves stood on the corner of 147th Street and looked up
Seventh Avenue at the six NYPD forensics officers who were
working in three teams. The first was examining the body of
Louis Egan, who'd been shot on the sidewalk, the second
working around the shredded Buick and the body of Taye Gatlin,

who'd been killed in the car, and the third checking the body of a man killed in a white Honda. Seventh Avenue had been closed and police officers were taking statements from those who'd witnessed the firefight. The lead detective was a grey-haired guy called Saul Oriol, who wore a crisply pressed suit and exuded care and confidence. Reeves didn't know him, but he seemed thorough. He was busy coordinating the search for a silver BMW that had been spotted leaving the scene. Multiple witnesses said they saw a woman flee the Buick and escape the shooters in the BMW, and Reeves hoped they were right, because it meant that Ash might still be alive and free. He was about to approach Oriol to see what he could do to help when his phone rang. The screen displayed a New York City number he didn't recognise.

'Deon, it's me,' Ash said. She sounded breathless and nervy and Reeves could hear heavy traffic in the background.

'Chris?' he asked incredulously, ducking beneath the police cordon and walking up the access ramp of the neighbouring brownstone. He didn't want anyone overhearing their conversation. 'Are you OK?'

'I think so,' Ash replied.

'Where are you?'

'I can't come in,' Ash said. 'I trust you, Deon, but the Bureau or the USM is compromised. Maybe both.'

'We'll—' Reeves began, but Ash cut him off.

'I can't come in, Deon. I need you to pass on a message. I'm hoping you're going to get a call from someone looking for me. If you do, I want you to tell him that I'll meet him at the penthouse suite.'

'Chris, please—'

'The penthouse suite. You got that?' Ash pressed.

'Yeah, I got it,' Reeves said. 'You be careful, and if you need anything, you call me. I've got your back.'

'I know,' Ash said sadly.

Reeves pocketed his phone and stood quietly for a moment as he considered whether to share knowledge of the call with Saul Oriol, Harrell, or anyone else at the Bureau. His eyes were drawn to the photographer who was cataloguing the crime scene, and as he watched her moving around, intently focused on capturing an accurate record of the mayhem, he realised he couldn't fault Ash's logic. Someone had given her up or their protocols had been compromised. Either way, she was right not to trust the system. Resolving to keep their conversation secret, he walked down the access ramp and slipped beneath the cordon.

'Detective Oriol,' he called out, 'what can we do to help? Finding Agent Ash and the men responsible is our top priority. The Bureau will give you whatever you need.'

Reeves was sifting through witness statements with Detective Oriol when his phone rang again, and another unfamiliar New York number flashed on screen. He stepped away from Oriol to take the call.

'I'm looking for Christine Ash,' a man said, his voice unfamiliar, his English accent unmistakable. 'She told me to call you.'

Reeves thought about quizzing the caller, but he suspected he already knew the man's identity, and having it confirmed would only put him in a difficult position. 'She gave me a message. She says you should meet her at the penthouse suite.'

'Thanks.' The line went dead.

Reeves shook his head. He hoped Ash knew what she was doing.

Wallace replaced the receiver and scanned the lobby. Reeves hadn't stalled for the time to run a trace, and the message sounded genuine. The world was full of penthouse suites, but there was only one that meant anything to Wallace and Ash. It seemed unlikely this was a trap. He headed for the cabs that waited in a rank outside the hotel, eager to reach Manhattan.

34

Bailey lay in the darkness, his throat raw, his eyes burning. He was too numb to cry, too near breaking point to do anything other than pray for it all to end. His head felt light, almost detached from his battered body, and his mind drifted, floating over times past, peering down at his memories as though his life belonged to someone else. He saw a cocky boy playing footie on a warm summer's day, a gaggle of friends pounding the tarmac between the semis that flanked Gracefield Gardens, collecting the ball and giving drivers a bit of London lip whenever a passing car interrupted their game. That same boy with Salamander, the two of them using sharp, narrow straws to pierce the film lids of plastic squash cups as they sat in the park and gave voice to their dreams, certain they could conquer the world through sheer optimism. The boy's grandmother comforting him, the smell of her lavender perfume soothing away his humiliation as he recounted the trauma of being bullied on his way home. A girl, her name almost forgotten, a date at the cinema, his first kiss, pretending he was a man of the world. His heart broken the very next day when he saw her, his girl, across the playground, her arms around someone else. That same boy, now grown, bitten by reality, choosing a path that took him into darkness, alienating him from his friends, making it difficult to find love. The boy trapped inside the body of an adult, huddled in the ever encroaching darkness, his knees pulled closer with every new investigation, hands over his face as though trying to blot out the horrors faced by the man he'd become. The boy mutilated by a shooting at the hands of a masked killer. Death's bony fingers tearing shreds out of him, trying to take him entirely. The disfigured boy now a trembling wreck inside the body of a man who pretended he could handle what life had thrown at him. *What had he done to that boy? What had he done to himself?*

Of all the moments that rose unbidden in the darkness, of all the faces, one stayed with him. His grandmother, her cheeks so full and round, her skin so smooth, her eyes so warm, glowing with love. She seemed so real that Bailey tried to reach out a hand to touch her, but his arms were bound, so he could only watch as she smiled.

'Whiners aren't winners,' she said softly.

And then she was gone.

Bailey wanted to cry out, but his throat was so swollen that he couldn't swallow to give himself voice. He wanted to go with her, to feel her embrace, smell her perfume, taste her food, to return to a time when life had been nothing but smiles. But even in his tormented confusion, Bailey knew she wasn't really there. She'd died years ago, swallowed by cancer, smiling even as it ate away at her. She was gone. There would be no easy escape. He was faced with a simple choice: tell his tormentor what he wanted to know and hope for a quick death, or continue to resist the worsening torture and hold out until the pain became utterly unbearable.

Escape.

The word eased into his mind so gently, Bailey was convinced his grandmother had whispered it in his ear. His concept of time had been lost to flashes of blinding light, raging noise and savage torment, and in the terrifying darkness, his mind had been overwhelmed by fear and self-pity. Unlike his anxiety attacks, which came without cause, he'd been forced inside his mind as part of a calculated strategy designed to wear him down. Robbing the subject of any sense of reality was a key element of torture, and he suddenly grew angry with himself for falling into the role of victim so easily.

He forced himself to focus on his senses, to try to gauge the world around him. He knew he was lying on a bunk, his arms, legs and torso restrained. The room was soundless, cut off from the world, the only noise the blood pulsing through his ears. The darkness was deep and impenetrable, and no matter how hard he looked, he could see nothing but black. He twisted his fingers towards the straps that bound his wrists and felt hard leather cuffs – the sort one would find in a secure psychiatric ward. Bailey knew from experience that few restraints could resist a determined captive. YouTube was littered with videos that demonstrated how to escape from handcuffs, cable ties, ropes, tape, and even psychiatric straps. He recalled one of his Hendon instructors saying that restraints only worked when combined with supervision, and wondered how long it had been since he'd last seen his tormentor. If he was caught trying to escape he had no doubt he'd be punished, but could it be worse than anything he'd already faced?

There was no art to escaping straps; it required brute force and determination. The hard leather cuff was secured to the wrist, set at a gauge too narrow for the palm, but few people knew just how pliable the hand was, how the bones could twist, contort and snap when needed.

Bailey took a deep breath and pulled his left arm down, straining with all the strength he could muster. The pain was intense but he'd endured far worse at the hands of his torturer, and the prospect of further suffering spurred him on. The cuff bit into the heel of his palm, but Bailey ignored the stabbing agony, telling himself that flesh and bone were malleable, that force could reshape them. He swallowed the pain and used it to fuel the engine of angry frustration that motivated him. Sweat sprung from every pore as his broken body came alive with effort and finally, as he bit his tongue in an attempt to distract himself from his harrowing task, he felt a crunch in his palm, and a shooting sensation raced down his arm into his very core. He ignored it, and continued pulling his slippery hand into the cuff. Excruciating agony scaled down to intense pain as Bailey's fingers slid through the hard leather and his hand flopped free. *Ignore it*, he told himself, as sweat poured down his face.

He forced his left hand down to his chest and searched for the buckle of the strap that bound his torso. His fingers felt strangely disconnected and disobedient. Tingling and numb, they didn't want to do his bidding, and instead seemed intent on lying limply at the end of his damaged hand. Bailey couldn't indulge them, and knew that if his tormentor returned to find one arm free he'd make sure it could never be used again. He concentrated and forced his way past the pain. His fingers touched metal, and traced the outline of the loose end of the strap. Forcing it through the buckle took real willpower, and as the moments passed, Bailey grew ever more fearful that his tormentor would return before he was ready, flooding the room with light, noise and pain. But the room stayed dark, and he freed himself from his second restraint, then quickly rolled on to his side and felt for the cuff that bound his right arm.

Hope surged, smothering pain and sending electrifying adrenalin coursing through his body. His twisted, swollen fingers worked as quickly as they could and finally unbuckled the cuff, freeing his undamaged right hand. Bailey froze, his ears straining, convinced he'd heard a muffled sound somewhere outside the room. Greeted with silence, he realised there was nothing to be gained from being caught mid-escape, and quickly found and undid the restraints binding his feet. Having been unable to see anything but blinding white light or pitch darkness, he had no idea of the layout of the room. He rolled off the bed and his feet touched rough, cold concrete. As he stood upright and his body supported its own weight, he was almost overwhelmed by pain. His abdomen had been battered by countless punches, his groin, legs, arms and chest likewise, and all joined a swelling chorus that urged him to lie down, to give them respite. But Bailey knew that he couldn't, and he forced himself into the darkness, moving slowly, his right arm outstretched, his left hanging limply beside him. After a few carefully taken steps, he felt a cool wall, and started to move along it.

Light!

Blazing, blinding light filled the room, and Bailey turned to see the man in the Pendulum mask standing beside an open door, staring at the empty restraints as though in shock. Bailey's eyes acclimatised and he took in the two HMI lights angled towards his 'bed', which was actually an emergency room trolley, pushed against the bare concrete wall furthest from the red metal door – the only exit. Loudspeakers were suspended from each corner of the room, and were now blaring thrash metal at a painful volume. Beyond the lights, set flush against the wall opposite him, was a metal trolley covered with workman's tools and surgical instruments, which would doubtless be used to take the torture to a new level.

The man in the doorway surged forward, his expression hidden behind the emotionless Pendulum mask, his trainers driving into the concrete floor, propelling his stocky body across the twelve-feet-square room. Bailey knew that in his current condition, he wasn't strong enough to fight such a powerful opponent. He concentrated on the timing of his move. His assailant was within arm's reach when Bailey sidestepped to the left and grabbed the man's right shoulder, pulling him forward and off-balance, sending him crashing into the concrete wall. The collision bought him the time he needed to cross the room and grab a claw hammer from the trolley. His tormentor lunged for him, and Bailey turned and swung with his right arm, watching as the hammer travelled through the air, arcing towards the masked man's head. His assailant was a skilled fighter and brought his left arm up to block the blow, and the impact almost knocked the hammer free, but Bailey held on, grasping the handle tightly. As the man drove his shoulder into Bailey's abdomen, knocking the wind from his lungs, Bailey brought the hammer down and drove the claw deep into his back. His guttural cry could be heard above the thrashing music. Bailey wrenched the claw free and as his tormentor stood, his gloved hands pawing ineffectually at his wounded back, he swung the hammer again and struck his assailant square across the cheek. The masked man spun round and collapsed in a motionless heap.

Bailey breathed deeply, trying to calm himself. He sensed movement to his right, and turned just in time to see a tall, muscular man rush into the room holding a pistol. Bailey lashed out with the hammer, striking the gun, which fired as it was knocked from the man's hand. The bullet went wide of Bailey, who pressed forward and swung the hammer once more, hitting the man's shaved head with a satisfying crunch. The man's eyes rolled back in his head and his body crumpled beneath him as he fell to the floor.

Bailey dropped the hammer and grabbed the smoking pistol, a Sig Sauer P228, special forces issue. He checked the magazine, which felt satisfyingly heavy, before clasping the gun awkwardly under one arm and reloading it. Ears pounding with the noise of the music, his body weak with pain, he moved towards the stocky, masked man, keeping the pistol raised. His left hand was starting to seize up, so, after checking the doorway, he set the pistol down and quickly removed the man's mask. The face that stared back at him was unfamiliar. An IC2 male with black hair, a scar bisecting his left eyebrow, and another running across the bottom of his chin. The hammer had left a deep indentation in his cheek which was starting to ooze blood, but the blow hadn't killed him, and Bailey could see his chest rising and falling with each laboured breath.

Bailey searched the man's pockets and confiscated a set of keys, an old Nokia phone and a wallet. Part of him longed to lash out and make the man suffer as he had, but Bailey knew he'd gain nothing from such violence. He hobbled across the room to the second assailant, whose face was swelling around a deep, mottled bruise. Figuring they were roughly the same size, Bailey stripped the man of his black boots, jeans, white T-shirt and navy hooded top. He dressed quickly, always keeping the gun within arm's reach, but no one else came. He left the room and glanced up at the door. There were neither bolts nor a keyhole, and a black transformer box attached to the top corner told him that the lock was electric, but there was no sign of the control switch anywhere nearby. He was uneasy at leaving it unlocked, but there was no choice.

Closing the door, he set off cautiously down the corridor. A quick search of the hoodie's pockets revealed another set of keys and a wad of cash. He reached a wooden door at the end of the corridor, its inset picture window covered by foil. There was a small patch where the foil had fallen away, and he peered through it, into an airy warehouse. A large table stood in the centre of the otherwise empty space, with two laptops on it, next to his iPhone, wallet and keys. Bailey couldn't begin to understand how these men had got his things. He slowly opened the door, and kept the pistol raised as he crossed to the table, where he pocketed his wallet, keys and iPhone before turning his attention to the laptops. One displayed an image of the interior of the torture cell, and his heart skipped when he saw that the shorter of the two, his tormentor, was starting to stir. He couldn't risk being recaptured, and knew he didn't have the strength to face more pain. He turned for the roll shutters that lay to his left, but before he moved away from the table, something caught his eye. There, on the second laptop, was the code Sylvia Greene had left in her suicide note. The machine was running it through a cracking program, trying to crunch the numbers that had so far resisted all his efforts. In a second window, Bailey saw an email addressed to him from Christine Ash, passing on information she'd had from Pavel Kosinsky, who suggested that the first six numbers in each section of code referred to a date. Bailey glanced at the cracking program again and noticed that it was focused on the second set of six digits in each batch of numbers. His confused mind struggled to make sense of what he saw. Why would these men want Sylvia Greene's code? What was the connection to Wallace?

The other laptop showed his tormentor getting to his feet and staggering around the cell, trying to come to his senses. The man reached behind his back to produce a pistol that had been concealed in the waistband of his trousers, and Bailey cursed himself for not searching him more thoroughly. As the man staggered towards the unlocked door, Bailey felt the desperate need to be somewhere else. He grabbed the code-cracking laptop and hurried towards the roll shutters, moving quickly, not looking behind him, fearful of what he might see.

When he reached the far wall, he stepped through a door cut into the shutters and found himself in a car park that contained three vehicles: a silver BMW 3 Series, a black Golf and a dark blue Ford Transit. He fished a set of keys out of his pocket and spotted a BMW fob hanging from the ring. He unlocked the car and threw the laptop inside, before easing himself into the driver's seat. To his relief, it was an automatic. He started the engine, then sped through the open gates, his dazed, disorientated mind trying to figure out where he was.

35

It took Bailey a few minutes to adjust to the real world and figure out that he was in South East London, near Goldsmiths University. He considered calling Superintendent Cross, to give him the location of the warehouse, and try to convince him that they were both victims of a larger conspiracy, but even if Cross believed him, what could he do to help? Bailey couldn't risk protective custody: those men had taken him from Belmarsh, Britain's most secure prison. They clearly had powerful reach, and Bailey knew that his safest option was to stay hidden from anyone or anything official. He suspected the men who'd kidnapped him worked for one of the security services, which meant there'd be an alert on the stolen vehicle. He checked his face in the rear-view mirror. Most of the damage had been done to his body, and other than some superficial bruising, palpable distress was the only thing that visibly betrayed his recent ordeal. So he ditched the BMW near the University, grabbed the stolen laptop and hailed a taxi on New Cross Road.

As soon as the vehicle was underway, Bailey pulled his phone from his pocket and dialled a number that wasn't stored in its memory.

'Haybale,' Salamander answered. 'What the fuck? I thought ya were locked up.'

'I need help, Sal,' Bailey responded quietly. 'I've hit real trouble.'

'Meet me at the tower,' Salamander instructed. 'I'll be waiting.'

'I'm going to need a doctor,' Bailey said.

'How bad is it?'

'Bad.'

'Just get here,' Salamander said seriously, before hanging up.

He and Salamander had taken opposing paths, but their bond went beyond the labels life had given them, and right now, Bailey could not think of anyone he'd rather be with. He willed the taxi through the afternoon traffic.

The driver tried to engage him in conversation, but Bailey felt incapable of normal responses and switched off the intercom. Desperate for something to take his mind off his painful injuries, he concentrated on the laptop. As the taxi rolled north-west, heading towards the heart of London, he opened the machine and saw that the screen still displayed the code-cracking program and the email he'd had from Christine Ash. His captors had obviously been through his phone, so they must have seen Sylvia Greene's suicide note in his photo library and known that it had nothing to do with John Wallace. Yet his torturer had asked about the code. The masks left little doubt that these men were somehow connected to Pendulum, and as such, Bailey could understand why they wanted Wallace, but what possible interest could they have in Sylvia Greene?

He minimised the windows containing his email and the code-cracker, and was about to open the file manager to see what else was on the machine, when the screen suddenly pixelated and turned blue. A pop-up window appeared momentarily flashing the words 'Remote Wipe', and then the machine went dead. Bailey tried to get it restarted but the laptop was unresponsive, so he put it on the seat beside him. Certain government computers were fitted with satellite uplinks to enable them to be remotely deactivated if they ever fell into the wrong hands, adding weight to Bailey's working theory that the men who'd snatched him worked for the security services. He checked his torturer's wallet and discovered a thick wad of cash, but no cards or identification of any kind. Then he felt around the stolen clothes for any sign of bugs or tracking devices but found nothing, not even labels, which had all been cut out. He counted the money he'd taken from the two men: £840 in crisp twenties. He pocketed the cash and stuffed the wallet down the side of the bench seat, where it would remain hidden from all but the most determined searches. Bailey winced as he settled back. He tried to take his mind off the pain by studying passing pedestrians, filling out the details of their lives from their faces, creating stories that occupied him as the taxi drove towards the river.

Bailey took the first taxi as far as Farringdon Road, then walked the back streets to Chancery Lane, where he hailed a second cab to take him the rest of the journey. It was a basic tactic, but would make it slightly more difficult for his captors to pick up his trail if they managed to get hold of the first driver. The second taxi took him to Edgware Road, where he got out and headed west. His left arm hung limp and jolted agony with every jarring step. He forced his way along Kendal Street, stopping a couple of times to ensure he wasn't being followed. Finally, in the face of increasing pain, he turned the corner and saw his destination: a twenty-two-storey high-rise on Porchester Place.

Bailey staggered towards the tower, past manicured beds bursting with spring blooms, before leaning against a cold steel handrail and hauling himself up a flight of concrete steps. Beyond the sliding glass doors, a porter sitting behind the reception desk eyed him sympathetically. Bailey forced a smile which he locked in place as he stepped into the lobby.

'I'm here for Mr Sohota.' Bailey grimaced.

'He's expecting you, sir,' the porter replied. He was young, maybe twenty-five, and full of earnest concern. 'He said you'd just been robbed. Do you need me to call the police?'

Bailey's smile broadened. 'It's OK. I am police.'

The porter was momentarily flummoxed by Bailey's response. 'Mr Sohota's on the twenty-first floor, sir. Please go right up,' he said finally, indicating the elevators.

Bailey walked as naturally as possible, but his movements were becoming jerkier.

'Would you like a wheelchair?'

A wave of angry humiliation washed over Bailey, and he forced himself upright and paced the last few steps to the nearest elevator. He was glad to see it was waiting with its doors open.

'I'm OK,' he replied proudly.

He pressed the button marked '21' and slumped against the full-length mirror the moment the doors closed. The swelling had come up on his face, and his left hand looked like someone had run it through a mangle, but Bailey knew that the worst of his injuries were concealed beneath the clothes he'd stolen.

The elevator rose quickly and ejected him into a windowed lobby on the twenty-first floor. The view alone was worth millions, the city spread out before him in glorious miniature, any ugliness beautified by distance. Bailey and Salamander took great care never to ask about each other's work for fear that professional obligation might one day wreck personal loyalty. Bailey knew his oldest friend had made a lot of money, and that this was one of many properties he owned around London. Salamander had bought the penthouse flat years ago, during the last economic downturn, registering it in the name of Reena, a gorgeous but flighty cousin Bailey had once been involved with.

Bailey turned south, leaning against the wall as he headed for one of four apartments located on the floor. His feet knocked each other as he struggled with each agonising step, and he was infinitely relieved to see Salamander's front door swing open. Familiar faces ran forward, calling his name, and he felt strong hands catch him as he fell.

There were no dreams. No bright lights. No flashed moments of his life. There was nothing but darkness. A blank that could have lasted a moment, or forever. Then Bailey was needled from unconsciousness. He opened his heavy eyes to see a middle-aged man with wild grey hair, rough stubble and jowls that were covered by a roadmap of tiny burst blood vessels. The man was holding a syringe.

'My name's Timson,' the man slurred, quite clearly drunk. 'Or Alistair. Either will do.'

'Doctor Death, more like,' a voiced sneered, and Bailey's eyes were drawn towards it.

He focused on Danny, leaning against a large table near a floor-to-ceiling window. The lights of the city sparkled and dark clouds drifted across a bright moon.

'Is he awake?'

Bailey recognised Salamander's voice immediately, and saw his friend step into view.

'Haybale. What the fuck? Ya scared us shitless.'

'Sorry,' Bailey croaked.

His eyes were suddenly drawn towards a large needle held by the drunkard looming over him, and he tried to scrabble backwards. But his limbs were weak and unresponsive, and he hardly moved.

'Relax,' Doctor Death gave him an inebriated grin. 'It's an antibiotic. You took a pounding.'

The doctor drove the needle into the muscle of Bailey's left arm, and he realised that he was naked save for his underwear. His left hand was in a splint, and there were bandages around his midriff and his right thigh.

'And this is a painkiller,' Doctor Death said as he picked up another syringe and hurriedly drove the sharp into Bailey's arm.

'What is it?' Bailey asked.

'My own recipe. A little of this, a little of that,' the doctor laughed. He caught Salamander's eye and suddenly feigned serious professionalism. 'It's perfectly safe. I think your hand is broken,' he advised, withdrawing the needle. 'But it needs an X-ray. You've got some internal bleeding, but nothing too serious. And three broken ribs. Normally I'd advise a trip to hospital, but given how popular you are, I don't think that's an option.'

Bailey was puzzled until Danny showed him his phone: the lead story was the nationwide manhunt for hero cop turned terror supporter, Patrick Bailey, who'd escaped from Belmarsh Prison the previous night.

'Fuck,' Bailey sighed.

'Fuck is right,' Salamander agreed. 'It's a stitch-up.'

'False flag,' Danny interjected. Salamander looked at him. 'What? I watch a lot of movies.'

'Are we done here?' Doctor Death asked. 'Because I—'

'Ya not going anywhere,' Salamander interrupted. 'There's beer in the fridge.'

'Beer?' Doctor Death didn't try to conceal his disappointment.

'Frank, fix this degenerate a drink,' Salamander said peevishly.

Bailey looked across the room and saw Frank Nash, one of Salamander's closest associates, sitting behind Danny. Frank's age was a mystery. Salamander joked that the guy had come up with the Krays. His hair was dyed jet black, and his pasty white skin was covered with scars from terrible childhood acne. Frank had served five years for armed robbery and attempted murder and was well known to the police. Seated along from Nash was Jimmy Cullen, a monster of a man who was famous for two things: only wearing tracksuits, and having beat a murder charge when the key witness for the prosecution changed his testimony mid-trial and acted as a character witness for the defence.

'Come on, pisshead,' Nash sighed, rising from the table.

Doctor Death followed him across the open-plan living room, through an archway that led to a vast, modern kitchen.

Salamander pulled up a leather footstool and sat next to Bailey, who finally worked out where he was – lying on a huge L-shaped couch in the corner of the living room.

'Ya boy, Wallace, said ya been taken,' Salamander began.

'Where is he?' Bailey asked, aware that the pain that assaulted his body was being smothered by warm relief. He hoped Doctor Death hadn't got his maths wrong when figuring out the dosage.

'The States,' Salamander replied.

'Ask him,' Danny urged his boss excitedly.

'He wants to know how ya broke Belmarsh,' Salamander informed Bailey. 'Ya his new hero.'

'I didn't escape,' Bailey revealed. 'I was abducted by two guys in the middle of the night. They took me to a warehouse. Did this.' He indicated his battered body.

'Where?' Salamander asked.

'New Cross.'

'Where exactly?'

'On Blackhorse Road, three buildings up from the railway bridge,' Bailey replied. 'But they were pros. They'll be long gone.'

Salamander ignored his friend and turned to Cullen. 'Give Lek a call. Ask him to send some of his boys down there. See what they can find.'

Cullen nodded, the huge red skull tattooed on the side of his head seeming to smile at Bailey as the giant man rose from his seat and stepped on to the balcony. Moments later, he had a phone to his ear.

'Lek?' Bailey asked, the detective in him burning with curiosity.

'Ukrainian friend of ours. Works that part of town,' Salamander replied, and Bailey instantly found himself wondering just how rich and powerful his friend really was. 'They want Wallace?'

Bailey shook his head uncertainly, his mind trying to cut through the heavy effects of whatever Doctor Death had pumped into his arm. He caught sight of the smiling doctor following Frank out of the kitchen, a tumbler full of golden liquid in his hand.

It's perfectly safe.

'That's what I thought,' Bailey replied, aware that he was starting to slur. 'At first. But then I think they went through my phone. Found the code, the email. Worked out I was on the Greene case.'

He looked at Salamander and registered his friend's puzzled expression, but couldn't formulate the words to explain. Clarity. For the first time in months, Bailey felt calm, the world around him clear, but the price of such peace was isolation. His soul had withdrawn from reality. He felt as though he was wrapped in layers of heavy protection which bore down on him, making every movement difficult, every breath an effort.

'It's here,' Danny said, stepping over to Salamander, showing him his phone.

Except it wasn't Danny's phone, Bailey realised, it was his own. How did they access it?

'Fingerprint ID,' Danny explained to the bewildered detective, nodding at Bailey's hand. He turned his attention to Salamander. 'They wanted to know about the death of that lady reporter. She left a note and a code, which some Yank friend of the detective's cracked. Well, part of, at least.'

'No connection to Wallace,' Bailey slurred.

'He'll be out soon.' Doctor Death sounded like he was making a toast, and when Bailey looked at his warped, shimmering form, he couldn't be sure the man didn't have his glass raised.

'Got to get the code,' Bailey found himself saying.

'No worries.' Danny looked down at him with a distorted, Cheshire Cat grin. 'It's obvious, really. Where's a reporter gonna hide things?' He paused for dramatic effect, but to Bailey it felt like an infinite silence. 'In stories. Dates give you the newspaper. The other numbers give you the page, column, word an' that.'

Even in his soporific stupor, Bailey registered Salamander's surprise. He'd have expressed some himself, if he'd been able to operate his body, which now seemed utterly detached and at rest.

'Boy done well.' Salamander slapped Danny on the back.

'I got to get up,' Bailey tried, but the words came out as an incoherent drawl.

'No ya don't,' Salamander assured him.

'Some of these dates are well old,' Danny revealed. 'The papers ain't online. Probably in a library or something.'

'Archive,' Bailey murmured. 'Must get . . .' His words drifted into the air like lazy curls of smoke from a dying fire.

'Ya will,' Salamander's face became unnaturally broad, his smile shifting from comforting to disconcerting as it continued to widen beyond Bailey's field of vision. 'Just not tonight.'

Bailey tried to resist his heavy eyelids, but they were unstoppable. As he drifted away, he recalled the flushed face of the sloshed doctor and his last thought was, *I hope I'm not dying.*

36

Wallace asked the cab driver to stop on the corner of Second Avenue and Houston. He paid the fare and stepped on to the sidewalk near the subway station. As the April sunshine warmed his shoulders, soaking through the parka he'd found in the bag Salamander had given him, he headed along Houston, scanning his surroundings for anything out of the ordinary: people who didn't seem to fit, strangers whose gazes lingered a little too long. But all he saw was the bustle of a busy Thursday afternoon, a city alive and indifferent to his troubles. Traffic pulsed along the wide artery beside him, and Wallace tried to recall the last time he'd walked this street. He'd been with Ash, and it had been after their rooftop confrontation with Pendulum. He'd been battered, dazed and barely able to move, but they'd made it across the city somehow. He remembered snow piled high on the sidewalks, the brutal cold chilling his bones.

He almost collided with two young women as he turned left on to Bowery. They smiled at his apology and stepped out of his way as he continued past Whole Foods Market, along the busy street which was flanked by a mismatched assortment of multi-coloured buildings, most of them no more than four or five storeys high, some of them old and in need of repair, others new and gleaming. Wallace forced himself to focus as he passed the All-Nite pharmacy and neared the Fresh City Hotel. If this was a trap, it would be sprung soon.

The hotel entrance was unchanged, the 'F' and 'C' still missing from the sign hanging above the doorway which was squeezed between the All-Nite and the Fireball Kitchen. There was no one hanging around on the street, and the nearby parked cars were all empty. Wallace scanned the windows of the surrounding buildings, but he couldn't see anything to suggest that the place was being watched. Bright sunshine glared off the glass door, making it impossible to see into the tiny lobby. As he walked towards the entrance, he couldn't help but imagine a gang of heavily armed men lying in wait for him.

He pulled the door open and saw that the lobby was empty. The receptionist sat behind the bulletproof Plexiglas screen, and barely glanced up from her iPad as he entered. Wallace headed straight for the stairwell, which seemed smaller and more dilapidated than he remembered it. The stairs were covered with large flakes of paint that had fallen from the walls, and the whole place reeked of decay. He climbed cautiously, his senses alert. As he rounded the first flight, a door burst open and two men spilled through it. Wallace's heart leaped into his throat, but his fear quickly subsided when he realised that they were students, goading each other remorselessly as they passed him, bantering loudly about each other's inability to hold liquor. They skipped down the steps, their voices echoing off the crumbling walls, diminishing to nothing as they left the building.

Wallace carried on. When he reached the next floor, he noticed a puddle of grim brown liquid pooling in the stairwell doorway. It had grown since his last visit. He stepped over it, into the decrepit corridor that lay beyond, and moved slowly towards room 217. He could feel his pulse rising and his breathing quicken as he neared the scuffed, chipped door. He glanced along the dismal corridor, peering in both murky directions for any sign of danger. He knocked. There were sounds of movement inside and he saw the peephole go dark for a moment before the door swung open to reveal Christine Ash. She wore a grey vest, which revealed her toned arms, and a pair of jeans. She looked pale and tired, but to Wallace she was still beautiful.

'The penthouse suite.' He smiled awkwardly.

Her bare feet made no sound as she stepped towards him.

'John,' she said, pulling him into a warm embrace. 'I'm so glad to see you.'

Her hair was tied in a lank ponytail, and smelled of smoke and grease. Wallace recalled the time they'd embraced outside a subway station to avoid the police. He could still remember the scent of jasmine and the overwhelming urge he'd had to kiss her. Ash pressed her soft skin against his cheek and Wallace was suddenly aware of her warm body and the tingling sensation of her breath against his neck. When he reached a hand up to return her embrace, he felt rough fabric and stepped back, surprised to find that a thick, dirty bandage encircled her throat.

'What happened?' he asked.

'You'd better come inside,' Ash said.

37

Ash sat cross-legged on one of the two narrow beds. She was paper white, and fatigue seemed to burden her every move. Wallace couldn't tell whether her condition was the result of her injury, overwork, or the fact that her investigation into Pendulum had been thwarted. He was sitting on the floor, his back against the wall beside the folding bathroom door, watching her closely as they traded stories. He couldn't be sure exactly how long they'd spoken, but the sun had fallen behind the neighbouring building, and as the last rays of light faded, Ash leaned over and switched on the unshaded bedside lamp. Wallace had talked of Afghanistan, of the men, women and children who'd died in the mountains, of Vosuruk and Kurik, and the discovery that Mike Rosen had been behind the assassination attempt.

Ash had chronicled months of frustrating obsession, working alone, robbed of the resources of the Bureau, coming close to losing her mind as the weight of evidence led to the crushing conclusion that she'd imagined the second man in the Twin Lakes facility, and that Pendulum had been working alone. She'd told the tale of Babylon, Pendulum's biggest fan, and how he'd led her to the base where she'd seen two other men, finally providing her with unassailable proof that she hadn't imagined an accomplice. They'd both spoken of their concern for Bailey, Wallace focusing on the selfless sacrifice that led to the detective's incarceration, Ash on the worrying communications which reflected their friend's damaged state of mind.

They shared their experiences of violence, Wallace first listening intently as Ash told him how she'd almost been beheaded in Babylon's dank, festering lair, how she'd fought, utterly determined that her life would not be lost to a brutal maniac. He had offered words of comfort when emotion washed away her composure, and she returned the sentiment when he'd choked on the tale of Kurik and Vosuruk dying in his arms. They both knew what had happened to Connie, her shadow looming so large that it would chill Wallace's remaining days, but neither spoke of the parallels, and when they were finally done trading tales of brutality, Wallace sensed that their relationship had shifted. Pendulum had forced them together and given them shared experiences that no one else could possibly understand. There existed between them a warped intimacy so deep that it could never be matched. As darkness rolled across the city, when they'd finally exhausted all they had to say, Wallace and Ash sat together, listening to the muted sounds of Manhattan, knowing that there was no better place to be than that infested hotel room, and no person they'd rather share their rotten sanctuary with.

'Truth or happiness?' Wallace asked at last.

Ash looked blank.

'If you had the choice, which would you pick?' Wallace explained. 'We can find out who did this, or we can leave, disappear. Go somewhere they wouldn't find us. We'd never know the truth, but we might have a chance at happiness.'

'When I was a kid,' Ash began, 'I wanted to be like everyone else, to be stupid enough to believe my father's lies, to nod my head, smile and be happy. But even then I knew that happiness can't be built on lies. I need to know who did this and we both need to make sure that they're never capable of doing it again.'

She smiled, and Wallace realised he'd made a mistake. She was an FBI agent. The truth was her job and she had no interest in escaping with the broken wreck of a man he'd become. Maybe, one day, he'd ask her the question again. If he lived that long.

'So, what do we do next?' he asked, concealing his disappointment.

She glanced at him before looking away, her eyes settling on the tiny window and the silhouette of the city beyond. 'I don't know,' she replied wearily.

He'd seen Ash lost once before, at the motel on the Wilbur Cross Highway where she'd watched in horror as her childhood had been dissected on television, but this was different. She seemed so fragile, vulnerable, the tough veneer worn away to reveal a delicate core. She'd given so much of herself to her lone crusade that when she finally had confirmation she was right, the spark that fuelled her had been extinguished by the terrible effort.

'I've been seeing my father,' Ash confessed, her eyes filling. 'In my dreams. The pills used to keep him away, but they don't seem to work anymore. Most of it I can live with, but if I see her . . . If I see what he did . . .'

Wallace could sense Ash's anguish at the horrific memory she carried deep inside her. As a child, living under a different name, she'd witnessed her father shoot her mother dead.

'I don't think I could cope,' she continued, choking out the words.

Wallace pulled himself on to the bed, and wrapped his arms around her.

'It's going to be OK,' he assured her, telling himself that it wasn't really a lie.

Ash smiled up at him awkwardly. 'I know,' she said quietly, gently extricating herself from his embrace. She wiped her eyes and stood. 'I'm gonna grab us something to eat. There's a pizza place across the street.'

Wallace was bewildered. After everything they'd shared, she

still didn't feel comfortable around him. 'Do you want me to come with you?' he asked.

'No. I'll be OK on my own. No point risking us both getting caught.' She slipped on a pair of sandals and hurried from the room.

Wallace felt a turmoil of emotion. There was no doubt that he had feelings for her, and he cursed himself for confusing the situation. He saw such sadness in her eyes, but it wasn't simply that they were kindred, flawed spirits who might find comfort with each other; there was something about her that had changed. She'd opened up to Wallace, exposing herself in a way that made it impossible to ignore the beauty that lay within. He knew that it had taken a lot for her to be so honest, and that trust had only strengthened the attraction.

'I'm sorry, Con,' he said quietly, swept by guilt as he realised he was feeling something he hadn't experienced since he'd been with Connie: longing.

Ash pulled the door closed and leaned against it, partly in response to the pain shooting up from the shredded soles of her feet, but mostly because she needed a moment of calm in the eye of an emotional storm. They'd established a genuinely powerful connection, and it scared her. She hadn't ever let anyone get this close. Even as a child she'd sensed something warped in her parents' relationship, and knew that her mother's loyalty was split between maternal devotion and religious obligation. She'd never been able to totally trust anyone, not even her own mother, who might betray a confidence to her all-seeing, all-powerful father. Ash had never been herself; she'd always hidden behind achievement and used constant activity as a way to avoid forging any real bonds. Her relationship with Wallace was unlike anything she'd ever experienced. Uncomfortable with being anything other than open, unwilling to give him anything but honesty, unable to erect the customary barriers that she used to keep people at a distance, Ash had let Wallace know her as no other. And he hadn't recoiled or run. He hadn't tried to use the knowledge to his advantage, or manipulate her. He'd just listened, and when he saw she was hurt, sought to comfort her. Even if he didn't exploit or betray her, Ash still had reason to be fearful of this unique relationship. She was in uncharted, unfamiliar territory. She'd never had a real friend and she didn't know how to handle it; she had no idea what was involved.

Don't be afraid, baby.

Her mother's words rose in her mind, and Ash smiled to herself. Of all the things facing her, having a true friend was the least troubling. She eased her weight on to her pained feet, making a mental note to stop at the pharmacy on her way to the pizza place. As she slowly shuffled down the gloomy corridor, she thought about Wallace's question. *What do we do next?* She already knew the answer. They'd have to start taking risks, and convince a brilliant man to break the law.

38

The kiss of bare feet on a polished wooden floor. Tiny, fragile fingers trailed along a whitewashed wall. A light cotton dress, crisp and cool against the skin.

Not this. No.

Sunlight warm on her back. A line drawn ahead of her, separating light from shade. She shivered as she crossed the border into shadow.

No. I can't go in there.

A door ajar. White wood framed by light. A young hand reached out to push it open.

Don't. Don't do it.

Her father's room. She'd made this journey countless times. From the lush garden, into his bungalow, down the corridor, into his bedroom.

Don't go in there. You know what you'll find.

The little girl she once was couldn't possibly hear the warning, and stepped inside.

Please. Please don't.

'You sent for me, Father,' Alice said, fixing a practised smile to her face.

Don't look.

But this wasn't then; it wasn't the day she dreaded, the day her world turned to horror. This was another time. Nicholas was sitting on his vast bed, his arms around her mother, pulling her close to him in an unaccustomed display of affection that reminded Alice of a time long ago, when she'd been tiny, when life had been good, and simple, and sweet.

'We just wanted to tell you that we love you,' Nicholas announced. 'And to let you know that you're going to have a brother.'

'Or sister,' her mother chimed in.

This should have been a happy day. Alice wanted to hug her mother, but she knew that Nicholas was as changeable as a Pacific squall, and so she stood, waiting to be told how to react, looking beyond her parents, through the French doors, watching a blanket of California poppies as they swayed in the breeze, the thick yellow petals cupped tightly, as though trying to catch the air.

'Don't you have anything to say, Alice?' Nicholas asked, the bright, whitewashed room darkening as he spoke.

'I'm very happy,' Alice tried.

'That pleases me.'

Nicholas smiled and offered her his arm.

Alice stepped forward and he pulled her into a tight embrace. For a moment she almost believed that they were a normal family celebrating the impending arrival of a new baby.

'We should all be most grateful for the wondrous bounty that is life, for the great gifts that the divine bestows upon us all,' Nicholas whispered in her ear, his words reminding her that they weren't a normal family.

They weren't normal at all.

A shaft of light snuck between the ill-fitting drapes and highlighted her smooth leg, which was wrapped around the quilt. Her hand gripped the thick fabric, her knuckles white with tension. She was asleep, but instead of calm repose, her face was furrowed, and her body had trembled intermittently the whole time he'd been watching. Wallace sat on the edge of his bed and wondered whether he should wake her. He'd showered and shaved, but his movements had been insufficient to rouse Ash from her nightmare. They'd shared a six-pack with their pizzas, and Wallace had seen her swallow a couple of pills after her food. He wasn't sure whether they were painkillers to help numb her throbbing neck, or whether she'd picked up some sleeping pills from the pharmacy at the foot of the building.

He hadn't wanted to confuse the situation or add to her stress, so he'd spoken of inconsequential things, watching Ash for any sign that she shared his feelings. But she'd returned from the pizza place more like her old, guarded self and instead of relaxing her, the beer and pizza seemed to make her more distant, their conversation growing increasingly superficial until at last she'd announced that she needed sleep.

Wallace checked the phone Salamander had given him: 10:17 a.m. – they needed to get moving. He reached a hand towards Ash's exposed shoulder, but her eyes flickered open before he could touch her. Fear and anxiety clouded her face until she realised where she was and who she was with.

'Morning,' Wallace smiled.

'I was dreaming,' Ash replied quickly, her words running into each other with the haste of the recently woken. 'I didn't wake you, did I?'

'No. I've been up for a while. I was thinking of getting some breakfast.'

'We'll grab something on the move,' Ash advised him, shifting to her customary 'take charge' tone. As she pushed herself upright, the quilt fell away to reveal her slim, muscular body, which was ill-concealed by the grey vest and panties she'd slept in.

Wallace flushed and looked away.

'I'm going to shower,' she announced, stepping into the tiny bathroom.

Wallace watched the flimsy plastic door slide shut. 'I'll wait for you downstairs.'

They walked north from the hotel, losing themselves in the Manhattan crowds. They bought a couple of cream cheese and lox bagels, and ate them on the move.

'We've got to go after Steven Byrne,' Wallace said as they joined the Avenue of the Americas and picked their way along the busy sidewalk. 'I shot his son, and was at least partially responsible for what happened to his daughter. He's got plenty of motive. And we know he's rich enough to finance something like this.'

Ash shook her head. 'We checked him out thoroughly to see if he knew more than he was saying. There was nothing to link him to the murders.'

'But—' Wallace began.

'I'm not saying he's not involved,' Ash cut him off. 'I'm just saying that I don't think we should start with one of America's richest men. You're wanted and I've been targeted twice. Maybe we should stay off the radar for a little longer?' She shot him a mollifying smile.

'OK,' Wallace conceded. 'So what's the plan?'

They were parted by a polished businessman shouting into his phone.

'I put in three requests but I couldn't get access to Max Byrne's military records,' Ash revealed when they came together. 'Mike Rosen said they'd served in the same unit, but I don't remember seeing his records either. So much was lost in the aftermath of what happened in California . . .' She trailed off at the memory of her colleagues. 'I can't be certain we vetted him properly, and by the time things were back to normal, Rosen was in the wind. I want to see their military records, see who else they served with.'

★

The Kosinsky Data Services reception hadn't changed. Puffball clouds eased across a cobalt sky, and the city gleamed in the sharp sunlight, but Wallace only glanced at the view from the eighteenth-floor windows. He could feel Ash's anxiety and watched as she paced back and forth. Todd, the young receptionist, had offered her a seat, but she'd rejected it impatiently. Wallace couldn't tell whether her fearfulness stemmed from their current predicament or whether she was afraid of the man who haunted her dreams. Ash hadn't said any more about her father and Wallace hadn't wanted to pry, but he sensed a change, as though the spectre of her past had been rendered more potent by her recent ordeal.

He was struck by the thought that it might be him, that Ash had sensed his growing feelings for her and that he was making her uncomfortable, but as he looked at her, she flashed him a sad smile that seemed devoid of discomfort. Wallace recognised that he wasn't in the best state of mind, that he might be confusing feelings of safety and familiarity with something more. He resolved not to say anything until their ordeal was over. Only then would he know how he truly felt about the beautiful FBI agent.

They'd given false names to the building security guard. Wallace had been hunted by the authorities before, first in Afghanistan, after the Marwand massacre, and then, when he'd been implicated in the Pendulum killings. His experiences had made him more than a little paranoid. He imagined that being the subject of an Interpol terror alert would have put his photo in the hands of every receptionist, concierge and security guard in the country, but the man had hardly glanced up from behind his high counter as he'd directed them to the elevators. Security alerts were only as good as the people enforcing them, and even in troubled times, some people suffered from poor attention spans, fallible memory and a general lack of interest in the world around them.

'You have no idea how much ass pain you've unleashed.'

Wallace turned to see Pavel Kosinsky enter the lobby, his sharp features twisted in irritation.

'The guard called up to warn us,' Pavel went on, shooting Todd an angry look.

'I wasn't sure if I should tell them,' Todd said guiltily, concern flashing across his youthful face as he realised he'd made a mistake.

'There's a nationwide alert out for him,' Pavel announced, pointing at Wallace, who felt an immediate pang of fear, but also perverse relief that the watch list worked. 'The cops are on their way. Probably the Feds too.'

'We need to go,' Ash said flatly.

'My thoughts exactly,' Pavel agreed. 'I'll drive. We'll take the stairs.' He began to stride towards a door marked 'emergency exit', then registered the surprise on Ash's face. 'What? You must have had a good reason to come here. I'm intrigued.'

'You're crazy,' Ash smiled. 'Come on,' she said to Wallace. 'You heard the Mad Hatter.'

He followed them into a wide concrete stairwell.

Pavel skipped down the stairs. 'I heard about your brush with death. Harrell had me consult on the program the perp, Charles Haig, was running. Quite clever.'

'Reeves said it was denial of service attack,' Ash responded, her discomfort showing as she struggled with the pace.

'No, no. Haig had modified some facial recognition software; he was scanning every publicly available image source for pictures of Max Byrne,' Pavel revealed. 'Facebook, Twitter, Instagram – do you have any idea how many images he scanned? Billions. More brute crunching than finesse, but still effective.'

Ash had told Wallace about finding the photograph of Max

Byrne in Charles Haig's lair. She'd also told him about the pictures of Pendulum's victims, which Haig had obtained from Max's hideout. Wallace felt queasy thinking of the images, considering the care and preparation that had been put into each murder.

He was surprised by Ash's laboured breathing and worried whether she should be exerting herself. But there was no sign of any wavering resolve, just her customary determination to succeed.

'What's the favour?' Pavel asked, his trainers lightly kissing each step.

Wallace guessed Pavel was wealthy, but the black jeans and open-necked white shirt were economically anonymous, and he could have passed for a server in any one of New York's restaurants.

'You only come to see me when you want something. Like the worst type of cat.'

Ash ignored the dig. 'I need Byrne's military record. I've put in three requests, but they've all been refused. I need someone to hack the Pentagon.'

'Hack the Pentagon!' Pavel laughed. 'You people make everything sound so dramatic.'

'Can you do it?' Ash asked.

'Maybe your requests were refused to save embarrassment,' Pavel replied cryptically. 'I tried myself, shortly after Pendulum was identified. I was interested to see where he'd acquired his considerable technical expertise. But his records aren't classified, they've been disappeared. Whatever was there before has gone. Now there's just a name and service number. His file's been emptied and orphaned. Most strange.'

'Who could do something like that?' Wallace chimed in.

'DOD, NSA, CIA: pick your acronym. Or it could have been a hacker.' Pavel smiled at Ash as he emphasised the last word.

'But it would have to be a good one. I couldn't find any markers. No sign of who'd erased the file or that it had ever existed.'

'We've got the name of someone who served alongside Byrne: Mike Rosen,' Ash said. 'You think you could check him out?'

'Sure,' Pavel replied. 'But I can't just mind-meld. I'll need a computer,' he added with a broad grin.

Ash looked as though she was about to say something, but she just shook her head and smiled as they continued down the stairs. They raced past the ground floor, into the bowels of the building. Finally, when they reached basement sub-level three, Pavel hurried through a metal fire door and led them into an expansive parking garage.

'Come on,' he urged, jogging towards the rows of parked vehicles.

Wallace was struck by the collective value of the surrounding cars, but surmised that few poor people could afford to park in Midtown Manhattan. The underclass that cleaned and lubricated the city relied on public transport.

They approached an unmarked black Chevrolet Express, its interior shielded by dark privacy glass.

Pavel unlocked it. 'Get in.'

Ash took the passenger seat while Wallace climbed in the back, surprised to find himself in a cabin that reminded him of the Millennium Falcon. A pair of captains' chairs were set between two banks of monitors and control panels lining both sides of the vehicle.

'This is our mobile unit,' Pavel explained, sliding into the driver's seat and starting the engine.

Wallace said nothing as the van rolled up the main access ramp, heading for the surface. He imagined a fleet of patrol cars screeching into view in front of them, and guessed that Ash, who was equally tense and silent, had similar concerns. After three steep turns, he saw the light of 50th Street through a chain-link shutter. Pavel drove towards it, touching the brake, slowing the van's progress to give the sensor time to register its presence. As the shutter rose, Wallace watched the street intently but saw no sign of police, just the steady flow of Manhattan traffic.

The van lurched as Pavel stepped on the accelerator.

'Everyone stay calm and there'll be no problem,' he advised. Wallace followed his gaze to see three blue-and-whites parked by the main entrance. A couple of uniformed police officers stood by the cars, laughing and talking with the easy manner of men discussing sports scores. 'We're going to have to go past them,' Pavel said.

His heart racing, Wallace had to resist the urge to duck as the Chevy turned east and joined a line of traffic edging slowly towards Seventh Avenue. One of the cops, a tall, heavy-set man, seemed to stare directly into the van, but when he adjusted his peaked cap, Wallace realised that the officer had simply been studying his own reflection in the darkened windows.

The traffic eased, and the van gathered speed. Nobody said anything as they passed the towering glass-and-steel Allianz building which dominated the block, but as they finally reached the intersection with Seventh Avenue, Pavel blew a prolonged whistle.

'See, I told you, no problem,' he said, swinging the steering wheel right.

Ash punched him playfully. 'We were lucky.'

'There's no such thing as luck,' Pavel replied. 'Only fate.' He smiled, and the van joined the traffic speeding south.

39

'Rosen's file is orphaned and empty,' Pavel announced, leaning back in the captain's chair. 'Just like Max Byrne's. Someone doesn't want people connecting these guys.'

They'd crossed the East River on the Williamsburg Bridge and had parked the van on Driggs Avenue. The narrow street cut through McCarren Park, a quiet patch of open space surrounded by low buildings. Wallace couldn't tell whether Pavel was playacting the part of a paranoid technology freak, but he'd pointed out that their location gave them clear visibility in all directions, and the mature trees on either side of the park prevented aerial surveillance.

Pavel had fired up the very expensive, liquid-cooled computers that ran off a bank of hotwired batteries taken out of a Tesla. He'd established an encrypted link to a DOD satellite, using an old operator code, and had hacked into the Department of Defense from within its own system. But his efforts had proved fruitless. He'd found Rosen's personnel file, but it was empty and had no unit or service markers to tie him to anyone else.

'We know Byrne was in the Seventy-fifth Rangers,' Ash said.

'Which unit? When?' Pavel asked. 'We're talking about thousands of people.'

Wallace was surprised to feel something vibrate in his pocket, and he reached in to find the phone Salamander had given him. As far as he knew, only one person had the number.

'Should I answer?' he asked.

Pavel shrugged and Ash nodded.

He went ahead and took the call.

'John, it's Patrick Bailey.' The detective's voice sounded strained.

'Let me put you on speaker,' Wallace replied. 'It's Pat Bailey,' he told Ash.

'Pat, it's Chris. We've got Pavel Kosinsky with us.'

'No names. No names,' Pavel cautioned. 'Don't you people know anything?'

'They said you were in Belmarsh,' Wallace observed.

'I got taken out. Two guys abducted me. Wanted to know your location. They started asking me questions about the case I'm working. The one with the code I sent you.'

'Pendulum?' Ash asked.

'I think so,' Bailey replied. 'There's something bigger going on.'

'Agreed. I found Pendulum's base. There were two guys there, but the place was booby-trapped,' Ash explained. 'They've tried to get me twice, which means just knowing about this is dangerous.'

'We think we've got a lead on the code,' Bailey said.

Wallace thought he heard a groan when Bailey finished speaking, but it might have been a flaw in the connection.

'We're working our own angle this end,' Ash revealed. 'Is this a good number to reach you?'

There was a brief pause. 'No. It's a burner. My friends are pretty paranoid.'

Wallace could guess who those friends were.

'Good. Paranoid is good,' Pavel chipped in.

'I'll call you,' Bailey added. 'Be careful.'

'You too,' Ash advised, and before Wallace could say anything, Bailey had hung up.

Wallace's attention was drawn towards a school athletics team practising on the track to the south of them. He watched the faces of the diligent young athletes running around the blood-red lanes, envying their normality. He wondered when he might be able to return to the real world, and suddenly found himself questioning whether he'd ever be able to. Had his experiences warped him in a way that made a normal life impossible? He thought of the life he might never live and the family he might never have. Everyone had family, right?

'What about family?' he asked. 'Byrne's parents won't talk to us about their son's service, but what about Rosen's family? Did he have a wife? Parents? Cousins? There will be someone out there who knew his unit, the people he served with. You can't erase a person's life.'

'I'm not sure I like this. Getting out in the real world. Talking to people,' Pavel said mockingly, but he was sitting up and typing on the terminal. 'It sounds old-fashioned.'

'It's called investigation,' Ash joined in. 'Detective work. It's what we real cops do when you web puppets strike out.'

Her arms mimicked those of a flailing marionette, and she eyed Pavel, his arms dancing above the keyboard in similar fashion. He suddenly froze.

'I'm happy to assist you, Agent Ash, but I will not be mocked.' His tone was deadly serious, but he could only maintain it for a moment. 'Nah, I'm kidding, mock away. I'll console myself by crying in a bath full of money and thinking about how little you real cops get paid.'

'Touché,' Ash observed.

'Indeed,' Pavel replied, studying the screen. 'Not many people know that the Military Postal Service keeps extensive contact details of personnel and their family. I've got an inactive record for a Michael Rosen of the Seventy-fifth Rangers, which means he's been discharged.'

Wallace peered at the screen and saw that Rosen's name was part of a long list. Pavel clicked on the entry.

'The Department of Defense is nothing if not methodical,' he noted. 'Most recent operational address is Fort Benning, but there are two personal ones in West Virginia and Kentucky.'

Ash squeezed into the cabin and patted Pavel on the shoulder. 'You did good, Kos.' She smiled at him. 'We're going to need a vehicle.'

'No chance,' Pavel replied immediately. 'No way are you taking my baby.'

Ash fixed him with an unwavering stare, but he was equally intransigent.

'I know where we can get a car,' Wallace said. 'They probably won't have anything as fancy as this, but they take cash.'

40

The old cop sat in the back seat, moaning every time they hit a pothole. He wasn't really old, at least no more than Sal, but it was his outlook: he was proper.

By the book.

Mind the gap.

You have twenty seconds to comply.

Rules made people seem old. They were fine for the sheeple, those who wanted to daydream, chew grass and get fleeced by the farmers. But Danny had told the rules to go to fuck long ago, and had never looked back. He'd grown up on a council estate in Elephant & Castle, one that had long since been demolished, and he'd never bothered with school. It was a junior pen where young sheeple were trained to be afraid of the bosses, the government, people who told you what to do and robbed you blind for the privilege of being in charge. You make your own way in the world, something Danny often imagined his father might say if he'd been around. He was a legend. A king among men. But he'd been gone for most of Danny's childhood, serving at Her Majesty's pleasure. So the only male figures in his life were his mother's steady stream of damaged boyfriends, losers, drug addicts, drunks and perverts. None of them had shit-all to say that was worth hearing, so Danny's true role models flickered at him from the TV his mum had scored from work. Cowboys. Gangsters. Maverick cops. These were the men that shaped

Danny's world. Movie stars. Silver screen heroes. His mum spent her days at the local Cash for Gold, a pimped out pawn-broker's that traded treasures for dirty notes. But if the sheeple were stupid enough to accept ten quid for a TV or twenty quid for an iPad, they deserved their fleecing.

Danny had started dealing aged twelve, running weed through school. Couple of greasy Year Five goons, Chris Brown and Billy Kane, thought they'd rip him off, but Danny was no fool. They'd come at him with fists, not realising he was tooled up, and when he shanked Kane-o in the leg, the two of them backed off sharpish, Kane-o crying like a little girl whose puppy had just died. Most mugs would have gone for the gut, but Danny knew that would've been murder, and there was no point killing a fool over a bag of weed. Besides, Kane-o's limp was a permanent advert against messing with Danny's business.

And it was a business. He'd downloaded a bunch of audio books on to his phone, business gurus, biographies of famous criminals, anything that might have a bearing on his operation. He learned more from those stories than he ever did from school. While his school mates were shoplifting from the local offy, Danny was building a distribution network, using older guys to take his product on to the street. That's how he'd come to Sal's attention, and they'd clicked immediately, each recognising the other's sharpness, the shared ambition. The spark, Sal had called it. Some people had it. Most didn't. Salman Sohota definitely had the spark.

A few years older and smarter than him, Sal was more polished than anyone Danny had ever met. He'd come up from the streets, but life had smoothed out his rougher edges, which meant he could easily move from the gutter to the boardroom and not look out of place. Danny never got on with anyone at school, so he didn't really understand the friendship Sal had with the cop. It seemed fucking risky staying pals with the law, but

Bailey – Haybale as Sal called him – seemed cool enough not to ask the wrong questions. Danny had once suggested they try to put him on the payroll, but Sal had refused. They had plenty of police working for them, so it wasn't a point of principle; Danny guessed that Sal didn't want to tempt his mate down from his pedestal.

They were in Frank's Range Rover, and the old villain was driving them along Victoria Embankment. Danny shifted uncomfortably in his suit. He hadn't worn the thing since his Uncle Ian's funeral, but Sal had insisted nobody would take him seriously if he wasn't in sheeple uniform. Danny caught Sal glancing back from the passenger seat, watching his old friend with rare concern. He looked across at the cop, who'd borrowed some of Sal's clothes – a crisp tailored grey suit, sky blue shirt and a pair of black Derbies. He was tough, Danny had to give him that. Apart from a little swelling on Bailey's face, and the splint holding his left hand together, there was no outward sign of the man's injuries. The way Doctor Death had been talking – contusion, haemorrhage, fracture, laceration – there's no way he should be upright. And if Sal hadn't stopped him, the nutter had planned to handle the day's business alone. Danny had volunteered. Why not? It sounded like a right laugh, a low-risk cakewalk mugging off some librarian. Sal had talked Bailey into agreeing, but the cop had insisted on coming with them.

'You alright?' Danny asked.

'Yeah,' Bailey replied, but his face was clenched tighter than a fist, making a liar of him.

'Well, that's OK then,' Danny said, but he gave Sal a worried look: *the cop should be laid up*.

Sal nodded but said nothing.

They pulled into an empty driveway in front of one of the three-storey terraced houses on the eastern side of Porter Street. Danny popped the door open, but the cop reached out and grabbed him. Danny could feel weakness in the man's grip, and when he turned to give him some verbal for inappropriate touching, he saw a face twisted with pain. Only a complete asshole would kick a wounded dog, Danny thought, so he stayed silent and waited to hear what the crazy cop had to say.

'You sure you know what to do?' Bailey asked.

'You don't have to worry, man,' Danny assured him. 'I ain't thick.'

'He's got it,' Sal added.

'He is fucking thick,' Frank needled.

'Fuck off, you greaseball,' Danny snapped back, as the old geezer reached for him.

He skipped out of the car and slammed the door, knowing how much Frank hated people doing anything that might damage his motor.

Frank raised a fist and Danny replied with his middle finger before turning north and heading towards the river. He made a left and hurried along Park Street towards the *London Record* building, a short, fat, dirty brown brick pile that squatted right by the Thames. He pulled a pair of shades from his inside pocket and slipped them over his eyes as he entered.

The reception was like the entrance to every other sheeple factory. Lots of glass and marble, a few plants, some paint splats framed as art, a lazy fatso play-pretend cop posing as a security guard, and a couple of honey dolls sat behind a long desk: a brunette and a redhead. He went for the brunette.

'Detective Sergeant Deckard,' Danny announced, producing a forged warrant card, which he flashed at the receptionist. Harrison Ford had been one of his matinee role models. 'I'm working with Detective Murrall on the Sylvia Greene case.'

The smile fell from the brunette's face and she nodded seriously.

'He's asked me to take a look at the paper's archives,' Danny continued.

'The Archive Department is in the basement,' the brunette replied. She toyed with a strand of hair that had worked free of her loose ponytail. 'Would you like me to show you the way?'

Danny got a definite flirty vibe, but she did nothing for him. He'd swung for guys ever since primary school. He kept his love life low-key and private, but he was pretty sure Sal had guessed which way the dice rolled.

'I'm alright, thanks,' he said. 'Just down in the lifts, right?'

The brunette nodded. 'I'll give them a call, let them know you're coming.'

'Thanks.' Danny spun on his heels and sauntered past the security guard towards the heart of the building.

A tall blonde in brown sandals, sandy trousers and a white shirt was waiting when the lift spat him into a small lobby. The air was dead still and stale as though it had been through a billion lungs. It reminded him of the Natural History Museum, which had been saved from being written off as the dullest place in London by two things: the animatronic dinosaurs and his first furtive kiss with a boy called Hugh, a posho from another school, who'd got talking to Danny in the basement lunch room.

'Detective?' the blonde asked, her voice suggesting she'd sooner believe Danny was the Pope.

'That's right,' Danny said, flashing the warrant card. 'Detective Sergeant Deckard.'

'My name's Mary Stephenson,' she said, offering her hand. 'I'm the assistant manager of the archive.'

Danny shook her hand, which was the softest and warmest he could ever remember touching.

'How can I help?'

'I need to look at some of your back issues,' he said.

'A lot of them are online,' Mary countered. She clearly didn't like people coming down to her dungeon.

'I know. I need to see some from the nineteen-twenties and thirties,' Danny said coolly. 'They're not online, are they?'

'No, they're not. You'd better come with me.' Mary moved towards a set of double doors, her sandals squeaking against the polished floor. She brushed a key card in front of a reader and pulled one of the doors open to reveal a vast vault that ran the entire length of the building.

'Wow,' Danny remarked, looking at the rows of archive shelves that stretched into the distance.

'It's not as bad as it looks,' Mary told him. 'We've digitised almost all of it.'

A middle-aged woman and a nerdy young guy eyed them from inside a glass-panelled office as Mary led him into the archive. They turned right into a narrow gulley that ran between two long shelves, and emerged into a small cubbyhole. Three computer terminals stood on a counter set against the far wall.

'The system's simple enough,' Mary said, approaching the nearest machine.

She toggled the mouse and the screen sprang to life to reveal an old-fashioned browser which was badged as 'Arcfile'.

'You can search by subject, date, keyword, anything really. And if you need a bespoke search, Simon, our resident expert, can write you one.'

'Date will be fine.' Danny slid into the adjacent chair and rolled it towards the computer. 'Thanks,' he added. 'I'll let you know if I need anything.'

He was glad to see Mary was smart enough to sense that he was politely telling her to get lost.

'OK,' she said, backing away. 'I'll be in the office if you need me.'

Danny waited until she was gone before pulling a folded piece of paper from his pocket. He laid it flat on the counter to reveal Sylvia Greene's code. Lines now divided the block into its component parts. Fucking ball-ache, Danny thought as he typed in the first date. It was fun posing as a cop, but doing real police work was nothing but a drag.

Danny had been at it for over forty minutes and was down to the final two words when he heard footsteps behind him, and turned to see Mary approaching.

'How are you getting on?' she asked.

He carefully covered the deciphered message he'd scrawled on the back of the piece of paper.

'All good,' he replied. 'Nearly done.'

'Were you expecting any colleagues?' Mary continued. 'Only reception just phoned to say there's another couple of detectives on their way down.'

Danny felt the familiar bang of adrenalin as his heart tick-tocked up a notch. According to Bailey, the men who tortured him were the only other people who knew about the code. They'd been trying to decipher it when he'd escaped. Maybe they'd cracked it?

'They aren't police,' he said, getting to his feet and pocketing the message. 'They're villains posing as the law.'

He registered Mary's dismay as his brain whirred through his options. 'Is there another way out of here?'

Mary hesitated.

'If they know the real police are on to them, we'll all be in danger,' Danny added.

'The fire stairs,' Mary told him. 'They're by the lifts.'

She hurried towards the exit and Danny followed.

'Tell your mates to call nine-nine-nine,' he said as they passed the glass-panelled office.

'Call the police!' Mary shouted at the nerdy man Danny assumed was Simon.

He looked perplexed.

'Do it!' Danny yelled.

When they entered the lobby, Danny saw a door marked 'emergency stairs'. Mary hurried forward, but Danny froze when he heard a chime announce the arrival of one of the lifts.

'Get out of the way,' he said, pushing Mary clear as he drew one of his VBR machine-pistols and strode towards the lift. The doors slid open and two heavy guys in badly fitting suits stepped out. They were both wearing the cuts and shiners of a recent fight. *Cops, my fucking arse*, Danny thought as he surged forward. He cracked the shorter of the two with the butt of the pistol, knocking him cold. The guy dropped like a deadweight punk, and Danny levelled the pistol at his buddy's head.

'Don't you move,' Danny snarled. 'Or I'll fuckin' drill you.'

'Detective?' Mary asked doubtfully.

'I'm no detective,' Danny admitted. 'And neither's this guy,' he added, frisking the barrel-chested guy and finding a Sig in a concealed underarm holster. 'Unless the Met's lettin' its troops out with heavy artillery. Who you working for?' he demanded.

The goon glared, but said nothing. Danny raised the VBR and was about to strike, when the security door opened and the nerdy guy burst in.

'The police are on—' He stopped short when he realised what was happening.

The goon smiled like a meth-head who'd had his first hit of the day.

'So you like the police,' Danny observed. 'I don't,' he added, slamming the pistol into the man's face and feeling the satisfying crunch of bone as he fell.

'If I were you, I'd get his gun,' Danny suggested. 'It's unlikely, but they might wake up.'

Mary was frozen like a child who'd just caught her parents having sex. She wouldn't be any use to anyone.

'You,' Danny said to Simon. 'Take his gun, and if either of them move, just shoot. Thanks for your help,' he added with a twinkling smile, before racing into the emergency stairwell and bouncing up the steps three at a time.

A red squad car drew up outside the main doors as Danny entered the lobby. Armed police, he thought as he sucked in a deep breath of air and made an effort to calm himself. Sure enough, two bullet boys emerged from the vehicle, side arms showing, vests puffing out their chests. They jogged past Danny on their way to the reception desk. He spun on his heels and gave the brunette receptionist a cheeky salute, but she didn't notice; she was too busy trying to understand why the building was now the epicentre of a cop convention.

Bailey was out cold when he returned to the Range Rover.

'Is he . . .' Danny let the question hang as he climbed on to the back seat.

'No, I am not dead,' Bailey said, opening his eyes. 'I was just resting. Did you get it?'

'We heard some blues,' Sal added. 'Everythin' alright?'

'I had to call the cops. Couple of heavies showed up. Short one had a couple of scars, one on his eye, the other on his chin, and a big fuck-off hammer-shaped bruise on his cheek. Big guy had a shaved head and a broken nose. Sound familiar?'

Bailey nodded.

'We should pick 'em up,' Frank suggested.

Danny shook his head. 'Cops'll have 'em now. We need to bounce before they start looking for me too.'

Frank looked at Sal, who nodded, and the Range Rover started moving. The old villain threw it into reverse, swung out of the drive and headed south along Porter Street.

'Did you crack the code?' Bailey asked.

'I like that. Makes me sound like Bond,' Danny observed.

He produced the piece of paper and handed it to the cop.

Bailey squinted at it for a moment. 'I can't read this,' he protested. 'It's like a spider crawled through a pot of ink.'

Danny snatched back the paper and was about to say a few words when he caught sight of Sal, who signalled calm.

'I'll read it for you,' Danny said, telling himself he was being the bigger man. 'You're reading this because I believe you're a good man and I trust you. I've been the victim of blackmail and I don't think I'm the only one. My investigation leads me to believe there are other victims. I've been working with one of our reporters who knows as much as me. If you're good at your job, you'll figure out who. What I know ended my life, so don't go down this path unless you're prepared. Be . . .' Danny trailed off.

'Be what?' Bailey asked.

'I don't know. Your friends showed up before I got the last two words,' Danny replied.

The cop muttered something indecipherable.

'I'll take that as a thank you,' Danny said.

'Thanks,' Bailey offered grudgingly.

'D'ya know who she's talking about?' Sal asked Bailey.

'I think so,' the cop replied thoughtfully. 'I need to get to Geneva.'

41

It was a little after ten and they were an hour away from their destination. The air conditioning was faulty, so they had the windows down, and cool air was gusting into the car. It carried the fresh scent of the lush green trees that covered the surrounding hills. Pavel had taken them to Five Star Auto Sales, the used car lot near JFK where Wallace had purchased the ancient Explorer the January before last. He and Ash had ignored Pavel's advice to buy Japanese, and had selected a sixteen-year-old navy blue Chevy Blazer with cracked grey leather seats. Pavel had decried it as ugly and unreliable, but Ash had countered that it was a common model that was unlikely to draw any attention. They had paid cash, using some of the money Wallace had taken out of his safety deposit box. Pavel had given them a private number to contact if they needed anything else from him and told them to be careful.

Ash had driven the Blazer into Manhattan, to the Fresh City Hotel, where Wallace had gone to the room and grabbed the holdall Salamander had given him, while she checked out. They'd left the city and headed west. When they'd reached a place called Montgomeryville, they'd stopped at the mall and Ash had bought some new clothes, cosmetics and toiletries. They'd found a payphone and Ash had called the two numbers Pavel had given them. The first belonged to the address in Louisville, Kentucky, but the man who'd answered had never heard of

Mike Rosen and said he'd been renting the house alone for the past three years. The second number, which went to an address in Summersville, West Virginia, had been far more promising. When the call was over, Ash had told Wallace that the man who'd answered had said, 'Six-four-five-two, Rosen.' But the moment she'd asked about Mike, the guy had clammed up and denied any knowledge of him.

They'd taken turns driving west, and had finally stopped in Clarksburg, a small town in the north of the state. They'd found a place called the Greenbrier Motel, and, posing as a couple, had taken a king room in the three-storey, shoebox-shaped structure. They'd had dinner in a Chinese restaurant near the motel, but Wallace hadn't been much interested in food or Ash's dissection of the investigation. He'd been puzzling over the nature of their relationship. They'd been thrown together by circumstance, but Ash was now closer to him than anyone. He'd watched her throughout the meal, studying her delicate features. Maybe he was projecting, but it seemed to Wallace that her eyes spoke of a life haunted by personal tragedy and the horrors presented by her profession, and he wanted to make it better.

Part-way through the meal, he had caught himself staring at her, watching her tease a loose strand of hair, studying her beautiful sad eyes, longing to catch her smile. He'd looked away, not wanting her to have any hint of his feelings until he could be sure of them himself.

'How are we supposed to eat these?' he asked, drawing attention to a platter of Chinese greens.

'I have no idea,' Ash replied, flashing him a smile that seemed to light up her face.

It had taken Wallace three attempts to pick up the slimy green bulb with his chopsticks, and each effort had made Ash chuckle. Finally, he'd managed to hold the vegetable, which was about the size of a baby's fist.

'Now what?' he asked.

'I think you just have to pop it in,' Ash suggested.

'There's no delicate way to do this. You might want to look away. Things could get ugly.' Pleased to be rewarded with another smile, he popped the oversized vegetable in his mouth. His cheeks had puffed up like a chipmunk's and he chewed as fast as he could to minimise embarrassment. After what seemed like an age, he'd been able to swallow.

'Pretty good,' he said, and the two of them giggled like innocent children.

The Chinese greens had set the tone for the rest of the meal, and they'd laughed and joked, as though there'd been an unspoken agreement that they take a break from their unhappy lives.

After Wallace had paid the bill, they'd walked across the small parking lot, neither saying anything, but the sense of carefree fun had died away as they'd approached their room. Ash had switched on the television, which helped make the silence less awkward. Wallace had been surprised when she had accepted his offer to sleep on the floor. He'd obviously read too much into their evolving relationship. Part of him had been grateful that Ash had kept it professional, but he hadn't quite been able to shake the desire to hold her, to pull her close and feel her warmth against him.

They'd created a makeshift bed using a quilt and some pillows. It had been reasonably comfortable, but Wallace had found it difficult to sleep, and he'd lain in the darkness listening to the soft sounds of Ash's breathing, until, sometime in the grey hours before dawn, he'd finally dozed off.

An early breakfast had put them on the road before nine, and now they were making good time, racing south along Highway 19 towards Summersville.

'You can't come with me,' Ash said, finally breaking a prolonged silence. 'You're wanted for Rosen's murder. They probably know what you look like.'

Wallace nodded. He'd been thinking as much.

'It's too risky staying out in the open for any length of time,' Ash continued. 'We need to find a motel.'

The Summers Inn was a long, low building located on the northern edge of Summersville. It wasn't much to look at, but the manager, a short, wizened guy called Jeb Harlan, was friendly, and the room was clean.

Ash felt a pang of regret leaving Wallace, but there was no way she could risk taking him. If, as she suspected, Rosen's parents lived at the address, there was no way they'd talk to the man accused of murdering their son.

'I'll be as quick as I can,' she assured Wallace. She hovered at the door, surprised to find herself reluctant to leave. She'd noticed how he hadn't been able to take his eyes off her during dinner, and his gaze had electrified her. She hadn't laughed so freely for longer than she could remember. She'd always pushed people away, but it was getting harder for her to ignore the feelings she was developing for Wallace. Were her emotions real? Did he feel the same way? Ash didn't handle uncertainty well. She had to be sure.

She approached Wallace, who was standing by the television, trying to figure out the remote. He turned, surprised to see her drawing close. They stood facing each other, and Ash felt a force more powerful than gravity pull her towards him. The world around her shrank into insignificance as she wrapped her arms around his waist and kissed him. There was no doubting his feelings for her. He pulled her close and held her tight. Ash felt a wave of excitement and longed to stay in Wallace's arms, but this was new territory for her and she needed to move slowly. Besides, she had work to do.

'I need to go,' she said awkwardly as she retreated from him.

He looked at her with a stunned smile on his face. 'Sure,' he responded, even more awkwardly.

'You going to be OK?' she asked.

'Yes,' he assured her. He shook himself from his daze, grabbed the remote and sat on the bed.

'Stay put, and don't open the door,' Ash cautioned as she left the room.

'Be careful,' Wallace returned. He switched on the TV and the room filled with the sound of a crowd cheering: *The Price is Right*.

She climbed into the Blazer, which was parked outside, and reversed away from the green and white building, before turning left on to Highway 41 and heading south. The quiet road wound through green countryside and mature woodland, and as Ash followed its lazy turns she found herself contemplating the kiss. There was no doubting how she felt about him, and he seemed equally drawn to her. She'd never been in this situation before and even in the first bloom of romantic excitement, Ash found herself worrying about how this would complicate their relationship. She should be focused on the Pendulum case, not daydreaming about a kiss, no matter how wonderful it had been. And how could she consider bringing another person into her life until she'd found a way to exorcise Nicholas from her dreams? she thought darkly. She and Wallace were going to have to talk when she returned to the motel.

Ash stayed on 41 for a couple of miles, passing only a handful of vehicles headed in the other direction. As she neared the centre of town, she saw Walker Avenue. She made a right and kept her eyes open for number 324. The unmarked road curled round manicured lawns, past houses that sat on expansive plots of land. Each of the homes was different, from small bungalows that seemed to shrink in the space around them, to huge, two-storey red-bricks that dominated their plots.

About a quarter of a mile from the intersection, Ash spotted '324' stamped on a battered mailbox which stood beside a potholed driveway on her left. She swung the Chevy into the drive and followed it past a short run of trees to find a dilapidated Arts and Crafts-style home. There were gaping holes in the red-tiled roof and white paint was flaking off the wooden walls. An old silver Ford pick-up was parked next to an even older navy blue Buick Skylark. Both vehicles were losing the battle against the rust that was spreading from their wheel arches.

Ash pulled to a halt beside the Ford, climbed out and started across the rutted drive. She saw movement in the house, and an old lady with full, drooping cheeks came to one of the upstairs windows and peered down at her. Her eyes were magnified by thick glasses, the edges of which were lost beneath scraggly curls of grey hair.

'Whatever you're selling, we don't want it.'

Ash looked towards the hoarse voice and saw an elderly man standing on the porch. He was so thin that he was almost lost inside his red-and-white checked shirt and frayed blue jeans. His swollen, red feet were wrapped inside a pair of orthopaedic sandals, and he tottered so unsteadily that Ash thought a harsh word might knock him down. The man's narrow eyes tracked her as she approached, his brow furrowed beneath his bald pate.

'I'm tellin' you, you're not welcome,' he said weakly.

'Mr Rosen?' Ash asked as she reached the foot of the stairs.

'I ain't givin' you my name, lady,' he replied. 'An' I don't wanna know yours either.'

'My name's Chris Alton, Mr Rosen. I'm with the West Virginia Veterans' Benevolent Fund. I'm sorry to trouble you during this difficult time—'

'Difficult time? What difficult time?' the old man interrupted. 'What the heck are you talkin' about?'

'He's dead, ain't he?' the old lady observed, her voice devoid of emotion. She looked like a wraith, standing behind an ancient screen door.

The old man glanced at her and then turned to face Ash, his mouth hanging open as though someone had just punched him in the gut.

'Well? I'm right, ain't I?' the old lady challenged Ash, stepping on to the porch.

Ash thought about the Interpol notice. It never mentioned Mike Rosen, it just said Wallace was wanted in connection with a terrorist attack. She only knew about Rosen from Wallace. His identity wasn't public. She'd screwed up. These people didn't know their son was dead.

'Well?' the old lady pressed, her tone hardening.

'I'm afraid so,' Ash replied.

'No!' the old man exclaimed, clutching his chest and steadying himself against the porch rail.

'Edward, you need to sit down,' the old lady observed, taking the man by the arm and leading him inside. 'You'd better come in, too,' she said, looking over her shoulder at Ash, who was suddenly weighed down by crushing guilt at the thought she'd inadvertently broken such terrible news.

Touched by their unexpected sorrow, Ash moved slowly up the stairs towards the tattered screen door.

42

Wallace flicked through the channels like a hunter stalking elusive prey. He couldn't settle. The kiss filled his mind, making it impossible for him to concentrate. He replayed the moment again and again, wondering what had prompted Ash, worrying about what it would do to their relationship, imagining falling into bed with her and spending the day in each other's arms. He felt guilt at the thought he had betrayed Connie's memory, but he needed to believe that love wasn't finite, that his feelings for Ash didn't diminish the way he felt about Connie. He wished he'd never let Ash go, and his mind suddenly filled with the multitude of horrors she could face when she arrived at the address in Rosen's file. Hostile parents? An angry sibling? An FBI trap? An armed gang in Pendulum masks? The rapid succession of flickering images did nothing to allay his fears, which only grew into a hungry feeling of regret: he should have gone with her.

He was surprised by how much he missed her already. The kiss had only cemented the feelings that had developed over the past few days. He longed to simply be around her, to hear her talk, saying anything just so that his ears would be filled by the sound of her voice.

Steven Byrne.

He registered the name, but, lost in his thoughts, kept clicking before he realised he'd just seen the face of Max's father. Wallace tapped his way back to the correct channel: C-SPAN. On screen, surrounded by a gaggle of camera-toting journalists who yelled a steady stream of questions, and a handful of imposing body-guards, Steven Byrne was climbing the steps of an imposing building. A lower third title read 'Senate Commerce Subcommittee Hearings'.

Wallace was unnerved by the sight of the man who'd lost so much because of him. His body crackled with nervous energy and he could feel his heart start to race as his emotions surged. Shame, fear, remorse, guilt, anger washed over him in successive waves, but all were nothing compared to the tsunami of regret. If he'd lived a different life Steven Byrne's children might still be alive. Connie might still be with him.

'Earlier this week, tech billionaire Steven Byrne arrived at the Russell Senate Office Building to testify before the Senate Commerce Subcommittee on Communication, Technology, Innovation and the Internet in relation to hearings it's been holding on the International Online Security Act, the so-called Blake-Castillo Bill.' The speaker had the deep, modulated tones of a network anchor. 'Mr Byrne's appearance before the committee has been contentious because many blame his son for sparking the call for internet regulation. The Pendulum murders led to widespread calls for an end to online anonymity.'

The camera cut to Steven Byrne, now seated behind a large table. Next to him sat an older, bald-headed, sharp-faced man in a suit, who was whispering in Steven's ear.

'Many were expecting the increasingly reclusive Mr Byrne to refuse to testify, but he attended the proceedings in Room SR-two-five-three with no sign of reluctance,' the voiceover continued.

A wide shot of the fifty-feet-square, wood-panelled room showed that it was divided into two halves. The first half, nearest the camera, was the auditorium, where press, politicians, lobbyists and members of the public sat and watched proceedings. The second half was effectively the performers' stage. Testifying witnesses sat at a baize-covered long table that stood between the auditorium and the dais. Ahead of it, raised above all else in the room, was a long concave bench where the twenty-two members of the committee were seated. Wallace saw Steven's companion whisper something in his ear, and wished the television microphones could pick up what was being said.

'Mr Byrne's testimony did not go the way many had predicted, and some commentators say that it has transformed the bill's chances of being passed,' the voiceover explained.

A chubby middle-aged blonde in a smart navy blue suit stepped through the large door behind the ranking senator's seat. She was followed by a furtive aide, who whispered some hurried words before scurrying away. The camera cut to a close-up as the woman took her seat, and a lower third title appeared on screen: 'Barbara Manchin – R, Nebraska'.

'Mr Byrne, I'm pleased to have you before the committee here today,' Manchin began. 'What I'm going to do is briefly summarise why you're here before we move on to your sworn testimony. The International Online Security Act is currently before Congress and proposes changes to the way we regulate the internet. The two most sweeping changes are the introduction of digital passports, which will be issued by the federal government to the citizens of the United States to bring an end to the era of anonymous commerce and activity online. The second proposed change is the creation of a central settlement system, utilising Blockchain technology to clear all online payments denominated in US dollars through the Federal Reserve. Blockchain is a self-contained digital audit technology that prevents fraud or tampering, creating a totally reliable, bulletproof transaction mechanism. The proponents of this bill, Representatives Blake and Castillo, argue that these two measures will ensure safety and transparency on the internet, and put a stop to the millions of harmful anonymous interactions that take place online every single day.'

Manchin paused, and the coverage shifted to Steven Byrne, who was impassive, but Wallace thought he looked wrung out. His skin seemed greyer than when they'd first met in Jean Mata's, and his eyes were ringed by dark shadows. He had the troubled air of a man who might be involved in murder. Or someone who'd lost his son and daughter, Wallace caught himself thinking.

The camera moved back to Senator Manchin as she continued. 'Mr Byrne, you have been invited here because of your particular technology expertise. After a distinguished career serving our nation in the First Ranger Battalion, you founded Erimax Security, one of the world's leading providers of digital security software. Your software guards many of the world's most prestigious institutions, including, I believe, this one, meaning the safety of my inbox is literally in your hands.' Manchin paused for the obligatory chuckle that rolled around the room, before continuing. 'A number of your peers have come before this committee and argued that the passage of this bill would stifle innovation in the technology sector. You have been a pioneer and an innovator, and your tragic personal experiences give you a unique perspective on how we might best protect ourselves from the very worst influences of technology.'

Manchin paused, letting her words linger in the air, and the camera returned to Steven.

'I support this legislation,' he said into the microphone, and his response drew a few gasps from the people behind him.

Wallace didn't completely understand what was happening, but the camera moved to Manchin, whose face expressed surprise as she looked down at her witness. Something important had taken place, and, as the commentator had noted, things hadn't gone the way people expected.

'The internet has always been a place of experimentation and exploration and we should embrace that, but there is no reason that commerce and communication needs to be carried out under a cloak of anonymity,' Steven added as the camera reverted to him. 'Concealing our identities only protects those with something to hide. The Panama Papers showed us what people will do when they are shielded by anonymity. People are simply more likely to break the law if they think they can't be identified, and my own experience tells me that even the most respectable, civilised people can behave reprehensibly when given anonymity. I lost my family . . .' He trailed off, his voice fading with emotion, and Wallace felt a pang of guilt.

Steven took a sip of water. 'But that's not the only reason I support this bill,' he continued. 'The internet should serve society, not the other way round. The concerns of big businesses like mine should not trump the needs of society. Business will always find a way to thrive.'

Manchin's face filled the screen, her expression one of pleasant surprise. 'Your industry colleagues have accused the legislation of being misguided at best, and at worst, downright irresponsible. They say that millions of people who cannot or will not obtain digital passports will effectively be denied access to the Net, because the legislation will forbid ISPs from connecting people who don't have one. Do you think that this bill will rob people of their freedom?'

'No, I don't,' Steven replied. 'As I understand it, every American will be issued with a digital biometric passport, in the same way we get social security numbers. The only people who would lose out are those who are here illegally, but I think the laws you make have to serve the interests of our citizens.'

'And you're not worried about the fact that people will be tracked and identified at every site they visit?' Manchin challenged.

'It's already happening, senator,' Steven responded. 'Most people just don't know about it. Your ISP knows exactly where you go and which sites you visit. All this bill does is make it absolutely clear that our online activity is being monitored, and I believe that awareness will encourage people to take greater responsibility for their actions.'

'I see,' Manchin observed. 'And you don't see any issues over implementation? What about the foreigner question?'

'Technology can do whatever we want it to. If my digital passport is linked to my fingerprint, my identity can be confirmed every time I go online. Whichever way we choose to do it, implementation will not present a problem,' Steven said. 'As for the foreigner question, I believe this issue is being debated at the UN Digital Security summit in Geneva, with a view to using the Blake-Castillo Bill as a model around the world. Japan has already signalled its intent to follow our lead. In future, digital passports may just become passports – the way in which we identify people whether they're online or in the real world.'

Wallace began to think he'd misjudged the man. Steven Byrne was trying to salvage something positive from his personal tragedy. He was supporting an attempt to make the internet a safer environment for everyone. Wallace didn't understand the logistics of what was being proposed, but he was certain that, no matter how drunk he'd been, he would never have been so cruel if he hadn't been able to hide behind a shroud of anonymity. Would a man with a multi-billion-dollar business, someone who was involved in a mission to transform the digital world, have the time or inclination to coordinate an assassination attempt?

'And what are your thoughts on the proposed Federal Central Settlement System?' Manchin continued.

'I have to believe that a central, secure ledger maintained by the Federal Reserve would prevent a lot of fraud and corruption,' Steven replied.

Manchin leaned over to confer with her neighbour, and the two of them exchanged whispered words before she returned to her microphone. 'Thank you, Mr Byrne. The committee would like to extend its appreciation of the time you've taken from your busy schedule to come here today. We're going to take a short recess before the next witness,' she said, her voice oozing gratitude.

The camera returned to the wide shot as the room erupted in turmoil. Steered by his older companion and surrounded by bodyguards, Steven tried to push his way to the exit through a throng of journalists who shouted questions, all of which went unanswered.

'Many in the industry were shocked by Steven Byrne's testimony and wonder whether his personal tragedy has clouded his judgment,' the voiceover continued.

The screen was suddenly filled by the face of a blond-haired man in his early twenties. He was wearing a black T-shirt that bore the legend 'Digital Freedom Forever'. A group of young protestors in replica T-shirts stood in the background chanting, 'Hands off our Net!'

'Steven Byrne made a fortune from a free internet, and like the worst kind of pioneer, now that he's got his ranch and homestead, he wants everything regulated so that others can't follow in his footsteps,' the man said angrily.

The camera cut to a short, red-cheeked woman with russet hair, who wore a baseball cap bearing the Texan star. Behind her stood a diverse group of men and women, many of whom were waving the Stars and Stripes.

'The families of America have lived with this menace for too long,' she said excitedly. 'Our children have been exposed to filth and violence and we've given the worst kind of people a place to meet and hide. I can't walk down the street without people seeing my face. Why shouldn't people have to say who they are on the internet?'

On screen, the image changed to show the anchor, a thirty-something black man in a dark suit, sitting behind a glass counter, as a lower third ticker scrolled the latest news. A title in the top corner of the screen identified the programme as 'Bob Mundy's News Review'.

'With the vote imminent, emotion is running high on both sides,' he observed. 'In other news this week, Congress has been considering an emergency infrastructure investment budget . . .'

Wallace switched off the television, trying to make sense of what he'd just seen, wondering whether a man with the gravitas of Steven Byrne could possibly have been involved in the attempt on his life.

43

Large sections of the greyish-pink wallpaper were peeling away from the cracked plasterboard. Ragged purple zigzags ran along the paper, reminding Ash of an ECG readout. She sat on one of a pair of sagging sofas covered with an old patchwork pattern that might have once matched the ECG zigzags. The faded colours were marked by dark stains, and both couches were so frayed and dirty that it was hard to believe they'd ever been consciously designed. A splintered, shabby tallboy stood beside a heavy eighties television that was encased in a cracked veneer cabinet. A framed photograph of Mike Rosen in his dress uniform had pride of place atop the tallboy, and looked out at a room that had clearly seen better days. A pair of prints hung on the wall opposite, anonymous paintings of high mountains that might have been beautiful once, but which were now edged by dark, encroaching mould. Ash glanced through an archway into a similarly dilapidated kitchen and saw the old woman leaning over Edward Rosen, who sat at a chipped table. She was embracing him and whispering into his ear. Ash looked away, uncomfortable to be intruding on their grief.

'He's just having a glass of water,' the old woman said, entering the room.

'I'm sorry for your loss. Your son—'

'He wasn't our boy,' the woman interrupted. She sat down on

the couch opposite, her movements laboured and slow. 'We're his grandparents. Michael's father was our son, Edward Junior. Eddie, we called him. I'm Martha, but there never was no Martha Junior, Eddie was our only child.'

'Is Eddie . . .' Ash left her question hanging.

'Nah. Maybe. I don't know,' Martha sighed. 'He and his girl were a couple of junkies. Lived in dark places. Took us down with 'em sometimes. They skipped town one day. Left little Michael with us. We ain't never heard from 'em. Raised the boy as our own.' Martha's voice was hollow and flat, as though the vibrancy of life had been ground away by years of trauma. 'I never wanted him signin' up. But Ed Senior was an Army man, engineer, and Michael idolised his grandpa.'

'I don't mean to be insensitive,' Ash began.

'Go ahead. I've had nightmares 'bout this day for years. I knew it was comin',' Martha revealed.

'I'm sorry to hear that.'

'He's in the Army. Front line. Not the engineerin' corps. Those boys die for this country,' Martha observed.

'Do you know what Michael's been doing these past few months?' Ash asked.

Martha shook her head. 'He never tells us nothin' 'bout his missions.'

She didn't know her grandson had been discharged, Ash thought.

'We didn't see him for around a year an' a half,' Martha continued. 'He said he was deep cover. Then he paid us a visit. Stayed a few weeks, an' then split. Said he was on a mission that would make the front pages.'

'Did he ever talk about his unit?'

'This benevolent fund . . .' Martha hesitated. 'You think it up before you got here, or on the spot when you saw us?'

Ash felt her face redden.

'I spent too much time around lyin' junkies to be hoodwinked, Miss . . .'

'Ash. Christine Ash,' she admitted. 'I'm with the FBI.'

'I see,' Martha said, without giving anything away.

'How'd he die?' Edward asked, shuffling into the room. His throaty voice crackled with every word and the rims of his eyes were a shiny crimson.

'There was an incident in Afghanistan. Kabul,' Ash replied. She saw no point in telling these poor people that their grandson had killed a number of innocent people in an attempt to murder John Wallace.

Martha nodded and took Edward's hand as he sat next to her.

'When?' Edward's face contorted as though the single word pained him.

'A few days ago,' Ash replied. 'I assumed you'd been informed.'

'Nobody's told us nothing,' Martha said.

'Did Michael ever talk about his friends?' Ash asked.

'He never had anyone besides his unit.' It took a moment of pointed silence for Martha to realise that was exactly what Ash meant. 'Like I said, he never talked about what he did for the Army.'

Ash stared at the bereaved couple, trying to figure out how she could persuade them to let her examine Michael's belongings.

'What you asking all these questions for?' Edward's voice was suddenly full of aggression.

'We're hunting a killer, Mr Rosen,' Ash replied honestly. 'We believe that he might have been part of Michael's unit.'

'This is . . .' Edward began angrily. 'How do we even know he's dead? Huh? Who are you? Where's your ID?'

'She don't need ID,' Martha said calmly. 'I remember her. There was that Nightfile report. And then the Pendulum case. I didn't recognise you at first. You look thinner. An' your hair's longer.'

Ash was full of admiration for this smart old lady. Life might have beaten her down, but the relentless run of misery hadn't dulled her mind.

'I got something you might wanna see,' Martha continued, heaving herself to her feet with a sigh.

'Martha, don't you do anything stupid,' Edward cautioned.

'Why don't you mind your grievin', Ed? Let me do what's right,' Martha replied, her voice edged with steel. 'Follow me,' she told Ash.

She led Ash up the creaking stairs, pausing for breath every three steps. The bannister was loose and wobbled every time Martha leaned on it. Ash had visions of the rail giving way and the old woman tumbling over the edge, her tatty floral dress cascading as she fell head first. But the rail held and Martha didn't fall. Instead, she struggled to the top of the staircase and along the landing to one of four closed doors, then pushed it open to reveal a small boxroom with a steel-framed single bed. The thin mattress had been rolled up and placed against the baseboard, exposing a mesh of springs. A chest of drawers stood beneath a small window that overlooked a large, wild backyard.

'This is Michael's room,' Martha announced. 'He didn't much care for creature comforts.'

There were no paintings, no trinkets, no photographs, no awards, nor trophies, just the bed and dresser.

Martha shuffled over to the window and groaned as she bent down to open the bottom drawer. Ash peered over her shoulder and saw a metal canteen, a dog-eared James Patterson novel and a journal, which Martha extracted. She placed the thick square book on the rolled mattress and brushed some dust off its grey fabric cover.

'He wasn't one for writing, but he kept pictures,' she told Ash, flipping the book open.

The first image was of a young Rosen in camo trousers and

boots, top off, with a group of young soldiers who were all grinning up at the camera, full of youthful dreams of glory.

'This was when he was in training,' Martha said. 'I never blamed Ed,' she continued as she turned the pages. 'I asked him to talk to the boy, encourage him to find a different path. But Ed loved servin' his country, and when he talks about it, he lights up, even now.' She looked up at Ash and smiled sadly. 'Best years of his life. Well, Michael never had a chance with all those stories fillin' his head. It was only ever gonna be the Army, but he didn't have Ed's cunning. Front line, first in, guns blazin', that's what Mikey wanted.'

Ash noticed that Martha's eyes were moist with tears.

'I knew how it'd end,' Martha said. 'Doesn't make it any less painful.' She began to sob.

Ash put her arms around the old woman. 'I'm sorry. I really am.'

Martha pressed her hand against Ash's. 'I appreciate it, honey.'

They stood there for a moment, listening to the creaks and groans of the old house.

'I'm not doing much good standing here gettin' all nostalgic.' Martha had regained her composure and her flat, matter-of-fact tone had been restored. 'Why don't you have a look? I'm gonna go check on Ed.'

As she watched the old woman slowly leave the room, Ash wondered how many people had seen her true emotions. Her very being seemed covered in hard calluses, as though her soul had been toughened by a lifetime of misery, but, for a brief moment, she'd revealed the raw tenderness that lay beneath, and Ash was moved, not only by Martha's grief, but by the solitary existence such strength demanded. No one, not even her husband, would ever be allowed to see how things really affected her. Martha reminded Ash of herself.

When she heard Martha's laboured footsteps on the stairs,

Ash turned her attention to the journal and started flipping through the pages. There was at least one photo on each page, sometimes two or three. Most featured Mike Rosen posing with his comrades, weapons up, deployed overseas, on R&R, hanging around base. Ash felt she was seeing a time-lapse of a man's career, and as she neared the middle of the book, Rosen transformed from a wide-eyed wannabe hero to a jaded soldier, his face mapped by furrows and lines that reflected his experiences. He was no longer a naive recruit, he'd seen combat, and had taken on the serious quality of people who'd lived through war. Further on, and the faces around Rosen changed. He'd moved to a different unit, and the black, red and white shoulder insignia indicated he'd joined the 75th Rangers. These were some of the toughest men in the world. They trained . . .

Ethan. Ethan Moore.

That was the name the man had given. Ash looked at the photo in shocked disbelief. Mike Rosen was posing with a group of Rangers. There were fifteen men in the picture, and judging by the easy atmosphere, this might have been Rosen's platoon. They were standing outside a tent, squinting in the blazing sunlight of a desert nation. Rosen had his arm around Max Byrne, and the two of them looked so similar they might have been brothers. But Ash wasn't interested in Rosen; her attention was fixed on the man two along from them, the man who'd been working at the Cromwell Center, caring for Rosen as he impersonated Max Byrne, and who'd introduced himself as his nurse, Ethan Moore. All three had been in the same Special Forces unit: Byrne, Rosen and Moore. She closed the journal and hurried from the room, her body tingling with a rush of adrenalin. She was holding incontrovertible proof that Max Byrne had not been working alone: the killings were part of a bigger conspiracy.

44

'Edward Rosen, what have you done?' Martha exclaimed. 'What Mike told us to do,' her husband replied coolly.

Ash heard the exchange as she hurried downstairs, and glanced across the hallway to see them both staring out of the parlour window.

'This is nobody's business, Ed. Nobody's!'

As she crossed the hall, Ash saw what had made the old woman so angry. A late-model silver Chevy Tahoe blocked the driveway. Black letters emblazoned on the side of the vehicle proclaimed it belonged to the Summersville Police. Ash leaned into the parlour and craned her head to look into the front yard, where she saw two uniformed police officers approaching the house.

'What's it matter? If she's tellin' the truth?' Edward asked pointedly, glaring at Ash.

'You bitter old man,' Martha muttered. 'Mikey gave us a number to call if anyone ever came askin' for him,' she told Ash. 'I'm sorry. You're gonna need to explain this to them.'

'I can't,' Ash replied hurriedly. 'I'm sorry. I was trying to protect you from the truth, but your grandson was involved in all this. He was part of—'

'You're lying!' Edward yelled. 'She ain't no FBI!'

'I am. And there have already been two attempts on my life,' Ash protested, focusing on Martha, who was studying her intently, sizing her up. 'I don't know who you just called, but if it was a number Michael gave you, it probably wasn't the good guys.'

'You're lying,' Edward countered angrily.

'Your grandson got involved with some bad people. I'm sorry about that, I really am,' Ash responded. 'But I need to go. Please help me.'

'You're not going anywhere,' Edward said, clasping Ash's wrist, but his grip was so feeble that she easily yanked her arm free.

There was a loud knock at the door.

'Mr and Mrs Rosen, it's officers Doyle and Perry. Open up, please.'

Ash stepped back and looked along the hallway to see the two officers through the screen door, a muscular young man with close-cut dark hair, and an older colleague with a head of grey stubble, jowly cheeks and a paunch. They looked at Ash uncertainly.

'Come with me,' Martha told Ash, bustling her into the kitchen.

'Officers . . .' Edward began, moving towards the front door.

'Edward Rosen, don't you dare!' Martha yelled sternly. 'Open that door, and I'm leaving you!'

'Mrs Rosen, we can't help you if you don't let us in,' Ash heard one of the officers say, as she watched Martha open a battered kitchen drawer.

'Are you in danger, Mr Rosen?' the officer asked. 'Let us in, sir.'

Ash looked towards the front door and saw Edward hovering nearby, glancing from her to the police officers as he tussled with his conscience.

'Can you handle a motorbike?' Martha asked, rifling through the drawer.

'Not well,' Ash replied. 'But I can ride.'

'Here,' Martha said, dangling a key in front of Ash. 'It's Mikey's. It's in the yard just out back. Ed starts it every day, so I know it runs. Take it,' she added, thrusting the key into Ash's hands.

'Thank you,' Ash nodded gratefully.

'I don't care what Ed thinks. If our boy did wrong, I want to know the truth,' Martha assured her. 'I've had too much lying in my life. You'd best go. He can't stop from being a son of a bitch for more'n a minute.'

Martha knew her husband well. When Ash glanced into the hallway she saw that Ed's dilemma was over and he was trudging towards the front door.

'Woman in here claims to be an FBI agent,' he told the officers through the screen door. 'Says Mikey's dead.'

'Go,' Martha commanded, as Edward pushed the door open.

As the officers entered the house, Ash escaped through the back door and found the motorcycle, a KTM Duke, in a lean-to beside the kitchen. She placed the journal in one of the panniers and pushed the key into the ignition, then wheeled the bike off its kickstand and jumped on. She hit the starter button as the back door swung open and the two police officers ran into the yard.

'Freeze!' the older man yelled, his voice almost lost beneath the roar of the engine.

Ash kicked the gear pedal and turned the throttle, and the bike shot forward. She glanced behind her to see the young officer draw his pistol, but he decided against pulling the trigger. His older colleague spoke furiously into his radio. Ash sped across a strip of dirt that ran alongside the house, crossed a patch of grass and skidded on to the rough driveway. The bike almost came to a halt as she turned towards the road, and she glanced back to see Edward standing in the porch, glowering at her. The two police officers came bursting out of the house, pushed past the old man and ran towards their patrol vehicle as Ash sent the bike lurching forward.

She turned right on Walker Avenue, and the powerful machine threatened to buck free, but she fought gravity and shifted her weight in the seat to bring it back under control. She kicked into second gear and twisted the throttle, gaining speed as she heard the sound of a siren wail behind her. She glanced over her shoulder and squinted as sunlight gleamed off the hood of the silver Tahoe.

Hearing another siren, she looked to her left, and through the high trees of the adjacent garden, saw a silver Ford Fusion in black Summersville Police Department livery racing along a road that intersected Walker Avenue. Ash kicked into third and sped on, beating the Fusion by a matter of yards. She turned right and accelerated with the Ford almost kissing her back wheel.

The Tahoe swung in behind the Fusion, and as the road straightened, Ash turned the throttle and the bike roared clear of the two police vehicles. The houses that lined the road fell away, and after a short stretch of open country, Ash found herself riding into a cemetery. High gravestones flanked both sides of the road, cutting off any chance of escape, forcing her on. Ahead of her, the road ended in a turning circle which was surrounded by a thick forest where the trees were packed so tightly that their branches intermingled. Ash's only escape was a steep chalk rise that bisected the forest like an old scar. Over one hundred feet high, the incline was almost steep enough to make Ash want to call it a cliff, but her flight wouldn't be served by making herself more afraid, so she ignored the thought and rode the bike towards the exposed soft rock. As she raced across the turning circle, she heard the familiar throbbing of a chopper, and looked up to see a helicopter approaching.

She kicked down into second gear and forced the bike up the

incline, hitting it on a diagonal to give herself the best chance of coping with the gradient. The heavy off-road tyres chewed the soft rock and propelled the bike forwards. The rutted landscape made the ride choppy and erratic. Ash felt out of control as the KTM climbed, but when she glanced down she saw that the chasing vehicles had stopped at the edge of the turning circle. The cops were running towards her, and one of them was shouting something, but the growl of the bike's engine was too loud for her to hear. Ash reached a small outcrop and banked left, climbing at an angle in the opposite direction. She was almost halfway to the summit when she looked up and saw the West Virginia State Police helicopter hovering above her.

'Stay where you are!' a voice said through the chopper's loudspeaker.

Ash ignored it and pressed on, the bike's powerful wheels throwing up clouds of pale dust. She turned again, almost losing control of the machine as the front wheel collided with a spearhead of hard rock, but she squeezed the throttle and the bike shot up the remainder of the rise, and caught some air as it crested the summit. Ash's whole body shook, and sharp pain shot through her neck as the motorcycle landed with a heavy thud. She was on a small plateau, and the tyres chewed the soft, tufty grass as she made for the forest beyond, ignoring the helicopter buzzing low overhead. She banked right, joining a trail that snaked into the trees, then accelerated, standing on the foot rests as the bike bucked and shuddered over the uneven ground. Within moments, she felt the cool shadow of the forest upon her, and glanced up to see that she was covered by thick canopy. She was pleased to hear the chopper moving away. It zigzagged through the sky as its occupants tried to catch sight of her, but the thick mesh of leaves offered Ash shelter, and she slowed the bike as she carefully followed the trail that led her away from her pursuers.

*

The trail took Ash east and she emerged from the treeline into the backyard of a large country house. There were no vehicles in the half-moon driveway and no signs of life inside, so Ash sped across the lawn, along the driveway and down the private road that led away from the building. She could hear the distant purr of the helicopter, but saw no sign of it as the bike devoured the narrow road that cut between ranks of high trees. She slowed as she rounded a bend and came to an intersection. She recognised Highway 41 and turned left, heading north towards the motel.

She passed a number of cars but there was no sign of the police. As she followed the winding highway through the rich countryside, Ash tried to compose herself. Realising she was no longer in immediate danger of being captured, she set her mind to figuring out how she and Wallace would leave town. They couldn't use the motorbike for any length of time. By now a description would have been circulated throughout the state. The local police department would almost certainly canvass the area, so the motel wouldn't be safe for much longer. Their best bet would be to head into open country until nightfall and then try to hitch a ride out of town. North or south, it didn't matter, they just needed to reach somewhere they could pick up a new car.

The woodland to Ash's left gave way to a modern mini-mall, and its brash store signs came and went in an instant before being replaced by an exclusive housing development. As the bike raced on, the houses blurred into yet more forest and the road banked right, before the trees thinned, and then suddenly opened to reveal the Summers Inn. Ash slowed and turned left, pulling into the motel driveway. She'd just straightened up and was heading for a parking space when she heard an engine roar behind her. A siren screamed to life, but before she could react, the motorcycle was shunted out from beneath her, and she flipped high into the air before landing heavily, the force of the impact knocking the wind from her lungs. As she lay, face down in the dirt, Ash heard movement behind her. She glanced over her shoulder and saw a police officer emerge from another Ford, the sun shining on his skinhead.

'Freeze!' he yelled. 'Put your hands where I can see them!'

The skinhead drew his pistol and aimed it at her face as he approached.

'Dispatch, this is two-seven, I have the suspect in custody. I repeat, I have the suspect in custody,' he said with the swollen pride of a big game hunter. 'If you so much as blink, I'll shoot you dead,' he told Ash. 'Put your hands behind your back.'

Ash complied. There was no way she was going to die face down in the dirt at the hands of some trigger-happy flatfoot.

45

Wallace was on his way out of the bathroom when he heard the commotion. He went to the window but couldn't get a clear view of what was happening, so he opened the door to the room and immediately regretted his decision. The parking lot was filling up with police: there were already two cruisers, and an SUV was joining them. Wallace thought about slamming the door shut, but that might draw the attention of the growing number of onlookers. People stood outside the adjacent rooms, and a small crowd had gathered at the edge of the parking lot, drawn from the home improvement shop across the street. Wallace's stomach lurched as he saw who one of the police officers, a bald, hard-faced man, was hauling off the ground: Christine Ash. Her dust-encrusted face scanned the motel, and when she caught sight of Wallace standing in the doorway, she held his gaze and gave an almost imperceptible shake of her head as if to say, 'Don't do anything stupid.'

Wallace wanted to rush out there, disarm the men, rescue Ash and escape together, but he knew that in reality, he would end up in cuffs beside her. His mind ran through the possibilities but he couldn't think of anything that he could do. He didn't have a weapon, he was outnumbered, and Ash had made it clear that she didn't want him to jeopardise his safety. Ash was strong, the strongest person he knew. She had a resilience that Wallace had never seen in anyone else, and he felt certain she knew what she was doing. As he tried to process what was happening, his head went light. He was struggling to understand how Ash had wound up in handcuffs, battered, dazed and under arrest.

He blinked and focused on Ash, who was trying to catch his attention before the bald officer led her away. She looked at him intently, as though she was willing him to understand something, and he saw that her hands, which were cuffed behind her back, were clasped together and that her index fingers were pointing to a dirt bike that was lying on its side on the edge of the motel parking lot. *There's something in the bike*, Wallace thought, and he nodded at Ash as she was pushed into the back of the police car.

The bald police officer climbed into the driver's seat and the cruiser pulled away. Ash didn't look back, but Wallace watched her until the car was out of sight, feeling hollow, as though his innards had been dragged with her. Two of the remaining four officers moved the motorcycle on to a verge, and one of them pulled the key from the ignition and stuck a police sticker on the fuel tank, while his colleague radioed for a tow truck.

Wallace watched as the four police officers got into their vehicles and drove away. Once they were out of sight, the on-lookers drifted back to their normal lives, the sensational interlude over.

He hurried across the parking lot towards the abandoned motorcycle. He searched the first pannier, which was empty, and then strained to flip the bike over, exposing the other side. He looked over his shoulder and saw that one of his neighbours, a grey-haired woman in a bright green pullover, was watching him from her window.

'You need a hand?'

Wallace glanced round to see Jeb Harlan emerging from the manager's office. His mouth was stretched in a smile, but Wallace could sense that the man was puzzled to find him plundering the impounded bike.

'I'm OK,' Wallace replied.

'Cops? What's been goin' on?' Jeb asked, noting the police sticker. 'I heard a ruckus, but I was in the john.'

'The police arrested a dangerous driver,' Wallace said. 'I thought they might have missed something hidden in the bike.'

'You're English,' Jeb noted. 'I didn't catch that when you checked in. Your girlfriend did most of the talking. But then don't they always?' he added with a cheeky wink. 'Don't let my wife know I said that.'

Wallace stood watching the old man, aware of the growing, uncomfortable silence.

'Well, go on then,' Jeb urged. 'Look in the saddle-bag.'

Wallace smiled awkwardly and nodded, before reaching inside. He felt something hard and rough, and pulled out a book. It looked like a journal.

'What is it?' Jeb asked as he approached.

Wallace opened the book to find a collection of photographs of Mike Rosen and his Army buddies.

'That's the Rosen kid,' Jeb announced. 'Local war hero,' he noted as he peered at the pictures. 'Green Beret,' he said conspiratorially.

Wallace flicked through the pages trying to figure out what lie he could tell the motel manager, realising that his options would be severely limited by the fact that Jeb knew Mike Rosen. His mind went blank when he saw a face that had haunted his nightmares. A little over halfway through the book was a picture of Rosen with a squad of men. Wallace recognised Pendulum – Max Byrne – and the man who'd said he was Byrne's nurse at the Cromwell Center, Ethan somebody, but none of the faces bothered him in the same way as the one he recognised from his time in Rikers. There, looking back at him was Smokie, the Blood gang member who almost gutted him during a riot in the notorious jail. Wallace's mind raced with the implications of what he held in his hand, and he realised why Ash had wanted him to have it: it was proof positive that Pendulum had not been working alone. He was transfixed by the image, his mind overwhelmed by speculation and conjecture. Why had these men helped Max? Had Smokie gone to jail deliberately in order to try to kill him? Why had Rosen tried to murder him in Afghanistan? What had the men been doing when Ash had disturbed them in Byrne's bunker? Was he up against the entire unit?

'We'd better turn it in,' Jeb suggested, intruding on Wallace's thoughts.

'Yeah,' Wallace agreed. 'I can run it down to the station if you give me directions.'

Something about the way Jeb eyed him made Wallace feel uncomfortable.

'I'd better do it. I know the chief pretty well. I can explain why we went rooting around the bike,' Jeb said pointedly. 'Let me just lock up the office.'

Wallace could almost have collapsed with relief as Jeb produced a set of keys and jogged towards the office. While the old man hung a 'Back in 5 Minutes' sign on the door, Wallace carefully peeled the photograph off the page and stuffed it into his back pocket. Jeb shut the office and by the time he returned, the journal was closed and there was no sign of anything untoward. Wallace handed it over with a forced smile, desperately hoping that there was nothing else Ash wanted him to see.

'Thanks,' Jeb said. 'I'll be sure to mention you were the one who found it. William Porter, wasn't it?' he asked, seeking confirmation of Wallace's false name.

'Yeah, but I don't need any credit,' Wallace protested.

'Well, you're gonna get some,' Jeb beamed broadly as he headed towards his truck.

Wallace watched and waved as the old man drove his battered

pick-up out of the lot. Jeb was the one person who could link him to Ash, and he'd just sent the man straight to the police. Once Jeb was out of sight, Wallace hurried into the motel room and shut the door. He pulled out his phone and checked the memory for the number Ash had emailed him. He fed the room payphone with quarters and dialled.

'Reeves,' a man's voice answered.

'I'm a friend of Christine's,' Wallace said. 'We spoke a couple of days ago.'

'Is she OK?' Reeves asked.

'No. She's been taken into custody by the Summersville Police. We're in West Virginia,' Wallace replied. 'I'm worried she might end up in the wrong hands.'

'I'll get on it,' Reeves assured him. 'And you? Do you want to come in, Mr Wallace?'

The sound of his name filled Wallace with panic. Had Ash told him? Had he figured it out? Was he part of Pendulum?

'I'm better on my own. Don't let anything happen to her.'

'I won't,' Reeves said.

Wallace hesitated. 'I mean it,' he added finally.

'You have my word,' Reeves replied. 'She'll be OK.'

Wallace hung up, feeling every inch the failure. Ash had saved his life multiple times, and he was going to leave her. He didn't have her training or knowledge, and any rescue attempt would almost certainly end in disaster, with both of them either in custody or dead. At least this way he had a chance of getting to the truth, and that was their best hope.

Praying that Ash knew what she was doing and that she was right to say he could trust Deon Reeves, Wallace stepped out of the motel room and fled north.

PART TWO

PART TWO

46

Smokie sat back and thought about the night that was never far from his mind. His mother's junkie boyfriend, Angel, had brought three gang bangers to their apartment. Each man paid Angel fifty dollars so that he'd hold Smokie's mother down while they raped her. Smokie was twelve. He'd been woken by his mother's screams and had come running, fists flailing, yelling for help from deadbeat neighbours who would never answer. He'd tried to grab a kitchen knife, but the gangsters, big men with heavy hands and hate-filled eyes, had beaten him senseless. As he'd lain on the floor, drifting in and out of consciousness, listening to his mother's screams turning to pained whimpers, Smokie had realised what he'd long suspected: the world was rotten.

Just thinking about that night made him boil. It was his spider bite, his Peter Parker moment of transformation, a memory that was always there to be called upon whenever he needed the power to be righteous. He'd used it to beat down kids at school, his anger fuelling him to take on thugs twice his size. He'd called upon it when he'd joined the Bloods, and his rage had earned him a fearsome reputation that had propelled him up the ranks. The memory had also driven him to track down Angel and the three men who'd set his mother on her path to an early death. In one bloody night of horror, aged sixteen, Smokie had killed all four of them. By then, Smokie had seen enough pain to know that the world really was rotten and that people were sick and deserved nothing but suffering.

He stared at the face of Steven Byrne, which was frozen on the screen in the corner of Smokie's office. He had just finished watching a recording of Byrne's testimony at the Senate hearing and was surprised that the weak man hadn't changed his tune. He'd kept his promise and supported the bill. *That's because he doesn't know what's coming*, Smokie told himself. *He still thinks he can salvage something good.*

He looked across the office that Steven Byrne's money had bought and watched his men shooting the breeze. BB and Jackie were chatting shit about the Mets, and Downlo was checking his phone. He didn't trust any of them, not even Jackie, the vicious, toothless brawler who'd had his back in Rikers. Life had taught him that every friend was only ever one fix away from betrayal. It didn't need to be drugs. Money, girls, religion, everyone had a weakness that would eventually turn them traitor.

'Can you believe this motherfucker?' Smokie asked.

All three men instantly faced him.

'Look at him carrying on like normal. After the shit he tried to pull?'

Jackie, BB and Downlo nodded agreement, but before they could say anything, there was a knock at the door, and Pope, one of the old guard, entered.

'We found Christine Ash,' Pope announced.

'Where?' Smokie asked.

'Summersville, West Virginia,' Pope replied. 'I'm on my way.'

'No,' Smokie said. 'I'm gonna handle this personally. It's time she and I met. I want you focused on finding Steven Byrne. Me and that old motherfucker need to talk.'

Ethan Pope could only nod. As he surveyed the three gangsters who sat around the coffee table, he wondered how something that had started with such high ideals could have got so lost. He'd genuinely believed in the Foundation, that it was a force for good, but after the things he'd seen, he'd finally realised that he'd helped to create something truly dangerous. And his eighteen-month absence, posing as a nurse, had enabled Smokie to consolidate his power.

Smokie. They'd had him all wrong. Ethan looked at him across the large office. The gangster turned soldier turned demagogue's face now seemed locked in a permanent sneer, as though he could no longer be bothered to mask the evil. There had been a time when he and Smokie had been close, when, like the rest of the unit, Ethan had believed him to be genuine in his desire to help the poor, to do something to fight inequality.

Now Ethan suspected there had never been any benevolent aim and Smokie had always only been interested in the acquisition of power. Power which he now had, thanks to the support the unit had given him, and the money he had talked out of Steven Byrne.

'I should be there when you bring her in,' Ethan suggested.

'No,' Smokie replied coldly. 'I told you, I want you on Byrne. I'm gonna handle Ash myself.'

Ethan suppressed a shudder and nodded again, before withdrawing and closing the door behind him. As he walked along the corridor that led to his office on the other side of the building, he tried not to think about the dangerous game he was playing. Instead, he concentrated on his need to fix the terrible mistake he'd made.

47

'My name is Christine Ash. I'm a senior special agent with the FBI's New York Field Office. You need to call Special Agent in Charge David Harrell. He'll vouch for me.'

The skinhead said nothing as he steered the police cruiser into the heart of Summersville. The chatter of a radio dispatcher filled the silence.

'Are you listening to me, Officer Bernard?' Ash challenged him, recalling his name-badge. 'Hey!'

'Settle down, Missy,' Bernard drawled, his voice oozing overconfidence. 'You've been read your rights. That's all I'm obliged to do. Rest is for the higher-ups.'

'Listen to me, officer . . .'

'No, you listen to me,' Bernard spoke harshly, glaring at Ash in the rear-view mirror. 'If it were up to me you'd be . . .' He trailed off, his words stifled by the strength of his hatred.

'I'd be what?' Ash asked.

'Never mind.' He shook his head. 'They warned us you'd be tricky. Now why don't you go ahead and shut up till you ain't my problem no more.'

Ash was silent, thinking about what he'd said, trying to figure out how to escape the situation. *They warned us* . . . the people Edward Rosen had telephoned. The officer's unshakeable preconception that she was somehow bad meant two things: whoever Rosen had called was in a position of authority, and it

306

was someone connected to Rosen's recent past rather than his military service. If it had been a Homeland Security alert line, or Department of Defense security team, the local police would not have been dispatched with any preconceived notions about Ash. The person Rosen called knew who she was and had warned the police not to listen to anything she said.

Her hands were throbbing because Bernard had manacled her too tightly, and her back was starting to ache as the pain of the fall set in. Her neck was sore, but she tried not to think about the scored wound.

Now why don't you go ahead and shut up till you ain't my problem no more . . . He could have been talking about handing her into custody, or he might have been referring to the people Edward Rosen had called.

'Where are you taking me?' she asked, and she saw Bernard roll his eyes.

'Are you dumb? I got nothin' to say to you.'

Whatever the Summersville Police Department planned to do with her, the previous attempts on her life left Ash in no doubt that she'd be killed if she stayed in police custody. She couldn't rely on Wallace to do anything. If he'd understood her signals, he'd have found the journal and would be on his way to New York with the proof Harrell needed to open a full investigation.

The cruiser pulled into a parking lot beside an imposing two-storey building constructed of large caramel-coloured stones. The Stars and Stripes fluttered above the entrance and a nearby sign identified this was the Nicholas County Courthouse. She was reminded of her father.

'Where are you taking me?' she repeated, as Bernard eased the Ford into a parking space.

'Where they told us to take you,' he replied, switching off the engine.

Bernard hauled himself from the vehicle, straightened his

pants and opened the back door. He grabbed Ash by the arm and pulled her out. She resisted the urge to yelp as the cuffs bit into her wrists, and fell to her knees.

'Get up,' Bernard commanded, looming over her.

Ash stood suddenly, using all her strength to drive the top of her head into his chin. She felt the painful but satisfying crunch of bone, and heard Bernard cry out as he toppled backwards. He fell on his backside, his eyes dazed and wide, blood oozing from his mouth. His hands pawed ineffectually at his holster, but he was teetering on the verge of unconsciousness, and couldn't compel his body to do what he wanted.

Ignoring her own pain, Ash charged him, barging him with her shoulder and knocking him down so that his head hit the asphalt with a heavy thud. He passed out immediately, and Ash turned around and forced her hands into his pocket, searching for the key to the handcuffs. She pulled out his wallet and tossed it aside, before pushing deeper into his pants. As her fingertips touched the cold metal of a keyring, she heard the sound of heavy footsteps approaching at speed and craned her neck to see three burly men in black uniforms, sporting the six-pointed stars of county sheriff's deputies.

'Stop where you are,' the lead runner yelled.

Ash tried to get to her feet, but it was a struggle with her wrists bound behind her back, and when she felt strong hands on her shoulders, she realised her escape attempt was over. Two of the deputies grabbed Ash and hauled her to her feet. As they dragged her towards the courthouse, she watched the third man tend to Bernard and radio for an ambulance.

'I'm really sorry. This is all a mistake. You've got to let me make a phone call,' Ash pleaded with the deputies, but they ignored her and manhandled her into the building.

The automatic doors swung open and the strong men pulled Ash inside. As she felt her feet hit the smooth marble floor, she stopped struggling and hung limp. She knew how this looked: she'd fled the police, assaulted an officer and tried to escape. She'd find no friends here. She cursed herself for having botched her bid for freedom. As she watched the courthouse doors close, she realised that she might never get a second chance.

The painkillers had worn off and Ash now felt wrung out. Her head pounded, her neck throbbed, her back ached, and her ribs protested every breath. The deputies had dragged her into the bowels of the building and deposited her in a holding cell. There'd been no custody process, no phone call, no lawyer, and she guessed she was being held until whoever Edward Rosen had called could come to claim her. There was a low bench in the cell, but she resisted the urge to sit, and instead paced the tiny space, counting out her steps as a way of marking time. She'd learned the technique when her father had sentenced her to the disciplinary cells. Robbed of time, people could quickly lose their minds, and counting the passing seconds not only tied her to reality, it distracted her from her predicament. She'd tried hammering on the door, shouting her name, her rank, calling for help, but these local cops had clearly been ordered to ignore her.

She estimated she'd been in the cell for a little more than three hours when the door finally opened and a sheriff's deputy stood aside to let a Latino man in a tan suit enter. He had thick black hair that curled around the tops of his ears, neatly clipped stubble flecked with the odd spike of grey, a lean, narrow face, and hard eyes that studied Ash as he drew near. His shirt rippled as tight muscles moved beneath it.

'My name is Alejandro Luna, I'm with the Bureau's Pittsburgh office. I've been sent to bring you in.'

Something about the man felt wrong. If this was the guy Rosen had told his grandparents to call, he was almost certainly not someone to be trusted.

'Don't let him take me. Don't let this man take me,' Ash urged the deputy.

Luna stepped forward calmly. 'Please, Agent Ash. I'm here to help.'

She peered over his shoulder and stared at the sheriff's deputy.

'Please. Please don't do this,' she begged, but her words had no effect and the young man looked away.

When Luna's hand touched her arm, Ash jumped back. The same lie. The same lie that destroyed her mother would kill her. This man was pretending to be nice, to be her friend, but he wasn't. He was here to hurt her, maybe kill her. She wouldn't let her life end the way her mother's had. She lashed out, striking Luna in the face. After recovering from the initial shock, he grabbed her firmly.

'Don't make this difficult, Agent Ash,' Luna said. 'There's no need. I'm here to take you to safety.'

Don't believe the lies, Ash told herself. She planned to make it as difficult as possible. She threw a punch at Luna's neck, but he was too quick. He blocked the blow and jabbed her in the gut. As she doubled over, he drove his elbow into the back of her head, stepping out of the way as she hit the deck face first.

'It didn't have to be like this,' she heard Luna telling the deputy as the edges of her vision frayed. 'What the hell was she thinking?'

'Don't sweat it. After what she did to Bernie, no one's gonna miss this bitch.'

The deputy's words were the last thing Ash heard before she lost consciousness. The last things she felt were Luna's hands around her arms as he dragged her towards the cell door. *Towards death*, she thought before she passed out.

48

Bailey felt pressure building in his ears as the plane descended. Geneva was set in a bowl encircled by snow-laden mountains. He wasn't a skier but he knew that April was the last of the good powder, and, judging by the ski bags his fellow travellers had presented at check-in, the aircraft was full of people desperate for a final week on the slopes. He shifted in his seat and a dull pain gripped his ribs and shot up his spine, but the worst of it quickly died away, numbed by the prescription-strength co-codamol Doctor Death had given him. Salamander had tried to talk him out of making the trip, but, realising that Bailey was going to do it with or without his help, had managed to persuade his old friend to take a day to rest, prepare, and at least give them time to get a decent false passport. So Bailey had spent Friday in Salamander's penthouse while Danny went to obtain the forged document. Bailey had tried not to think about how many laws he was breaking, nor how unsettling it was to see the ease and speed with which such an essential piece of identification could be sourced by the underworld.

Salamander had sent Frank out to buy clothes, and then called the *London Record*, posing as Superintendent Cross, and had been able to talk Francis Albright, the beleaguered acting editor, into revealing the name of Melissa Rathlin's hotel. As day had drifted into night, Salamander had broached the subject of Bailey's health, eventually steering the conversation to his state of mind.

Bailey felt nothing but warmth and affection for Salman Sohota, his oldest and dearest friend, but he hadn't been able to prevent himself from clamming up. He'd given one-word answers, playing down his anxiety, and had tried to convince his friend that the worst was over.

In a way it was. He hadn't suffered a panic attack since being kidnapped, and was starting to believe that the bitter reality of the pain that assaulted his body left no scope for dark imaginings. His mind had been overloaded by his terrible ordeal; the shame and hurt, the puzzle of piecing together what Sylvia Greene had to do with Pendulum, and the desire for revenge, all forced him to rise above himself. It was as though adversity had brought him to life. He shifted again in his seat, and took comfort from his aches. He wondered whether it was sick to believe that real pain would keep his anxiety at bay.

Salamander had eventually given up probing. He had the good sense to know that Bailey wasn't going to talk about it. He hadn't been happy, but he'd left it there, and after a respectable period of idle chat, he'd made his excuses and left, claiming he had business to attend to. Bailey had taken a couple of Doctor Death's co-codamol and some other pills that the degenerate medic had said would help him sleep. Bailey couldn't recall losing consciousness, but he did remember how he'd enjoyed the dreamy embrace of the drugs as he'd lain in the master bedroom and looked out over the starry streets of London.

The following morning, Danny had returned, telling him the passport would take another day. Secretly grateful for the delay, Bailey had spent Saturday mooching around Salamander's penthouse, willing his body to heal. The following morning, Danny had arrived with a Belgian passport, and the photo that stared out from beneath the digital watermark was Bailey's, but the document belonged to one Davide Morel. Bailey had been surprised at the passport's authenticity, and had been even more shocked when Danny had assured him it was bulletproof: the photo would match the one on file. As a police officer, Bailey was unsettled to know that one of their criminal connections had access to the Belgian passport system, but given his situation, all he'd done was to express his gratitude. Danny had already bought a ticket and completed the online check-in. Frank had arrived soon afterwards with a small Samsonite full of clothes, and they'd waited for Salamander, who'd insisted on driving Bailey to the airport.

They'd left Frank and Danny at the penthouse and taken the Range Rover. Bailey had assumed that his friend was going to try to continue their conversation of Friday night, and had prepared a catalogue of evasive responses. But Salamander had been silent, and Bailey got the sense that something between them had changed.

'Ya know, we've been mates through thick and thin,' Salamander had said finally as they stopped at one of the drop-off bays outside Terminal Five. 'We've survived ya being a villain, and me being righteous. But this – what this is doing to ya . . .' He trailed off. 'It's the first time I ain't been able to reach ya, Haybale.'

His friend had been right. He'd erected a barrier to keep people out, and it was working.

'Ya need to get ya shit together,' Salamander had added. 'And however ya do it, be careful, ya hear me?'

'Thanks, man,' Bailey had responded sheepishly, clasping his friend's proffered hand.

Salamander had patted him gently on the back.

Bailey had resisted the strong confessional urge to unburden himself of his fears and share his torment with his friend. He'd simply nodded and climbed out of the car, holding the bag full of clothes, not looking back as he'd walked towards the huge glass and steel terminal building.

★

The British Airways 767 taxied to its stand at Geneva Airport, and after a final few minutes in the aircraft's stale recycled air, waiting for the gangway to be connected, the passengers were finally released, and streamed into the building. The shining expanses of metal-framed glass and anonymous corridors were common to every airport Bailey had visited, giving every arrival the same sense of dull familiarity. Only this one was different, and, as he shuffled towards passport control with a crowd of enthusiastic skiers who were trading optimistic snow forecasts, he felt a slick sheen of perspiration cover his body, a manifestation of pain and stress. His body was shouting at him to sit down, to rest, and his mind was screaming fearful predictions that his fake passport had been flagged at Heathrow and that Swiss police would be waiting to take him into custody. He peeled off from the crowd, took out a packet of co-codamol and necked two pills, before taking a moment to focus on his breathing, inhaling deeply until he felt sufficiently relaxed and revived to continue.

The long queue at passport control was a blessing. By the time Bailey reached the front of the line, the painkillers had taken effect, and he barely registered any nerves as a stern official scanned his passport. Davide Morel survived the scrutiny of the Swiss system, and the humourless man waved Bailey through.

Bailey's relieved smile was broadened by the co-codamol, and he made a conscious effort to dial it back as he wandered through baggage reclaim. He found the Samsonite Frank had given him and lifted it off the carousel. He extended the handle, grateful for the wheels that would spare his damaged left hand any heavy lifting. Doctor Death had removed the splint and wrapped round a semi-solid bandage, but it was still unusable.

The familiarity of arrival continued when Bailey stepped through automatic doors into a hall filled with friends, relatives and placard-waving drivers. He picked his way past them, following signs for 'Taxis'. His legs felt heavy, but even though he seemed to be moving a little slower than usual, each step was painless. When he reached the front of a line of taxis, all of which seemed to have been made in Germany, a stubby man with a bulbous stomach struggled out of a new Mercedes and took Bailey's bag.

'*Où voulez-vous aller?*' he asked, popping the boot.

'*Merci,*' Bailey replied, grateful to be relieved of his load.

'Where do you want to go?' the driver asked.

'The Intercontinental.'

'Jump in.' The driver returned to his seat.

Bailey eased himself on to soft, black leather. The car pulled out of the taxi rank and rocked gently as it gathered speed, lulling Bailey to sleep.

'*Monsieur?*' the man's moon face was close enough for Bailey to see flakes of dry skin crusting the corners of his mouth.

He had the back door open and was leaning into the car, gently shaking Bailey by the shoulder.

'Thanks,' Bailey said, his speech clipped by surprise. 'I must have dozed off.'

'Eighty francs.' The driver stepped back as Bailey staggered out of the vehicle.

'I've only got Euros,' Bailey replied.

'No problem,' the driver shrugged. 'Eighty Euros.'

Bailey suspected he was being done on the exchange, but thrust his hand into his pocket without complaint and produced the cash Salamander had given him. He peeled off two fifties and took twenty Swiss francs from the driver, who waddled round the car.

'Your bag,' he said, pointing towards the entrance, where Bailey's Samsonite stood beneath the hotel's illuminated logo.

As the Mercedes pulled away, Bailey registered his surroundings. He was standing beneath a high canopy supported by four stone columns. Bamboo reeds were planted between the columns, sprouting from a cobbled driveway that ran all the way up to gleaming glass doors. He found his feet after a few hesitant steps and wheeled his suitcase inside.

A liveried doorman standing in the small antechamber nodded a greeting. *'Puis-je vous aider?'*

'I'm OK, thanks,' Bailey replied, stepping into the rotating door that led to the main lobby.

The vaulted space was clad in cream marble and made Bailey think of a temple designed to impress and inspire. There was a fireplace on his left, behind a cluster of chairs and sofas. Its twin lay to his right, with a matching set of seats, but next to them was a grand piano. Beyond it, Bailey could see shelves of books lining the wall by the hotel bar. The reception desk was at the far end of the deserted lobby, and Bailey's heels echoed off the walls as he approached the lone receptionist.

She smiled up at him. *'Bonjour.'* Her long brown hair was pulled into a neat bun, exposing her smooth neck.

'Bonjour,' Bailey replied.

'How can I help you, sir?' the receptionist continued, switching effortlessly to English.

Bailey couldn't believe his accent was so terrible that it took only one word to guess his nationality, but apparently that was the case.

'I'm looking for Melissa Rathlin. I believe she's staying here.'

'Let me just check,' she replied, tapping a computer that was concealed behind the leather-topped counter. 'Yes. Can I have your name, sir?'

'Francis Albright,' Bailey said.

The receptionist lifted a receiver and dialled. She waited patiently, but the call rang out.

'I'm afraid she isn't in her room, sir. Would you like me to take a message?'

'No, it's OK, I'll wait,' Bailey replied, backing away. 'Thanks,' he added, flashing a smile as he headed towards the sofa nearest the grand piano. It would give him the best view of the entrance and the elevators.

One pricey sandwich, two bottled waters and three hours later, Melissa Rathlin came hurrying into the lobby. She was wearing a three-quarter-length formal herringbone coat, and elegant high heels. Her glossy brown hair hung over her shoulders and looked as though it had been freshly styled. She seemed quite different from Bailey's recollection of her in Albright's office: more sophisticated entrepreneur than hard-bitten newshound. Even through the haze of medication, he hadn't lost the sense to know that she looked gorgeous.

'Ms Rathlin,' Bailey called out as she passed him.

She seemed unnerved by the sound of her name and stopped dead, her fearful expression shifting to surprise as she clocked Bailey.

'What are you doing here, DI Bailey?' she asked, her heels tapping out a gentle rhythm as she approached.

'Sylvia Greene left me a message. Said she was working with one of her reporters,' Bailey revealed. 'I'm guessing it was you. Why else would Francis bring you into the meeting with me?'

'He didn't,' Melissa responded, and for an instant Bailey felt he'd made a mistake. 'I asked to be there. I wanted to see whether I could trust you.'

'And?' Bailey asked.

'You don't know, do you?' Melissa countered. 'Francis is missing.'

Bailey instantly felt guilty. He should have warned Albright that he might become a target. The men who'd tortured him, they wouldn't know who Sylvia Greene had been working with.

Once they cracked the code, they'd apply pressure in the right places to find out the name of her collaborator.

'I think I might know why he's been taken,' Bailey confessed. 'Can we go to your room?'

Melissa's room was located by the lifts on the fourth floor. Every exposed surface was spotlessly clean, and the double bed was neatly made, but the floor and chairs were covered with clothes and shoes, and the laptop on the desk was surrounded by scraps of paper.

'It's a bit of a state,' Melissa said as they entered.

'We're not staying,' Bailey told her. 'We need to go. Get your stuff and your passport.'

'What? What are you talking about? What do you know about Francis?'

'I think he's been taken by people who know Sylvia was working with you,' he revealed, registering her dismay.

'How? Francis doesn't know anything,' she protested, but Bailey noticed that she'd started packing.

'Sylvia left me a coded message,' Bailey said. 'She wanted me to know she was working with someone. They got hold of it.'

'How?' Melissa asked. 'How could you let them have it?'

She paused when she saw Bailey hesitate, and she looked down at his damaged hand.

'I was kidnapped from Belmarsh Prison,' he confessed. 'They had my stuff. They tortured me . . . I couldn't . . .' He choked on the words, recalling his ordeal. It wasn't the pain that bothered him, it was the sense of powerlessness.

'I'm sorry,' Melissa said, her tone softening. She resumed packing while Bailey told her about the investigation into Sylvia Greene's death, his arrest, abduction and ensuing torture.

As he spoke, the air in the room seemed to become inert, and Melissa eventually stopped packing and fell still, watching him intently as she listened to the horror of his experiences. The confession was cathartic, and by the time he'd recounted his escape, Bailey felt lighter, as though a burden had been shed.

'I'm sorry you've been dragged into this,' Melissa said. 'And you're right, we need to leave,' she added, tossing the last of her clothes into a scuffed brown leather holdall.

'Dragged into what?' Bailey asked.

'During your investigation, did you ever come across Freefall?' she asked, slinging the holdall over her shoulder and grabbing her laptop bag.

Bailey shook his head.

'There's a group trying to railroad the international community into adopting the Online Security Act, the Blake-Castillo Bill, as a global standard. I think Freefall is the code name for their operation.' Melissa began to head towards the door.

'Who's behind it?'

'I don't know,' she said as she stepped into the corridor. 'I'm due to meet David Harris in . . .' She checked her watch. 'Shit! Now. He's one of the British negotiators. I've been working with him for weeks. He said he'd found out about a blackmail plot. He had the security services do some digging and I think he knows who's behind it. Come on.'

Melissa started down the corridor at a blistering pace, and, inspired by her energy and the seriousness of what she'd revealed, Bailey ignored his aching body and hurried to keep up.

49

Deon Reeves had made the call to Harrell the moment Wallace had hung up. Harrell had told Reeves to phone Summersville and instruct the Sheriff's department to protect Ash and to only discharge her into the custody of a specific FBI agent who would be dispatched from the Pittsburgh office to collect her. Harrell had phoned ten minutes later to give him the name of the agent, Alejandro Luna, and Reeves had relayed the information to Summersville's sheriff, who seemed shocked to learn that Ash was what she claimed to be, an FBI agent. Reeves got the sense that she hadn't come quietly. But that was her all over, tough and troublesome.

Reeves believed that Harrell harboured a grudging respect for Ash, but the special agent in charge had no idea just how astonishingly brilliant she could be. Reeves had a serious professional crush on his boss. He wasn't interested in her romantically, she was far too damaged, but he'd fallen in love with her work ethic and ability. She was more creative, tenacious and inspiring than anyone he'd ever worked with, and he was determined to keep his word to Wallace and make sure she came home safely. Which was why the second call from Harrell had been so unsettling: Alejandro Luna's car had been run off the road and he'd been attacked by four masked men who'd abducted Ash.

The injured Luna had been airlifted to New York and admitted to Presbyterian Hospital, where he'd been placed under police guard. As Reeves pulled into a space on Spruce Street, he cursed himself for not insisting that he be the one to collect Ash. Part of him had believed that Ash's paranoia was rooted in her warped childhood. He'd never spoken about it with her, but most of the New York office had seen the Nightfile report which had exposed her true identity and the nature of her awful childhood. He kicked himself for dismissing her paranoia. It was now beyond question that her fears were grounded in reality. He prayed that he'd have the chance to set things right and get her back.

'Why don't you tell me what happened?' Reeves asked the groggy man who sat on the bed. 'If you feel up to it.'

Alejandro Luna was in a hospital gown that exposed his hairy legs, which dangled over the edge of the bed. He ran his hand through his thick black hair and winced. According to the doctor Reeves had spoken to, the Pittsburgh agent had a concussion, some minor bruising and abrasions, but nothing life-threatening.

'They want to keep me in for observation. I feel like a fraud,' Luna confessed. 'I should be out there looking for her.' He nodded towards the door, beyond which sat a uniformed cop. 'We were heading for Summersville Airport,' he continued. 'Your boss, SAIC Harrell, had arranged the flight. This van came out of nowhere and ran us off the road. Four guys in those Pendulum masks jumped me—'

'You get a look at any of them?' Reeves interrupted.

Luna shook his head. 'Masks, black clothes. Nothing distinguishing. I'll be honest, it all happened so fast, I'd struggle to even give you height and weight. I thought I was a dead man. They smashed the window, dragged me out . . .' Luna's voice trembled as he tried to find the strength to continue. 'And beat me until I passed out. I didn't think I'd be coming back, but I did. Maybe twenty minutes later. They were gone and so was Agent Ash. Were you guys close?'

'She's my boss,' Reeves replied.

'I'm sorry.'

'You tell anyone about the transfer?' Reeves asked.

'No. My boss SAIC Parry said Agent Ash needed to be brought to safety, so I volunteered. He ordered me not to tell anyone about the travel arrangements.'

Reeves considered Luna's response. That gave them three possible sources for the leak: Harrell, SAIC Parry, who ran the Pittsburgh office, and Luna himself. Reeves studied the man and tried to gauge whether he was lying. He was troubled by a nagging thought: the group that had taken Ash had killed her neighbour and slaughtered innocent bystanders in the street. Why had they left Luna alive?

'You don't think someone inside the Bureau is talking to these guys, do you?' Luna asked.

'Hard to see how else they found out,' Reeves replied, holding the man's gaze. 'Listen, I've got to get going. Here's my number if you think of anything else.'

He handed Luna his card.

'You don't think it was me, do you?' Luna said, his tone light and jokey. 'You New York types are all the same: suspicious and untrusting. I had a heck of a time trying to convince Agent Ash that she'd be safe with me.'

'And yet she wasn't,' Reeves noted. 'Sometimes it pays to be suspicious,' he added pointedly, before turning for the door.

As he reached for the handle, Reeves caught sight of Luna's reflection in the picture window. Something about the way the Pittsburgh agent was watching him didn't feel right, and Reeves resolved not to ignore the feeling and to subject Luna to the full force of Bureau scrutiny. By the time he was through, he would know absolutely everything about Special Agent Alejandro Luna.

50

Alice crouched behind the lawnmower, playing with a twig she'd found snared in one of its wheels. Light shone through a small window, creating a golden corridor in which dust danced. She imagined they were little people at a fairy-tale ball, the one bowing to the other before they began their whirl. Nicholas said stories filled the mind with nonsense, that they crowded out penitent thought. Years ago, her mother had ignored Nicholas's rules and had read stories to her in secret, but one night he'd discovered them huddled under Alice's covers laughing at *Green Eggs and Ham*. Alice had been given three days in a disciplinary cell and her mother had been beaten so badly that their secret pleasure died that very day. She never picked up a book again, and never once spoke to Alice of anything but the real world.

Without her mother to share them, secrets became a lonely business. The shed was one. When the Clan was engaged in group therapy, she'd usually be given two or three hours' worth of chores. She'd whizz through them as quickly as possible and retreat to the sanctuary of the shed, knowing that no one would ever come looking for the lawnmower, or a shovel or rake during one of Nicholas's sessions. Nicholas taught Alice the ways of the Clan, but she was forbidden from participating in services until her first bleed. In addition to group sessions, all members underwent individual instruction, which often left Nicholas tired and irritable, vexed by the hours he spent listening to their doubts and failings. He took his ministry seriously and worked hard to try to make his followers' lives whole, but for every two steps forward, he often complained that they would take a step back, and he begrudged them this wasted effort. He was showing them the path to enlightenment, a way of living that would change the world, but their small thinking prevented them from striding alongside him as equals. They stumbled and fell and he had to expend his energy helping them along the way.

Group therapy happened in the devotion hall. All forty-six members of the Clan were obliged to attend. Alice often wondered what happened in those sessions. She'd see people emerge weeping as though they'd lost a loved one. Other times, the Clan spilled out of the hall, bubbling like children high on too much sugar. Alice was wary of growing old enough to begin proper devotion, but a part of her wanted to know what could provoke such extremes of emotion.

She was also curious about what would become of her when she passed into adulthood. Would she still live with Nicholas and her mother, or would she be required to move into the main house with the acolytes? There were four bungalows in the compound and she and her parents lived in the nicest. The other three were inhabited by the most senior members of the Clan, including Seer and Muse, Nicholas's second and third wives. Newcomers lived in the main house, which had once been the home of a big movie producer who'd fallen in love with Nicholas and left him the compound and all her treasure when she'd finally made the great journey. Nicholas always talked of her fondly, as a model of serenity and selflessness that they should aspire to.

Alice could not find the serenity Nicholas often described. He said it was an emptiness that could be felt; it lay beyond bliss or any other human emotion; it was pure existence that cared not what happened to it nor whether it continued. Freed of desire, one was freed of all sin, no more capable of wrongdoing than a tree. Alice had tried but she'd never felt the emptiness; her mind was always bubbling with dreams, her imagination cramped by the confines of the compound. She longed to play on the beach, to see the vast city that lay beyond the mountains, to experience the world from which her parents had withdrawn. Of course, she never shared such thoughts with anyone, not even her mother. After they'd stopped reading stories, Alice knew that her mother would never have the strength to resist Nicholas. There were to be no more shared secrets.

She looked down at the twig to see that her thumbnail had gone green from peeling away the bark. The exposed heartwood reminded Alice of bone, and she dug her nail deeper to see what lay beneath.

She froze when she thought she heard a noise. It was a sound so slight that she would later believe she'd sensed rather than heard what was coming. The dust danced, untroubled, but she stayed utterly still, adrenalin rising, familiar fear heating her body. The tiny dancers vanished as their world was cast into shadow: someone was peering through the small window directly above her, blocking the light. She couldn't see who it was, but she didn't have to. There was only one person who could leave a group session. He never had, so she'd thought he never would.

The door swung open to reveal Nicholas, standing silhouetted against blinding sunlight.

'What are you doing in here?' he asked.

Alice trembled at the sound of his voice. It was low and hard, the overture to rage.

'You were given chores,' he continued, his voice slowly swelling, anger inflating it. 'I thought we could trust you, Alice.'

He stalked forward, stepping into the corridor of golden light, and Alice could see his face was twisted and red. She knew the signs. This wasn't about her. Someone else had angered him.

'I give myself to you. All the knowledge I have, hard won by me at great cost. Do you have any idea how much I have suffered so that I can commune with the divine?' he spat, the walls seeming to shake with his passion. 'I give and I give, and all you do is take, take, take! No more!'

A slap punctuated his tirade. It was the first time he had hit her, and Alice was in such shock that she couldn't even be sure that it had happened. The second and third left her in no doubt, and when his hands balled into fists and began pounding her the same way he hit her mother, Alice tried to focus on the dancing dust, knowing that crying, resisting, pleading only made things worse.

The pain almost compelled her to yelp, but she swallowed the urge, and when his fury was finally spent and her body was tender and bruised, he turned for the door without looking back.

'Three days' discipline,' he said, passing judgment on her failings.

He didn't check to see whether she'd heard. He knew that his pronouncements were divine law and that they would be followed as such. When she was sure he had gone, Alice wept, sobbing uncontrollably as the pain finally found release. She cried with horrible anticipation, knowing that this would be the first of many beatings to come.

The blow startled Ash, and for a moment she straddled the border between reality and nightmare. She thought she'd buried her father's memory in the deepest recesses of her mind, imagining it would vanish like smoke on the wind. But his dark shadow would always be with her, its tendrils reaching into every part of her life. Another slap, and as her eyes focused she half expected to see his twisted, hateful face, spittle on his lips, about to spew yet another zealot's tirade. Instead, the blurry world took shape and presented her with another figure from her nightmares.

The dim light caught the features of the Pendulum mask, as the man who wore it leaned towards her.

'Where's John Wallace?' he demanded, his voice angry and raw.

Ash ignored the question, trying to channel the adrenalin that flooded her system to productive ends. She looked beyond her interrogator and saw two other men, dressed all in black, their faces covered by replica masks. They were in a dark space covered with pockmarked tiles, and it took Ash a moment to realise that they were the kind used to soundproof recording studios. A metal cable cover ran around the room at waist height and frayed wires poked through broken sections. Splintered remnants of furniture lay on the floor, and a few fragments still clung to the walls, attached by screws too stubborn to have been broken by whoever had demolished this place. Ash couldn't see any windows; the only light came from a desk lamp that had been placed on the floor in the far corner of the room. Despite the soundproofing, she could hear the deep rhythm of a pounding bass: she was in or near a club, probably in the basement, which had once been used as a recording studio.

'I said, where's John Wallace?' her interrogator continued.

She turned her attention to the man, who wore the same black uniform as the others. He had a pronounced New York accent, but it wasn't the nasal, clipped speech of Wall Street or Madison Avenue; this was the languid drawl of the street.

'Where's John Wallace?' he repeated, drawing closer.

The slaps had been to wake her. He hadn't touched her again, which unsettled her. Thugs and gangsters usually believed they could beat their way to what they wanted, and would pile on the violence. Professionals knew that anticipation was the best way to break a mind.

'You know how this is going to go,' the man whispered.

Ash stared at him defiantly. She tried to raise her hands but they were tied, and she could feel something soft beneath her fingers. She looked down to see that her wrists were bound to the cushioned arms of an old-fashioned chrome and red leather barber's chair. Her legs were tied to the baseplate. The man was right, she did know how this would go. If she gave them what they wanted, she'd be killed. Her only hope was to hold out long enough to find a way to escape.

Her interrogator backed away, moving towards something concealed in the shadows. He took hold of the object and pulled it forward. As it rolled silently across the carpeted floor, Ash saw a glint of shiny metal and realised that she was looking at a dentist's tray, but instead of the customary array of tools, it held a set of barber's clippers and a curved cross. The cross was comprised of two strips of metal with what looked like electrical sensors embedded at one-inch intervals along each strip. The device was shaped to fit a human head and a cable ran off it and snaked into the darkness.

'You could take the easy way,' the man observed as he picked up the clippers.

I won't die quietly, Ash thought, glaring at the expressionless mask.

Her interrogator flipped a switch and the insectoid buzz of the clippers filled Ash's ears. Years of her life were represented by the hair that fell away in thick clumps, and she knew that removing it was part of an attempt to dehumanize her and break her down, but she'd learned from her father that any reaction, no matter how trivial, was a sign of defeat. So she sat silently and eyeballed the man who shaved her.

51

David Harris was staying at the Four Seasons on the Quai de Bergues, a short cab ride from the Intercontinental. Bailey tried to question Melissa but she was evasive, signalling the driver as the reason they shouldn't talk. Bailey suspected her reticence was really because she didn't trust him, so they sat in silence as the taxi rolled along the lakeside past the magnificent baroque buildings.

The Four Seasons was an imposing six-storey neoclassical building constructed of bone-white stone. It sat squat on the corner of the busy Rue du Mont-Blanc and the Quai de Bergues, a narrow street that ran alongside the Rhone, marking the point where the grand river flowed into Lake Geneva. The hotel entrance was on the Quai de Bergues, and when the driver pulled up, Melissa's door was instantly opened by a liveried attendant.

'Checking in?' he asked in faultless English.

'Maybe,' Melissa answered, collecting her laptop case as she clambered out of the car. 'Could you pay the driver and take care of our bags?' she asked, pressing a hundred-Euro note into his hand.

'Of course.' He bowed his head.

Bailey marvelled at the ease with which Melissa played the entitled Euro-traveller. He wondered how many personas journalists had to inhabit, and whether, like cops, it was difficult to keep track of who they really were.

A huge flower arrangement dominated the lobby. Multiple vases stood on a rosewood table, filled with magnificent blooms, long reeds, rushes and rare leaves that reached up towards the golden candlestick chandelier that hung from the ceiling. White columns flanked every archway, and a black Moravian star was inlaid in the white marble floor.

'Stay here.' Melissa indicated a seating area next to the lobby. 'Harris is already jumpy. He doesn't need to see a strange face.'

Without waiting for a response, she walked straight towards the elevators. Bailey watched her get swallowed by the golden doors before taking a seat on one of the plump floral sofas. Surrounded by marble, flowers and heavy drapes, he could easily have imagined himself in a stately home. Aware that his battered body longed for respite, he swallowed a couple of Doctor Death's painkillers. After a few minutes' watching the hotel's hushed comings and goings, a tanned receptionist made a beeline for him.

'Mr Bailey?' she asked. 'There's a call for you.'

Bailey resisted the urge to groan as he pushed himself to his feet and followed her. The click-clack of her heels on the polished marble sounded like a ratchet being wound, and he couldn't help but feel nervous as he approached the phone which lay on the front desk. He picked up the receiver and heard fast, shallow breathing.

'Hello?' he asked.

'It's me,' Melissa replied. 'You need to come up. Room four-six-one.'

'What's happened?'

'Just come,' she responded firmly, before hanging up.

Bailey had to fight the urge to leave the hotel immediately. There were plenty of reasons why Melissa might have summoned him and none of them were good. His biggest fear was that she was merely doing the bidding of someone else, being held against her will and used as bait. Even if that were true, he knew he couldn't abandon her.

'Thanks,' he said, forcing a smile for the receptionist.

Everything's OK, he lied to himself as he stepped away.

The golden doors made the elevator seem like a pharaoh's sarcophagus, and Bailey couldn't help but feel that they were sealing his fate when they slid shut. He turned, trying to shake the sense of foreboding, and caught sight of himself in the full-length mirror that lined the back wall. His dark skin seemed to have a grey tinge to it, as though he was covered by a fine layer of dust. His eyes were yellow and bloodshot, and the mottled, puffy bruises on his face and his bandaged arm accentuated his shabby and dishevelled air. He was exhausted and needed extended bed rest, but there would be none until he identified the men who had abducted him. So he steeled himself and turned towards the doors as they wafted open.

A thick, ornately patterned carpet silenced his footsteps as he moved slowly towards room four-six-one, which lay at the very end of the north corridor, on the river side. Bailey cast around for a weapon, and saw a gilt vase standing on a half-moon table in an alcove. He took the flowers out, poured the greenish water on to the carpet and continued towards the room with the vase held like a club. About ten feet from the door, he noticed it was ajar.

He sensed movement behind him and glanced over his shoulder to see an elderly couple emerge from their room. They didn't even notice him as they sauntered towards the elevators. The door to their room slammed shut with a bang that seemed capable of waking the long dead. He waited until they had disappeared from sight before continuing.

He crept on, his hand trembling as he reached out and pushed. The door swung open and Bailey edged into the room. It was opulently decorated and dominated by two floral sofas, their patterns matching the one in the lobby. Official papers were spread across a low coffee table, next to a half-full tumbler of amber liquid.

'Bailey?' Melissa whispered, poking her head through an archway.

Bailey's pulse soared and he almost cried out, but managed to control himself.

'You almost gave me a heart attack.'

'Sorry,' she replied. 'In here.' She withdrew from view.

Beyond the archway lay a large bedroom, with a sumptuous king-size bed and carved wooden furniture. Bailey looked to his right and saw why he'd been summoned. A half-naked man was hanging from the bathroom door, a noose throttling his neck. The rope ran ramrod straight up and over the top of the door. Bailey placed the vase on a cabinet and approached the man, who could not have been more than forty. His dark hair was wet and tousled, as though he'd recently emerged from the shower, and his fingernails reminded Bailey of the smooth, polished white marble in the lobby. When he reached out to touch the body, he found it tepid; the warmth of life had not quite ebbed away. Melissa crouched nearby, using her phone to take a picture of something.

'What do you think this is?' she asked, stepping aside and drawing Bailey's attention to three metal balls and three spikes that lay on the floor.

'*Awen*. It's Welsh,' he said. 'It means truth. The same arrangement was found next to Sylvia's body.'

'Jesus.' Melissa sighed. 'We should get out of here. I've got photos,' she added.

'Give me a minute.' Bailey crouched down and examined the deceased's fingers.

'What are you looking for?' Melissa asked.

'Fibres, torn nails, any signs of a struggle. Even when it's suicide, in those last moments, people will try to tear off the noose. Survival is a powerful instinct. Sylvia's nails were ripped, but his are clean, which means . . .' He trailed off as he felt around the back of the man's skull. 'Got it,' he continued, when he felt a bulbous lump. 'He was knocked unconscious. A sloppy pathologist would say he did it falling against the door, but the size of the lump is consistent with a forceful blow to the head.'

As Bailey stood, he realised the painkillers had kicked in. His injuries were no longer troubling him, and his mind felt clear and alive with the tantalising mystery of a puzzle. It felt good to be doing real police work again.

'When I saw the symbol that had been left by Sylvia's body, I assumed it was part of her message, but seeing this, I think it was left by someone else.'

'Why would someone go to the trouble of staging a suicide and then leave a message?' Melissa asked.

'I don't know,' Bailey conceded. 'But I don't think this man killed himself, which means there's a good chance Sylvia Greene was also murdered.'

'Of course she was murdered,' Melissa responded, as though there had never been any doubt. 'We need to find somewhere to talk.'

When the elevator doors slid open Bailey froze. Three uniformed police officers were by the entrance, talking to the attendant who'd taken their bags. The man was looking their way, and pointed directly towards them.

'Hey!' one of the policemen yelled. '*Arrêtez!*'

Bailey ignored the command and hit the 'close' button. The doors slid shut as the three officers raced across the lobby. Bailey ran his hand over the buttons for all six floors.

'I can't get caught,' he explained to Melissa.

When the elevator stopped, they squeezed through the opening doors and ran along the first floor.

'Do you have your passport?' he asked.

'Always.' Melissa indicated her laptop case.

Bailey spied what he was looking for, a door marked '*Réservé aux Employés*'. He pushed it open to reveal a service area full of housekeeping trolleys. Beyond them lay a large industrial elevator. He hit the call button, looking nervously at the door.

'Did you know Sylvia was going to ask for me?' he asked.

Melissa shook her head. 'We never spoke about her plans, but I knew she rated you. What you did on the Pendulum case really made an impression.'

A single large silver door slid open to reveal an elevator lined with hard plastic.

'You think it's a coincidence? The police showing up?' she asked as they stepped inside.

Bailey pressed 'basement'. 'No. I think Harris was killed because he was going to talk to you. The police were supposed to find you with the body. They might not be able to tie you to his death, but the scandal would be difficult to shake off, and by then whoever set this up would have got you transferred to their custody.'

Melissa was quiet as the elevator descended. 'That sounds like black ops,' she observed at last.

The door slid open with a clank and they found themselves in a tiled lobby. An industrial laundry lay directly ahead, and huge washing machines spewed steam into the vast space. When Bailey spied a police officer approaching through the vapour, he grabbed Melissa's wrist and pulled her towards some dark double doors. They led to a raised platform that ringed a deserted loading bay. Bailey jumped down, ran across the bay and found the round green button that raised the roll shutter. He and Melissa watched the double doors as the slatted metal rose at what seemed an impossibly slow pace. When it was a couple of feet off the ground, Bailey urged her forward.

'Come on,' he said, dropping to his knees.

Even through the numbing effects of the co-codamol, he could feel his body protest as he lay on his side and rolled through the gap. He stumbled as he tried to stand, and Melissa, who'd followed him, offered him her hand.

'Thanks.'

He clasped her wrist, grateful for the support, and hauled himself to his feet. They'd come out on the road that ran parallel to the Rue du Mont-Blanc. Bailey saw a police car race past the southern end of the street, along the river bank. He kept hold of Melissa's wrist and they headed north, away from the hotel.

52

The bitch's screams were making him angry. Smokie had read her record. She was smart enough to know that everyone broke eventually. Some people believe there's honour in suffering. Honour is an illusion manufactured so people can feel good about doing the wrong thing. He'd slain enough people to know that honour doesn't count for shit. Take what you can, and make sure you hold on to it.

The metal headpiece was doing its thing, sending high-voltage electricity directly to the pain centres of her brain, not outwardly injuring her, but inwardly, it was inflicting more agony than any physical torture.

'You're strong,' he observed, switching off the device. 'But that was level two. This thing goes up to ten.'

She moaned and her head rolled around, a thin sheen of sweat glistening on the rough stubble.

'You think on that a while,' he suggested, before leaving the room.

Once outside in the cool basement corridor, Smokie removed his mask and lit a cigarette. He nodded towards Marty, a giant hulk of a man, who kept watch from a chair by the stairs. He and Echo had screwed up the snatch from the US Marshals and had killed two of them, and a civilian, in broad daylight. They'd been seen by a number of witnesses, so Smokie was keeping them here, off the streets, until the heat had blown over.

'She's strong,' Jackie observed, stepping out of the room and removing his own mask.

'Yeah,' Smokie agreed. 'But everyone breaks eventually.'

Downlo shuffled out behind them and pulled the blackout curtain over the doorway.

'You want us to get physical with her?' he asked.

'No,' Smokie replied. 'It wouldn't work.'

He'd seen it in the bitch's eyes, the morbid obstinacy that he recognised in himself.

One of the three phones he carried with him rang. He didn't recognise the New York number.

'Yeah?' he answered.

'It's me,' came a familiar voice. 'They're going to start checking me out, looking for connections. They're throwing everything at finding her.'

'Then maybe we should let them,' Smokie suggested.

'She given you what you need?'

'Not yet. But she will. I'll take care of it. It's time for you to come in. Time for you to join us. Show everyone whose side you're really on.'

'OK.'

Smokie could sense reluctance, but that was to be expected. Not everyone could be as strong as him.

He hung up and inhaled deeply, dragging the hot cherry down the cigarette.

'Feds are tearing shit up looking for her,' he told Jackie. 'We've got to get what we need, and then dump her.'

Jackie and Downlo put on their masks, pulled aside the curtain and returned to the dark room. Smokie inhaled one more lungful before stubbing out his cigarette on the damp basement floor. He blew a smoke ring before donning his mask.

I'll break you, bitch, he thought. *I'll break you and then I'll kill you.*

53

There was something magical about the painting, as though it had captured the spirit of a long-forgotten fairy tale. A red-haired woman in a long white dress knelt on the edge of a grassy cliff, her arms outstretched like the wings of a bird, her head flung back as though pleading with an unseen god. Three eagles soared high above the valley spread out below, tracking the course of the silvery river, which flowed towards a picturesque castle that was surrounded by high mountains. A tree, possibly eucalyptus, cast a shadow over the young woman, and to the far left of the image, dark clouds gathered over the highest, most distant mountain.

What was the symbolism of the eucalyptus? Did the artist paint eagles for aesthetic reasons or because they were part of the story? Was the woman an exile, longing to return to the castle? Bailey thought the painting beautiful, and pondered its secret meanings as he waited for Melissa to come back from the bathroom.

They'd wound their way through Geneva, moving swiftly this way and that, and once they were certain they were not being followed, they found the Café Art's on the Rue des Paquis. It was a small, double-fronted place with a dozen tables arranged across the pavement and an equal number inside. A handful of people sat outside, tourists enjoying the spring sunshine, and a few locals relishing a lazy Sunday afternoon. Bailey and Melissa had opted for the deserted interior and selected a table near the back, away from the windows. Living up to its name, the café was devoted to art, and the walls were crammed with sketches and paintings.

The waitress was covered in tattoos and piercings and didn't raise a smile as she deposited their coffees on the small table.

'*Merci*,' Bailey tried.

'*Je vous en prie*,' the waitress replied, but there was nothing welcoming about her tone.

Melissa returned as the surly goth retreated towards the bar. She checked the street nervously as she sat.

'I think we're OK,' Bailey assured her.

He was rewarded with a half-nod and a thin smile.

'So . . .' he dragged the word out, 'you think you can trust me?'

Melissa's smile widened. 'Do you trust *me*?'

'You're a reporter,' Bailey countered. 'Of course I don't.'

'And you're police,' she said accusingly. 'You think I'd sell you out for a story, and I know you'd turn me over to make a case.'

Bailey broke a wry smile and the two of them sat in silence studying one another.

'So, why don't we forget our prejudices?' Bailey suggested. 'Just be people. Two strangers who know they've only got each other and that if they don't work together, there's a good chance they'll wind up dead.'

Melissa nodded slowly.

'You want to start?' Bailey said.

'Sylvia was approached about a month ago,' she began. 'She received an email threatening to expose her.'

'Expose what?' Bailey interrupted.

'I don't know,' Melissa replied with a shake of her head. 'She never told me. It must have been bad, because I've never seen her so rattled. The next email offered her a deal: silence in exchange for Sylvia's support of the Online Security Act. She was to have the paper present the initiative in a positive light and promote the cause at every opportunity, not just with our readers, but with politicians and decision-makers. That's when she came to me.'

'She put you on the story?' Bailey asked.

Melissa nodded. 'She told me she was being blackmailed. She wanted me to dig into the initiative, to find out who was behind it and why someone would go to such lengths to ensure it passed. She also suspected she wasn't the only one being blackmailed. I was to find out if there were any other victims.'

'Were there?'

Melissa shook her head. 'Not that I could see. But something was going on. We found rumours of an operation on the dark web. A post on a hacker board referred to something called Freefall. That symbol we saw in Harris's hotel room was on the post.'

'Why didn't you say you'd seen it before?'

'Trust,' she replied simply.

She hesitated, and for the first time Bailey saw her strength waver and her mask slip. Her eyes filled with tears, but she quickly wiped them away.

'Sylvia was tough. The toughest person I've ever met. She refused to give in to their demands and we ran articles questioning the legitimacy of regulating the internet. Whoever was black-mailing her found out she'd launched an investigation. They threatened her family, the one place they knew she was weak. She never told me what she had planned, but she said she'd come up with a way to get out of the trap. An escape trick, she called it.'

'Suicide would have neutralised the threat,' Bailey began. Melissa was about to protest, but he continued, 'But Harris didn't kill himself, and Sylvia probably didn't either. My guess is that Sylvia pushed the right buttons, maybe threatened to expose the blackmail, and allowed herself to be murdered to stop them going after her family.'

Melissa's hand went up to her mouth.

'She obviously didn't tell them you were working on the story, otherwise you'd already be dead, but once they had the note she left me and broke the code, well, given that they've killed Harris, we should assume that they suspect you were the one working with Sylvia.'

'God, I hope Francis is OK,' Melissa said.

Bailey eyed her sympathetically. 'If he's lucky they'll keep him alive until they confirm you're the one working on the story. My guess is that David Harris was killed because he was going to talk to you. How did you arrange your meeting?'

'In person, right after the last negotiation session ended,' Melissa replied.

'So no emails to intercept. Where were you? Could you have been overheard? Were there any bugs?'

'We were in a corridor in the UN building. We were alone.'

'Maybe he told someone?'

Melissa's face suddenly animated with inspiration. 'His boss, Diana Fleming, she's the ranking civil servant from the Department of Trade. She's leading the British delegation. David hero-worshipped her.'

'You think we can talk to her?' Bailey asked.

Melissa's vulnerability vanished and her mask of bravado returned. 'Getting access to the rich and powerful is what I do.'

54

Diana Fleming was staying at the Four Seasons with the rest of the British delegation, but returning there was out of the question. Melissa had been given the negotiator's schedule and knew Fleming was due to dine with the head of the American delegation at Le Chat-Botte, a Michelin-starred restaurant on the Quai du Mont-Blanc, less than five minutes' walk from the hotel. She and Bailey knew that there was every chance Fleming's schedule had been changed as a result of Harris's death, but he'd suggested they stake her out anyway. It would be too risky to attempt to reach her inside the hotel, and they didn't have any immediately obvious alternatives.

Melissa believed the dinner was scheduled for seven o'clock, so they left the Café Art's at quarter to six and made their way through the city.

They hurried along the Place des Alpes, a broad, quiet street, past souvenir shops and high-end boutiques. A park lay to their left, its pristine lawns encircling a high gothic monument. When they reached the river, they turned right on to the Quai du Mont-Blanc, joining the crowds of locals and tourists who were enjoying the warm evening. Couples meandered along the riverside, holding hands, heads bowed like cooing doves. Bailey tried to recall the last time he'd shared a moment like that.

'Over there,' Melissa suggested, interrupting his line of thought.

She was pointing towards a pier complex that was an embark-ation point for the pleasure boats that cruised the lake. There were two sets of steps leading down to the riverside path, separ-ated by a raised platform that was approximately one hundred feet long and five feet high. The top of the platform was a patio overlooking the river and lake. One half was covered with chairs belonging to a little café, and the other was bare. A glass ticket office fronted the pavement and bisected the two halves of the patio behind it.

'The far stairs,' Melissa suggested, pointing to the furthest set of concrete steps, which dog-legged down towards the river.

Bailey nodded, and they weaved through the evening traffic to cross the road. He followed her along the pavement, past the ticket office and the bustling patio, to an information sign that stood beside the western steps. He leaned against the wall, and Melissa took up position next to him. She was smart: the restaurant lay a quarter of a mile to their east, and from their vantage point, they could see the corner of the Four Seasons, the riverside path below, and both pavements that flanked the Quai du Mont-Blanc. If Fleming passed them, they'd see her.

He shifted his weight, aware that he was starting to feel his nagging injuries. He reached into his pocket and freed another two pills from the blister pack. He couldn't be sure exactly how long it had been since the ones he'd taken in the lobby of the Four Seasons, but the returning pain indicated that they'd worn off, so he popped the liberated co-codamol into his mouth and crunched them down. Melissa watched him, clearly curious, but she was sensitive enough not to pry.

He swept the street, looking for any sign of police, while Melissa kept a keen eye on the Four Seasons. The nagging pain subsided and was replaced by dreamy warmth, which flooded his body and made his head feel heavy. He found himself staring at a couple seated on the pavement outside the Restaurant Casanova, a small place across the street. Both were in their late twenties, the man with the chiselled good looks of a sixties movie star, and even at this distance Bailey could see that his watch was worth more than most cars. The woman was catwalk gorgeous, with long brown hair that rippled over her shoulders in beautifully set layers. She wore a short white lace dress, which reminded Bailey of the girl in the fairy-tale painting in the café. Her companion wore a double-cuffed tailored shirt and slacks. They held hands and talked while they waited for their food to arrive, smiling to reveal their perfect white teeth, gazing at each other with eyes full of love.

'Are you OK?' Melissa asked.

Bailey was startled by a sudden change in light. The street lamps were on, and the sky was dark purple, coloured by the fading sun. He could see Melissa staring at his mouth and reached up to find himself drooling.

'You've been looking at them for ages,' she continued.

He was grateful when Melissa returned her attention to the Four Seasons, giving him the opportunity to wipe his lips. He might have misjudged the timing of the pills, or was suffering their cumulative effects. Either way, he suddenly felt light-headed and unsteady, and when he looked at the couple outside the Casanova, the movie star was on his feet putting a jacket around the fairy princess's shoulders. They'd finished their meal and were on their way to paradise. It seemed like only a moment ago they'd been waiting for their food to arrive, and as he watched the waitress clear away their dishes, Bailey grew unsettled at the apparent lost time. Was it possible to black out without even realising?

'What's the time?' he asked.

Melissa checked her watch. 'Five-to-seven.' Almost an instant later, she whispered, 'There she is.'

Bailey looked across the road and saw a tall woman in her

mid-forties, her hair cut into a bob. She wore three-inch heels, beige tights and a dark skirt suit.

'Who's he?' he asked, indicating the suited man who accompanied Fleming.

'Scott Barnes,' Melissa replied. 'Her assistant. Come on.'

She grabbed Bailey's arm and pulled him away from the wall. His legs felt weak and slow, but they kept him upright, and he allowed himself to be steered across the street on an intercept course. They stepped on to the pavement directly in front of Fleming and Barnes.

'Ms Fleming,' Melissa began. 'I need to talk to you.'

Fleming looked around nervously. 'The police want to question you,' she revealed. 'They say you were in David's room.'

'We had nothing to do with his death,' Bailey protested.

'Come on, Diana,' Barnes urged, taking her by the hand.

He tried to pass, but Bailey squared up to him. 'David was murdered, but not by us,' he assured them.

'Murdered?' Fleming was genuinely surprised. 'The police say it's suicide. They're under the misguided impression that you and David were having an affair,' she told Melissa.

Melissa shook her head and snorted in derision. 'It's a set-up. David was going to share some information he had about a blackmail plot.'

Even through the haze, Bailey saw Fleming stiffen. 'You know about it?' he observed.

'Can you give us a moment, Scott?' she asked her assistant.

Barnes hesitated, before backing away to take up position near the Casanova, his eyes watching them the whole time.

'I know about the blackmail,' Fleming revealed. 'David told me he'd been threatened by someone who was going to expose his homosexuality if he didn't ensure the British delegation advocated the Online Security Act. It was ridiculous, David's sexual preferences were well known and were neither here nor there. It's not the bloody sixties. David needed my authorisation to initiate an investigation.'

'The Box?' Bailey asked.

Fleming nodded. 'Who are you?'

'It's better you don't know.'

'Yes. I asked MI5 to look into it. They're investigating as we speak. If you want to know more, talk to them.'

'Who's leading the investigation?' Bailey inquired.

'A man called Samuel Mayfield,' Fleming replied. 'Now, if you'll excuse me, I can't be seen with you.'

She waved to Scott, who hurried forward, and the two of them were about to leave when Melissa touched Fleming's arm.

'I'm sorry about David,' she said. 'He was a good man.'

Fleming nodded sombrely before heading east.

'Shit,' Bailey muttered as he watched them go. He couldn't believe the mess he'd made. Bomber jacket, Sam Mayfield. Bailey had been to hell and back, when all the answers might have been found in an interview room in Heathrow Police Station.

'What?' Melissa asked.

'I know this Mayfield,' Bailey replied. 'I've fucked up. He tried to help me, and I wouldn't listen.' He looked around, suddenly alive with adrenalin. 'We need to get to London.'

55

Tears ran down Ash's face not as a result of the unbearable pain, but because her own screams sounded so distressing. They were loud and raw and bristling with despair. She could tell that the agony and desperation were genuine because she could feel nothing but fire in her bones and anguish in her head. She knew they'd broken her because she was crying, and only the defeated showed weakness. It was as though she was looking down at herself, watching through her father's eyes, seeing the feeble wretch he'd tried to save her from becoming. The power of the divine would go nowhere near such an abject excuse for a human being. She was a failure on every single level and all she wanted to do was die. To be rid of it all. To end the pain. The suffering. Even if she survived, she couldn't cope with the burden of these memories. What these men had done to her combined with the suffering of her childhood would be too much to bear.

Better an ending.

Release.

Freedom.

These men would give it to her. These men in masks. The leader, or Drawl as she'd thought of him before the pain had started. It had been a way of remembering his identifying accent in case she escaped. But she now knew there was only one way to escape. She was to die here in this rotten room, at the hands of these evil men.

'Tell us where he is,' Drawl yelled above her screams as he increased the severity of the device attached to her head.

All she had to do was give them an answer and it would all end. Just words. Air. Nothing really. It wasn't a betrayal. It was freedom. For her, and for Wallace.

'Stop,' she pleaded, her voice hoarse.

The pain subsided instantly, but echoes of it coursed throughout her being.

'I'll tell you what you want, on one condition,' Ash said, gulping in air. 'You make it quick.'

Through her tears she saw Drawl nod. She couldn't shake the feeling that behind the Pendulum mask, he was smiling.

56

The call came when night was at its darkest. Good news was never delivered at this hour, and it was with a sense of dread that Reeves answered the phone.

'Reeves,' he said.

'It's Harrell.' His boss's voice was leaden. 'We've found Christine.'

The journey from his small Brooklyn apartment to the promenade beside John Lindsay Park took a little over twenty minutes. Reeves felt empty when he saw the flashing blue lights lining the access road north of the tennis courts. There were four NYPD cruisers, a couple of unmarked sedans and, most disturbing of all, a coroner's truck.

Reeves bit his lip as he parked behind the truck. He felt the suffocating weight of sadness as he climbed out of his car. He ran his hand over his face and started walking towards the East River. To his right, the three a.m. traffic on the Williamsburg Bridge emitted a steady, pulsing rhythm, as people went about their lives, unaware that a short distance away people were mourning the loss of a colleague and friend.

Reeves followed a path which traced a circle around some trees, and he was soon confronted by the sight of half a dozen uniformed NYPD officers conducting fingertip searches near the edge of the promenade. Silent and sombre, they eyed him warily.

As law enforcement officers, these men and women were used to the horror of losing one of their own, and Reeves could sense their sympathy as he walked towards the river bank.

A lone figure stood at the very edge of the promenade and looked over the barrier towards the river below. Reeves recognised Harrell's silhouette, but the man looked smaller somehow, more tired and frail. Reeves took a deep breath and joined his boss.

'Agent Reeves,' Harrell observed. 'Miller and Romero are on their way.'

Reeves steeled himself, taking a moment to try to bring his emotions under control before he peered. It was useless, and when he put his head beyond the railing, looked down and saw what Harrell had been watching, he couldn't stop the tears forming in his eyes. A few feet below him, a pair of police divers corralled a body that was floating face up in the cold, dark water. Her head had been shaved and her throat cut, but the thing that upset Reeves most was that even in the dead of night, he could see that she'd been badly beaten. Her face was a bloody mess of cuts and bruises, the swelling turning her into something unrecognisable. Reeves felt pure rage as he thought about her suffering, and swore that those responsible would pay for what they'd done.

'NYPD got an anonymous call from someone who says they spotted the body. Male caller,' Harrell said. 'They're trying to trace him. You worked with her. Is there anyone we should call? Friends? Family?'

'I don't think so,' Reeves replied slowly. 'Her mother's dead, and her father, well . . .'

'I know,' Harrell interjected. 'Even if we could find him, she wouldn't want him involved.'

'There's no one else. Just us,' Reeves responded, suddenly struck by the tragedy of Ash's life. She was truly alone. He wiped his eyes and looked away from her body, concentrating on the jagged outline of the buildings on the opposite bank.

'They found Agent Ash's ID stuffed in her mouth,' Harrell said after a while. 'I know how hard this is . . .' He hesitated, marshalling the composure to continue. 'But it's a murder invest-igation now. I want you to take all that grief and anger and find the people responsible. NYPD are putting Saul Oriol on this. He's a good man and we should give him all the help we can.'

Reeves found himself backing away before he'd even registered the decision to move.

'Agent Reeves?' Harrell queried.

'There's someone I need to talk to,' Reeves replied before he started running towards his car.

I didn't see anything wasn't good enough. *I didn't get a look at their faces* wouldn't cut it. Alejandro Luna was the only direct link to the men who'd abducted Ash, and he had to give them more.

Presbyterian Hospital was a short drive from the park and Reeves shot through the city at speed, caring little for lights or traffic. When he got to the hospital, he bounded into the building and, lacking the patience for the elevator, ran up the stairs, emerging on to Luna's ward angry and breathless.

The moment he saw the uniformed officer guarding Luna's room, Reeves knew that something was very wrong. The man's head was cocked at an awkward angle, his eyes staring blankly at the floor. He was dead. Reeves raced over and pressed his fingers to the young cop's neck. The stillness and encroaching chill confirmed that he was gone.

'Nurse!' Reeves yelled. 'Somebody!'

He heard the sound of distant footsteps skipping towards him, but he didn't wait. Reeves opened the door to Luna's room and stepped inside to find that the bed was empty: Alejandro Luna was gone.

My boss, SAIC Parry, said Agent Ash needed to be brought to safety, so I volunteered.

Reeves recalled Luna's words. In another world, it might have been a coincidence, but Reeves didn't believe they existed in this one. Luna hadn't been chosen, he'd volunteered to collect Ash from Summersville. He'd volunteered because he planned to hand her over to the men who'd killed her.

Reeling from the implications of his conjecture, Reeves produced his phone and called Harrell. The first task in the investigation of the murder of Senior Special Agent Christine Ash was to find Alejandro Luna.

57

Wallace was looking west along 50th Street, studying how the early morning sunlight caught the edges of the high buildings, wondering when he'd next have the opportunity to catch such a moment on camera.

He'd hitched a ride with a trucker named Andy, who'd taken him from Summersville to a town called Charlottesville in Virginia. He'd missed the late train and been forced to stay in a seedy motel near the station. The following morning, he'd caught a train to New York, and, arriving late in the afternoon, had taken a cab to the Fresh City, where he'd been given the same room. Wallace spent a restless night riddled with guilt over abandoning Ash. He almost phoned Reeves to find out whether he'd been able to secure her release from police custody, but paranoia prevented him from doing so. Alone, Wallace knew he had to take extra care to avoid being caught and couldn't risk giving away his location. When he had eventually drifted off, he was tormented by nightmare images of Ash lying next to Connie, the two of them dying long, ugly deaths.

Feeling exhausted by his restless night, he had risen before dawn, dressed in jeans, a blue sweatshirt and black trainers, and caught the subway up to 50th Street. He'd spent two hours watching Pavel's building, stalking the streets, looking for any signs of surveillance. Satisfied there were no lingering pedestrians, out of place vans or passing drones, he finally slipped into the building through the basement garage and rode the elevator up to the eighteenth floor, where he asked to see Pavel.

He'd been waiting twenty minutes, studying the city from the vantage point of the eighteenth-floor windows, when his phone rang. He stepped away from Todd, who watched him from behind the reception desk with ill-disguised suspicion that bordered on hostility, and crossed the Kosinsky Data Services lobby to answer the call.

'Hello?'

'John, it's Pat Bailey.'

He was somewhere loud and busy, and Wallace could hear the garbled sound of a public broadcast.

'Let me talk to Chris,' Bailey continued.

'She's not here,' Wallace replied. 'She got arrested.'

Bailey muttered something under his breath. 'Where are you?'

'With a friend. You?'

'I'm also with a friend. We're on the move,' Bailey replied.

'We found something,' Wallace revealed. 'Max Byrne was being helped by members of his unit. Mike Rosen, Ethan Moore and Smokie, the guy who attacked me in Rikers, they were all in his platoon.'

'I've found a blackmail plot tied to the International Online Security Act,' Bailey responded. 'If you're with a good friend, ask them to check out "Freefall", see what they can find.'

Another indistinct announcement blared in the background, and Bailey said, 'Gotta go. You be careful. I'll call you soon.'

Bailey hung up and Wallace pocketed the phone. He turned to see Pavel Kosinsky watching him from the other side of the lobby.

'What are you doing here?' Pavel said, stepping forward aggressively. 'How can you show your face?'

Wallace had never seen the slim professional so agitated, and backed up, but Pavel kept closing and only stopped when he was inches away.

'You don't know, do you?' he observed, studying Wallace's bewildered face. 'Christine Ash is dead.'

Wallace stumbled like a punch-drunk fighter as the world went mute and distant. He could hardly breathe, and felt his legs go, but gravity didn't take him. He was caught by Pavel, who opened his mouth to bark something at Todd. Wallace could see the sinews on Pavel's neck but heard no sound, as the young receptionist ran over. He grabbed one of Wallace's arms, and he and Pavel bustled Wallace through the adjacent offices, past a man in uniform, into the secure area. The lights on the servers became incandescent streaks as Wallace's vision failed, and the world morphed into a swirling mess of colour, much like the oils on an artist's palette. He only had the vaguest sense of where he was, who was with him, what was happening, before everything went white.

Then came the slap.

Another.

And another.

Reality flooded in as his senses rebooted. He was in the insulated, windowless room where he and Ash . . . he felt his stomach churn acid as he thought of her . . . where he and Ash had watched Pavel hack Pendulum's email account. He was propped up against the wall and a concerned Pavel was watching him to see if his blows had snapped Wallace back to consciousness. Todd was nowhere to be seen.

'How long was I out?' Wallace asked.

'A few minutes,' Pavel told him, somewhat relieved.

'What happened to . . .' Wallace trailed off, unable to say her name.

Pavel's chest swelled as he heaved a huge sigh. 'I heard from a source in the Bureau. They found her body last night. Floating in the East River,' he said quietly. 'It was badly disfigured. They believe she was tortured.'

Wallace choked back a cry. He'd left Ash. He'd left her to face her death alone. She'd borne the horrors that had been meant for him. He'd abandoned her. Betrayed her. After Connie . . . He struggled to think rationally, his mind filling with images from his nightmares, the two women closest to him dying in anguish and agony.

'The Bureau identified her from her dental records,' Pavel continued. His voice was hoarse and he struggled with each and every word. 'They're looking for you. They say you were the last person seen alive with her. They want to talk to you.'

Pavel's words marshalled Wallace's mind around a single thought: revenge. He embraced the memory of Connie dying in his arms, forced himself to imagine the horrors Ash had endured, and as he pictured their ordeals, he felt a rage so pure and powerful that it scared him. He forced himself to his feet.

'I would never hurt Chris,' he said flatly. 'She was arrested in a place called Summersville. They must have taken her from the police.'

'Who?' Pavel asked.

Wallace produced the photograph he'd taken from Mike Rosen's journal and showed it to Pavel.

'That's Max Byrne, Pendulum,' he said, pointing to the picture. 'This is Mike Rosen, the man who tried to kill me in Afghanistan. Ethan Moore, the guy who posed as Max Byrne's nurse. And the black guy in the middle is Smokie. He almost murdered me in Rikers. I don't know if any of the others are involved, but Byrne's military unit is at the heart of this.'

'Can I make a copy?' Pavel asked.

Wallace nodded and gave him the photo. Pavel took it to the computer terminal in the centre of the room, and touched a panel to reveal an alcove that housed a scanner.

'I can run a facial recognition program,' he explained as he activated the device. 'It will identify everyone in the image, and we can pull up everything we can find on them. You can stay here in my office until—'

'I need you to check a name for me,' Wallace interrupted. 'Pablo Matias. He's twenty-six, maybe twenty-seven. He was in Rikers last year, charged with dealing meth.'

Pavel was already at the terminal, his fingers tapping the keyboard.

'He's still there,' he revealed. 'His trial date has been postponed twice. Why?'

'I can't stay here,' Wallace replied. 'I'm the reason Chris was caught. I saw the police take her away and I did . . .' He choked on the admission.

'I did nothing,' he said finally. 'I watched them take her away.' Wallace felt tears flowing down his cheeks, but he didn't wipe them away. He deserved far worse ignominy. 'I watched them take her away and I did nothing.' A surge of self-loathing swept over him. 'I'm not going to stay here doing nothing. There's a chance Matias knows where Smokie is.'

'You're nuts!' Pavel countered. 'You can't go to Rikers. You're on the FBI's most wanted list.'

Wallace shrugged. 'And if they catch me? Am I going to get any less than I deserve?' He took out his phone and pressed the 'show own number' command. 'Here's my number. Call me if you find anything.'

When Pavel had finished noting the number, Wallace moved towards the door and pulled the handle, but it didn't budge.

'You can't blame yourself,' Pavel said.

'Let me out,' Wallace growled, his anger bubbling to the surface. He thought of all the things he should have said to Ash. All the things he should have told her so that she would have known there was at least one person in the world who loved her before she died.

Pavel shook his head sadly. The scanner had finished, so he gave Wallace the photograph, and ran a swipe card over a reader. The latch clicked and Wallace pulled the door open, but before he could leave, Pavel clasped his arm.

'Christine wouldn't want you to do this,' he cautioned.

Wallace stared at him. Knowing that it would be impossible for this man to understand what he was going through, he didn't waste the time or breath trying to explain. He freed himself from Pavel's grip and set off through the server room, propelled by pure, white-hot rage.

The rhythm of the city was unchanged. Traffic rolled along West 50th Street, and the sidewalks were crowded with the pounding feet of awestruck tourists and bustling locals. Nobody stopped to stare at the pale man who emerged from the sky-scraper, the blood drained from his face, his eyes wide with shock and raw with grief. No one registered his loss, nor gave him so much as a second glance. Wallace was struggling with a storm of emotions – remorse and regret, demanding to know why he hadn't insisted on going with Ash to Mike Rosen's house, or tried to rescue her from the police. Rage, scorching him with anger at himself, at those who'd killed Ash, at the world for allowing such injustice. Shame, at the awareness that this wasn't the first innocent person who'd died in his place. Guilt, eating away at his psyche with the knowledge that he'd set himself on this path, and that all the evil that had befallen those he loved could be justly laid at his feet.

He tried to clear his head, to concentrate, but found himself unable to focus over the storm of emotions. Eventually he recovered the presence of mind to flag down a taxi. The city passed in a blur of buildings and faces, and Wallace lost track of how long he sat in the cab, watching everything but seeing nothing.

'John Wallace is a coward.' He recalled Pendulum's last words. 'A weak man who could not live with the guilt of his cowardice.'

He'd been right. John Wallace was a coward. He'd run from everything – the massacre at the Marwand compound, Connie's death, Vosuruk, and now Ash. A better man would have protected them, or made their deaths mean something. He only seemed able to drag people into the turmoil that had upended his life, and watch them die as he did nothing.

'Are you listening, man?'

The voice intruded on Wallace's dark reflections, and he realised that the taxi had stopped. They were in the huge parking lot on the south side of Rikers Island, near the Perry Control building. Wallace felt a jolt of nerves when he noticed the Eric M. Taylor Center on the other side of the lot. The block had been the scene of so much misery, and he began to feel that Pavel was right. He was tempting fate coming to New York City's largest jail.

'I ain't got all day.'

The cab driver's heavy jowls quivered with irritation. He ran his hand over the stubble that flecked his head.

'I'm sorry,' Wallace replied. 'I was somewhere else.'

'That's thirty-six fifty,' the driver noted, checking the meter.

Wallace handed him two twenties. 'Keep the change.'

'Thanks. I appreciate it. You can get a bus back to the city,' the driver advised, indicating a small group of people standing at a stop near Perry Control.

Wallace nodded his thanks and got out. He crossed the parking lot and presented himself at the visitors' check-in, where his William Porter passport was scrutinised and his false details fed into a computer.

★

Thirty minutes later, Wallace found himself being led into the Eric M. Taylor visitors' room. He'd never seen it before. Ash was the only person who'd come to see him when he'd been incarcerated, and they'd met in a tiny interview room he could hardly remember. Another time she'd saved him from grave danger. He owed her so much and now he could never hope to . . . Wallace never finished the thought. If he carried on thinking about Ash, he would break down entirely, so he focused on his surroundings. The visitors' room was huge. A long line of white PVC stools sprouted from the floor like rigid mushrooms. They stood in front of a partition that stretched the full width of the sixty-foot space. The partition was divided into carrels just wide enough for a single person, and there was a telephone receiver in each one. Visitors could see the inmates through panes of reinforced glass and speak to them via a paired receiver on the other side of the partition.

Wallace passed men and women of all ages visiting the young men who were trapped on the other side of the room. As he walked the line, he heard sobs, harsh words, sweet nothings, tenderness, hostility, the full range of human emotions delivered in this least private of settings.

'In here,' the guard gestured to a carrel halfway along the line.

Wallace took a seat and nervously scanned the faces around him, looking for anyone, guard or inmate, that he recognised.

There was movement on the other side of the carrel, and he turned to see Pablo Matias settling on the stool beyond the partition. If his former cellmate was surprised to see him, his face gave no inkling of the emotion; in fact, his eyes hardly seemed to register anything at all. Matias looked thinner than Wallace remembered, his cheekbones so pronounced that they threatened to tear through his craggy skin.

Wallace reached for the receiver and Matias did likewise.

'Hey, man,' his old cellmate said. 'Thought you was dead.'

'It was close. But I made it out.'

'That's good,' Matias observed, in a tone that suggested he couldn't care. He stroked his chin and his eyes focused on some distant place.

'How have you been?' Wallace asked.

'Oh, you know. Survivin',' Matias replied. 'I found a connect. Makes the days easier.'

Meth, Wallace thought, suddenly wondering whether Matias would even make it to his next court date.

'You should be careful, Pablo,' he cautioned.

'I know, man. Else the devils will chew my face off,' Matias sighed. 'It's life, homes. I gotta take the rough with the smooth, right? But sometimes I jus' need a little something to help the craw go down. Warm my eyes, help 'em see that things ain't all that dark.'

Wallace stared awkwardly at the man who'd helped him survive Rikers, wondering what he could do to repay the kindnesses Matias had shown him.

'Do you need anything?'

Matias's head drifted from side to side. 'What I need, you ain't got.'

They sat in silence for a moment.

'That it?' Matias asked finally.

Wallace shook his head. 'You remember Smokie?'

Matias's lips tightened into a strained smile. 'Yeah, man. I remember him. He made bail right after you disappeared.'

'Do you know his name? His real name?'

Matias focused on Wallace, looking at him for the first time, his expression that of an alien species studying a primitive life form. 'Smokie,' he said at last. 'His name's Smokie.'

Matias replaced the receiver in its holster and heaved himself to his feet. Wallace watched him sway for a moment, his brow furrowed as though he was trying to recall a deep memory. He stepped away, but stopped suddenly and backtracked, reaching lazily for the receiver.

'The Bunker. It's a place in Harlem. They all hang out there,' Matias drawled.

'Thanks,' Wallace replied gratefully.

Matias nodded and then staggered towards the exit, which was flanked by two watchful guards. He didn't even glance back.

Wallace looked down at the chipped laminate that covered the carrel and tried to control his building fury. He hated himself. He loathed the cowardice that made him run from Ash instead of going to save her. He detested everything about what he'd become, and when it was all over, when he'd found the person who'd killed Ash and avenged her, he knew he'd put an end to his blighted life. The only question was whether he'd take the long road out, like Matias, or the short one, like Erin Byrne, the girl whose suicide had first made Wallace a target.

It was eight-thirty by the time Wallace found the Bunker, a squat, rectangular building located on the corner of 10th Avenue and 202nd Street. The grey structure stretched back almost two hundred feet and was fifty feet wide. It was situated in a run-down neighbourhood, surrounded by convenience stores and places that encouraged people to trade gold for cash. As he clung to the shadows in the doorway of a boarded up shop across 202nd Street, Wallace watched a steady stream of people join a queue that snaked into the loud club. The building had hardly any windows, but even through the thick walls, the pounding bassline made the night air tremble.

Four hard-nosed bouncers guarded a small doorway cut into the wall halfway down the street. They frisked everyone entering the club and turned away anyone found carrying weapons. Wallace saw five such refusals in twenty minutes, and wondered what the hell he was doing staking out somewhere so dangerous. None of the people denied entry took rejection well, and stalked off muttering puffed-up threats of violence. It was the sort of neighbourhood where people got buried for giving the wrong kind of look. He knew he shouldn't be there on his own, and even if Matias was right, he had no idea what he'd do if he saw Smokie. He felt a chill of fear as he recalled how dangerous the man was, how he'd almost died at Smokie's hands. Knowing that he had military training, that he was once part of Max Byrne's Ranger unit only served to swell his menace.

Wallace was weighing up the possibility of calling Agent Reeves and asking for help, when a black SUV stopped directly outside the entrance. One of the bouncers hurried forward and opened the rear passenger door, and Wallace saw a face he recognised from his past: Toothless, one of Smokie's lieutenants. He looked taller than Wallace remembered him, but was still short enough to be dwarfed by the bouncers. His wiry frame was concealed beneath an expensive black suit, but the biggest change was his mouth. When he scrunched up his wrinkled face to smile at a beautiful woman waiting in the queue, instead of gums, Wallace saw the glint of metal. He was wearing twenty-four carat dentures and each golden tooth looked like a tiny tombstone. Neither his gaze nor his smile lingered, his eyes darting around like those of a hungry predator, and Wallace could tell that the vicious man was alert to his surroundings. Toothless glanced over his shoulder as the SUV pulled away, and Wallace shrank into the shadows. He felt Toothless's sharp eyes upon him, and shuddered with panic. Recognition meant death. Wallace held his breath and tensed, preparing to run.

They seemed to lock eyes, but eventually Wallace realised that Toothless couldn't penetrate the darkness. He pulled his hood up, hunched himself over and staggered into the light, muttering and swaying like a drunk. He lurched towards 10th Avenue, and when he was near the corner, he glanced over his shoulder to see Toothless heading into the club.

Wallace didn't straighten up until he was fifty yards from the corner and well out of sight of the Bunker. He could hear his rapid pulse as his racing heart sent blood thundering into his ears. His clothes were damp with sweat. He told himself that he didn't care if he died, the only thing that mattered was avenging Ash – but deep down he knew the truth. He was terrified of the death that awaited him at the hands of such violent men.

58

Bailey and Melissa had only just made the last train to Paris. They'd arrived at the Gare de Cornavin at seven-twenty, and had raced through the restored Empire-style building to buy their tickets for the seven forty-two departure. Bailey had been unable to resist the soporific effects of the painkillers, and the gentle rhythm of the train had soon rocked him to sleep. He'd woken a couple of times, when his lolling head had been jolted into an unnatural position, and he'd caught a snapshot of Melissa working on her laptop before sleep had quickly reclaimed him.

She'd shaken him awake as they'd rolled into the Gare de Lyon, and surprised him by having taken care of their accommodation. Shortly after half past eleven they'd been buzzed into a grand old building within a few minutes' walk of Notre Dame Cathedral, and had climbed the wide, sweeping staircase to the top-floor flat, where Melissa's friend, Pravesh Malviya, a video game designer, lived.

Pravesh had offered them a simple but delicious spread of sourdough bread with charcuterie and provincial cheeses that were so ripe and runny, their potent aroma had filled the whole flat. The food had been washed down with a Cahors that was so smooth, Pravesh had to open a second bottle. Bailey had been temperate, limiting himself to a single glass, which he felt mix with his pain medication, transforming the world into a muffled, dreamy place.

Melissa and her university friend had tried to include him, but their conversation had soon turned to old times and they'd traded stories about people he'd never met. Pravesh had probed the nature of Bailey's connection to Melissa, but she'd been pointedly vague, saying he was helping her with a story. Pravesh had eyed Bailey over the top of a pair of thick black-framed glasses, which matched his New York poet black shirt and jeans. His gaze had been rich with scepticism, but whatever judgment he'd come to, he had kept it to himself.

After propping his head up for almost an hour, Bailey had excused himself, and Pravesh had shown him to the smallest of the two guest bedrooms. It was actually Pravesh's home office, an airy space built into the eaves of the attic, which had a view of the top of Notre Dame through a tiny picture window. Bailey had thanked Pravesh for his hospitality and the food, and had stripped to his underwear and collapsed on the bed, falling asleep so quickly that he couldn't even recall having closed his eyes.

Melissa had woken him just after nine. Pravesh had already gone to work and they'd had the run of the flat. Feeling groggy and wrung out, Bailey had been glad to step into the shower and wash off the grime of the past few days. When he'd emerged, refreshed and feeling slightly more human, Melissa revealed that she'd managed to persuade Pravesh to lend them his car. She figured they had a better chance of getting to the UK via the Channel Tunnel than they did by plane, and Bailey hadn't been able to fault the logic. Plane tickets required credit cards, passports and checks. They could buy Eurotunnel tickets in cash, and unless there was an Interpol alert on Melissa, which seemed unlikely given that Diana Fleming had told them the Swiss police believed Harris's death was suicide, they shouldn't face more than a cursory check of their passports at Calais.

They'd taken Pravesh's one-year-old Peugeot 308 from a nearby underground parking garage, and Melissa had driven them three hours north to Calais, where they'd purchased the Eurotunnel ticket and, after an anxious wait, had been waved through passport control. Bailey's false passport was still good.

Inside the terminal building, Bailey had made two phone calls – the first to Salamander and the second to John Wallace, who'd given him the disturbing news that Chris had been captured. She and Wallace had been through a lot together and Bailey hoped that they'd both be OK.

When the public address system had announced final boarding, Bailey and Melissa returned to the Peugeot and joined the long line of predominantly British vehicles that snaked into the massive train. Twenty-five minutes later, they'd been speeding into a dark tunnel bound for home.

Salamander met them at the Stop service station just outside Folkestone, off the M20. Bailey saw him, Frank and Danny milling around the Range Rover, as Melissa eased the Peugeot into the car park. Salamander smiled as Bailey hauled himself out of the car.

'Haybale, ya one lucky bastard,' he noted as they embraced.

Danny and Frank nodded their respect.

'Thanks, Sal,' Bailey replied. He gestured towards Melissa. 'This is Melissa Rathlin, she's a reporter. And this is an old friend of mine, Sal—'

'Salman Sohota,' Melissa interrupted. 'I know who you are.'

The remark unsettled Bailey, who was disappointed to learn that his childhood pal was big enough to be on the press's radar.

'I got the burner,' Salamander said, eyeing Melissa as he reached into his pocket and produced a phone. 'Ya sure ya know what ya doing?'

'No,' Bailey replied, taking the mobile and dialling a number. 'But Fleming says he's one of the good guys, so . . .' He trailed off.

'Home Office,' a voice said.

'Yes, Special Services, please.'

'Do you have a unit?' the disembodied voice asked.

'No, but I've got a name: Sam Mayfield,' Bailey replied.

'Just one moment.'

'Who's he calling?' Danny asked, between draws on his e-cigarette.

'The Home Office,' Bailey explained, while he waited for the call to be connected.

'MI5,' Melissa added with a wry smile.

Danny's eyes narrowed as he tried to gauge whether she'd just made a joke, but when Salamander nodded confirmation, the young gangster glanced around nervously before peering into the sky.

'What the fuck are you doing?' Frank asked him.

'Looking for drones,' Danny replied with a grin.

Bailey heard a click on the line, and then there was suddenly background street noise.

'Mayfield,' a voice said.

'It's DI Bailey.'

'Where are you?' Mayfield asked.

'Someone told me I can trust you,' Bailey replied. 'I want to meet.'

'Where?'

'St Paul's Cathedral.'

'Do you need a priest, Patrick?' Mayfield observed sarcastically. 'Or are you ready to let me help?'

'Just be there,' Bailey responded coolly. 'Five o'clock,' he said before hanging up.

Bailey directed Melissa to St Andrew's Hill, and they found a space on the narrow street, opposite the Cockpit, an old-fashioned black-and-gold-fronted pub. Raindrops flecked the

368

pavement as Bailey and Melissa climbed the hill. He'd spent the journey up the M20 trying to convince her to go home, to lie low until it was all over, but Melissa had been firm. Sylvia had been her friend and mentor, and she was determined to find her killer. Besides, this was her story and she'd been on it longer than he had. And she needed to do whatever she could to help Francis, who was still missing.

They walked briskly, turning on to Creed Lane, another tiny, crooked street that dated back to London's distant past. They started to pass people as they neared Ludgate Hill: a couple of suited men in their late twenties, full of the brash energy of celebration, halfway to being completely legless; a group of tourists peering into the windows of the souvenir shop on the corner; and a frazzled mother leading her chatty young son south, towards the river.

When they emerged on to Ludgate Hill, islands of tourists clustered on the wide pavement in front of the cathedral, while local professionals charted swift routes around them. A steady stream of vehicles flowed along the wet street, and even though the sun hadn't set, the heavy clouds meant most had their lights on, their brightly coloured beams reflecting off the surfaces of the deepening puddles. The rain started to fall harder as Bailey and Melissa crossed the road. They hurried into the cathedral courtyard, towards the grand steps that led up to the visitors' entrance. Bailey was glad he'd chosen somewhere so public: there were plenty of witnesses, and CCTV cameras protruded all around them. He also knew that the City of London police had one of the fastest response times in the capital. If Fleming was wrong, and Mayfield couldn't be trusted, then they were meeting the enemy in one of the safest possible environments.

Bailey's back and ribs ached as he climbed the stone steps up to the West Portico, but the worst of the pain was absorbed by the pills, and he kept up with Melissa as she entered the cathedral.

They went through a large circular door and came to a small lobby where uniformed security guards were searching people's bags. Melissa was ushered to one side and her laptop case checked before they were allowed to proceed into the vaulted nave.

A small congregation gathered in prayer on chairs that were arranged in rows across the wide space. Most of the chairs were vacant, and what worshippers there were had gathered near the altar at the heart of the cathedral. It was impossible not to feel moved in such a building. The white marble and gold detailing, the ornate stucco reliefs, the high arches, the distant, domed ceiling all combined to give a sense of majesty that time had not diminished. The faint scent of sandalwood lingered in the still air, and made Bailey think of all the midnight masses his grandmother had taken him to as a child. As he and Melissa crossed the black-and-white flagstone floor, he kept his eyes open for any sign of Salamander, Danny and Frank. He was unsettled not to see them anywhere, but told himself that his old friend had vowed to ensure they were safe.

When they were level with the classically styled, imposing Wellington Monument with its heroic statues and ornate crypt, Bailey spotted Mayfield standing in the south transept. He was wearing the same leather jacket he'd worn when Bailey had overpowered him to help Wallace escape. He felt slightly foolish as he led Melissa towards the short, powerfully built man, but consoled himself with the thought that paranoia had kept him alive. Mayfield nodded as they approached, and Bailey was relieved to see that the man was alone. If he'd listened to the MI5 agent, he'd have been spared the horrors inflicted by the men who abducted him from Belmarsh, and he and Wallace would have been in protective custody together.

'Detective,' Mayfield observed. 'Miss Rathlin. Are you ready to listen to me now?'

Bailey nodded sheepishly.

'We believe a radical anti-capitalist group known as the Foundation is blackmailing key decision-makers around the world. We think Sylvia Greene and David Harris were killed to prevent them from talking. They also served as warnings to the other blackmail victims.'

'Which is why the "truth" symbol was by the bodies,' Bailey noted. 'The killer probably took photos to send to people and the symbols were signatures to prove they were responsible for the deaths.'

'There have been another four such killings, two in Japan, one in Australia and another in Germany,' Mayfield revealed.

'Why hasn't this made the news?' Melissa asked.

'Apart from my team, you're the only ones to have linked any of the deaths,' Mayfield replied.

'What has this got to do with the attack on John Wallace?' Bailey asked.

'We don't know, but we're convinced it's tied to the Pendulum killings. That's why I needed to talk to him. That's why I put you in Belmarsh. I was trying to get you to crack,' Mayfield explained. 'I'm sorry about that,' he added quietly. 'I had no idea what would happen.'

'The guys that took me – how'd they do that?'

Mayfield shook his head slowly. 'We don't know. The Foundation has reach. They've been able to do things we didn't think were possible.'

'What do you need us for?' Melissa asked.

Mayfield seemed puzzled.

'You know all this stuff,' Melissa went on. 'You know the organisation that was behind Sylvia's killing. You know way more than either of us. Why do you need us to come in?'

'You having second thoughts, Miss Rathlin?'

Mayfield's tone was light, but Bailey thought he detected a little unease.

'There might be some nugget of information locked in your heads that will help us connect the dots,' Mayfield explained. 'You're assets. You don't know what we might find valuable.'

The lull in the conversation was filled by the sound of hushed prayers from the nearby churchgoers.

'So are you ready?' Mayfield said at last. 'We want to take you to a safe house.'

Bailey glanced at Melissa, who seemed uncertain. They were staking their lives on their assessment of this man.

'Did you find the warehouse?' Bailey asked.

'What warehouse?' Mayfield seemed puzzled by the question.

Either he was a brilliant actor, or he genuinely knew nothing about the scene of Bailey's interrogation. Bailey wanted to trust the man, but years of being a detective and his experiences with John Wallace had honed his needle-sharp paranoia.

'We're going to need time to think,' Bailey said at last.

Melissa nodded. 'The trouble with spies is you can never tell when they're lying.'

Her pointed remark provoked a smile.

'I can't protect you out there,' Mayfield countered.

'We'll be OK,' Bailey assured him, backing away.

As he and Melissa started retracing their steps through the nave, Bailey glanced over his shoulder and saw Mayfield following them, like a lion stalking its prey. *Something's wrong*, Bailey thought, and his senses went into overdrive. His gaze darted over the congregation and he saw two men, their heads no longer bowed, watching them with cold eyes. Another man, a black guy with a skinhead, was standing by one of the massive pillars that lined the south of the nave, studying them intently.

'It's a set-up,' he told Melissa, grabbing her arm and urging her forward at speed. The guards at the visitors' entrance might provide some protection.

When Bailey looked over his shoulder, he saw the two

men had risen from their seats and joined Mayfield and the skinhead in a measured pursuit. As they rounded the Wellington Monument, Bailey felt a rush of panic. The visitors' entrance was shut and the three guards were waiting for them, batons in hand.

'Patrick Bailey, Melissa Rathlin, you're under arrest,' Mayfield called out as he approached. 'Put your hands up.'

Bailey turned to see that the three thugs trailing Mayfield now had pistols drawn. He glanced at Melissa, who was looking at him nervously. Bailey shook his head, regretting his stupidity. His only hope was Salamander, but his old friend was nowhere to be seen.

Mayfield grabbed Bailey's wrist and manacled him.

'Shout terrorism, and you can do anything,' Mayfield whispered. 'Even take over the security of a cathedral.'

'There's nothing to worry about, people,' the skinhead called out to the members of the congregation who were watching nervously. 'You're safe now.'

'I was hoping to avoid a scene,' Mayfield said as he cuffed Melissa. 'But you're too stupid to know when the game is over.'

'Diana Fleming said we could trust you,' Bailey returned, his tone almost pleading.

'You assumed Harris was the one being blackmailed,' Mayfield replied. 'We never go after the monkeys, just the organ grinders. Fleming's in our pocket. Harris simply found out about it. That's why he had to go. That's what he was going to tell you,' he said to Melissa. 'We told Fleming where to send you if you made contact.'

'You bastard!' Melissa spat. 'Did you kill Sylvia? Did you? Answer me.'

Mayfield smiled. 'Get her out of here,' he ordered the two hard-faced men.

Melissa tried to resist as they dragged her towards the north transept. 'Bailey! Help! Someone help me!'

Bailey flinched as one of the men struck Melissa, dazing her into silence. He tried to move towards her, but Mayfield pushed him back.

'I watched you, detective,' he whispered into Bailey's ear. 'I watched you interview Wallace's neighbours. I saw you visit that pretty thing who lived above him. Some kind of dancer, wasn't she? When you brought in the forensics team, I was worried you might find some trace of us. But you're just like the rest of them. You saw what we wanted you to see. A lone man, a crazed serial killer working alone. No matter how exceptional, one man could not have launched such an operation by himself. But you're beginning to realise that we are not just one. We are an army. And this war is just getting started.'

Bailey was momentarily stunned by Mayfield's revelation. He was talking about the Pendulum murders and had just confessed to being an accomplice.

'You fuck!' Bailey yelled, snapping his skull forward to deliver a bone-crunching head-butt.

Mayfield crumbled, cradling his nose.

Bailey tried to run, but only managed two steps before the skinhead cracked him across the back of his head with the heel of his pistol.

Everything went black.

59

Bailey felt himself falling. He hit something hard, and the impact jolted him awake. His senses tumbled into overdrive. The sound of thunder pounded his ears. His tongue recoiled at the metallic taste of fresh blood. His ribs stabbed his sides with pain. A powerful smoky aroma filled his nostrils. When his eyes finally focused, he saw that he was lying on the semi-circular steps that led away from the cathedral's north transept, over-looking Paternoster Row, the tree-lined pedestrian alleyway that abutted the grounds. His captors had dropped him, and when he looked up, he saw the skinhead firing his machine-pistol. Mayfield stood next to him, his broken nose covered in blood, his gun spitting fire.

Bailey followed the bullets and saw Danny, Frank and Salamander. Danny was crouched behind the bonnet of a dark blue Mercedes SUV, which was parked by the high wrought-iron gates that opened on to Paternoster Row. He was shooting at the skinhead, trying to provide cover for Salamander, who was helping Melissa to her feet. The two men who had taken her were lying on the ground. One was motionless, the other had his hands pressed against a bloody wound in his side.

All around them, men, women and children were fleeing the scene. Bailey could see suited City workers running east along Paternoster Row, and when he looked west, he saw people scattering like struck bowling pins. He sensed movement behind him, and saw the three men who'd posed as security guards drawing pistols as they stormed out of the cathedral. He knew he had to do something and tried to push himself up, but as he forced his protesting body off the ground, he caught a flash of movement and saw the huge figure of Jimmy Cullen come steaming round the eastern edge of the transept, and rush up behind the guards. The red skull on the side of his head looked fearsome as Cullen set about them with an ice axe. He swung the serrated point of the silver head up into the first man's groin, and a spine-chilling scream burst from the guard, which had the immediate effect of terrifying the others.

Cullen moved quickly for a big man. His victim crumpled as he yanked the ice axe free. Bailey watched blood run down the metal handle as the huge man drove the vicious point into the second guard's gut. The third man managed to get a shot off, and the bullet caught Cullen in the flank, but didn't slow him down. He smashed the guy in the face with his wrecking-ball fist, and slung the pick into his shoulder, dragging him back for another punch, which knocked him out. The dead weight of the guard pulled the ice axe down with him, and the deeply buried point was tightly bound by sinew and bone, clasping it hard and resisting Cullen's attempts to yank it out.

Bailey saw the skinhead turn his attention to Cullen, and moved just as the man was about to shoot, rising, clattering into the back of his legs, forcing the shot to go wild. Skinhead wheeled round, surprised to see Bailey on his feet, but he didn't get the chance to react. His missed shot had got Cullen's attention, and the giant charged and tackled him. The two men went tumbling down the short run of steps, struggling all the way, but when the mass of muscle stopped, it was Cullen who had the advantage, and he pressed it hard, battering the skinhead until he stopped moving.

Mayfield grabbed Bailey and pulled him into a chokehold. He

tried to get his gun up to Bailey's temple, but the detective resisted, elbowing him in the gut. The blow winded Mayfield, and his grip loosened just enough for Bailey to get away. As he moved, Bailey heard the crack of a pistol and felt a bullet whistle past him. He turned to see Mayfield stagger back, clutching at a hole in his leather jacket, just above his collar bone.

Bailey felt hands on him and saw Salamander's face crowd his vision.

'We need to go, man,' his friend urged, pulling him towards the black metal gates.

The sound of sirens filled the night air, and Bailey saw a flash of fluorescent yellow as the first uniformed foot patrols arrived. They were keeping their distance at the edge of the courtyard, pushing back anyone foolish enough to be gawking.

'Come on!' Salamander exclaimed.

'Not without him,' Bailey replied, his mind finally kicking into gear.

He gestured towards Mayfield, who was leaning against the wall, beside the huge wooden doors of the cathedral.

'Get him,' Salamander instructed Cullen.

Mayfield tried to raise his pistol as the huge man closed, but his arm wouldn't work, and the gun slipped from his fingers and clattered on the stone slabs. Cullen ignored the small man's feeble resistance, pulled him into a chokehold and dragged him towards the Mercedes.

'Pat, we've gotta move.'

Bailey hadn't heard Salamander use his real name for years. He nodded and allowed his friend to help him forward.

'Thanks,' he said, as he staggered away from the cathedral.

'Save it until we're clear,' Salamander cautioned.

Cullen forced Mayfield into the boot, and climbed in on top of him. Frank was in the driver's seat, revving the engine. Danny sat next to him, guns at the ready, keeping a watchful eye on the hesitant police. Melissa was in the back, and looked relieved as Salamander helped Bailey slide in next to her.

'Let's go,' he said, as he jumped in.

Frank didn't even wait for him to close the door: the car shot back, the adjacent black railings becoming a blur as they sped along Paternoster Row.

'We'll need to ditch this quick,' Danny observed, indicating the Mercedes.

Salamander nodded.

The SUV lurched as Frank put it into a violent, tyre-screeching turn, swinging it on to New Change, the wide road that ran behind the cathedral. He flipped into 'drive' and there was a moment of inertia as the engine screamed through the gears, before a violent jolt sent the car racing forward. Frank ignored the red lights, cut across the intersection and turned right on to Cheapside.

As they sped east, Bailey heard the muffled sound of Mayfield moaning, and prayed that the wounded man would stay alive long enough to give them the truth.

60

They'd escaped quickly enough to evade the police, speeding down to one of the lower levels of the underground car park on Aldersgate, where they found Frank's Range Rover. Frank complained about bloodstains and insisted on laying a tarp on the flatbed before they transferred Mayfield from the boot of the Mercedes. The injured man groaned and muttered incomprehensibly as they tossed his bleeding body in the back of the car. Keen to avoid drawing attention to an already overcrowded vehicle, Salamander praised Cullen's bravery and dispatched the huge man to see Doctor Death with instructions to get his bullet wound treated. When he was done, he was to meet them in Radley Green.

As they drove out of the car park, Salamander apologised for leaving them alone inside the cathedral, explaining that he hadn't wanted to risk being disarmed by the security guards at the door. Bailey expressed his gratitude, a sentiment Melissa had echoed. They were just glad to be alive.

No one said much else as they made steady progress through Central London. All eyes were alert to danger, and the first ten minutes of their journey was a rollercoaster ride of tension, as half a dozen squad cars and a couple of vans passed in the opposite direction, sirens blaring, blues flashing.

The further they travelled from the cathedral, the more relaxed they became, and soon Danny was filling the car with his rapid-fire chatter, reliving the confrontation and speculating on whether the men Cullen had attacked would live or die. Even though they had saved his life, Bailey couldn't share Danny's pride. He was uncomfortable being on the wrong side of the law, and tried not to listen. He watched Melissa for a while, but she didn't return his gaze and simply stared out of the window, lost in her own thoughts as Frank steered them through the suburban fringe of London. Salamander's attention was swallowed by his phone, and his thumb jumped across the screen as he tapped out urgent messages, so Bailey mimicked Melissa and turned his eyes to the passing scenery, focusing on it in an attempt to drown out Danny's words, Mayfield's groans, and the pain coming from his own throbbing head.

They'd been driving for about an hour, heading north-east into Essex. Monochrome countryside flashed past, barely illuminated by a cuticle moon. They were blistering along the A414, and were about two miles out of Chelmsford when they came to a tiny roundabout. Frank slowed and turned left off the main road, following the sign for Radley Green.

Even in the darkness, Bailey could see that it wasn't much of a village. A few disparate farms, a rural warehouse complex that was home to some small businesses, and then field after open field. They drove for a couple of miles, twisting their way along the narrow road, the wing mirrors brushing the high, unkempt hedges. He saw the silhouette of an owl swoop over the car, but said nothing to the others. Eventually, Frank turned off the road on to a dirt track, and the headlights briefly illuminated a signpost that read 'Radley Hulme Farm'.

Something had been bothering Bailey since they'd turned off the main road, and as they approached the large farmhouse, he was finally able to identify the cause: Danny was silent. Bailey couldn't see the young gangster's face, but he could sense the nervous tension emanating from the front seat.

'Your dad knows we're coming, right?' Frank asked.

'Course,' Danny replied, full of bluster. 'I called him.'

'I just don't want him thinkin' we're villains,' Frank countered.

'We are bloody villains,' Danny told him.

'The wrong kind of villains,' Frank clarified.

Bailey looked to his old friend for an explanation.

'Why don't ya tell my man here ya surname?' Salamander suggested.

Danny glanced round at Bailey, his face weighed down by resignation.

'Kane,' he said quietly.

'Kane,' Bailey repeated. 'You're not Terry Kane's son?'

Danny nodded. 'I haven't seen him for years.'

'Shit,' Melissa sighed.

'Exactly,' Salamander said. 'Even if anyone found us, they'd think twice about coming up here.'

Terry Kane was a legendary underworld figure. He and his two brothers had run large parts of London during the eighties and nineties. He was a violent man with a savage temper, but was reputed to be the nicest of the three siblings. They'd lived large, running drugs, prostitution, extortion rackets, arms dealing – hustling anything and everything, keeping the streets in line and crushing the competition. Their reign came to an end when the two older brothers were kidnapped and executed. Terry had retaliated with a vengeful one-man rampage. There were whispered stories of bodies fed to pigs, buried in disused coal mines, sealed in the structural supports of buildings, disintegrated in smelting plants. Bailey had heard that as few as twenty and as many as eighty men had died at Terry's hand, but in the end the Met could only tie him to the murders of three men: low-level enforcers for the Hackney Mob, a rival gang. The evidence had been overwhelming, but somehow Terry managed to pull a masterful trick that had become part of London folklore. He managed to avoid a life sentence because, despite being in protective custody, the fourth man Terry had attacked and badly injured disappeared, simply vanishing from his bed one night. The lack of eye-witness testimony had been sufficient to have the charge reduced to manslaughter and Terry only served eight years.

'There he is,' Frank noted.

Terry Kane stood in the doorway of the farmhouse, silhouetted by warm, golden light. He stood maybe an inch or two shorter than Danny, but was wider, his body almost filling the frame. Even at a distance, Bailey noted his big, brutish hands.

Frank parked next to a Bentley Arnage Concours, and they all exited. The cool air was rich with floral scents, but beneath them hung the odour of manure. Danny jogged forward, crunching over gravel, head low as though trying not to meet his father's eye.

'Alright, Dad,' he said, trying to sound as nonchalant as possible.

'Alright? Alright, Dad?' Terry boomed, his voice dry as desert sand. 'Get over here, you bloody muppet.'

Danny slowed, hesitating as he came within his father's reach. Bailey saw him flinch as Terry lashed out with both hands, but instead of striking his son, the old villain pulled him into a tight embrace.

'Was that you on the news?' Terry asked, oozing pride like the parent of a prodigy.

'We didn't make the fucking news, did we?' Frank asked.

'Course you did. A shoot-out at St Paul's? You boys are famous,' Terry replied. 'They've got your mugshots everywhere. Terrorists, right? Wanted in connection with an' all that bollocks. Come on in. You can have a brew and introduce me to your mates. Katie's just put the kettle on.'

★

Katie turned out to be Terry's girlfriend, an attractive woman in her late fifties who introduced herself as Katherine, her clipped, upper-class accent making Bailey want to stand that little bit straighter. She was slim, blonde and three or four inches taller than Terry, who mauled her with affectionate pats and embraces whenever she came within reach. She wore a pair of pegged tweed trousers and a light blue blouse and looked every bit the aristocrat that her accent suggested she was. Bailey guessed the furniture, and possibly the house, belonged to her. It was as though the contents of a stately home had been disgorged into the farmhouse, crowding every available space with antiques, paintings, elegant chairs, tables, marble clocks, grandfather clocks: the place was like a museum. Only the living room was vaguely homely. A couple of blood-red Chesterfields faced each other across an open hearth, a low coffee table between them bearing the burden of a fine china tea set.

Terry sat in the middle of the sofa nearest the kitchen, an oil painting of a fox hunt hanging on the wall behind him. Danny was on his left, and Katherine on his right, leaning back against Terry's coiled arm. Salamander sat opposite, with Bailey on his left and Melissa on his right. Frank leaned against the arm of the Chesterfield next to Bailey. The TV was on mute, and BBC News was broadcasting mobile phone footage taken outside the cathedral, which showed the gun battle. The incident had been labelled a terror attack, and all of them had been identified as suspects who were also wanted in connection with the disappearance of newspaper editor, Francis Albright. Bailey had encountered a few conspiracy nuts on the job, but this was the first time he'd seen the ease with which a bold lie could be swallowed by a docile audience.

He watched the rolling news coverage, while listening to Salamander apprise Terry of the situation. He and the others chipped in when necessary, and when Bailey revealed that he was police and Melissa was a reporter, Terry had suddenly bristled and become guarded, glaring at Danny until Salamander had assured the old gangster that they could be trusted. When he'd heard everything they had to say, Terry turned to Danny.

'I thought you'd come to nothing, boy,' he said. 'I thought your mother had ruined you while I was inside. Turned you soft. But look at you. You've done well.'

Terry slapped his thighs.

'Right,' he said, hauling himself to his feet. 'Sounds to me like we need to talk to the toerag you've got in the boot. Find out where he's stashed your boss. Get him to spill about everything else. You,' he said, pointing to Melissa, 'you run a story blowing the whole thing wide open, and they ain't got no more leverage. And you,' he thrust his thick index finger in Bailey's direction, 'you get all the info you need to build a case. Much as it sickens me, you'll be a hero cop by the time we're finished.'

Bailey looked at Salamander, who smiled. His old friend was as sharp as an addict's needle. Not only had he brought them somewhere safe, he'd also introduced an unstable element, someone Mayfield didn't know, a man who would take great pleasure in breaking him. Terry's face said it all. He was looking forward to reliving his glory days.

'Come on then,' Terry said, striding from the room.

Bailey necked a couple of painkillers as Frank and Danny hauled Mayfield from the boot of the Range Rover, and followed Terry across the farmyard towards a renovated red-brick barn. Salamander and Melissa followed, and Bailey could see reluctance writ large on the journalist's face. He jogged to catch up with her, his head pounding with every step.

'You don't have to, you know,' he said, gesturing towards the barn.

'He was going to kill us,' she replied. 'I want to hear what he has to say.'

Terry unlocked a small door that was inset in one of two large slatted gates, and switched on the lights as he stepped inside. Frank and Danny manhandled Mayfield into the barn and the others followed.

Three red tents dominated the large space, each connected to a long, wide, flexible tube that fed into a dehumidifier. Inside the tents were three cars: a gold sixties Mercedes Pagoda, a black Ferrari 308, and a silver Aston Martin DB6.

'My babies,' Terry enthused, gesturing towards the cars. 'Put him on the bench,' he added, indicating a long, laminated workbench that was set against the north wall of the barn.

An assortment of tools hung from pegs above the smooth surface, and they shook slightly as Frank and Danny deposited Mayfield.

'Wake him up,' Terry said as he reached for a hacksaw.

Danny balled his hand into a fist and drove it into Mayfield's groin. Bailey shuddered as the man snapped to life with a shriek of pain. Mayfield curled up and tried to soothe himself, his movement releasing a stench that wafted from the folds of his leather jacket: blood, sweat and misery.

'Hold him down,' Terry instructed, and Frank and Danny unfolded the feeble man and pinned him to the counter.

Bailey's mouth ran dry, parched by the memory of his own ordeal. He felt uncomfortable watching Mayfield subjected to torture, but reminded himself that the man was at least responsible for, if not involved in, his own suffering.

'Right,' Terry said, placing the saw blade against Mayfield's little finger. 'This is to get your attention.'

Mayfield's scream shocked Bailey, and he was taken aback to

see Terry hacking through the man's flesh. He looked at Melissa, who'd turned away, her hand pressed to her mouth as though trying to suppress vomit. Frank and Danny held the struggling man, as Terry finished the job. Salamander kept his attention fixed to his phone, his thumb working as furiously as the blade, tapping out messages to unknown recipients. It was all over in less than twenty seconds, but Bailey knew the moment would last a lifetime. He had crossed a line.

'Shut him up,' Terry told Danny.

His son stuck his hand over Mayfield's mouth and pressed down hard, until the spy's scream had withered to a whimper.

Terry held up the severed digit.

'Right, now you know I'm not fucking about, you're gonna answer every single question we ask you. Play silly bugger an' I'll cut off another finger. I get a sniff you're not telling the truth, or that you're fucking us about, and I'll get my circular saw, you see it there?' He nodded towards a fearsome-looking machine mounted on thick pegs. 'Bloody sharp, it is. I'll use it to cut your arms an' legs off and let you watch as we feed them to my pigs. You got me?'

Sweat beaded Mayfield's brow, and his eyes were wide with pain and fear, but he had the sense to nod.

'Let him talk,' Terry said, and Danny removed his hand.

Mayfield gulped like a dying fish taking in huge breaths of air.

'What you told me in the cathedral, about the Foundation, was it true?' Bailey asked.

Mayfield nodded, his red, tear-filled eyes looking towards the detective.

'Are you a member?' Bailey continued.

'Yes,' Mayfield replied, his voice weak and hoarse.

'How many of you are there?'

'I don't know. I was recruited by Max Byrne – Pendulum.'

'Who handles you now?'

'I don't know his name. It's run from the States. Organised into cells. None of us see the full picture. They got me to recruit a bunch of guys from the Box.'

'MI5,' Bailey explained to Terry. 'Why?' he asked.

'You're a cop,' Mayfield rasped. 'You see how it's going. The rich are getting richer, and the rest of us are left fighting over the scraps.'

'Why the Online Security Act? How's that going to strike at capitalism?' Melissa interjected.

'I don't know,' Mayfield replied, looking nervously at Terry. 'I just follow orders.'

'You said you saw me at Wallace's place,' Bailey continued. 'You were helping Pendulum?'

'We all were. He was one of us. A comrade. What happened to his sister . . . when he told me about it, I offered to kill them myself,' Mayfield revealed.

'How do you make contact?' Bailey asked.

'Secure private network. Encrypted with a daily key.'

'Where's Francis? Is he still alive?' Melissa asked.

Mayfield hesitated, his face twisted by pain and indecision.

'Let me help you remember,' Terry said, pressing the saw blade against Mayfield's ring finger.

'He's at a safe house near Oxford,' Mayfield said hurriedly. 'Three guards. Ground floor, back left room.'

'How many have you compromised?' Bailey asked.

'My cell? Maybe two dozen. Politicians, journalists, police.'

Bailey shook his head in disbelief. 'How?'

'I get sent information. Your friend Greene,' Mayfield said, directing his remarks to Melissa. 'Early in her career she was involved in the cover-up of a paedophile ring.'

'You're lying.' Melissa stepped forward, and Bailey thought for a moment that she was about to strike the man. 'Sylvia would never do something like that.'

'She did. She was just as corrupt and rotten as the people she exposed,' Mayfield said.

Terry punched him in the mouth.

'Did you kill her?' Bailey asked.

Mayfield stared back, full of indignation, until Terry applied a little pressure with the saw.

'We knew she was going to expose us. She wouldn't back down.'

'And David Harris?' Melissa interjected.

'That was your fault,' Mayfield said spitefully. 'We had to shut him up before you got to him.'

Bailey shook his head in disgust and stepped away from the bench, signalling to Melissa and Salamander to join him.

'Terry's right,' he told them. 'We need to break this story. It's the only hope we've got of clearing our names and exposing this blackmail ring. And when we've done that, I'm bringing this guy in to stand trial.'

'You sure?' Terry asked quietly. 'People like him don't see jail. I'll serve justice better.'

'I can't do that,' Bailey replied. 'I'm already over a line I said I'd never cross. People need to know what he's done. I have to believe the system won't fail us.'

'But we need to rescue Francis first,' Melissa insisted. 'If we put this on the front page they might—'

'Yeah,' Bailey agreed. 'They might kill him in retaliation. You in?' he asked Salamander.

'Of course,' his friend replied. 'We can't do business with our faces all over the evening news. We gotta fix this.'

'OK. Melissa—'

'It's Mel,' Melissa interrupted. 'After what we've been through, I think you know me well enough now.'

'Mel,' Bailey smiled. 'How'd you feel about staying here and questioning this guy? Get the names of everyone he recruited, all the people they've blackmailed, details of how they helped Pendulum – anything and everything he knows.'

'OK,' she replied.

'Make sure Terry don't kill him,' Salamander said. 'Least, not right now,' he added darkly. 'Frank. Danny,' he called to the two men. 'Get the safe house address off our friend there and then meet us outside.'

Bailey heard a vehicle rolling across the gravel and hurried to the door to see the bright lights of a car. Salamander joined him.

Cullen heaved himself out of the vehicle. He was in a fresh red tracksuit, which clung tightly to his muscular frame.

'Ya get ya'self patched up?' Salamander asked.

'Just about. Doctor Death's off his head,' Cullen announced. 'Almost stuck me in the eye with a needle.'

'They're in a place called Cuddesdon,' Danny announced. 'Sounds like something off Harry Potter.'

'Jimmy, how bad was it?' Salamander asked, placing a hand on the huge man's arm.

'Alright, Sal,' Cullen replied. 'The bullet passed right through. Didn't hit nothin' vital.'

'Just your brain, then,' Danny noted, provoking Cullen's ire.

'Ya feel ready for work?' Salamander asked.

Cullen nodded.

'Ya comin' with us. Danny, I want ya to stay with ya dad. Get this guy to spill,' Salamander said.

Danny nodded and went to join his father at the workbench.

'Let's go,' Salamander told the others.

'Bailey,' Melissa said, as Salamander, Frank and Cullen went outside.

The detective hung back.

'Be careful,' she warned, her eyes alive with concern.

Bailey nodded. 'You too.'

He hurried across the gravel and joined Salamander in the back of the Range Rover.

'We can go alone. Ya sure ya want to do this?' his friend asked.

Bailey nodded and swung the door closed. 'I'm in.'

Salamander pursed his lips thoughtfully and signalled to Frank, who put the car in gear and drove away from the farm. Bailey glanced over his shoulder and saw Melissa standing in the doorway of the barn, her silhouetted curves making him wish they'd met under different circumstances.

There's still time, he thought, as the car sped into the night.

61

A dark corridor, the walls wet to touch, the air fetid. Light ahead, the faint outline of an open door. The sound of someone whimpering just loud enough to hear. Wallace's feet trudged on, even though his mind told him to run the other way. He wasn't in control of his body, but nonetheless, he tried to swallow the rising fear which was building to a scream. He was by the door, his hand reaching out, touching the moist wood. When he glanced at his fingertips, he saw they were covered in sticky blood. The door swung open silently, revealing a filthy bare mattress in the middle of a room whose edges were shrouded in endless shadow. Wallace's autonomous feet carried him closer to the mattress, towards a battered naked figure who lay on its squalid surface, hunched in the foetal position. He knew who it was. He recognised her legs, her arms and her hair, which fell in lank tresses against patches of dried blood. *Run*, he screamed inwardly, willing his legs to comply. But they carried on, forcing him within sight of her face. He tried to look away, but his head wouldn't move. It was as though rock-steady hands were holding his jaws, and, like an unruly dog, he was being compelled to confront the mess he'd made. He welled up when he saw her: Christine Ash, lying broken, near death. He tried to reach out a hand, but his arms stayed firmly by his sides.

A thunderous bang shook the space, jolting Ash's body.

Wallace heard the sound from another place, a world beyond his nightmares.

Another jolt, and this one shattered Ash and the mattress, dispersing everything into blackness, as his conscious mind woke.

Wallace opened his eyes, convinced the noise that had roused him from his nightmare had been real. He tensed, listening closely, his eyes growing accustomed to the dim, orange light of his Fresh City Hotel room. His body trembled with the lingering effects of his terrible dream. When he heard another loud crash, and the splintering of wood, he sprang from the bed. Three shadows were rushing into his room. As they emerged from the dark hallway into the dim light that bled through the thin drape, Wallace was immediately transfixed by the sight of their Pendulum masks.

Two of them pressed forward while Wallace's mind struggled to comprehend what was happening. His heart thundered and his legs shook as they laid heavy hands on him, pulling him forward by his arms. Wallace's stomach flipped, and his head went light as he saw the third man draw a silenced pistol. The other two masked men were pulling him towards the gun, which was being levelled in his direction.

The first gunshot shocked Wallace almost as much as it did the man holding his right arm, who whipped round to see his companion fall down dead, a smoking hole torn through the front of his mask.

'Hey!' the shocked man exclaimed, wheeling round to face the shooter.

His cry was the last thing that passed his lips. A bullet tore through his cheek and burst through the back of his skull. It was swiftly followed by another that ripped through his neck. His arms flew up instinctively and he clutched at his throat, making a grim wet choking sound as he fell to the floor.

Wallace watched in shock as the man writhed at his feet.

'We need to go,' the shooter said calmly, but his voice seemed muted and distant.

Wallace was reminded of the explosion outside the Marwand Compound in Kandahar when the shock and severity of what had happened seemed to thrust him into a dream. His breathing was shallow and rapid, his heart thundered and his body was shaking, but his mind was clear, detached and suddenly full of purpose.

He had to know.

'Come on,' the shooter urged.

Wallace ignored the man and reached a trembling hand down towards the man dying at his feet. He brushed the man's feeble hands away and felt for the edge of the mask. He had to see.

'We don't have time for this.'

Wallace sensed the shooter's gloved hand on his shoulder, but he resisted the pull and lifted the Pendulum mask, peeling it away as though he were skinning a chicken. The face beneath was contorted in pain, a gaping wound in its left cheek. The gold that grimaced back at him left the man's identity in no doubt. It was Smokie's lieutenant, Toothless.

'What did you do to her?' Wallace cried, surprising himself by grabbing the wounded man by his bloody throat. 'What did you do to her!'

The shooter pulled Wallace off the dying man. 'Don't do this, John.'

Wallace stumbled back, suddenly very aware of the blood on his hands. When he looked down, Toothless had stopped moving, and his eyes were lifeless and still.

'Come on, we need to get out of here,' the shooter reiterated, but Wallace fell on to the floor, broken by the experience.

The shooter pocketed the pistol as he crouched down. He removed his Pendulum mask, and Wallace registered the man's face but couldn't piece together what had happened and why he'd killed two of his own.

'Ethan Moore?' Wallace asked uncertainly, recalling the name of the man who'd posed as Max Byrne's nurse.

He launched himself with the savagery of a wild animal, but Ethan sidestepped the attack and Wallace fell flat on his face.

'You're one of them!' Wallace yelled. 'I saw you in the picture with Max, Rosen and Smokie!'

'My real name is Ethan Pope,' the shooter replied, trying to pull Wallace to his feet. 'And yes, I did serve with those men. I've been led down a dark path and I'm trying to make it right. Come on, John. There's still a chance we can save her.'

Wallace looked up, hardly daring to hope. 'Who?'

'Christine Ash,' Pope said softly. 'She's alive.'

62

Alice sat on the low bunk, clasping her knees. The sound of indistinct voices permeated the cell. The building used to be a garage. It was made of cheap concrete blocks, and was located at the very edge of the Clan's land. The windowless cells lined the west of the building, and small high windows were cut into the north and south ends of the corridor that ran alongside them. There was a desk set into an alcove near the door, where the duty steward was allowed to read his or her devotions, setting an example for those in the cells. Only Manny watched television, and Alice wondered how he avoided being put in one of the disciplinary cells himself. Maybe his sly smile kept him out of trouble?

Sitting in the cell nearest the door, Alice was far from the bright sunshine that came through the high windows, and she had spent three days living in twilight. The nights were worse. If Manny wasn't on duty, the cell block was pitch black, and her mind conjured terrible monsters to fill the deep darkness.

She could feel her cell starting to warm up. The California sun baked the block, and by midday the air became so thick with heat that Alice spent the afternoons gulping down shallow breaths, sweating, and praying for cooling nightfall, even though the darkness would fill her cell with terrors.

She heard more voices, and thought of the people outside, carrying on with their lives, completing their devotions, finishing their chores, smiling and laughing, while she sweltered in her disciplinary cell. She was the only one in the block, and for today at least, she was the only failed soul in the entire Clan.

She wondered whether her mother ever thought about her while she was locked up. Would Nicholas ever catch her glancing towards the building, fretting about her daughter? Alice doubted it. Her mother was now a very obedient woman, devoted to Nicholas and his faith.

Alice hoped that Manny would soon take over as duty steward. She longed for television to distract her from the roasting heat. Esther was sitting in the alcove, her eyes closed, her palms pressed flat against the desk as she rocked gently back and forth, her lips moving rapidly in prayer. The block door opened, blinding Alice with bright light, and when her eyes adjusted, she saw her father standing in the doorway, the golden sunshine blazing through his kaftan. Alice shivered and shrank into herself.

'Father,' Esther said, hurriedly getting to her feet.

It unsettled Alice to hear all these grown-ups calling Nicholas father. Maybe he would be a better father to her if he wasn't spreading himself so thin?

'Leave us, Esther.' Nicholas's voice was melodic and soft.

Alice saw that his eyes were wide and distant, as they sometimes were after ministry.

Esther bustled out of the building, bowing as she passed Nicholas. When she was gone, he approached, allowing the door to slam shut behind him. The cell block was returned to twilight, and the clang of metal on metal made Alice jump.

Nicholas took a key from the alcove and unlocked the door to Alice's cell. She felt the crunchy concrete wall against her back as she recoiled. If he saw her fear, he pretended not to notice, and crouched beside the low bunk.

'Do you know why you're here?' he asked, his voice little more than a whisper.

Alice took a deep breath, suddenly aware that the wrong answer would be painful. 'Because I've been bad,' she replied hesitantly.

Nicholas shook his head and smiled. 'No, little Alice. You're here to help you become a better person.'

She wasn't sure how to respond, and Nicholas stared at her the way he often did, as though he was burrowing inside her, stripping her soul bare. She had to look away.

'It's why I do everything, Alice. It's not punishment. It's to make you better. I do it all for you,' he said, his eyes wide and unwavering. 'You won't understand it now, but suffering makes us stronger.'

When Alice glanced at her father she saw his bottom lip quiver and uncertainty creep across his face. It was one of the only times she had ever seen him express any vulnerability.

'You can go now.'

Nicholas stood back and signalled the open cell door. For a moment Alice wondered whether it was a test, and sat completely still.

'Go on. Go to your mother,' he urged.

Alice nodded and hauled herself off the bunk. She hurried forward, crossing the corridor and putting all her weight against the cell block door. When it swung wide open, she glanced over her shoulder and saw her father sitting on her bunk, his head in his hands. If she forgot every unkindness he'd done to her and her mother, Alice might have been able to feel sorry for him, because he looked like a man weighed down by trouble. The bruises had faded, but the memories hadn't, and she couldn't think of him kindly. She dashed on, leaving the door to swing shut behind her, shrouding her father in the darkness he deserved.

★

The silence woke her. She longed to burn her memories to prevent them infesting her dreams, but at least they had light. The room she was in was beyond black, the darkness so rich and deep that she could feel it on her skin. There were no shadows, no highlights, no hint of anything beyond her body, but even though she couldn't see it, she knew the world was there. She'd been stripped of her clothes, and dressed in a pair of ill-fitting shorts and a dirty old T-shirt. She could feel the damp seat beneath her. Every few hours, she was released and led to the foul bucket in the corner, but sometimes, need got the better of her. Her bonds chafed where she had rubbed her wrists and ankles raw, desperately trying to loosen the cords that snared her, but her efforts had only seemed to tighten their embrace. A perpetual sheen of perspiration covered her, a physical manifestation of her pain, fear and fatigue. It had nowhere to go so it lay on the surface of her skin, thickening, blending with the darkness, making her part of it.

Don't be afraid, baby.

Her mother's last words, delivered lying in a pool of her own blood, as her life leeched out of the puckered bullet wounds.

There's plenty to be afraid of, Ash thought. *If you'd been more afraid and less trusting, you might still be alive.*

The silence. No pounding bass, thudding through the walls like an erratic heartbeat. Ash had tried to keep track of time, but her tormentors were professional and knew that disorientation and detachment were very effective at softening the spirit, preparing it to be broken by more direct methods. She had no idea how long they'd held her in the darkness. Her connection to time and reality had been severed. She was lost.

Tears rolled down Ash's cheeks as she thought of the device. She could still feel the vestiges of an agony that was beyond anything she'd ever experienced. She had heard rumours of such implements, designed to tap directly into the brain's pain centre, bypassing inefficient nerves, and unleashing immeasurable suffering without leaving a single mark. At least not externally. Her father had prepared her for a cruel world, taught her how to endure torment without showing weakness, but she'd encountered nothing like this. When the masked man placed the device on her shaved head and switched it on, it was as though she ceased to exist. Even closed, her eyes saw blinding fire, the stench of burning hair filled her nose, her ears throbbed to breaking with a shrill siren, and every nerve in her body was cut by a blunt blade. The pain smothered her in its brutality, making a mockery of sense and time. And with a flick of a switch, it was all gone, a horrifying illusion, perpetrated by a foul machine on her malleable mind. Only the echoes remained, tormenting her with reminders of what was to come. After what her father had put her through, what she'd experienced of the world, she thought she could endure anything, but that machine had broken her, and, trapped in the darkness, she wept at her failure, knowing that she would do or say anything to prevent them using it on her again.

Her eyelids squeezed fresh sorrow from her eyes as she tried to recall what she'd already told them. The pain was so complete that she lost herself utterly; all she knew was that her tongue, which felt as though it was burning, was loosened by the device and worked hard to give the men what they wanted, knowing that the right revelations would extinguish the fire. Her conscious mind, her memory, her civilised psyche had been destroyed, betrayed by bestial self-interest. She couldn't recall what she'd told them, but had a hollow sense that she'd revealed everything.

Sound.

The bolt being drawn back on the door, clanging like a perverse gong proclaiming the arrival of a terrible emissary.

The door opened and dim light brought Ash's dismal,

confined world to life. She squinted as two men entered, both wearing Pendulum masks. The larger of the two waited by the door, while the other, her familiar interrogator, walked over to the desk lamp and turned it on.

Ash tried not to show fear, but could feel herself recoiling as the man stalked towards her. She glanced at the dentist's tray, and trembled as she caught sight of the curved cross.

'Where else would he go?' the hateful man drawled, his voice sour and angry. 'Tell me about Wallace. Where else would he go?'

Her gut heaved with a sudden flash of memory. She heard herself screaming out the name of the Fresh City Hotel. She'd told them where she and Wallace had stayed. She'd given him away, betrayed him. Ash wept, despising herself and the weakness that gave others such power over her.

'I don't know,' she whimpered. 'I've told you everything.'

The masked man reached for the curved metal cross.

'Please,' Ash cried. 'I'll help. I swear.'

'I know,' he replied, picking up the device.

Ash dug her fingernails through the soft leather of the barber's chair, trying to force her bonds loose, but her resistance was short-lived, and as Drawl placed the chill metal on her head, she broke down entirely.

63

They fled the hotel via the fire escape, avoiding the fourth man, the driver, who was waiting outside in a stolen car. When Ethan bundled him out of the building and pushed him north, Wallace considered punching the man and sprinting in the opposite direction, but he couldn't shake Ethan's words. *She's alive. There's still a chance we can save her.* Wallace knew what it felt like to fail Ash, to abandon her and think her dead, and he would give anything to correct his mistake.

Questions crowded his mind as they sprinted north, but he had not been able to give them voice, such was the pace set by the muscular, athletic man next to him. They spilled out of the alleyway on to Houston, Wallace's stomach heaving, his body shaking as he finally realised how close he'd come to death. He wasn't able to resist his body's spasms and leaned against a lamp post, retching with dry heaves that wrung his every muscle. Ethan pulled at his arm.

'Come on,' he urged.

Wallace forced himself on, running across the quiet street towards Second Avenue Station, where Ethan hailed a cab.

They took it to Times Square and waited for the driver to pick up another fare and disappear from view before hailing another. The second cab delivered them to the corner of 53rd Street and DeWitt Avenue, on the edge of a deserted commercial district, opposite a small park. As the cab's tail lights became distant specks, Ethan doubled back the way they'd come, and led Wallace into an underground parking garage one street north.

'Where are we going?' Wallace asked as they pounded their way down the stairs.

'I've just been told to bring you,' Ethan replied. 'I can't answer your questions.' He led Wallace out of the stairwell towards a gleaming gold Toyota Camry.

Ethan cruised out of the garage, winding through the city streets until he was certain they weren't being tailed. He took the Lincoln Tunnel beneath the Hudson River, and they stayed on the 495 through Union City. As they sped along the two-lane westbound carriageway, Wallace looked at the dark windows of the passing apartment buildings, trying to recall what it was like to have a normal, peaceful existence, going to bed, sleeping through the night, waking for work, surrounded by friends and family. He wondered whether he'd ever be able to return to such a life.

Suburbs gave way to rough parkland that was peppered with the odd warehouse or discount hotel. Further on, they came to a massive interchange system. Ethan navigated the tangled roads, and steered them off the highway into a vast industrial estate populated by huge warehouses. As they drove along the estate's wide, deserted roads, Wallace was unsettled by the obvious signs of high security: double fencing, surveillance cameras and guard patrols. They should have made him feel at ease, but such measures were only comforting if the people in charge were on your side.

Ethan pulled into a warehouse complex that lay at the heart of the estate. The man in the guardhouse would not have looked out of place in the starting line-up of an NFL Team. His tan shirt rippled as he waved at Ethan and lowered the crash barrier that blocked the drive. The metal wedge was the same as the ones the US and British military used to guard their bases in hot zones, and as he watched it descend into the earth, Wallace looked at the building that lay beyond, and once again thought of escape. His misgivings grew as Ethan drove forward and Wallace glimpsed what he thought was a sniper lying prone on the roof of the warehouse, his night-vision sight winking green for a split second as it swept the area.

'There's a guy on the roof,' Wallace observed nervously.

'I know. He's a friendly,' Ethan replied, following the driveway, which curved into a large parking lot.

There were four cars parked near the building. Two black Mercedes SUVs, a blue BMW 5 Series, and a silver GMC Sierra with opaque windows. Ethan drew into a space beside them and jumped out. Wallace hesitated, studying the building for any clues as to what lay inside. Long and low, it stretched for about fifty yards in both directions. A strip of high windows was cut into the wall on both sides, but the glass was mirrored. The main entrance, which lay directly opposite, was built of panes of high, wide, similarly reflective glass, which gave no hint of what lay within. There was no corporate livery, not even a small sign to indicate who occupied the building.

'Come on,' Ethan said. 'I could have killed you back at the hotel if I'd wanted to.'

Wallace nodded and clambered out, then followed his rescuer towards the building. Ethan pressed his hand against a wall-mounted fingerprint scanner. The machine flared with red light and moments later the adjacent automatic doors slid open.

Ethan glanced up at a high camera as he led Wallace into a security lock. Another set of opaque double doors blocked their way and didn't open until the outer pair closed. Beyond them lay an expansive, vaulted lobby, decked with planed timber, which made it look like a luxury yacht. Wallace followed Ethan across the polished floor, past the deserted reception desk, through another security lock – this one accessed with a swipe card – into a long corridor that seemed to run the breadth of the building. Dark wooden doors lay either side, cut into the whitewashed walls, but there were no windows, and Wallace felt the building pressing in, squeezing his leaden legs until his pace slowed, and a gap had opened between him and Ethan. Anxiety spawned dozens of ugly scenarios that all ended with him and Ash covered in blood, being wrapped in a plastic sheet. With each nightmare, his legs moved more slowly, until he was reluctantly forcing himself forward by inches, creeping along the maple wood floor, propelled by the thought that he would rather die next to Ash than live in the knowledge that he had failed her.

Ethan stopped and opened one of the doors. 'In here,' he said, indicating the room that lay beyond.

When Wallace reached the doorway, his legs instinctively went into reverse, trying to carry him away from the danger that lay beyond.

Standing inside a large, windowless conference room was Pendulum's father, Steven Byrne.

64

Wallace felt heavy hands at his back, and Ethan pushed him forward, forcing him into the room. Steven Byrne stood halfway along a twenty-four-place conference table which was flanked by high-backed leather chairs. Max Byrne's father watched Wallace, who fidgeted anxiously as Ethan shut and locked the door behind them. Directly opposite Steven sat a black man whose stony face was covered with grey-flecked stubble. Both men wore the same black uniform as Ethan.

Steven Byrne said nothing as he approached Wallace. His boots made no sound as they moved across the thick carpet. Wallace trembled, and stepped back until he collided with the wall, his mind struggling to process the fact that he was finally going to die. This was the man who, more than anyone on earth, had reason to want him dead. As he neared, Wallace noticed that time had taken its toll on Steven. His lean face looked gaunt, his eyes buried deep inside his head, behind dark, troubled shadows, and even his once jet-black hair was marred by flashes of white.

'John Wallace,' Steven began, his deep voice so quiet that it hardly carried at all. 'Don't be afraid. I'm not going to hurt you.' He hesitated, clearly wrestling with powerful emotions. 'There was a time when I would have killed you. But not now. Now I see you're just like me. It's written on your face. You're haunted by those you've lost.'

★

Wallace was seated opposite Steven at the head of the table. The other man hadn't moved and kept a close eye on them both, while Ethan leaned against the wall near the door.

'You ever made a bargain you regretted?' Steven began. 'Something you wished you could take back?'

Steven's tone was wistful, and Wallace stared at him, uncertain whether he was supposed to answer.

'I was with my son that day in Twin Lakes. I read Agent Ash's report. I was the second man she saw,' Steven revealed. 'I falsified my travel documents and got three of my employees to give me a false alibi. But I was there.'

Wallace felt his stomach twist into a knot: a confession was dangerous. Steven wouldn't be telling him his secrets if he planned to let him live. He glanced at Ethan, whose sombre features gave nothing away.

'Max called me while my ex-wife and I were being interviewed by the Feds, by Agent Alvarez. He asked for my help with the final stage of coding. I offered him a deal, my help in return for a promise to leave the Foundation, to exile himself to some foreign country and live out his life in anonymity.'

Tears welled in Steven's eyes, but he didn't give in to them.

'I didn't know what he was going to do to those agents in California. He told me he had a way to make sure they'd never track him down. I didn't know!' Steve slammed his palm against the table and took a moment to compose himself.

'And yet in some way I did,' he admitted at last. 'I didn't know exactly how, but I knew it would be violent. I've always known. You don't have kids, or much in the way of family, but you must have had friends. You ever had a bad one? Someone you make excuses for? Someone whose behaviour you look away from because it's too ugly for you to confront? Imagine if that was your son.' Steven's voice faltered. 'He was always different. It was like there were two people sharing his body, one happy, the boy we'd birthed, the other, something else. Something malevolent. I should have been there . . .' He trailed off. 'You understand regret. I read your witness statement. I know what happened to Constance. I know what my boy did.'

Wallace felt his throat swell with sorrow, but he held Steven's gaze.

'There's nothing we can do about the past. But it defines our future. Unless we're strong. But I wasn't strong,' Steven confided. 'After you . . .' He hesitated, his eyes suddenly flashing with anger. 'I wanted to tear it all down. See it all burn. They came to me. Ethan, Mike, Craig. They asked me to help them do something good, to honour his memory. I agreed. I was angry. I couldn't see the danger that was staring me in the face. What do you know about the Foundation?'

Wallace shook his head.

'It's an underground group. It was born in Max's unit.'

Wallace reached into his pocket and produced the photo he'd found in Mike Rosen's journal. He pushed it across the table, and saw Steven's eyes cloud with sadness as he studied the picture.

'That man there,' Steven pointed at Smokie. 'Craig Weathers. You'll know him as Smokie. He was the one who started it. He wasn't like the others. He came from the street. A career criminal. He joined the Army under duress, because a judge gave him no other option. But he has an aptitude for killing, and he excelled. The Army never realised what they'd done, what poison he was spreading. See, Smokie's sharp, and it didn't take him long to figure out that ideas are like a virus, that once they're out in the world, they take on a life of their own. And his idea was simple: that the world is a hell-hole of violence and iniquity because too much wealth is concentrated in the hands of too few. His comrades had travelled the world using thousand-dollar guns to blow peasants out of their fifty-cent shoes. They saw Smokie as some kind of visionary Robin Hood and started meeting and organising. They were almost caught when the unit commander found some of Smokie's literature, but Max said it was his and took the rap.'

Wallace glanced at Ethan, who nodded.

'And so Smokie continued. Every man in that photograph was a member of the Foundation,' Steven revealed. 'And they've recruited many more. A secret army in the military, the intelligence agencies, government, preparing themselves for the day when they can bring down the system.'

'What's this got to do with me?' Wallace asked.

'When Max found out what happened to his sister, he asked Smokie for help,' Steven replied. 'None of them had forgotten the sacrifice Max had made, taking the fall for them, so they agreed to help him take his revenge. They used the trust fund I'd established to finance the operation. Smokie said it was a trial run, a test of their capabilities. They used their intelligence assets here, in the UK and the other countries to help Max track you all down, to help him . . .' Steven hesitated. 'To help him murder. Smokie treated it like a military exercise. You were a sideshow. A warm-up to the main event.'

Wallace looked at Ethan, who couldn't hold his gaze. 'You knew? When we came to see you at the Cromwell Center, you knew?'

'You were a target,' Ethan replied, finally looking up. 'You were the enemy. That's all I knew.'

'Smokie got himself arrested on trumped-up charges so he could get to you in Rikers, but you survived, and you . . .' Steven took a long breath. 'You stopped Max.'

He looked round the room, taking a moment to compose himself.

'Smokie told me he was going to force the government to

regulate the internet, to end the era of anonymity, bring order to the Wild West. He said it was a way to honour Erin's memory. I agreed to finance them, to give them access to Erimax's security software.'

Steven shook his head and sighed.

'I regret doing that with all my heart. Smokie's people rewrote my anti-virus software so that it mined people's computers, revealing whatever dark secrets they had concealed on their hard drives. It's the sort of thing foreign governments have done to high-profile individuals for years – chief executives, politicians, presidential candidates – but my modified software enabled us to do it on an industrial scale. He's using that information to blackmail people to force the Online Security Act into law. When I found out he'd started killing people who refused to cooperate, I tried to stop him, tried to get the other members of the Foundation to listen. Smokie despises me for it. He called me a traitor and said that when it came down to it, I love my money more than the memory of my children. He cut me off. Ethan was the only one. The rest follow him blindly. Ethan agreed to stay with Smokie, to become a double agent. That's how we know Ash is still alive.'

'Where is she?' Wallace asked.

'I don't know,' Ethan replied. 'Smokie's paranoid. He doesn't trust people at the best of times, and I think he suspects me. I only know the order he's given: she's not to die until he has you.'

'Why? Why does he want me?'

'When they came for you in Afghanistan, what did you think?' Steven asked. 'Who did you think was behind it?'

Wallace lowered his gaze as he replied. 'You.'

'He knows if he kills me my estate, all the money he's using, my technology, everything gets parcelled up and given to charity. But if he frames me for your death, I'd go to jail and he'd find a way to rule my business unchallenged. Nobody would ever question me having a motive to kill you, and I've got the means to reach you anywhere in the world. So he made your attempted assassination as loud and expensive as possible. Like I said, he's sharp. He's also malignant. He took it as a personal affront that you killed . . .' Steven trailed off. 'That you killed Max. Smokie doesn't handle failure well.'

Wallace felt tremendously awkward at the mention of Steven's son. Even though Max had been a killer, and Wallace had acted to save himself and Ash, there was no getting around the fact that he had been the one who'd ended Max's life. 'Who did they find in the river?' he asked, eager to change the subject.

'Some poor girl they found who looks like Agent Ash,' Ethan replied. 'They hacked and replaced Agent Ash's dental records. Smokie wanted people to think she was dead so they'd call off the search.'

'How come you don't know where she is?'

'Like I said, I don't think he trusts me. We used to be close, but . . .' Ethan trailed off. 'I was watching the equipment room, where we store weapons and combat armour. I knew they'd gear up before coming for you and I convinced Jackie, the guy with gold teeth, that they were a man short.'

The room fell silent, save for the gentle sound of air flowing through the vent above them.

'Smokie isn't going to all this trouble to stop anonymous trolling,' Steven said. 'He's planning something else. We don't know what.'

'I don't care what he's planning,' Wallace replied. 'I just want Ash back.'

Ethan shrugged. 'I'm out. By now, Downlo, the driver, will have checked your hotel room. He'll have told Smokie what happened. They'll know I turned.'

'Not if you say I shot them, that I escaped and you tried to chase me down,' Wallace countered.

Ethan looked at Steven for guidance, and the older man nodded slowly.

'It's a big ask,' Steven noted. 'You've already done so much.'

'She doesn't deserve to die,' Wallace continued. 'Not because of me. Not because of this. You can find her and we can save her.'

Ethan wavered. 'I'm gonna need an injury.'

'You sure you want to do this?' Steven probed.

Ethan nodded. 'I have to set things right.'

'Tyrese, can you take care of it?' Steven asked.

'Flesh wound to the shoulder?' Tyrese suggested.

'Yeah,' Ethan replied reluctantly. 'And you'd better knock me around a little.'

'OK.' Tyrese shrugged as he moved towards the door.

Steven stood and approached Ethan, placing a hand on his arm. 'Find her,' he said. 'But be careful.'

Ethan nodded and followed Tyrese out of the room.

When they were gone, Steven returned to the table and eyeballed Wallace as he slid into his seat. They sat silently, watching each other.

'I've got to ask you something,' Steven said at last. 'Did you have to shoot him?' His eyes were glistening, tormenting Wallace with memories of what he'd done.

'He'd have killed us both,' he replied flatly.

Steven wiped his eyes and nodded sadly.

'You must be tired,' he said in an artificially formal tone. 'I'll show you somewhere you can rest.'

Wallace followed Steven's lead and rose from his chair. His legs felt weak and unsteady and his heart was thundering in his chest, trying to keep pace with the thoughts racing through his mind. There were so many questions, so many implications of

what he'd just learned, but the one that troubled him most, as
Steven led him from the room, was that his life was now in the
hands of a man whose children he had killed.

65

Tyrese took Ethan into one of the basement plant rooms and used a suppressed Sig Sauer P239 to drill a hole in his left shoulder. The bullet tore into his black jacket and cut a ragged wound through the fleshy ball of muscle above his bicep. Ethan retched and thought he might be sick, but Tyrese took his mind off the pain with a couple of hard slaps to the face, which brought his cheeks up in ripe bruises.

Tyrese Bishop had served with Steven Byrne in the First, and was fiercely loyal to his wealthy friend. If Steven had asked Tyrese to shoot him in the skull, Ethan had little doubt he'd already be dead, but thankfully, after the slaps, the big man offered his hand.

'Nothing personal,' he said, giving Ethan a firm handshake. 'Be careful with Smokie. He ain't right in the head.'

He steered Ethan through the building, and by the time they hit the cold night air, the searing agony had faded to a painful throb. Tyrese wished him good luck before retreating inside, leaving Ethan alone to place a call to Smokie. Feigning a frantic tone, Ethan used the code they reserved for unsecure lines, and arranged to meet.

As he steered the Camry north along Amsterdam Avenue, navigating Manhattan's sparse pre-dawn traffic, Ethan thought about Tyrese's diagnosis. Smokie wasn't right in the head. Ethan hadn't noticed it when they'd first served together in the Rangers, and he'd naively thought that Smokie's tough exterior concealed a decent man.

Ethan came from North Carolina, and his people had a long tradition of military service. He'd been given his first shotgun for his eighth birthday and knew how to stalk game by the age of twelve. For him, the Army hadn't just been a job, it had been a very real manifestation of his love of America, a sacrifice he bore so that others could enjoy the rights and privileges that made it the most incredible nation on Earth. Ethan had always assumed that his comrades were motivated by variations on that theme, and his positive prejudice had tainted his ability to understand Smokie.

Even after his discharge Ethan hadn't realised the true nature of the man leading the Foundation, because he'd taken the job at the Cromwell Center to help sell Max's deception, to give him an unassailable alibi. Ethan hadn't been exposed to Smokie as he'd built the Foundation, recruiting new members and creating a private army that was embedded in powerful institutions across the globe. Only Smokie knew how far it extended, and when Ethan finally emerged from the Cromwell Center and rejoined the operation, he realised that he was witnessing the creation of something truly terrifying.

Smokie had fooled them all. His tough exterior didn't conceal a decent man. It strained to hide the true horror of what he was: a ruthless psychopath who had taken a simple, undeniable platitude – equality – and used it to garner support from people who were too idealistic to recognise the darkness that lay at his heart. They'd all believed that his upbringing, his rise from the streets, his understanding of real poverty gave him an unassailable claim to be the voice of the Foundation, but looking back he'd used the facade of authenticity to beat down rivals and cement his position. And now only he knew the full extent of the

Foundation's reach, and, like the dictators they'd so often mobilised against, no one individual or cell could see the whole picture, making it impossible for a rival to emerge.

Once he'd started to have doubts about Smokie's true agenda, Ethan had questioned why the Foundation had devoted its resources to Max Byrne's personal vendetta, and found himself wondering whether Smokie might have recognised the opportunity it presented. Ethan and Mike probably had the next strongest claims to leadership, and exiling them to the Cromwell Center for the duration of Max's operation was a strategic masterstroke. It seemed altruistic, but supporting their former comrade took his two biggest rivals off the board while he consolidated his power.

Ethan had seen Smokie's true face when he'd received news of Mike Rosen's death. This was a man who'd served with him, who'd helped him start the Foundation, one of their brothers who deserved their honour and respect, but Smokie had barely skipped a beat and immediately mobilised to cover up Rosen's identity and set another team to work tracking down Wallace. When Ethan had read about the hanging of the British journalist, Sylvia Greene, he'd challenged Smokie and the man's reaction had confirmed his suspicions that the Foundation was involved. Ethan was glad he'd chosen to side with Steven Byrne, who had also come to regret his decision to give Smokie assistance.

Ethan had felt relief killing the two men in Wallace's hotel room. Their deaths had brought his double life to an end, and he would no longer have to suppress the constant fear that he'd be discovered. The stress of facing Smokie, knowing how the violent man would react to betrayal, had been almost too much to bear. Now, wounded and exhausted, he was returning to the viper's pit, having killed two of his lieutenants. Ethan knew he couldn't afford to give anything away. *One last mission*, he told himself. *One last dance with the devil and you can put things right.*

★

Beneath his jacket, Ethan could feel his T-shirt was sodden with blood, but he ignored the pain of the wound and resisted the urge to apply compression. A grotesque mess would help sell his story. He slowed as he passed the large stone school that lay to his east and made a right turn on to 141st Street, continuing for a couple of blocks before pulling into a parking spot outside the Mobilisation Initiative. Born of Smokie's genius, the Mobilisation Initiative was a charity he'd established that gave the Foundation cover for its operations in the US and overseas. He'd talked Steven Byrne into financing the organisation with an eighty-million-dollar donation, some of which had gone towards the purchase of the four-storey stone slab building on the corner of Convent Avenue, opposite St Luke's Church. The rest of the world had swallowed the feel-good tale of a former gang member turned military hero who'd started a transformational charity that lived up to its motto, 'Working for a better world'. It was sufficiently bland and wide-ranging to cover almost any activity in every corner of the globe, giving the Foundation a presence wherever it needed one.

Ethan staggered out of the Camry and crossed the sidewalk, before grabbing hold of the cold metal handrail and pulling himself up the stone steps. The world took on a distant, airy feel as he neared the main entrance and he wondered whether it was a symptom of his wound, or the result of stress. If Smokie didn't buy his story, he had no illusions about what would happen. He punched the entry code into the keypad beside the double doors and they slid open, allowing him to cross the small lobby and take the elevator up to the fourth floor of the silent, deserted building.

The elevator released him into a small reception area where the bright faces of myriad children beamed down at him from framed photos lining the wall. Ethan smiled darkly, marvelling at the ease with which Smokie had created an illusion of benevolence. He staggered down the corridor towards the executive offices, aware that his sodden jacket was dripping a trail of blood along the carpeted floor. Little crimson splashes that might signal to others that the charity was not all it seemed.

He slowed as he approached Smokie's office, which lay at the very end of the corridor. He could hear muffled voices as he neared, and trod silently as he drew up to the closed door. He placed his hands on the frame, ignoring the stab of pain that radiated from his shoulder as he pressed his ear against the door.

'They were both drilled at close range.'

Ethan recognised Downlo's voice.

'I'm gonna need someone to cover Jackie's load.' Smokie's deep, drawling voice was unmistakable. If he was grieving for Jackie, he was keeping his feelings buried deep. 'I'll keep pressing the Bureau bitch for something on Wallace. She ain't got no fight left in her. You and Deuce take on Archangel. I don't want nothin' knockin' us off track.'

Deuce had served with them in the 75th, but Ethan had lost all respect for his former comrade, who seemed incapable of doing anything other than blindly following Smokie. Deuce was a cut above Smokie's gang bangers, and if he was being tasked with a job, it would have to be important.

Ethan became aware that Smokie and Downlo had fallen silent, and thought he could sense movement on the other side of the door. If they caught him listening to their conversation . . .

He reached for the handle and fell against the door, tumbling into the room for added effect. He collided with Downlo, who immediately frisked him, checking for a potential threat to their leader.

'Fuck, man!' Downlo exclaimed. 'You're bleedin' everywhere.'

Smokie was leaning against his huge desk. 'Why didn't you say you'd been shot?' he asked angrily.

'I didn't think,' Ethan replied. 'I fucked up. It's been a long night,' he added, collapsing into one of the two leather couches that dominated Smokie's large office.

'Call the doc, tell him we're sending him some more business,' Smokie instructed Downlo, who immediately produced his cell phone. 'What the fuck happened?'

'He shot Jackie and BB before I could get to him. We fought but he clipped me and then ran. I chased him down, but the man moves. I tracked him west, tried to tail him, but he's sharp. He changed cabs, then hit the subway. I couldn't keep up, and the bleeding got so bad it started to draw attention. That's when I called you.'

Ethan could feel Smokie's intense gaze upon him.

'Yeah, Doc,' Downlo spoke into his phone. 'Yeah, I know what time it is. We got a casualty. Yeah, I'll bring him over.'

'Shit,' Smokie sighed as Downlo hung up. 'Killing Wallace was meant to take Byrne off the board. But from what that FBI bitch has said, Wallace knows enough about the Foundation to be a threat. I want everyone lookin' for him.'

Downlo nodded. 'I'll spread the word.'

'Downlo's gonna get you to the Doc. Why don't you wait down the way? There's somethin' we need to talk about,' Smokie said.

Downlo helped Ethan to his feet and steered him towards the door. As he stepped into the corridor, Ethan was relieved that Smokie had bought his story, and glad to be leaving the office alive. But something nagged at him, and as he retraced his steps to the elevator, he wondered what Smokie and Downlo were talking about.

66

The adrenalin flowing through Bailey's body couldn't fight his fatigue, and he slept most of the journey west, his head lolling against the car window as Frank drove them to Oxfordshire. He woke as they were speeding through the Stokenchurch Gap, a steep chalk cutting that took the M40 from the Chiltern Hills down to the Oxfordshire plain. Dawn's ethereal fingers were reaching across the patchwork landscape, and the hazy sunlight made Bailey squint.

'How ya doing?' Salamander asked him.

'I've been better,' he replied, his mouth gummed up with thick saliva.

'Don't I know it,' Salamander smiled.

Frank pulled into the services at Junction Eight, and while he was filling up with fuel, Salamander brought Bailey up to speed.

'I've checked the place out. It's a detached house in the middle of the village,' he said, showing Bailey a Google Map image on his phone.

The house stood in the centre of a walled garden that abutted the churchyard, at the heart of the tiny village of Cuddesdon. Even though he was tired and wrung out, Bailey was still sufficiently alert to recognise that something seemed wrong.

'Doesn't feel like a safe house,' he observed. 'It's too central. Too many eyes watching people coming and going.'

'Ya reckon he was lying?'

419

Bailey's brow furrowed. 'He knows Terry will chop him up.'

'I found an old listing on Rightmove showing some of the interior,' Salamander continued. 'It's a big place. Five bedrooms, four rooms downstairs. The floorplan shows they're set on the corners, doors in the main hall.'

'If it's a three-man team, I'm guessing one will be on exterior, and the other two will be inside,' Bailey observed.

'Our chances would be better at night.'

Bailey nodded. 'But waiting is too risky. We don't know how long they'll keep Albright alive. Let's do a drive by. See how high the wall is, check out the gates.'

'OK,' Salamander replied thoughtfully.

Cuddesdon stood at the top of a hill five miles from the motorway. Frank steered the Range Rover along narrow country roads that cut between dew-drenched fields. The route up to the village was deserted – it was too early for even the most dedicated commuters – and they met no other vehicles as they turned on to Denton Hill, the road that snaked into the village. They passed beneath the bowed branches of trees that were rich with young leaves, and Bailey's alert eyes spied big properties dotting the hillside, hidden behind the thick hedges that flanked their way. As the road eased into a gentler slope, the hedges gave way to open land, and then came the gardens of the houses that lay on the outskirts of the village. Soon, Bailey could see a church tower rising above the surrounding properties, and his whole body tensed, knowing they were close.

'This is it,' Salamander said as they passed the churchyard and drew alongside a high stone wall. Frank slowed as they came level with the property's heavy wooden gates, which stood so tall that they obscured the house beyond.

'It's a bloody fortress,' Cullen observed.

'We're gonna have to wait till it's dark,' Salamander said

reluctantly. 'There's a pub in the village. Let's park up and do a walk around.'

Frank nodded and stepped on the accelerator. The Range Rover gathered speed as they passed another grand old house which stood adjacent to the village green. As the road opened out and the green came into view, Bailey's heart raced. Three police cars and a police van blocked both routes around the green, and armed officers stood behind them, poised for action, weapons drawn.

'It's a fucking trap,' Frank spat, throwing the car into reverse.

The engine roared as the gears shifted, and Bailey heard one of the policemen garble something through the van's PA system, but the words were indecipherable. Bailey's head whipped back, sending a jolt of pain down his spine as the tyres bit into the road and sent the Range Rover lurching back the way it had come. He cradled his injured hand as the big 4x4 was thrown around.

'Fuck!' Salamander yelled. 'I'm gonna kill that motherfucker!'

Bailey turned and saw the reason for his outburst. An unmarked car emerged from beyond the high gates and blocked the road, and two armed police officers leaped out and crouched behind its bonnet.

'Hold on,' Frank advised, flipping the car into drive.

The engine screeched and the heavy vehicle shuddered before jerking forward, accelerating as it headed towards the green. A low concrete wall marked the edge of the triangular patch of grass that lay at the heart of the village, and Frank aimed straight for it. The police opened fire on the Range Rover's tyres but some of their shots flew wild and struck the bodywork, thudding into the metal like hailstones.

Cullen's window shattered and he cried out and grabbed his side. The car hit the wall, and there was a terrible crunching sound as metal collided with concrete, but the vehicle's weight and momentum propelled it forward and up, and it crested the lip of the small wall, before its tyres found purchase on the soft grass. The car bucked and swayed as its suspension struggled with the extreme manoeuvre, but it didn't break, and an instant later, the back wheels hit grass and the Range Rover shot across the green.

Cullen was moaning in the front seat, his head lolling. He looked dangerously close to passing out. As Frank headed north across the green, Bailey glanced over his shoulder to see police cars moving, trying to cut them off.

'Fuck!' Frank yelled, and Bailey turned to see another police car up ahead, moving towards them from beyond the pub.

'We're gonna have to fight our way out,' Salamander told Bailey.

He leaned over the back seat, into the boot, and produced a machine-pistol.

'No. We're not shooting police,' Bailey told him firmly. 'We let ourselves get taken.'

'After what they did to ya?' Salamander challenged. 'Jimmy, ya okay?' he asked, noticing the state of the big man.

'I've been hit,' Cullen replied weakly.

'We're gonna get ya to the doc,' Salamander assured him.

Frank surprised them all by executing a sudden turn. The village pub, the Bat and Ball, was built into a row of stone terraces, but the car park was located down a narrow alleyway which had been cut between the pub and its neighbour. Frank crashed into the pub wall but quickly reversed and straightened up, before stepping on the accelerator and sending the Range Rover speeding down the narrow drive. Bailey looked behind to see one of the police cars block the alleyway, as three armed officers rounded the corner.

The driveway widened into a small car park, which was bounded on all sides by a wooden fence. Frank didn't slow, and the Range Rover leaped the kerb and smashed through the fence before hurtling down a steep grassy bank towards a children's playground. There were no vehicles following, but Bailey heard the low hum of a helicopter and looked out of his window to see the unmistakable outline of a police chopper overhead.

'Get to the woods,' Salamander instructed Frank, pointing to a copse of trees that marked the start of a large expanse of woodland on the other side of the vale.

The car listed violently as one of the tyres was shot out, and Frank struggled with the steering wheel, fighting the high vehicle's urge to flip. The engine screamed as he applied more power and drove into the unwanted turn, bringing the driver's side within sight of the shooters. Bullets thudded into the car as Frank fought for and finally won control, spinning the wheel and turning the Range Rover back towards the trees.

Moments later, they were speeding beneath the thick canopy, out of sight of the helicopter, far beyond the range of the police marksmen, racing on until the forest became impassable. Frank pulled the Range Rover to a shuddering halt, and Bailey and Salamander jumped out.

'Come on,' Salamander yelled at Frank, who hadn't moved.

The scarred man simply shook his head, and Salamander returned to the vehicle and tentatively opened the driver's door to find Frank's hands wrapped around his stomach, his face pale.

'Just not my day,' he muttered, blood oozing between his fingers.

Bailey could see the dismay on his friend's face as he looked from Frank to Cullen, who was unconscious, possibly dead.

'Go on,' Frank told him. 'Get out of here. We ain't no use to you.'

'I gotta get ya to a doctor,' Salamander responded desperately.

'They'll find us soon enough,' Frank replied calmly. 'Go.'

Salamander hesitated.

'Don't get soppy on me, Sal,' Frank said coldly. 'I'm countin' on you to kill that fucker.'

Salamander nodded and backed away from the Range Rover. The first sounds of vehicles and voices drifted towards them on the April breeze. Bailey felt for his anguished friend as the two of them ran into the forest.

They'd been running north for twenty minutes before Bailey's body finally rebelled and forced him to slow to a walk. As they picked their way through the ancient trees, crunching over fallen branches and mulched leaves, Salamander produced his phone and dialled a number.

'Danny?' he asked.

After a moment, he stopped in his tracks and put the call on speaker.

'—is otherwise engaged.'

Bailey recognised the voice. It was Mayfield.

'I'm gonna kill ya, motherfucker.' Salamander could hardly contain his fury.

'I'm out of your league,' Mayfield replied. 'This morning should have taught you that. But if you're too stupid to learn, come find me. I'll teach you a proper lesson.'

The line went dead.

'How the . . .' Salamander trailed off, incredulous.

'Was that Danny's phone?' Bailey asked, and his friend replied with a nod. 'I don't know how he did it, but he's right, he's in a different league.'

Salamander glared in reply. 'I left my two boys dyin' back there. And Danny's probably gone. I'm gonna find this fucker and then I'm gonna kill him. Only question is whether ya gonna be there with me.'

Bailey held his friend's gaze for a moment before nodding.

'OK then,' Salamander said, softening.

They resumed their journey through the forest. Soon the trees thinned and they came to a single-lane road. They waited for ten minutes before seeing a car; an old navy blue Jaguar X300. Salamander flagged it down. The driver was a friendly, elegant woman in her fifties with a short blond bob and a perfect smile, which fell the moment Salamander brandished his pistol.

'Get in the back,' he told her.

'Please don't hurt me,' she pleaded.

'Do what he says, and you'll be fine,' Bailey assured the terrified woman as he ushered her on to the rear seat and slid in beside her.

Salamander climbed into the car, slipped it into gear and drove on, brooding with grim determination.

67

Danny kept his eyes shut and tried not to think about the dead weight pressing on his chest. He lay completely still even though he wanted to howl with the anguish that tore through him and made his guts burn. He knew that if he moved, he was dead, so he lay, blind, listening to the sounds of the men he was planning to kill. He'd relived the moment a thousand times already. If he'd been faster, stronger, more alert, maybe they'd all be alive. He knew it was bullshit. Nothing could have stopped them.

They'd come at dawn, moving so quietly that he hadn't known what was happening until the first bullet hit him in the leg. Terry had reacted quickly, pushing him out of the line of fire, taking the volley himself, his face contorting in agony as the shots shredded his back. The old man had fallen forward, sending them both tumbling to the floor. He was sure the reporter had screamed. Danny had tried to draw his pistol, but Terry, his face white as a bleached sheet, had signalled his son to be still.

'Play dead,' he'd wheezed, as dark figures had crept into the barn.

Military types, special forces with black uniforms and Pendulum masks covering their faces, guns raised. One of them had run straight over to Melissa Rathlin and smacked her across the face with the butt of his rifle, knocking her out cold.

Danny had taken his father's advice and shut his eyes, wishing he could also seal his ears to the sound of his father's wet, forced breathing. He'd heard Mayfield roll off the workbench, his feet landing close to Danny's head.

'What took you so long?' Mayfield had asked, his voice croaking like an old engine.

'System trouble,' one of the military men had replied. 'Took us a while to home in on your chip. You OK?'

Danny had almost cursed. They chipped everything nowadays: cats, dogs, cars. They'd been stupid not checking Mayfield for a tracker. He'd lain perfectly still when he heard Mayfield's feet scuffing against the floor. A moment later, there had been a sudden pressure, and Terry had groaned. Danny had risked exposure and cracked his right eye open to see Mayfield pulling a chisel from his father's back. Terry's face was frozen in anger and his empty eyes seemed to be staring accusingly.

Danny shut his eye and remained still, his heart thundering in his chest as Mayfield said, 'Check this one, and search his pockets.'

A cold hand had pressed against Danny's neck, feeling for a pulse, but was only held there for a moment.

'He's dead,' the voice had pronounced, before searching Danny's pockets. He felt his phone and both pistols go. 'Handy,' the voice had said, referring to the guns.

'We'll take the phone, crack it for numbers. There was a woman in the house,' Mayfield had said.

'Dead,' the voice had replied. 'What do you want to do with the reporter?'

'Bring her with us. We may need her to reel the cop in. I want you to call in a terror alert. I've given Bailey the address of the assistant chief constable of the Oxfordshire Police. He and his villain friends will be there soon.'

Fuck! Salamander, Frank and Jimmy would be walking into a

trap. Danny's thoughts had raced as he tried desperately to come up with a way to warn them.

'Bravo Six, this is Ops Group Alpha, I have a level five alert,' the voice had said.

Danny hadn't been able to hear anything else, as the voice had drifted outside. He had continued to lie still, convinced there was someone off to his left, another gun-toting goon. He lost track of how long he'd been there, his legs tingling with terrible pins and needles, the awful smell of his dad's blood filling his nose.

A while later, Mayfield had returned and Danny had heard his voice from somewhere near the door.

'Danny is otherwise engaged,' he'd said, and Danny, who'd guessed he was on the phone, had resisted the urge to cry out, to scream for help from whoever he was talking to.

'I'm out of your league,' Mayfield had continued. 'This morning should have taught you that. But if you're too stupid to learn, come find me. I'll teach you a proper lesson.'

There'd been another pause, before Mayfield had walked away, saying, 'Run a trace on that number. It was the wannabe kingpin. The cop's probably with him.'

At least Sal and Bailey were still alive. *Now all I have to do is get to a phone to warn them*, Danny had thought, willing Mayfield and the others to leave.

When he finally heard motors leaving the yard, Danny heaved his dad off his chest and staggered to his feet. As he looked down at Terry, he realised he was crying and mentally told himself off for being such a soppy git. Terry had been inside for most of his childhood, and they'd only met a handful of times in his entire life. He was an old school hard nut who would have been ashamed to see his boy bawling, but Danny couldn't help it. Even though they were pretty much strangers, Terry had saved him, instinctively sacrificing his own life for his son's, and it was hard not to get emotional. Especially when he'd been forced to live through his father's death and hadn't been able to do a damned thing about it.

He grabbed a large rag from a box next to the bench and carefully placed it over Terry's head.

'Goodbye, Dad,' he whispered.

He picked up another rag strip and tied it around his left leg in an attempt to staunch the flow of blood from the bullet wound. He staggered out of the barn and looked towards the road, where he saw three Mercedes SUVs disappearing into the distance. He knew he didn't have long. If they made it to the main road, there'd be no way of knowing where they were headed.

When Danny turned towards the house, he noticed a device attached to the wall of the barn: a parcel of C-4 with a timer. There was another one stuck to the metal gas tank that stood on the other side of the farmyard, and a third next to the front door of the house. The countdown read 01:29. He had less than ninety seconds.

He ran into the house through the open front door and found Katie's blood-soaked, bullet-ridden body in the lounge. He said a silent prayer, grabbed the cordless phone and dialled a number while he searched for his dad's car keys. The phone rang as he ran into the kitchen and scanned the surfaces.

'Yeah,' Sal said.

'Sal, it's me,' Danny replied.

'Danny?'

'I'm OK, but Terry's gone. So's Katie. They killed them both. Took Melissa,' he said rapidly, running through the house, into the farmyard.

The counters now read 00:58, and Danny started to feel panicky.

'They're trying to trace your number,' he warned Sal as he ran into the barn. 'You gotta ditch the phone. Go to the old lock-up. Wait for my call.'

'You be careful, Danny,' Sal began, but Danny cut him off and dropped the phone, which clattered against the hard floor.

He shivered as he thought about searching his dad's body, but was saved when he spied a key locker beside all the tools. He grabbed a large hammer and hit the locker repeatedly until it smashed open. Danny's hand whipped towards the Prancing Horse, and he ran to the middle tent, pulling at the zipper, tearing it open, before climbing into the black Ferrari and thrusting the key into the ignition. The engine roared. He slipped the car into gear and the wheels spun loudly before gaining traction and sending the car rocketing towards the gates.

The first bomb detonated as the wheels hit the road, and Danny felt the car buffeted by the blast. The next two explosions rocked the Ferrari as it raced down the narrow lane, gathering speed. When he looked in the rear-view mirror, Danny was horrified by what he saw. The quiet little corner of England where his dad had chosen to live out his final years was burning in a firestorm that was sending a huge column of smoke into the sky.

He tried not to think about his dad's body being incinerated, and instead focused on taming the Ferrari, which wanted to maul the narrow, winding road. As he trod on the powerful throttle and worked to close the gap, Danny considered what he was going to do to the men in the vehicles ahead of him.

68

For a few blissful moments he was a mind drifting without place. Then memory flooded in and dragged him down, pinning him to harsh reality with its smothering weight. Wallace felt the familiar dirty burden of depression as he propped himself up on his elbows and looked around the silent bedroom. A skylight was covered by a thick blind, but enough sunshine seeped at the edges to illuminate the large space. Built into the eaves, the bedroom was part of a residential unit that Steven had constructed in the secure warehouse. The king size-bed was located in the centre of the vaulted room, which was about thirty feet long and twenty feet wide. A large closet stood against the back wall, next to the bathroom.

Wallace hauled himself to his feet and stood still to allow his protesting body to settle. He took a hot shower and dried himself with a towel so soft and rich that he longed to lie down and lose himself within its folds. He padded out of the bathroom, his feet massaged by the thick pile carpet, and opened the closet to find a stock of simple clothes in a variety of sizes. He selected black jeans, a matching T-shirt and heavy, military-style boots, before checking himself in the mirror. He'd lost weight and his pale skin looked like it had been stretched tight over his face, as though the strain of life was pulling it taut.

When he opened the heavy, oversized door, Wallace heard the sound of a television drifting along the dark corridor, the urgent, serious tones of a newscaster echoing off the black panelled walls as she discussed the Blake-Castillo Bill.

'With clear majorities in the House and Senate, and no sign of a presidential veto, the International Online Security Act should pass into law on Thursday. Negotiators at the UN Digital Security Summit are expected to recommend the adoption of the bill as a global standard, and preparations are already being made for implementation.'

Wallace walked towards a bright light at the end of the corridor, which also seemed to be the source of the newscaster's voice. 'The Department of Homeland Security is believed to have been tasked with coordinating the issuance of digital passports, giving each and every American a unique online identity. And the Federal Reserve has already begun beta testing its new central settlement system, with the first stage of the rollout expected within hours of the bill passing.'

The black corridor gave way to a wide, open-plan living space. Beyond a glass wall lay a terrace which overlooked the Hackensack River. The muddy water cut a lazy path across the landscape, meandering around a residential estate of red-roofed houses.

Three large couches formed a horseshoe in front of the TV, and an island kitchen stood a dozen feet away. Wallace saw Steven Byrne sitting on the couch at the centre of the horseshoe. His eyes were on the TV, but Wallace suspected that the man's mind was elsewhere. Steven's brow was furrowed, his eyelids darkly shadowed, and his mouth curled down, the sense of sadness so profound that Wallace could feel it seeping into his own skin. His eyes drifted off the solitary figure to the cloud-filled sky beyond the window, as Steven's melancholy brought his own loss bubbling up through his mind, and Ash's face crystallised, her eyes so deep and beautiful, her skin so soft and warm, that he would have given every remaining instant of his life just to hold her for one more moment.

'It doesn't get any easier.' Steven's voice blew the memory away.

Wallace turned and saw familiar grief on the man's face.

'They say time heals, but they're wrong,' Steven continued, switching off the TV. 'You might pretend, force yourself back into the world, but every now and again something will remind you of them, and you're right back there, remembering what was, and getting all caught up in what might have been.'

He looked down at the floor as he sought to master his emotions.

'There isn't a day that goes by that I don't wish I could take back what I did,' Wallace said. He crossed the room and lowered himself into the soft plush leather of the couch to the right of Steven. 'I think about her . . . Connie . . . and now Christine . . . Agent Ash . . .'

Steven nodded and smiled sadly. 'It's the regret, right? All the things you didn't do, the words you didn't say. I wonder what would have happened if I'd been a better dad. If I'd spent time with my kids, instead of chasing fortune. Erin was sick, she was so, so sad, and I never even noticed.'

'I'm . . .' Wallace tried, choking on the words. 'I'm so sorry,' he managed finally. 'I wish I could rewrite the past, undo what I did.'

'If it hadn't been you, it would have been the others,' Steven replied. 'I should never have let things get that bad. I should've been there for her.'

Silence crowded in, and Wallace sat watching his mournful host and marvelled at the cruel irony of the connection he had with this man. Meeting someone who shared his heavy grief didn't make his burden any lighter, but that was the point; he didn't deserve relief, he needed to feel more pain, and Steven's losses added to his load. There was sick satisfaction to be found in the heaviness. The weight was a gift. It was his due.

'I read your emails,' Steven said softly. 'Your friends Bailey and Ash think you went to Afghanistan to die.'

Wallace wasn't surprised by the revelation. He'd learned from bitter experience that nothing digital was safe. He nodded slowly. 'Maybe,' was all he could say.

'I've got my exit planned. I just wanted to do one good thing before I went. One thing to make up for all I've done wrong. Something good I could point to, something for Erin, for Max. To make sure this never happens to another family . . .' Steven's voice cracked and he fell silent for a few moments, then began to speak once more.

'I knew Smokie was bad news, but I was so desperate, I looked away from his flaws, hoping things would work out, even though deep down I knew I was being used. I could see it in his eyes. All he wanted was my money and the power it gave him. He told me whatever I needed to hear, just so he could get his hands on it.'

'Can't we grab him, force him to tell us where she is, what he has planned?' Wallace asked.

Steven shook his head. 'You've met him. He's a psychopath in the truest sense of the word. He cares about no one and nothing. Men like him don't break. He'd die to prove a point.'

'Why didn't you walk away?' Wallace asked. 'When you found out he wasn't being straight.'

Steven sighed. 'Because I believe in what we're doing. If I can just stop him, and whatever he has planned, the Blake-Castillo initiative will make the world a better place. Would you have said the things you did if people had known who you were?'

Wallace flushed with shame at the thought of the words that had helped drive Erin Byrne to suicide. He shook his head.

'I should have lobbied, pushed for change, but I know that for every dollar you spend, someone else is spending two trying to keep things the way they are,' Steven said. 'Smokie convinced me this was the only way to be sure. But I never signed up for murder.' He hesitated. 'You ever get the feeling that you can't stop making bad decisions? Like something inside you is broken?'

'All the time.' Wallace tipped his head in agreement. 'I can't remember when I didn't feel like something was wrong with me.'

'Afghanistan?' Steven suggested. 'I read the Masterton Inquiry report that looked into the shooting incident. You were set up to fail, but you still took on the fight.'

'I had to. I saw those kids . . . someone needed to be held responsible.'

'Captain Nash?' Steven said, surprising Wallace with his detailed knowledge.

'He should never have been commanding the assault platoon. It was hubris.'

'He knew it,' Steven remarked. 'At least that would be my guess.'

'There was an FBI agent Ash put me in touch with,' Wallace observed. 'Maybe we could get him to help with the search?'

'And how do you know he's on the level?' Steven challenged. 'Even if he is, what do you think would happen when Smokie got wind of a Bureau operation? His guys shot up a street in broad daylight, killed a couple of US Marshals. You think your G-Man would be safe? If you want Agent Ash back, our best chance is to find her ourselves.'

'Don't you have anyone close to him? Someone who might know where she is?'

'Ethan's as good as I've got. Smokie's smart. He uses the same methods as a terror group. No one sees the full picture but him. I'm guessing he wouldn't have given Ash to any of the ex-military recruits or his Ranger buddies. Some of them might have had a problem kidnapping an FBI agent. He's been picking up activists from colleges, the Occupy Movement, Anonymous, for low-level grunt work, but something like this would be too heavy for them. My guess is he's put his gang bangers on it.'

Wallace thought about his time in Rikers, and the vicious men who'd tried to help Smokie kill him, and immediately regretted it as he pictured them hurting Ash.

'The guy Ethan shot, the one with no teeth,' he began.

'Jackson Rowe,' Steven interjected. 'He was one of Smokie's most trusted street bosses.'

'I went to see my old cellmate. He told me Smokie and his crew hang out at a club in Harlem; the Bunker. I checked it out, saw Jackson going inside. You ever heard of it?'

Steven shook his head. 'Like I said, Smokie keeps everything separate. I've tried surveillance, but his countermeasures are state of the art.'

He produced his cell phone and dialled. 'Ty? Yeah. John has a lead. Get the car ready. And get hold of Pope. We may need him.' He hung up and got to his feet. 'We're going to go check this place out. You make yourself at—'

'I'm coming,' Wallace interrupted. 'She's my friend. I'm not leaving her to someone else.'

Steven nodded. 'Fine. We go in five.'

69

The sound of the phone woke Ethan, pulling him out of a nightmare that had him trapped in the Cromwell Center, surrounded by the poor, troubled inmates. He opened his eyes to find himself topless, lying in a small treatment room built in the basement of a brownstone Harlem block. It belonged to Caleb Perry, a quiet, gentle man, who'd served as their unit medic. Smokie had financed his community clinic, which offered free medical care to local people, on the condition that the Foundation could use it for off-the-books treatment.

'Pope,' Ethan said, answering his phone.

'It's me.'

Ethan stiffened, recognising Tyrese's sonorous voice.

'Go,' Ethan replied.

'Meet us outside the diner in an hour,' Tyrese said.

'Got it.'

Ethan hung up. The diner was code for the New York Historical Society, one of a number of pre-arranged meeting points they had across Manhattan. And an hour meant half that. Caleb's clinic was located on 180th, so he'd have to move fast.

'You're awake,' Caleb observed, ducking as he entered the room.

Ethan had almost forgotten how tall the guy was.

'I brought you some clothes,' Caleb added, depositing a grey

T-shirt and blue sweater at the end of the bed. 'I guess your buddy's trying to find the dude who shot you,' he noted.

The words struck Ethan like a slap. He surmised Caleb was talking about Downlo, who'd driven him to the clinic and must have been waiting outside. 'Why?'

'He's out there looking at photos of you and some other guy on a street somewhere,' Caleb revealed. 'Looks like security footage,' he continued, checking the dressing on Ethan's shoulder.

They knew the hotel. They knew the time. They had everything they needed to pull footage from any nearby cameras. That's why Smokie had held Downlo back. He'd told him to check out Ethan's story. They'd see him fleeing with Wallace, helping the man he'd been sent to kill, and they'd know he was a traitor.

'You're all good,' Caleb remarked. 'Try not to get yourself in any more trouble.'

Ethan flashed a feeble smile, but his body was suddenly awash with nervous energy. He looked at the high windows, which opened on to a well that ran alongside the sidewalk, but was disappointed to see thick iron bars made them impassable.

Downlo entered the treatment room and leaned against the wall near the door, eyeing Ethan with a dangerous half-smile on his lips.

'You guys OK showing yourselves out? I got a bunch of patients I need to see. Back end of flu season,' Caleb observed, stepping towards the door.

Ethan considered stalling him, maybe even revealing the threat he now faced, but, even though they'd served together, Caleb was Smokie's, and he'd be gambling everything on the man's loyalty. If Caleb sided with Downlo, Ethan would face two enemies instead of one.

'Thanks, man,' he said to Caleb, his eyes fixed on Downlo.

With Caleb gone, Ethan suddenly became conscious of how

vulnerable he was, his bare chest exposed to the world, his left arm weak, his shoulder torn by a bullet. Downlo was silent, but the room was full of the sounds of the city, the steady drone of passing vehicles, someone shouting in the street, feet pounding by the windows. Somewhere in the clinic a baby wailed, and a woman tried to soothe it.

'Yo,' Downlo said finally. 'Get dressed. We gotta take a ride.'

Ethan nodded slowly, acutely aware that Downlo had his hands in the pockets of his hooded top, his fingers probably wrapped around a gun.

Ethan swung into a seated position and reached for the T-shirt and sweater, grateful for whatever painkillers were in the syringe Caleb had stung him with. He felt horrible anticipation as he pulled on the T-shirt. The air in the room seemed charged with electricity, but if he felt it too, Downlo showed nothing. When Ethan's head emerged from beneath the thin cotton, the tough Puerto Rican's expression hadn't changed.

'Where are we going?' Ethan tried to keep his voice light as he hopped off the bed.

'Smokie wants us to check somethin' out,' Downlo replied. He'd doubtless been instructed to take Ethan somewhere he could be interrogated, and there was no question that they'd be able to break and then kill him.

'OK,' Ethan said, shuffling slowly towards the door, his heart pounding like a jackhammer.

Downlo stepped back. To the untrained eye it would have looked like he was being polite, but Ethan knew he was simply maintaining his firing line.

'I almost forgot the sweater,' Ethan exclaimed, quickly backing up to grab it from the bed. 'It's cold out there.'

The manoeuvre brought him within striking distance of Downlo, who didn't adjust his position. Ethan moved quickly, leaping across the linoleum floor, dodging the suppressed shots that came bursting through Downlo's pocket. His shoulder was torn, but his legs were fine, and the powerful muscles drove him forward, propelling him into Downlo. The impact sent the angry Puerto Rican crashing against the wall. Having both hands in his pockets might have helped him look nonchalant, but it was a bad tactical decision, and Downlo was still trying to free his hands, when Ethan punched him in the face. The first blow dazed, but the second knocked Downlo out cold, and he collapsed.

Ethan reached into Downlo's smoking pocket and pulled out a lightweight Glock 43, complete with silencer. In the other pocket Ethan found the keys to Downlo's customised Ford Mustang. He pulled on the sweater, slipped the Glock into his waistband, and then lifted Downlo on to the bed, before leaving the room. Heart racing, breathing hard, he hurried along a short corridor and stepped into the packed clinic waiting room. The receptionist was busy booking people in, and didn't even glance at him as he picked his way through the crowd and made his way to the door. Moments later, Ethan was bounding up the steps, the cool April air soothing his burning lungs as he put danger behind him.

The bustling city rolled by, but Wallace barely noticed the traffic-filled streets or crowded sidewalks. His mind was directed towards shaping the future, willing the universe to present him with certain facts: that Ash was alive and unharmed and that they'd find her at the Bunker. What he was doing went beyond prayer, it was sheer bloody-mindedness, but deep down he suspected he was like an ant trying to topple a skyscraper. The towering building would stand or fall irrespective of the ant's efforts, just as the universe would be unmoved by his desires, no matter how fervently they were expressed.

The GMC Sierra was a large double-cabbed pick-up, but Tyrese navigated Manhattan's streets with ease. Steven sat next to the taciturn driver. Equally laconic, he spent the journey checking equipment in a black flight case that sat at his feet. When they turned on to 76th Street, Wallace saw Ethan pacing nervously outside what looked like a gothic church. Tyrese slowed to a halt, and Ethan jumped into the rear cab, sliding on to the seat next to Wallace. Tyrese accelerated as Ethan slammed the door shut, and within moments they were headed north on Columbus Avenue.

'Downlo made me.' Ethan was shaken and disappointed. 'He had footage of me and Wallace. I had to put him down.'

'Permanently?' Steven asked.

'No. It was a public place. Caleb's clinic.'

Steven pursed his lips and nodded slowly. 'OK. You did what you had to.'

'I'm sorry, Steve,' Ethan said. 'I heard Smokie telling Downlo to stay on Archangel. That mean anything to you?'

Steven shook his head. 'Tyrese, you want to look into it?' he asked his old friend.

Tyrese nodded. 'I'll get on it once we're done.'

Steven turned to Ethan. 'John saw Toothless going into a club in Harlem. A place called the Bunker. Smokie ever mention it?'

Ethan shook his head.

'Good,' Steven observed. 'Then it's almost certainly a gang hangout. We're going to check it. We might be able to pick up one of his lieutenants and extract Agent Ash's location.'

Twenty-five minutes later, Tyrese turned on to 202nd Street and parked opposite the Bunker. The club didn't look menacing in daylight. The battleship-grey paint had peeled away in places, revealing powdery, crumbling concrete. This was a cheap, functional building that was already past its prime.

Steven reached into the footwell and produced what looked like a stubby green and black telescope from the flight case. He held it to his face and flipped a switch that activated a power source which made the device hum.

'Let's see who's here. I've got eyes on three,' he noted. 'And . . .' He hesitated, his surprise palpable. 'I think it's Agent Ash.'

Steven handed Wallace the device and pointed to the northwest corner of the building. 'This is a thermal imaging camera used for earthquake rescue. You can see into the building. Check out the basement on the left.'

Wallace held the camera to his eyes and focused on the strange, colourful image. The street and building were blue, while heat sources such as interior lights and people glowed red, orange and yellow. Wallace saw three shapes that were clearly men. Two seated in a room on the ground floor and a third in the basement. Along from him was a red and orange lump that could have been a person slumped in a chair.

'You see her?' Steven asked.

Wallace nodded, not daring to hope that Steven was right, fearful that he was. The figure wasn't moving and his treacherous mind conjured pictures of the horrors that Ash might have suffered at the hands of the men who held her. He returned the camera, and Steven passed it to Tyrese, who surveyed the building.

'We go in now, right?' he asked.

'The later we leave it, the more crowded the place is going to get,' Steven replied. 'Three against three is good odds.'

'Two on the ground floor should be easy,' Tyrese observed. 'Third guy's gonna be tricky, but I think we can manage it.'

'Ethan?' Steven asked, turning to Wallace's neighbour.

'I'm in,' Ethan replied.

'John, we're going in to get her,' Steven said. 'You think you can drive this thing?'

Wallace nodded.

'Then I want you here,' Steve said, indicating the driver's seat, 'engine running, ready to roll if we hit trouble. You follow?'

'Yes,' Wallace replied.

He was amazed how quickly everything happened. Steven distributed pistols and silencers to Tyrese and Ethan, who fitted them together, before accepting half a dozen ammunition clips, which they secreted in their pockets. Finally, Steven gave them black ski masks, which they rolled on to their heads like woollen hats.

'We good?' Steven asked.

'Yeah,' Tyrese replied.

Ethan nodded.

'Be ready, John,' Steven instructed as he, Tyrese and Ethan left the vehicle.

Wallace clambered into the driver's seat and looked across the street to see the three men roll down their ski masks as they approached the solid metal door that barred the club's entrance.

70

Ethan felt his hot breath percolate through the mask as they ran along the sidewalk towards the entrance. Steven massaged two patches of putty on to the door, before sticking the detonators in. He signalled Ethan and Tyrese to brace themselves, and, moments later, the tiny charges exploded, taking out the locks. Steven held his Glock 18 ready and pulled the door open. Tyrese followed him and Ethan brought up the rear. They moved fast, trying to cover the narrow, dark corridor as quickly as possible. This was the most dangerous part of the building. If they were discovered they'd be sitting ducks.

They bypassed the stairs that lay to their right. When they reached the end of the corridor, Steven raised his hand and signalled them to stop. They pressed flat against the walls, Steven against the east, Tyrese and Ethan on the west. Steven signalled himself and Tyrese and held up two fingers, indicating their targets, then raised five digits for the count.

Ethan took a deep breath and readied his weapon. He was back-up in case either of the others missed.

Steven folded his final finger and rounded the corner, with Tyrese flanking him. Ethan followed, and they moved into a large room full of tables and chairs. A bar ran the length of the far wall. Ethan raised his Glock, covering for Steven, who shot a short Latino man twice, once in the head, once in the chest. Ethan heard the quiet pop of Tyrese's gun and turned to see his target slump back in his chair, a single crimson hole in his forehead. Tyrese's victim was another Latino man in a suit. His curly black hair fell either side of the wound that had killed him.

Steven tapped Ethan on the shoulder and signalled the doorway behind them. Tyrese turned and pulled the door open, revealing a narrow stairwell.

'Hey.' Tyrese disguised his voice as he spoke into the dim light. '*Puede venir aqui?*'

'What's with all the fucking Mexican?' a voice called back.

Ethan saw Tyrese fire twice, and heard a grunt, and the sound of a heavy body falling against the ground.

Tyrese waved them forward, and Ethan followed Steven downstairs where they found the body of a huge white guy, his heavy frame stilled by the two bullets that were lodged in his chest.

The basement was lit by a single bulb hanging from the ceiling. A corridor ran the length of the building and derelict offices lay either side of the gloomy passage. Most of the doors were open, revealing the decay and disrepair of the adjoining spaces, but one door was covered by a heavy drape. Ethan pulled it back to reveal a bolted and padlocked door, and Tyrese, who'd been searching the dead man's pockets, tossed him a set of keys, which he tried in sequence, until, on the third attempt, the lock clicked open.

Ethan drew the bolt, pushed the door, and found himself peering into darkness.

'Here,' Steven whispered, tossing him a torch.

Ethan switched it on, and it cast a narrow, bright beam of light over a dank carpeted floor. When he stepped into the room, Ethan prayed he'd find Ash alive and unharmed. *But good things never come out of this kind of darkness*, an inner voice replied, so Ethan crept forward cautiously.

71

The kiss of bare feet on a polished wooden floor. Tiny, fragile fingers trailed along a whitewashed wall. A light cotton dress, crisp and cool against the skin.

Not this. No.

Sunlight warm on her back. A line drawn ahead of her, separating light from shade. She shivered as she crossed the border into shadow.

No. I can't go in there.

A door ajar. White wood framed by light. A young hand reached out to push it open.

Don't. Don't do it.

Her father's room. She'd made this journey countless times. From the lush garden, into his bungalow, down the corridor, into his bedroom.

Don't go in there. You know what you'll find.

The little girl she once was couldn't possibly hear the warning, and stepped inside.

Please. Please don't.

'You sent for me, Father,' Alice said, fixing a practised smile to her face.

Don't look. Please don't look.

The smile fell away the moment she saw her mother at the foot of the bed, lying trembling in a pool of her own blood, which was spreading from an angry wound in her stomach.

Nicholas sat on the bloodstained sheet, holding an old revolver. Smoke wisped from the barrel and drew serpentine shapes in the warm air. He looked pained and ashamed, much as she remembered him the day he'd sat in her cell.

Alice was numb with shock. She looked from her father to her mother, who was reaching out a blood-soaked arm, beckoning her. Horror fixed Alice's feet to the floor, and she could only look at her poor, terrified mother as her life ebbed away.

Wake up. Wake up.

Somewhere deep within her, Alice felt a scream building, and her mother must have sensed her dismay.

'Don't be afraid, baby,' Alice's mother said, a weak smile flickering across her face.

They were the last words she ever spoke, and moments later, her eyes went blank, and Alice screamed.

The decades-old scream lodged in Ash's throat as she woke. She despised the men who'd brought her here, hated the torment they'd put her through, loathed the memories they'd dredged up. She'd worked hard to suppress her mother's death, but it . . . he was back. He'd invaded her mind, infiltrated it, steeped it in his evil. She longed to scrub every shadow of her father's existence from her life, but his raw, ugly power was still with her.

She curled her fingers around the shard of plastic she concealed in her right hand. During the last interrogation, the pain had been so intense, so unbearable, that she had dug her fingers into the armrest of the chair, tearing her nails in the process. Beneath the leather cover she'd felt soft cushioning, and then discovered a plastic membrane, which she'd snapped. The crescent piece she'd extracted was about five inches long and an inch wide, and she'd used it to slice through her bonds, all the while making herself a promise that before she died she would kill the man who'd tortured her.

The flashlight blinded her, making it impossible to see any-thing other than the outline of the masked man who crept towards her. She sat still, hoping he wouldn't notice her severed bonds, which hung loose around her wrists and ankles.

'Agent Ash?' he whispered, his voice different, mocking her with false concern.

She felt her muscles tighten, and her entire body tense. She'd only get one chance, and she could see other shadows by the door belonging to the men who would doubtless kill her once they realised what was happening.

Don't be afraid, baby.

'I'm not afraid, Mama,' she mumbled quietly. 'I'm tired, and I want to be with you again.'

'Did you say something?' the man asked as he drew near.

The scream that had started in a child's throat burst from Ash's mouth and she leaped out of the chair and surged forward, swinging her arm and using all her strength to bury the plastic shard in the neck of the masked man.

'Agent Ash!' another voice cried, but she barely heard it, as she pressed her advantage and barrelled into her interrogator, knocking him off his feet.

The man clutched at his neck, his hands pawing ineffectually as she fell on him. She stabbed him repeatedly, her fingers growing slick with blood.

Ash felt strong hands on her and lashed out, but didn't con-nect with anything. She became aware of a loud, bestial sound and realised it was coming from her. She was growling, crying and screaming as the pain of her entire life flowed through her.

A blow, something hard against her head, and she was stunned into silence, the world dancing around her as though she was on a carousel.

'Fuck!' she heard one of the men say, as he crouched beside her attacker and removed his mask.

Torchlight illuminated a face she recognised: Ethan Moore, the nurse who'd posed with Mike Rosen in the Cromwell Center, a member of Max Byrne's Ranger unit. Ash renewed her struggle. If her captors were too stupid to kill her, she'd make sure they suffered for it.

The man kneeling by Ethan removed his own ski mask to reveal a middle-aged African-American face she didn't recognise. He made futile attempts to comfort Ethan, who was bleeding out, choking on his own blood, his face riven by anguish.

'Agent Ash!' the man holding her yelled. 'We're here to rescue you. We're with John Wallace.'

He removed his mask, and Ash recognised the familiar face of Steven Byrne.

'He's gone,' the other man said, and when she glanced over her shoulder, Ash saw that Ethan had fallen still.

'She's hysterical,' Steven replied.

Ash felt the men grab her by her upper arms and pull her from the room. As they dragged her past a large dead body that lay at the foot of a flight of stairs, she tried to figure out whether this was a delusion. When they reached the top of the stairs, she peered into the room opposite and saw two more men, one of whom she recognised from the Nicholas County Courthouse as the man who'd handed her to her tormentors: Alejandro Luna.

The Nicholas County Courthouse. Her father's name, the scene of her capture, another sick joke life had played on her. Ash felt her jaw spasm and heard herself laughing uncontrollably. These men, her new captors. They weren't her friends. They were taking her somewhere worse. Another nightmare. Another place of torment. She had to escape. She elbowed the African-American in the gut, but before she could capitalise on his loosened grip, Steven Byrne brought the butt of his pistol crashing into the back of her skull, knocking her out cold.

*

The door swung open and Wallace saw Tyrese and Steven emerge, carrying Ash between them. Her beautiful hair was gone, replaced by a shaven head that exposed much of her scalp. She looked filthy and malnourished, and seemed to be unconscious, her feet trailing behind her as the two men dragged her across the sidewalk.

Wallace put the pick-up into gear and swung a U-turn, stopping directly in front of the entrance. Steven opened the back door and he and Tyrese bundled Ash inside, before clambering in beside her.

'Go!' Steven urged.

Wallace was puzzled by Ethan's absence.

'Pope didn't make it,' Tyrese said, as though reading his mind.

'Move!' Steven said as he climbed into the front passenger seat.

Wallace looked at Ash's bloody hands, and tried not to picture the horror of what had happened in that building. He focused on the road as he accelerated away. Putting the ugly Bunker behind them, he glanced in the rear-view mirror and saw Tyrese's stony expression waver with momentary grief. Steven had turned away from him, and was gazing out at the city. When they made a right on to Ninth Avenue, a passing building transformed the window into a reflective surface and for a split second Wallace saw Steven's face, his eyes heavy with tears. Whatever had happened in there, it was clear that these two old soldiers had paid a high price for the return of the woman he loved.

72

Salamander had found the elegant blonde's driving licence in her purse and discovered that she was called Sarah Hillier and that she lived in Great Milton. Bailey had remained silent, but had felt distinctly uncomfortable when his old friend had threatened Sarah with violence if she ever spoke about what had happened. Salamander had just seen two of his friends shot, possibly killed, and there was a flinty edge to his demeanour that Bailey hadn't seen in years. He'd known it would not be blunted by reason.

They'd abandoned the Jag in North Acton, and had left a trembling, tearful Sarah to deal with the consequences of her abduction. They'd fled along Du Cane Road, a leafy residential street, and had found a tiny minicab office under the railway bridge. Danny's call had come as they'd been making their way across London in the back of a knackered old Vauxhall Zafira. Bailey had picked at the foam exposed by a ragged tear in the upholstery as he'd listened to Salamander speak to the scrawny gangster, his nerves jangling as his friend's mood had darkened. When the call was over, Salamander had removed his sim card and relayed what Danny had told him: Mayfield had escaped and Terry and Katherine were dead. Melissa had been taken. Bailey had struggled to process the news. He couldn't comprehend how Mayfield could have got the better of one of London's most notorious villains, and felt gnawing guilt at having exposed Terry and Katherine to such danger. Wherever she was, he prayed Melissa was OK.

Salamander had surprised him by opening the window and throwing his phone out. Aware that the cab driver had suddenly shifted position and was taking an interest in their conversation, Salamander had clammed up and the remainder of the journey had been spent in silence.

The taxi deposited them on Streatham High Road a little after five, by which time London was in full flow. The street pulsed with traffic that moved in a steady rhythm, and the pavements were thick with commuters, shoppers, derelicts, people of all shapes, colours and sizes, all absorbed in their own lives. As they stood watching the cab head north towards the city, Bailey took comfort in the normality of the people who surrounded him, longing for the day when he too could enjoy the sweet scent of the local Turkish supermarket without looking over his shoulder. Satisfied that, if quizzed, the cab driver wouldn't be able to tell anyone which way they went, Salamander signalled Bailey with a nod of his head, and the two of them started down Stanthorpe Road, heading east.

'What's the plan?' Bailey asked, noting two women in burkas who'd just emerged from one of the council flats that lay ahead of them.

Salamander waited until they'd passed before answering. 'Danny said we should wait for his call.'

'Is he OK?'

Salamander shook his head. 'He's tough. I mean, deep down. He's got what it takes.'

Bailey was overcome by nostalgia as they continued down one of the many streets they'd torn around as youngsters. 'You remember the time those kids, I can't even remember their names—'

'Karl Roker and Dave Arnold,' Salamander interjected.

'That's them,' Bailey continued. 'Remember when they chased us down for—'

'My bike. Yeah. And when they cornered us round the garages, backs against the wall, we kicked the shit out of them.' Salamander smiled wistfully. 'Yeah, I remember. These were our streets, Haybale. They still should be,' he added pointedly.

Salamander led them through their childhood turf until they reached Pilgrim Hill, a tiny rat run located beneath a Victorian railway bridge. Less than 250 yards long, the road was flanked by an old-fashioned pub, a large brick warehouse, a hand car wash and a scrap metal yard. This was old, pre-hipster London and as far as Bailey could remember, very little had changed. When they'd passed beneath the brick bridge, Salamander stopped by a key locker that hung next to a pair of solid metal gates. He input the correct combination, and extracted a key that opened the heavy padlock.

'This place is yours?' Bailey asked as he followed his friend into a small concrete yard that was encircled by a high steel fence.

'Yeah, first lock-up I ever bought,' Salamander replied, shutting the gates behind them. 'I could never bring myself to sell it.'

Corrugated metal sheeting covered two huge arches that were cut into the railway bridge, and there were double doors in each of the facades. Salamander used the key to open the nearest. Once they were inside, he switched on the lights to reveal a trove of memories. Old coin-op arcade games were lined up against the far wall, gathering dust. A couple of vintage green fabric G Plan sofas stood either side of a table-top PacMan. Toys, games, signs, posters, mirrors, computers filled every available space, apart from a large area at the heart of the arched warehouse, which was taken up by a mint condition gunmetal grey Mercedes G-Wagon.

'Remember how we always wanted one?' Salamander asked as he locked the door.

Bailey nodded. 'Proper gangster.'

'Ain't I just?' Salamander replied without smiling.

'You want a game?' Bailey asked, nodding towards the PacMan.

'Sure.'

They played for about an hour, but neither of them concentrated enough to get beyond the orange. Bailey could sense Salamander's quiet, menacing fury grow with every passing moment, and he struggled with his own dark thoughts. If Mayfield killed Melissa and Francis, there would be no way to get the truth out. He'd been discredited and, as career criminals, Salamander and Danny would be dismissed by anyone in authority. Their only hope was to recover Melissa and Francis, or hope that Wallace . . .

Bailey pulled out the burner Salamander had given him and dialled the number he'd called from the Channel Tunnel terminal building in France.

'Who ya callin'?' Salamander asked nervously.

'John Wallace,' Bailey replied, listening to the international ring tone.

'Hello?' Wallace's voice was quiet and hesitant.

'John, it's Pat Bailey. It's risky to talk long, but I wanted to check in.'

'We found her,' Wallace revealed. 'She's in a bad way, but we got her back. What about you?'

'I got screwed, and some of our mutual friends got caught in the crossfire,' Bailey replied. 'Can I talk to her?'

'She's out cold. She needs rest,' Wallace responded. 'You going to be OK?'

'Maybe. We're waiting to hear from someone.' Bailey was about to hang up, when he asked, 'Did you ever get anywhere with Freefall?'

'No. I got caught up in things. I'm with new friends. I'll ask them and call you if they know anything.'

'We think we know who's behind all this,' Bailey advised. 'It's a group called the Foundation.'

'I can't say how I know over the phone, but you're right,' Wallace confirmed. 'Be careful.'

'You, too,' Bailey replied, before hanging up.

'How's he doin'?' Salamander asked.

'Hard to say,' Bailey responded. 'He knows about the Foundation.'

'He say how?' Salamander asked.

Bailey shook his head. 'We should check the news. See if there's anything about Danny, Frank or Jimmy.'

Bailey used the phone to connect to the BBC News website and was looking at the London section when an old-fashioned phone came to life with a shrill ring that echoed off the stone walls. Salamander reached under the table-top PacMan and produced a shiny black circular dial phone. He lifted the receiver.

'It's me.' He listened carefully to whatever the caller had to say and then replied, 'We're on our way.'

He hung up and got to his feet.

'Come on,' he said. 'Danny's found them.'

73

The sun was setting when Reeves flashed his ID at the cop by the barricade. The paunchy man pulled the gate aside and allowed him beyond the cordon. Reeves parked across the street from the Bunker, a Harlem nightclub that was now a major crime scene. NYPD officers worked to keep people beyond the cordon. A local news crew was setting up on the corner near the forensics trucks.

Reeves crossed the street and showed his ID to the cop guarding the door. He was nodded through and stepped into a busy crime scene. A young woman was being interviewed by a couple of detectives, while an older man, presumably the manager, protested at the intrusion and demanded that he be allowed to phone his lawyer.

'Detective Oriol?' Reeves asked a cop who was milling nearby.

'Through there,' the cop replied, indicating a corridor that ran alongside a flight of stairs.

Reeves walked through the building until he reached an archway. To his left, at the bottom of a flight of stairs, lay the body of a large white male. A forensics officer was too busy examining the body to notice Reeves, so he walked on, turning right into a large bar.

Detective Saul Oriol stood with one of his colleagues, discussing the scene in hushed tones, while two forensics officers worked a pair of bodies. Reeves recognised one of them instantly: Alejandro Luna, the FBI agent who'd betrayed one of their own.

'Agent Reeves,' Oriol said as he approached. 'One of the bartenders came in to get the place set up and called us. I think her boss would prefer it if we weren't here.'

'Looks professional,' Reeves observed, indicating the single bullet in Luna's skull.

'Yeah,' Oriol replied. 'We've got forced entry using an explosive charge. Two shot here and one at the bottom of the stairs. This guy you know, Alejandro Luna out of the Bureau's Pittsburgh office. The guy next to him is a gang banger who goes by the name Echo, real name Jose Lopez. The man at the bottom of the stairs is Marty Wilkes, a street player who's been in and out of jail all his life. Lopez and Wilkes match the descriptions of the men who killed the US Marshals Egan and Gatlin trying to abduct Agent Ash. We're working on getting confirmation from witnesses.'

Reeves looked up at an old camera fixed in the corner of the room. 'Any security footage?'

'The manager says the cameras don't work,' Oriol responded. 'My guess is he doesn't want any record of the shady shit that goes down here.'

'You think this is where they kept Ash?' Reeves asked.

Oriol nodded. 'Yeah. I think she's been here. I want to show you something.'

The detective led Reeves out of the bar and down the basement stairs. They sidestepped the large corpse and entered a room that lay at the head of a long corridor. Inside, Reeves saw two forensics officers working the room. A powerful field light illuminated the large space, and Reeves saw a fourth body lying on the floor, face up. He'd been stabbed in the neck, and the surrounding carpet was drenched in his blood. Reeves didn't know the man, but he recognised the look of horror that was his death mask. He'd suffered, his fingers frozen near a jagged shard of plastic that protruded from his throat.

'We haven't ID'd this guy yet,' Oriol said.

He wandered past the body to an old barber's chair that stood at the back of the room. The seat was badly stained and the arms and footplate were tangled with thick cord, the ends of which had been severed.

Reeves noted a tray next to the chair. On it lay a curved metal cross that was connected to a power source. Some sort of torture device, Reeves surmised, and he suddenly felt sick at the thought that Ash had been held here.

'Agent Ash was found last night, correct?' Oriol asked.

Reeves nodded, recalling the terrible moment he'd seen her floating in the river.

'These men were killed a few hours ago,' Oriol said, crouching beside the chair. 'The blood on these bonds is still wet,' he added, indicating the severed cord.

Reeves tried to process the implications.

'This was a rescue,' Oriol continued. 'Someone was in that chair when these men died.'

'Who?' Reeves asked.

'We lifted one set of prints from the armrest,' Oriol continued. 'They belong to Christine Ash. And over here, we've got what looks like a woman's handprint in this guy's blood. I don't want to get your hopes up, but we're going to need to take another look at that body we found in the river. I think Agent Ash might still be alive.'

Reeves looked at Oriol in disbelief. Questions flooded his mind, the foremost of which was: if the detective was right, and Ash was still alive, where the hell was she?

74

Bailey's call had come at the end of their silent, paranoid, circuitous journey back to Steven Byrne's warehouse, just as they'd been carrying Ash into the bedroom in the residential quarters. Wallace had taken the call in the corridor, and when he hung up, he thought about relaying the limited information Bailey had given him, but Tyrese and Steven's sombre moods dissuaded him. They were still grieving for Ethan.

Entering the bedroom, he placed his phone on the bedside table and watched Tyrese check Ash with a medical kit. He declared that apart from slightly low blood pressure, which was probably the result of dehydration, and the obvious cuts and bruises, she was OK.

'Whose blood is that?' Wallace asked, indicating the congealing liquid that covered her clothes and hands.

'It's Ethan's. She was with him when he died,' Steven explained, before he and Tyrese left Wallace alone with her.

Wallace stood still and took her in. Part of him was terrified that this was a dream, that he would tumble out of this perfect reality and wake in a world where Ash was still dead. He'd been given another chance, redeemed by unknown forces, offered an opportunity to be with her again. The feeling of relief, of happiness was almost overwhelming. Finding it unbearable to see Ash looking so battered and soiled, he stripped her, stowing her filthy clothes in a linen bag he found in the closet. He had seen Ash naked when they'd shared a Connecticut motel room, and had marvelled at her body, but this time he felt nothing but sadness. Her skin hung off prominent bones and the deterioration went beyond her recent ordeal, suggesting months of skipped meals and lost sleep. As he walked to the bathroom, Wallace wondered just how hard Ash had been pushing herself.

He wet a towel and used it to clean the worst of the caked blood and dirt that crusted Ash's body. He worked carefully, ensuring he was gentle so as not to wake her. When he wiped her head, which was rough with stubble, Wallace noticed that circular patches of dirt marked her skull in regular intervals. Ash stirred as he tried to remove them, and groaned as though wrestling with some dark nightmare. Wallace sat back until she fell still, and when he leaned forward to continue, he finally realised the marks were actually blemishes on her scalp. The stubble made it hard to see whether they were bruises or burns, and Wallace choked up when he thought of what might have caused such injuries, wondering what suffering Ash had endured because of him.

He found a pair of blue boxer shorts and a white T-shirt in the closet, and gently dressed her, before pulling up the quilt. He looked at her face, which was twisted by whatever spectres invaded her mind, and as grey and gaunt as it was, he was simply overjoyed to have her back. He traded the main lights for the gentle glow of the small bedside lamp so that she wouldn't wake in darkness, and made sure the door remained ajar when he left the room.

He could hear the quiet murmurs of a hushed conversation, but it stopped as he approached the end of the corridor, and when he stepped into the living area, Steven and Tyrese were sitting in silence on adjacent couches. Neither man looked at him, as though they were ashamed to catch his eye, and Wallace immediately found himself wondering whether he could trust them. Had they simply used him to get Ash? Was Steven really the one behind it all?

'How is she?' Steven asked, finally looking at Wallace. The words seemed oddly stilted, reinforcing Wallace's concerns.

'Still out,' Wallace replied, studying the two men for any sign of danger, but their expressionless faces gave nothing away.

'Probably best,' Tyrese observed.

'What do we do now?' Wallace asked.

'I'm thinking of turning myself in.'

Steven's reply surprised Wallace.

'I thought I could do something good,' he continued, 'but this . . . what happened to you, to her,' he gestured towards the bedroom, 'to Pope. Ethan really suffered . . .' Steven trailed off, before continuing. 'I should never have given Smokie that kind of power. If I go to the Feds, I can tell them everything I know about the Foundation and make enough noise to stop him.'

'The Feds can't protect you,' Tyrese countered. 'Smokie will neutralise any threat. He'll reach you anywhere.'

'We can't just sit here,' Steven argued. 'We've lost Pope. We've got no way of knowing what Smokie's really up to. I've got to do something.'

'Have you ever heard of Freefall?'

Wallace's question was met with blank looks.

'Pat Bailey, the detective who saved me, said I should look into it.'

Steven nodded slowly. 'I'm glad you felt you could share it,' he said, before turning to Tyrese. 'Can you handle this, Ty?'

The powerful man got to his feet. 'He say what it was?' he asked Wallace.

'No. He just said I should look into it.'

'I'll see what I can find,' Tyrese said as he left the room.

'Why don't you have a seat?' Steven suggested, indicating the couch Tyrese had vacated.

Wallace accepted the invitation. 'What happened to Ethan?' he asked.

The memory weighed down Steven's eyes, dragging them towards the floor. 'He wasn't careful,' was all he said.

Wallace studied the older man and wondered how much loss one person could take. He knew what it was like to carry the burden of grief, and even after so many months, the memory of Connie's death was potent enough to cripple him. When Wallace had thought Ash was also gone, he'd lost his senses, so he could only imagine what it was like for this man to lose first his children and now his son's friend.

'I appreciate you trusting me,' Steven changed the subject. 'I think, if things had been different, we might have been friends.'

Wallace was saved from having to reply to the suggestion by the sound of a ringing phone. Steven rose and approached the cabinet underneath the large television. He opened a drawer and produced a satellite phone, similar to the ones Wallace had seen the military use.

'This is a Foundation line, only to be used for emergencies,' Steven said, before he answered the call. He listened for a moment and then set the phone to speaker.

' . . . and I know what you did.'

Wallace shuddered at the distinctive sound of Smokie's snarling voice. It was a voice he would never forget.

'So Pope was your boy? Well, he ain't nobody's boy no more. You shoulda just stepped aside, Byrne, cos I'm gonna get to where I'm going whether you're in my way or not.'

'This wasn't what we—' Steven began.

'Save your speeches, old man,' Smokie interrupted. 'You think it matters that Wallace is still alive? That you've got the FBI bitch? You think you can stop me? By this time tomorrow, it'll all be over, Byrne. You and everyone like you will be finished.'

With a click, the line went dead.

★

The kiss of bare feet on a polished wooden floor. Fragile fingers trailed along a whitewashed wall. A light cotton dress, crisp and cool against the skin.

Sunlight warm on her back. A line drawn ahead of her, separating light from shade. She shivered as she crossed the border into shadow.

A door ajar. White wood framed by light. A hand reached out to push it open, only this one wasn't young, it was older, fully grown.

Ash wasn't a child when she entered her father's room. There was no warning, no inner voice telling her to beware. In her dream, she relished what was to come.

When she entered, she saw her mother at the foot of the bed, lying trembling in a pool of her own blood, which was spreading from an angry wound in her stomach. Nicholas sat on the bloodstained sheet holding an old revolver. Smoke wisped from the barrel and drew serpentine shapes in the still air.

Ash felt something hard in her hand and looked down to see a long, sharp, crescent-shaped shard of plastic. She leaped across the room, slashing at her father's neck, but as the first blow landed, he was replaced by the man from the Cromwell Center, the man she knew as Ethan Moore. He unleashed a wet, rasping scream, but the sound only made her angrier and she drove the shiv home again and again, snapping her hand back and forth like the head of a sewing machine, until the man had fallen silent.

Ash wanted to cry out when her eyes snapped open, but she bit her lip. She didn't want them to know she was awake. Instead of darkness, she squinted into low light. She looked away, nervously, wondering whether what she was seeing was real or a dream, and realised that she was no longer in her cell, but was instead lying in a soft bed in a large, expensively furnished room. She felt soft, warm fabric against her legs and threw the quilt off to see that her filthy T-shirt and shorts had been replaced by clean ones. She swung her feet on to the soft carpet and sat up, wincing as a jolt of pain ran from her neck to her tailbone. Her skull felt as though it had been excavated with a dental scaler that had left the inner bone sensitive and raw. When she rose and crept to the nearest open door, she saw her reflection in a bathroom mirror. Her shaved head was an obvious disfigurement, and the loss of her hair accentuated her haunted appearance and made the cuts and bruises that covered her body seem even more severe. Her sunken eyes were wild and deeply shadowed, and her cheekbones were more pronounced than she'd ever seen them. She became possessed of the idea that if she exhaled too much she might be able to make her belly button meet her spine, but she dared not try it in case her weakened bones should shatter and snap. She was suddenly overcome by a flash of violence and saw her dream repeated, but this time she was stabbing Ethan Moore on the floor of her cell.

She steadied herself against the wall and examined her reflection – there was no blood or anything that would indicate such violence, but when she looked down at her right palm she saw two deep lacerations, the kind that might have been made by gripping a shard of plastic. It was a dream, she told herself, but her mouth muttered something unintelligible and she saw a smile flicker across her face. She felt uncomfortable looking at the broken figure in the mirror, and backed away, crossing the bedroom to the door on the other side of the room.

She pulled it open slowly and when she slid her head through the gap was surprised to find her room unguarded. She could hear voices, the indistinct words tumbling into one another as they made their way down the corridor. Ash crept forward, moving towards a large, lit room, and as she neared it, she pressed her back against the right wall, inching closer, taking great care to place her feet to ensure they made no noise against the deep carpet. As the conversation became intelligible, Ash thought she recognised one of the voices. It belonged to the man she'd suffered for.

'Tyrese is right. If you go to the Bureau, you'll be at risk. I know. They couldn't protect me,' she heard John Wallace say.

'Then we've got to do something about it.' The respondent had a deep voice and a strong New York accent.

Ash moved slowly, cautiously craning her head to peer round the corner. She stifled a gasp when she saw Wallace sitting opposite Steven Byrne, the man whose son had triggered everything. A lump swelled in her raw throat. She wasn't going to cry over this betrayal. She would be strong, like her father. People had feared him, and even in the face of his hateful violence, her mother had lacked the courage to betray him. Strength through fear, through solitude. People were craven and their treachery inevitable. She was done suffering for others. Ash quickly concealed herself and suppressed her hurt and anger with questions that tore through her mind with the pace and violence of machine-gun fire. The loudest of the volley of queries was whether Wallace had bartered her life for his.

'What about Archangel?' Wallace asked. 'What do you think it is?'

'Some kind of code name,' Steven replied hesitantly.

Who were they talking about? Why were they even talking? Who or what was Archangel? Ash saw a double door that looked like an exit. It was located halfway along the wall that lay to her left, beyond the kitchen area. There was no way she could get to it without being seen, and she wasn't willing to risk her life betting on the fact that Wallace hadn't been turned. She retreated towards the bedroom, and as she stepped silently away, the conversation returned to a low, indecipherable drone.

Ash pushed the door closed, and looked around the windowless room desperately, until her eyes fell upon the cell phone that lay on the bedside table. She hurried over to it and was relieved to find that the key lock had not been activated. She knew she was taking a huge risk, but she was out of options. She'd given everything to Wallace and the Pendulum case, and seeing him sitting with the killer's father was the ultimate betrayal. She couldn't believe that she'd harboured feelings for Wallace, that she'd allowed him into her life, and that she'd planned to bring him closer. The memory of the kiss sickened her. She'd given him so much, and it still wasn't enough to bind him to her, to guarantee his loyalty. She'd never known real love, not even from her mother who had chosen Nicholas over her, but she felt certain that this wasn't it. Lovers did not sit down with the enemy.

It made her angry to think of how much she'd given to those who didn't care for her. She wouldn't worry about the consequences any more. She couldn't stay here with these men. She didn't trust them and she couldn't live with the fear that they might return her to that chair, to the device that had broken her. She'd been betrayed and was truly alone. Like a scab picked from a pustulous wound, that bleak conclusion unleashed an oozing stream of corrosive thoughts that seeped through her mind. She'd tried to picture Wallace's face during her ordeal, believing that thoughts of him would give her the strength to resist the torture. He'd been her one good thing, the one person she'd thought she could rely on, her friend and future lover. She couldn't believe she'd been so foolish. Trust didn't exist, at least not for her. She'd felt such anguish at giving her tormentor the name of the hotel. If she'd known of Wallace's treachery, she would have surrendered sooner. The dark thoughts kept coming. Wallace had never liked her. He'd been involved in the Pendulum killings from the outset. He and Byrne had plotted the whole thing and worked Wallace into a position where he could manipulate her, and through her, the Bureau. Her mind raced and cartwheeled with the horror of her misjudgment. Her father had been right all along; she'd turned her back on the divine and this was her punishment for being a bad person. Maybe this was a brief period of respite to lull her into a false sense of security before they returned her to the cell for more torture. The dark thoughts gathered momentum and were soon flowing so quickly that Ash wanted to cry out, but instead she activated the phone's keypad, and her eyes misted with tears as she dialled a number she could never forget.

75

The sky was so dark that Bailey could almost feel the oppressive weight of night closing in around the Mercedes. They were in the eastern reaches of London, north of the Hackney Marshes, south of Walthamstow, an area that was a mix of residential estates and industrial sprawl. Salamander turned off Forest Road, steering through a pair of open steel gates marked 'Thames Water Walthamstow Fishery'. The narrow road ran alongside a banked railway line, towards a daisy chain of reservoirs. When they were fifty yards along the tree-lined route, a scrawny figure stepped out from the bushes and flagged them down. The car's headlights illuminated a troubled, bloodless face. The only colour came from dark purple bags that sagged beneath haunted eyes. His left trouser leg was bloody and a makeshift bandage circled his thigh just above the knee.

Salamander parked in a lay-by, and stepped out to embrace Danny.

'They killed him. I was right there,' Danny said, his voice broken by distress.

'I'm sorry, man.' Salamander spoke softly. 'Ya OK?'

Danny shook his head.

'How's ya leg?' Salamander asked.

'I think the bleedin's stopped.' Danny wiped his eyes. 'Where's Frank and Jimmy?'

Salamander looked down at the ground, unable to answer.

'They got shot,' Bailey replied. 'We don't know if they made it.'

Danny fumed. 'I'm gonna get that fucker,' he spat.

'Yeah,' Salamander said coolly. 'So what we got?'

'There's an old copper mill by the lake on the other side of the railway. Follow me,' Danny instructed, limping into the bushes.

Bailey trailed Danny and Salamander into thick hawthorn. A narrow path ran between the bushes, but they still had to contend with spiky branches which scratched at them as they forced their way to the other side. They emerged at the foot of a railway embankment, and Bailey's body ached as Danny led them up the steep incline. When they reached the summit, Danny signalled them to drop and the three men lay level with steel tracks that stretched into darkness in both directions.

A dozen yards to their west the embankment ran into a steel viaduct, which led to a bridge that crossed the River Lea. South of the bridge, the river curled round a bare patch of land in the heart of which stood a large Victorian mill. The tall building was flanked by a pair of old warehouses. The mill was a three-storey, square red-brick structure and the two-storey warehouses spread out to its west, reaching towards the river. The bare yard was surrounded by mature trees, and behind them was a dark body of water. Bailey surmised that it was the stream that once powered the mill. It ran south-west and must have joined the river at some unseen fork. The warehouses were dark but some of the mill's casement windows were lit, illuminating a solitary Mercedes SUV that was parked in the yard.

'There were three of them,' Danny said, pointing towards the car. 'The other two left about an hour ago. Full of heavies. Soldiers or pigs, I reckon.'

'You think Melissa's in there?' Bailey asked, gesturing at the mill.

Danny nodded. 'I saw 'em carry her inside. I've been watching the place ever since.'

'Ya been countin' bodies?' Salamander quizzed.

'Yeah. Reckon there's two of them in there,' Danny replied. 'Including that fucker, Mayfield.'

'Two on three,' Salamander mused. 'I'll take those odds. Come on.'

Salamander slid down the embankment and Danny and Bailey followed. The three of them retraced their steps through the hawthorn and returned to the Mercedes.

'Ya got any tools?' Salamander asked.

'Nah,' Danny replied. 'I had to leave Terry's place sharpish.' He hesitated, and Bailey thought he might well up, but after a moment he continued. 'I took the Ferrari. It's in a pub car park across the way, but I've already checked, there's nothing useful.'

Salamander opened the G-Wagon's boot and lifted the inlaid carpet to reveal a concealed locker where the spare tyre should have been. When he popped the lid, Bailey saw a cache of small arms and ammunition.

'This is all we've got then,' Salamander said.

'I'll take the MP7,' Danny announced, leaning forward and grabbing the small, snub-nosed Heckler & Koch sub-machine gun. He pocketed five extended clips and stepped away.

'What d'ya want?' Salamander asked.

Bailey hesitated, studying the weapons.

'We need ya, Haybale,' Salamander observed. 'And ya can't go in empty-handed.'

Bailey nodded and reached for a Sig Sauer MPX and a Heckler & Koch USP pistol. He took three clips for each of them.

Salamander picked up the last two guns, a Mossberg 500 12-gauge shotgun and a second USP pistol. He filled his pockets with clips and shotgun shells, shut the boot, and started loading cartridges into the Mossberg's breach as he headed towards Danny.

Bailey followed the two men through the thorny bushes and back up the embankment. This time, they crept along the railway tracks in low single file until they came to the start of the viaduct. They slid down the other side of the embankment and took cover behind a small shed that abutted the viaduct.

'Danny, ya take the back,' Salamander whispered, pointing to a solid wooden door directly opposite the shed. 'We'll take the front. We'll go on the signal.'

Danny nodded, and the three of them set off across the yard, moving quickly and quietly through the shadows. Bailey followed Salamander to the north-east corner of the building, while Danny stationed himself by the back door.

Salamander ducked low and scurried along the side of the building, and Bailey ignored his protesting body and did the same, clasping the MPX close to his chest. He flipped the safety off as they rounded the next corner and approached the main entrance. The dark stream lay about twenty yards to their rear, and a little to their west Bailey could see that it ran beneath a short, narrow bridge. He was about to point out the second route into the yard when he saw Salamander step back from the front door, flip the shotgun up and fire a single blast that shattered the lock.

As they rushed into the building, weapons ready, Bailey heard the rattle of machine-gun fire and guessed that Danny was tackling the back door.

The building had been stripped to its shell, and their footsteps reverberated off the bare brick walls as they hurried across the dusty wooden boards. There was no other sound as they moved into the dark hallway, and Bailey was surprised not to meet immediate resistance.

'I don't like this,' he whispered, and Salamander nodded.

Three closed doors were set in the north, east and west walls, and a narrow strip of light illuminated the stairs that led up to the first floor. Salamander moved to the east door and signalled Bailey to cover him as he turned the brass handle. Bailey took a deep breath and tried to steady his weapon against the adrenalin that was surging through his veins. He was blinded by light when the door swung open, but as his eyes adjusted, he saw that the bare room was empty.

They moved west and repeated the procedure to get exactly the same result. When they opened the north door, Bailey caught sight of a shadowy figure and his index finger tightened around the trigger, but he restrained himself just in time. It was Danny.

'The place is empty,' the young villain whispered as he joined them.

'There's another way out,' Bailey observed quietly.

'The little bridge?' Danny countered. 'I could see that from the tracks. Nothing came or went.'

'Upstairs,' Salamander said softly, leading the way.

Bailey held his breath as they crept up, but breathing was the least of their worries; each of the steps creaked loudly, marking their progress with loud, painful sounds that seemed to echo throughout the building.

The staircase led into a wide open space. Apart from a handrail to their right, and a retaining wall to their left, it looked as though all the interior partitions had been ripped out to create a single room that took up the length and breadth of the building. Salamander paused at the top of the steps, which marked the end of the retaining wall. He nodded to Danny to join him, and the scrawny criminal leaned out to provide cover as Salamander stepped into the open.

'Drop your weapons!' Mayfield's voice echoed off the walls. 'You think we wouldn't see you following us in a fucking Ferrari? Where's Bailey?'

Salamander edged further into the room, clasping his weapon.

'I said drop it!' Mayfield pressed. 'Or we'll shoot.'

'Six of ya. Two hostages,' Salamander observed as he put the Mossberg down.

Bailey knew his old friend was talking for his benefit. He saw Danny carefully place the MP7 on the lip of the final step as he entered the room with his hands up.

'Detective Bailey!' Mayfield yelled. 'Show yourself, or your friends are dead.'

We're all dead anyway, Bailey thought bleakly. The moment Mayfield had him, there was no reason to keep Melissa or Francis alive, and Salamander and Danny would go down too. Fighting was their only chance. He'd rather kick and scream than crawl meekly to his death, and for all the panicked moments of anxious anticipation, in truth it was a simple transition. One moment he'd be alive, and in the time it took for a gun to fire a bullet, he'd be dead. It was a journey made by billions before him, and as he stood on the staircase watching his friends, Bailey felt his nerves melt away. He finally realised there was nothing to be afraid of.

He moved slowly, keeping tight against the wall, praying the stairs wouldn't give him away. Salamander and Danny kept inching apart, creating space between them.

'I'm going to count to three,' Mayfield shouted. 'One!'

Bailey reached the penultimate step and wrapped his finger around the trigger.

'Two!'

Bailey lunged around the wall and opened fire, spraying bullets high into the ceiling. His intention wasn't to hit anyone, but instead to strike terror into his adversaries, while he surveyed the scene. His plan worked.

Wide brick columns rose from the floor at regular intervals. Melissa and Francis were gagged and bound to chairs in the far corner of the room, and Mayfield stood nearby. Five men in Pendulum uniforms were spaced around the room, each holding a sub-machine gun. They'd scattered when Bailey had opened fire, and regrouped as Bailey started to target them. He sprayed two of the men with bullets, and they dropped instantly.

'The hostages!' Salamander yelled, as he pulled the USP from his waistband and shot at Mayfield, who was heading for Melissa.

The other men started returning fire, and Bailey ducked behind the brick wall, narrowly avoiding being hit. Danny rolled, and stayed low as he grabbed the MP7 and unleashed a daisy cutter volley of shots that shredded the ankles of one of their assailants.

Bailey joined Danny's assault, and craned his head around the brickwork, targeting the remaining three men, who'd taken cover behind the exposed brick pillars. Shattered brick and dust filled the air as bullets chewed their way across the room.

Mayfield cried out as one of Salamander's shots struck home, clipping him in the shoulder. He went down when a second caught him in the right thigh.

Bailey shot a third man in the head, and with only two masked men remaining, he, Danny and Salamander ran into the room, using the columns as protective cover. Their opponents were positioned behind adjacent pillars near the windows, shooting wildly as Bailey and the others worked their way down the room.

Bailey darted to the next column and hid behind it as the brickwork exploded under a hail of bullets. He heard a volley of shots and the assault on him was diverted elsewhere, giving him the opportunity to glance round the bricks. He caught sight of the edge of a torso – just enough to take a shot. He sighted the machine gun before squeezing the trigger. His target bucked as the bullet struck him, revealing his head, which burst like an overripe tomato when Danny shot it.

The last masked man surprised them all by breaking cover.

Bailey opened fire, trying to adjust his aim as the armoured figure leapt through the nearest window, shattering the glass before plummeting earthwards. Bailey ran over to the jagged remains of the window and saw the shadowy figure limping across the yard, towards the trees. Salamander joined him at the window and raised his pistol, but before he could take the shot, the masked man had reached cover.

'Help me,' Mayfield cried weakly.

Bailey turned to see him cowering at Danny's feet, his hands raised in submission. His gun lay nearby, at the foot of Melissa's chair.

'Don't, Danny,' Bailey advised.

'He killed my dad,' Danny replied, his voice ragged with emotion. 'I've got to do this.'

'Please,' Mayfield pleaded. 'I'll give you the photos.'

'What photos?' Bailey asked.

'The ones we took of Sylvia Greene and David Harris. Of their bodies. I'll give you proof we killed them,' Mayfield said, his eyes darting nervously from Bailey to Danny. 'I'll give you the names of all the people we were blackmailing, the messages we sent them . . . everything. Just don't kill me.'

Bailey moved towards Danny, covering the ground slowly and deliberately. 'We need him alive, Danny. We've got to find out what he knows.'

'Sal?' Danny cried out.

'This is ya business. Ya do what ya think is right,' Salamander replied quietly.

Tears started to flow down Danny's cheeks as he wrestled with his emotions. Heavy silence filled the room, and Bailey stood still, hardly able to breathe as he watched the young gangster's finger waver on the trigger.

Finally, Danny lowered his gun, and the motion acted as an immediate spur to action. Salamander ran over to Mayfield and kicked his gun away, while Bailey rushed to free Melissa, first ripping off her taped gag, before setting to work on her bonds.

'Am I glad to see you,' Melissa said tearfully, as Bailey freed her hands.

He glanced over his shoulder and saw Danny collapse on to his backside, his head in his hands, his body shuddering with the release of tension.

'Likewise. I'm just glad you're alive.' Bailey pulled the rope clear of Melissa's wrists. 'Tie him up,' he said, tossing it to Salamander.

Melissa threw her arms around Bailey and pulled him into a tight embrace. 'Thank you.'

'How's Francis?' he asked.

'Beat up, but OK, I think,' Melissa replied, wiping away joyful tears.

Bailey rounded Francis's chair and saw that she was right. His face was covered in cuts and bruises and his wild hair was matted with blood, but his eyes were alert and watched Bailey, greedy for freedom.

Moments later the newsman had his wish and was rubbing his sore wrists as he thanked Bailey and the others.

'We should get out of here,' Salamander advised. 'In case the last one comes back with friends.'

Bailey helped Danny to his feet. 'I know exactly where we need to go.' He glanced across at Melissa, who was supporting Francis. 'Mel, how would you feel about running a story?'

76

A sh found a fresh pullover and a small pair of jeans in the
closet, along with sneakers that were only one size too big.
She put them on and sat on the edge of the bed and waited. Her
fingers teased the quilt folds and when she looked down at her
hands, she saw they were shaking. She felt hollow, as though her
innards had been replaced by a foul spectre that infused her with
shame and despair. She realised her bottom lip was trembling
and that tears had sprung anew and were sliding down her
cheeks. She pinched her thighs and squeezed her thumb and
index fingers hard, inflicting a reminder of what real pain was.
The sensation shot up her spine, shocking her out of maudlin
self-pity. Betrayal was a lie born from the illusion of trust. If she
never trusted, she could never be betrayed. The days of darkness,
spent baking in the disciplinary cell, finally made sense. Her
father was trying to teach her that she couldn't trust anyone. Not
him. Not her mother. Only by standing alone would she find
true strength.

Weak, toxic grief was replaced by a flurry of memories of her
past and projections of the future, a jumble of thoughts, all
racing, colliding, merging, melding, mutating into a massed
cacophony of violent conceptions, beginnings, endings, the hard
middle, making her want to laugh and cry hysterically, a barrage
of simultaneous emotion that was impossible for any one person
to express. Ash put her right hand to her mouth and bit the fleshy

side of her index finger until pain silenced the mental bombardment.

As the tumult died away, Ash's senses returned and she noticed that the cell phone on the bedside table was vibrating.

'It's me,' she said as she answered.

'Chris? John said you'd been taken.'

It wasn't who she was expecting, but she recognised Bailey's voice at once. The man who, like her, had sacrificed so much to save John Wallace. So, he and Wallace were in contact. Did he know about Wallace's involvement with Steven Byrne?

'I escaped,' Ash replied. 'I'm OK now.'

As the words left her mouth they took on a truth of their own, and by the time they reached her ears, she believed them. She was OK. Just a different kind of OK. Like a snake shedding its skin, her experiences had helped her grow. More than that, they were helping her evolve. She felt nothing, but maybe there was nothing to feel. Maybe this was how her father had faced the world, emotionless, detached, his isolation protecting him from harm, giving him the freedom to do exactly whatever he thought was right.

'Is John with you?' Bailey asked.

'No,' Ash said quietly. 'He's not with me at all.'

'I wanted to check it would be OK to break the story, that it wouldn't put you at risk, but you're free, so we're good to go,' Bailey continued excitedly. 'We've captured a member of the Foundation.'

'The Foundation?' Ash asked. She'd first heard of the radical anti-capitalist group almost two years ago, when Parker had been assigned to look into its activities. Ryan Silver, the student Pendulum had hired to create a diversion at the Manhattan Regent Hotel, had said in his deposition that he'd believed he was being recruited into the Foundation.

'Pendulum was part of it,' Bailey told her. 'The guy we've

caught is going to give us everything he knows. The news should break in a matter of hours, blowing the whole thing wide open.'

Ash felt the stirring of her past self, a ghost that wanted to congratulate Bailey and express relief, but so much had happened while she'd been held captive that the old world no longer seemed relevant. Besides, she had no way of knowing where Bailey's loyalties really lay. So she simply said, 'I'll let him know.'

'Are you OK?' Bailey asked.

Give him nothing, a voice said. A moment later, Ash realised her inner adviser sounded a lot like her father.

'Chris?' Bailey pressed, his voice tinged with concern.

'I'm fine,' Ash replied. 'I've got to go,' she added, before hanging up.

The phone rang almost immediately, but she left it unanswered, and it vibrated in her hands for what seemed like an eternity before finally falling still. It started again, and with it a flood of thoughts that had one common root: *doubt*. What if she was wrong? What if they were her friends? What if the true danger lay elsewhere?

What if the . . . ?

What if . . . ?

What . . . ?

She felt as though her mind might fry with the ferocity of her thoughts, and the nagging, insistent pulse of the phone only seemed to make things worse. She longed to hurl it against the wall, see it flying through the air, spinning wildly before a violent impact smashed it into shattered pieces. But she couldn't. This was how they would find her. They. Yet more people she couldn't trust, but at least these ones she knew she could manipulate . . . command . . . that was a better word. Command and control . . . to ensure the guilty were punished and justice was served. So she bit her lip until it bled, and the doubt that had flourished in her mind withered and died. Finally at peace with herself, she let the phone ring and waited for them to arrive.

Wallace was exhausted and on any other day he would have succumbed to sleep, but today was different. He'd returned to Ash regularly but she was still out cold, and Wallace was confident rest was what she most needed. Between visits to check on her, he and Steven had spent their time talking, and as unconventional as their relationship was, Wallace felt his host might be right. In a different life, they could have been friends. They'd spoken of their shared grief, how the desire to set things right had pushed them both down dangerous paths, Wallace with the Masterton Inquiry and Steven first with Max, and then with Smokie. Wallace knew that few people would be able to understand him the way Steven did, and was drawn to the man. It seemed that the sentiment was mutual; his host had researched him thoroughly, and was intimately familiar with the Inquiry and the massacre. He even knew about Captain Nash, and was fascinated to hear Wallace recount the truth of what had actually happened that day in Kandahar. The tale of his ordeal seemed to deepen their connection, and Steven murmured sympathetically when he heard how hard Wallace had fought to try to win justice for Elam, Mai, and all the other people who'd been killed that day. It seemed to help Steven to understand the process that had broken Wallace, turning him into the bitter drunk who had trolled Erin, ganging up with others and hounding her. He wasn't inherently evil. He'd been ground down by his tribulations and had lashed out, spreading his suffering to another innocent who'd been unable to cope with it.

The double doors behind Steven opened and Tyrese came in, carrying a laptop. He crossed the room with a sense of purpose.

'I found something on Freefall,' he revealed, placing the

laptop on the coffee table in front of the couches. 'This was posted on a dark web hacker board a couple of months ago.'

The web browser displayed a bulletin board from a web address that was a jumble of letters and symbols. It was a place only the initiates were meant to find.

User: GozertheGozerian
The Foundation is coming. Freefall will reshape the world.

Beneath the text was a symbol: three circles beneath three curved, sharp teeth, like a trio of warped punctuation marks.

'The symbol is Welsh,' Tyrese added. '*Awen*. It means truth.'

There were no responses to the post, but the board view count showed that it had been read 102 times.

'Can you identify the user?' Steven asked.

'Possibly,' Tyrese replied. 'But this might not be anything, could just be someone bragging. I got a hit on Archangel, though. It's the Secret Service call sign for Victoria Hawkins, the Chair of the Federal Reserve.'

'You think he's going to try to kill her?' Wallace asked.

'Maybe,' Steven responded uncertainly. 'Her death would send markets into turmoil, but I was expecting something bigger. Smokie said it would all be over.'

'We need more resources,' Tyrese observed.

'I'll talk to Christine,' Wallace said. 'There's an agent she trusts. Maybe we can take this to him.'

Steven thought for a moment, and then nodded.

Wallace left the room and walked down the dimly lit corridor to the guest bedroom, where he was surprised to find Ash awake. She had her back to the door and was sitting on the bed. As he entered the room, he could see that she was holding the phone Salamander had given him.

'You're up,' he observed. 'Who're you calling?'

Any relief he felt that she was awake disappeared the moment Ash turned to face him. She exuded despair. Her bloodshot, red-rimmed eyes were the gateways to a lost, broken soul. The fiery independence that had kept him alive, that made her such a vital, independent force, was gone, and in its place lurked a mutilated, dangerous creature.

'I'm so sorry, Chris,' he said, sitting beside her.

She flinched when he tried to enfold her in his arms.

'It's OK,' he reassured her, as he took her in his embrace. 'It's OK.'

Her whole body shook, and Wallace heard choking sobs as she pressed against him. He wished he could take her pain away. He thought about their meal together, the feelings he'd developed for her, the kiss they'd shared, and was overwhelmed by guilt at having abandoned her to such horror. He pulled her close, relieved she was alive, grateful to hold her.

'I should never have let them take you,' he confessed. 'I should've done something. We came for you as soon as we could.'

The shuddering stopped and Ash pulled away from him, the despair in her eyes replaced by something else, a hardness that bordered on hostility.

'You couldn't do anything,' she said flatly. 'Could you?'

The question sounded more like an accusation. Wallace waited for some reassurance, but none came and the two of them sat in awkward silence.

'What do you mean?' Wallace asked at last. He tried to ensure his tone was as gentle as possible. He could only imagine how she'd suffered at the hands of Smokie's people, but he knew that her ordeal would have warped her thinking.

'You let them take me,' Ash spat, her voice barbed, her eyes blazing.

'You told me to go . . . I couldn't . . .' Wallace began, but he didn't know what to say. He could sense Ash's rage building, filling the room. How could he explain himself? Even though she'd signalled him to do nothing, he knew he shouldn't have left her. He'd abandoned her to horrors that seemed to have changed her. She looked at him with open hostility. He could see that whatever feelings she'd once had for him were now dead. 'As soon as we knew where you were—'

'We?' Ash interrupted.

'Steven Byrne. He's been financing the Foundation. It's behind all this. But he wants out . . .'

'Does he?' Ash asked bitterly. 'And what makes you so sure?'

Wallace hesitated, unsettled by her darkly cynical tone.

'He wants to turn himself in. To help stop Smokie. The only reason he hasn't is because Smokie's infiltrated the government. The Foundation has built a network of members around the world. It's impossible to know who to trust.'

He saw Ash's eyes cloud with uncertainty, before the steel returned. 'And you believe him?'

'I've spent time with him,' Wallace replied. 'I don't think he's lying.'

'Then he's going to get his wish,' Ash said ominously.

'What do you mean?' Wallace asked, worried about his friend's demeanour. Whatever they'd done to her, she clearly wasn't herself.

'I called them.' Ash indicated the phone. 'I called the Bureau. They used the phone to trace my location. They're on their way.'

Wallace backed away, disturbed by the revelation.

'Your new friend can help all he wants,' Ash added.

'You said we couldn't trust anyone,' Wallace protested, getting to his feet.

'Advice you ignored,' she shot back accusingly. 'But I was right. I can't trust anyone.'

He staggered towards the door, almost overwhelmed by his

sense of loss. His friend, the woman who'd sacrificed so much for him, who understood him better than anyone else, was gone. He didn't recognise the mangled creature sitting in her place.

'I wish I'd let him take you,' Ash mused darkly. 'That night on the roof. I could have saved so many lives if I'd just let Max kill you. It would have been better all round.'

Wallace couldn't bear to hear her talk about him in that way and couldn't stand to look at the damage he'd caused. He backed away and fled the room, then raced along the corridor, his mind spiralling out of control. The woman he loved wished him dead.

'She's called the FBI,' he announced as he ran into the room. 'They've traced her location. They're on their way.'

Steven and Tyrese exchanged angry looks.

'After what it cost to save her,' Tyrese noted.

He'd hardly got the words out before he became aware of a familiar sound. The room vibrated with the low, deep hum of an approaching helicopter.

77

The sound of muffled gunfire filled the room.

'Tell security to stand down,' Steven instructed Tyrese, who produced a radio from his pocket and relayed the command. 'They're to give themselves up. We need to go,' he said, turning to Wallace. 'I think we can stop Smokie. But if we get caught . . .'

Wallace needed no further explanation. His experiences of law enforcement and protective custody had been unrelentingly bad.

'Give me a minute,' he said, racing down the corridor. He couldn't leave her. Not like this. He needed her to know how he felt. He had to make it better.

He burst into the bedroom and found Ash where he'd left her, sitting on the bed, her eyes wet with fresh tears. She was adrift, lost in misery like a parent grieving for a dead child.

'Chris, I'm sorry. I'm sorry for everything, but you need to trust me. We've got to leave,' Wallace pleaded. 'Come with us. Please. You mean so much to me. I don't want it to be like this. I love you.'

Grief was replaced with unmistakable rage as Ash glared up at him.

'Please,' Wallace said, clasping her by the wrist.

'Love?' Ash growled. 'Don't you dare use that word!'

The scream startled him, and he jumped back, narrowly

avoiding being struck by Ash's fist. She came at him, crying and shouting curses, intent on inflicting harm as she punched and kicked his body. Some of the blows connected, and Wallace staggered back in pain. He couldn't bring himself to fight back, but knew that if he didn't do something, this well-trained, ferocious woman would put him down. Ash caught him with a punch that sent him crashing against the wall, and he smacked his head against the hard surface, the impact sending the world into a wild spin. He put his hands over his face in a feeble attempt to protect himself, but was surprised to sense sudden movement beside him. Steven rushed into the room, grabbed Ash and knocked her to the floor. She tumbled on to her backside, but quickly recovered and sat up with a fierce look on her face, as though she was goading Steven to fight her.

'We've got to go,' Steven urged. 'Now!'

Wallace wavered, looking at the enraged woman. 'Chris,' he tried. 'You're right, I should have done more. I never meant to hurt you. Please come with us.'

Ash got to her feet and leaped at Steven, who reacted instantly, flooring her with a single, brutal punch.

'You can't help her, John,' Steven said. 'She needs professional attention. Let the FBI take care of her.'

Wallace allowed himself to be pulled from the room, but when he gave a backward glance he felt nothing but grief. She cut a tragic figure, lying on the floor, her body stirring as blood streamed from her nose. She'd been broken trying to protect him, and all the ills she'd suffered had crystallised as hatred. Whatever they'd once had, the warmth they'd felt, the connection they'd established, it was all gone. She despised him, and as he was pulled along the corridor, Wallace lamented all those shared moments and mourned what might have been. Maybe in another world, they could have had a life together. But not in this one. They should have died lovers, but the fierce contempt in her eyes was unmistakable. Finally, Wallace accepted that she loathed him.

Shock robbed Wallace of continuity. His flight from the residence became a series of snatched moments. Steven leading him to a concealed exit. Their steps echoing around a stairwell as they thundered down the stairs. Opening an exterior door and creeping across a courtyard that was swarming with police officers and FBI agents. Lights shining on the faces of Steven's security as they were rounded up. Tyrese thrust into the back of an FBI van. Steven leading Wallace to a storm drain. Removing the metal grate. Emerging from the fetid pipe that fed into the Hackensack River. Clambering through mud and grass. An apartment block. Waiting while Steven broke into a car. Driving along the highway, the car rising and falling rhythmically every time it rolled over the ridges that separated the slabs of asphalt. The gentle beat sending him into the welcome embrace of sleep. Feeling sick as he wavered on the cusp of consciousness. Traumatised as he recalled the hate in Ash's eyes. Consumed by bleak emptiness at the thought he'd lost the woman he loved. And then nothing.

78

INTERNATIONAL BLACKMAIL RING EXPOSED
By Melissa Rathlin & Francis Albright

A secretive organisation known as the Foundation has been blackmailing key public figures in an effort to ensure that the International Online Security Act, otherwise known as the Blake-Castillo Bill, is passed into law and becomes the international standard for regulating the internet. A member of the Foundation has confessed to the murders of the former editor of this newspaper and a senior British diplomat. This individual, known as 'M', has also confessed to his involvement in the Pendulum killings, and claims to have provided assistance that enabled Maximillian Byrne to commit the murders. 'M' is an MI5 officer and claims that the security services have been infiltrated by other members of the Foundation. Circumstantial evidence points to the possibility that such infiltration may have happened in other countries.

'M' claims that the Foundation is an anti-capitalist movement that started in the United States, and that it has a violent, radical agenda. The organisation seems to operate a cell structure similar to other terror groups, with no one except the group's most senior leaders having full knowledge of all its members and objectives. 'M' says that he received instructions via an anonymous encrypted messaging system and that funds to finance his cell's activities were delivered by courier in regular cash payments. He claims not to know why the Blake-Castillo Bill is key to the Foundation's objectives, but says that it was made clear to him that its passage was of the utmost importance.

'M' has admitted to blackmailing influential individuals by sending them anonymous emails using information he received from his Foundation conspirators, threatening to make it public if the victim did not comply with his demands. The blackmail instructions were authenticated with *Awen*, the Welsh symbol for truth.

This is an evolving story, but the *London Record* is taking the unusual step of publishing before we have concluded our investigation. The authors of this article were abducted by 'M' and others loyal to him, and would most likely be dead were it not for the bravery and perseverance of a few good men. We believe that the only way to protect ourselves from further violence is to expose the conspiracy and call upon the British government to treat these allegations with the seriousness that they deserve.

Subscribe to continue reading this article or more like it:
What is the Foundation?
Why we cannot pass the Blake-Castillo Bill.
How conspiracy has shaped the world.

Bailey exited the browser and pocketed his phone. He turned his attention to the busy London street, which seemed to glow in the bright spring sunshine. The secret was out, and life seemed alive with possibilities. His only concern was Ash. They'd spoken hours earlier and everything about her sounded wrong. He'd tried to call a number of times, but the phone had never been answered again.

Bailey and the others had spent the night at the *London Record* office, where Melissa and Francis had worked tirelessly to put the exposé together, holding up the paper's production for the first time in over thirty years. Word of the delayed print had spread, and soon the hastily assembled skeleton staff had been fielding calls from other journalists eager for some insight on the scoop. No one had blabbed, and the story had stayed within the walls of the riverside building, as it had been brought to life by two seasoned journalists. Whenever Melissa or Francis had hit a block, Danny had been more than happy to press Mayfield for information. Salamander had given him just enough medical attention to ensure he stayed alive, and Danny had taken great pleasure in forcing him to reveal the location of his embedded tracking device, and had then used a sharp pocket knife to cut it from Mayfield's muscular shoulder. The man had screamed, but after what they'd all endured, no one cared about his suffering, and they had simply watched as Danny had smashed the bloody chip with the heel of his knife.

The story was a sensation, and Melissa had been lost in a whirlwind of activity when Bailey and Salamander had decided to leave. They'd dragged Mayfield to his feet and hauled him out of Francis's office before she had noticed they were going.

When she'd finally seen them leaving, she'd hurried over and touched Bailey's arm tenderly. 'I just wanted to say thanks,' she'd said, before being dragged away by one of her colleagues, who had told her that she had the Home Office on the line.

'Ya sure ya want to do this?' Salamander asked as he steered the Mercedes along Edgware Road.

Bailey glanced over his shoulder and caught Danny's impassive gaze.

'This OK with you?' Bailey asked him.

The young villain looked at Mayfield, who was unconscious.

'Sure,' Danny replied. 'Let the pigs pump him for everything he knows. We can always get him on the inside.'

Bailey smiled, but Danny's expression didn't change and he realised that the kid wasn't joking.

'I want my life back,' Bailey said, turning to Salamander.

'It's a shame. I was just getting used to having ya around,' his friend replied. 'Ya'd make a good addition to the crew.'

Bailey smiled and shook his head. Salamander was in high spirits because Melissa had been able to discover that Jimmy and Frank had both survived and were being held under police guard in the John Radcliffe Hospital in Oxford.

The Mercedes passed into the shadow of the Westway flyover and crossed underneath the wide concrete structure. When they reached the other side of the Edgware Road, Salamander pulled to a halt beside the towering building that had been Bailey's base for so many years.

'Thanks, man,' Bailey said, offering Salamander his hand.

His friend shook his head and pulled him into an embrace. 'Handshakes are for strangers, Haybale. Ya family.'

Bailey felt a lump rise in his throat, but forced it back with a pronounced gulp. He turned to Danny. 'I'm sorry, Danny,' he said. 'I really am.'

'It's OK,' Danny replied. 'I didn't really know the geezer,' he added, trying to dismiss his father's death, but Bailey recognised what lay beyond the brash mask of a hard man, and saw a sad, hurt child trying to shield himself from further pain.

Bailey stepped out of the car, opened the back door and hauled Mayfield to his feet. Danny gave a forceful shove that brought Mayfield to his senses. He threw a feeble arm around Bailey for support.

'I'd offer to help you inside,' Salamander called out, 'but you know that place gives me the creeps. Besides, I need to take Danny to Doctor Death. Get that leg looked at.'

'You've done enough, man,' Bailey responded. 'Now get out of here.'

He slammed the door shut, but noticed that Salamander didn't drive away until he and Mayfield had crossed the threshold of Paddington Green Police Station.

The lobby was quiet. A haggard old man was slumped in one of the plastic chairs in the waiting area. The receptionist, a civilian called Jason Lake, noticed Bailey as he shuffled forward, straining under Mayfield's weight. Jason's mouth opened and closed a couple of times before it finally produced any words.

'Detective Inspector Bailey,' he remarked in astonishment.

'That's right,' Bailey said. 'I'm bringing in a suspect,' he continued, his voice thick with emotion. 'This is Samuel Mayfield. I'm arresting him for the murder of Sylvia Greene.'

79

Wallace woke to the sound of his own name being said by an unfamiliar voice. When he opened his eyes, he was greeted by the sight of a cracked and yellowed ceiling.

'Morning,' Steven said.

Wallace remembered the house, a small detached property on Belmont Avenue, a quiet residential street not far from the warehouse. They'd ditched the car about a mile away, and had covered the remaining distance on foot, before arriving at the run-down house, set in a tiny yard. Exhausted, Wallace had followed Steven up a short run of steps to the dilapidated porch and surveyed the neighbourhood while his host had retrieved a key from the tiny locker concealed by one of the structural supports. Most of the homes on the street were covered in painted aluminium cladding that had been designed to look like timber planks, but even at a distance, the way the street lights reflected off the metal surfaces betrayed the artifice. A few interior lights had been on, but most of the houses had been dark and peaceful, their occupants undoubtedly sleeping before the daily grind. Wallace had collapsed on the creaky old floral couch the moment they'd entered, and must have fallen asleep immediately.

He sat up and looked around a room that reminded him of a fifties parlour. Lace, china, flowers, throws, rugs, dark wood, patterned wallpaper, all old, all decaying, it was the sort of unreformed place that a previous version of himself might have used in a vintage photo shoot. But not any more. Now, the sight of so many old things only saddened him, reminding him that what was could never be again, that all things passed and eventually perished. He recalled Ash's hatred, the anger, the violence, a deep ravine of hostility that seemed beyond healing. Maybe Pendulum had been right. Maybe he was a coward and it was his cowardice that had lost her.

'You OK?' Steven asked.

Wallace glanced over to see him sitting in a frayed, floral wingback, hunched over a laptop, half-watching the news which was playing on an old television. Their faces were being flashed on screen, and the lower third scrolling titles informed viewers that John Wallace and Steven Byrne were wanted in connection with the Foundation blackmail plot.

'I don't know,' Wallace replied. 'I can't remember what OK feels like.'

'The news has broken out of London. The Foundation's blackmail plot has been exposed but the Blake-Castillo bill is still going through. The legislation is going to pass. Congressional leaders say the plot is irrelevant to their decision.'

'They would,' Wallace observed. 'Some of them will be desperately trying to prevent their secrets from being revealed.'

'We've been set up as patsies,' Steven observed. 'My guess is Smokie's given our names to people he controls. Making us the public face of the Foundation buys him the time he needs to complete his mission, and destroys our credibility. Who's going to believe anything we say now?'

Steven looked tired and troubled as he rubbed his face.

'I've been trying to figure out what Smokie's planning. He said there was nothing we could do to stop it. It's got to be something to do with the bill. I've been trying to identify whoever posted that message about Freefall, but it's been a while since I had to do this sort of thing.'

A voice nagged at Wallace, telling him to keep his mouth shut, to stay hidden until the crisis had passed, but he couldn't ignore the defeated look on Steven's face, nor the knowledge that he'd been partly responsible for the man's condition. If his daughter hadn't killed herself, if his son hadn't died at Wallace's hand, Steven Byrne would be sitting in some lofty Manhattan office instead of hiding in a safe house desperately trying to stop a dangerous psychopath. Wallace ignored his inner voice and said, 'We'll have to be careful, but I know someone who might be able to help.'

80

Electroshock. Concentrated jolts of charged ions shot directly into her brain. The doctor had said that from her description of the device, it sounded like a modified version of machines that were used to treat psychiatric patients, frying their minds with electricity in an effort to cure depression, psychosis, schizophrenia, any number of reality-altering illnesses. Recalling her last encounter with Wallace, Ash knew that her sickness had been cured.

She sat on the couch in her office, feeling like a stranger in her old world, looking out through the open door, watching bodies scurrying, bustling, striding, moving with purpose, unaware that they were decaying with every passing moment, that their time on the planet was finite and that everything they did was a futile distraction from the inevitable.

Don't be afraid, baby.

I'm not afraid, Ash told her mother's ghost, *I'm awake. At last, I see things as they truly are.*

The *London Record* story had spread across the world, and when Ash had given Harrell her report, the Bureau had been thrown into panic. Like the McCarthy communist witch-hunt, the entire agency was under suspicion. And it wasn't just the FBI. Anyone in any branch of government or the military could be a member of the Foundation. It seemed that Ash alone was above suspicion, her ordeal having earned her a free pass. Reeves,

Parker, Romero, Miller – everyone, including Harrell, would have to be vetted. Teams were being reassigned and people paired with new partners, and all duties had to be overseen by at least one other randomly selected agent. Fear of what might have been no more than a handful of infiltrators was hampering the effectiveness of an agency of 35,000 people. And this same paranoia had unleashed similar chaos across the country, throwing other government agencies into turmoil. The truth was, no one knew the full extent of the Foundation's reach. There were fifteen men in Max Byrne's platoon, and if they'd each recruited one new member per year for the past five years, and the new members had done likewise, the Foundation would be 480 strong.

The doctor had advised bed rest, but Ash had insisted on being taken to Federal Plaza. She had no idea whether the Foundation would still target her after the news broke, but figured that she was safer in a public place, surrounded by people. Harrell had strictly forbidden her from getting involved in the unfolding investigation, so, unable to sleep, Ash had sat on the couch watching her fellow agents hurry around while she contemplated the doctor's prognosis that she would likely suffer long-term psychological damage from the electroshock. Ash didn't tell him that he was wrong, that her ordeal had cured her. He would never have believed her.

'You OK?' Reeves asked, leaning against the doorframe, a folder in one hand, a plastic bag in the other.

Ash smiled and nodded. He had no idea how OK she was.

'I thought you might want some clothes,' he said depositing the bag. 'I went to your place and got you a selection.'

Ash crossed the room and began rummaging in the bag. There were a couple of tops, pants, a dress, underwear, trainers and some shoes.

'We identified Archangel,' he said. 'It's the Secret Service call sign for Victoria Hawkins, the Chair of the Fed. Did you hear Wallace and Byrne say anything else?'

Ash shook her head.

'Harrell thinks it might be an assassination plot to crash the markets. She's been taken to a secure location, and we're chasing down every lead we've got.'

Ash looked up at Reeves and her smile broadened, knowing their efforts would yield nothing. The members of the Foundation would go to ground. They might offer up a few sacrificial lambs, but the true villains would remain hidden.

'I'm sorry about Wallace,' Reeves said. 'I know what you went through for him.'

Ash said nothing. She stood up and took off the pullover she'd grabbed from Steven Byrne's closet. The fact that she wasn't wearing a bra seemed to make Reeves uncomfortable.

'You sure you're OK?' he asked, glancing over his shoulder towards the open-plan office that lay behind him.

Ash could see Romero and Miller working at the closest desks.

'I'm fine,' she responded, pulling on a tight blue top. 'Just tired.'

She stepped out of the oversized trainers and started unbuttoning her jeans.

'I wanted to see if you could identify any of the men from the club,' Reeves said, as Ash slipped into a pair of black pants.

'They wore masks,' Ash responded flatly.

'Body size, shape,' Reeves pressed. 'There might be something.'

Ash had no desire to look at the past, but before she could object, Reeves produced a sheaf of photos from the folder and started leafing through them.

'Him,' Ash said, pointing at the picture of Alejandro Luna. 'He's the one who took me from Summersville. He handed me to a group of men in Pendulum masks and they smashed him and his car up to make it look like we'd been hijacked.'

Reeves continued but Ash didn't recognise the next two corpses.

The fourth man lay face up, his features contorted in horror, his fingers reaching for a bloody shard of plastic that was buried deep in his throat. Ash swallowed hard.

'You know him?' Reeves asked.

Ash recalled the nightmare in which she repeatedly stabbed this man until he bled to death at her feet. It couldn't be real. She couldn't have done that.

'He went by the name Ethan Moore,' she said at last. 'He posed as Max Byrne's nurse at the Cromwell Center.'

'Thanks. I can only imagine how hard it is to see the faces of these men, but this guy didn't have any ID, and you've just given us something to work with.'

Ash stared into the middle distance, unwilling to give Reeves anything else. She didn't want to tell him that none of the men in the photographs matched the physique of the man who'd tortured her. Finding him would be her privilege. Punishing him, her pleasure.

'Try to get some rest,' Reeves suggested as he backed away. 'Well, I've got to get to work. You know where to find me if you need anything.'

He smiled awkwardly. Ash could tell that he sensed there was something different about her, but he lacked the courage to voice his concerns. He thought she was damaged, impaired in some way, but she was improved, stronger. She knew for example that the Foundation would not have gone to all this trouble for something as prosaic as a political assassination. Ash reflected that there was something else at play, and if she found out what it was, she would be able to confront the men who had tormented her, and in recognition of the improvements they'd made, thank them in kind.

81

Bailey staggered into the street, slightly bewildered by his freedom. He'd spent the morning being interviewed by Superintendent Cross and a man from MI5 who never gave his name. They'd listened to his story twice, an old trick designed to highlight any inconsistencies in the retelling, but Bailey's tale had the benefit of being true, so he didn't fall into the simple trap. Murrall had joined them for the second interview. Summoned as the lead detective on the Sylvia Greene case, he'd sat in astonished silence as Bailey had recounted his ordeal. Every so often, the interview had been interrupted by one of a number of other detectives who were now working the investigation into the Foundation. They'd pass Superintendent Cross a note, and he'd ask a question, clarifying some aspect of Bailey's story or checking a new lead. Bailey had got the impression that things were moving fast, that the *London Record* story had become the only news that day, and was being chased down by every other media outlet in the capital. He could only imagine the frenzy of the situation room, as the full scale of the task started to become apparent to the investigative team. He was glad not to be involved. His battered, exhausted body told him that he'd done more than his fair share.

The MI5 man, a tall, gaunt guy in his mid-thirties, had said little, but his face had betrayed his dismay, and by the time Bailey had finished his story for the second time, his expression was that of someone who'd realised life would never be the same.

Bailey had been left alone while the others stepped outside to confer. Moments later, Superintendent Cross had returned full of congratulations and smiles. He'd told Bailey that he was being placed on two weeks' compassionate leave to rest and recover. He'd instructed Bailey to stay in London as he'd almost certainly be required for further interviews, which could be conducted at his home. Cross had offered Bailey a personal apology and heartfelt congratulations before telling him he was free to go.

Surprised and somewhat stunned, Bailey had staggered through the station. As word of his work quickly spread, he'd been applauded by a group of his colleagues who'd gathered in the custody suite. He'd struggled to maintain his composure in the face of their congratulations, as waves of celebratory relief swept over him. He'd listened to words of praise until he could no longer resist the prospect of sleep, and he'd made his excuses and hurried from the building, staggering into the afternoon sunshine like a man with a terrible hangover emerging from a dodgy nightclub after a particularly hard night.

Everything seemed overly bright and surreal, and, robbed of galvanising adrenalin, Bailey suddenly felt fatigued.

'I was wrong about you,' Murrall said.

Bailey turned to see the chubby detective standing beside the entrance at the foot of the towering building.

'You did well,' Murrall added. 'I thought you should know that.'

'Thanks,' Bailey replied.

The phone Salamander had given him vibrated in his pocket. He pulled it out and saw that it was Christine Ash's office line.

'Hello?' he said, answering the call.

'Patrick,' Ash responded. 'It's me. Christine Ash.'

'Chris. How are you?'

'Fine,' she replied curtly. 'I need a favour. This source the

London Record has. This "M", were you involved in questioning him?'

'Yeah,' Bailey replied. 'I brought him in.'

'You think you could ask him something?'

'I don't know,' Bailey confessed, his limbs suddenly feeling even heavier at the prospect of more work. 'Every cop in London is going to want to talk to him.'

'But you could try?'

Ash left the suggestion hanging until Bailey filled the silence. 'I could try.'

'I appreciate it,' she said, but her tone was distinctly unappreciative. 'Ask him about Archangel.'

'Archangel?' Bailey asked.

'Yeah. Give me a call if he tells you anything.'

The line went dead, and Bailey found himself at a loss to understand why Ash had been so abrupt. There had been no pleasantries, no questions about his well-being, no sharing of experiences.

'Trouble?' Murrall asked.

'Just a friend wanting me to check something out,' Bailey replied. 'She's with the FBI. She wants me to ask Mayfield about Archangel. Do you know where he is?'

'St Mary's. He's under armed guard, but I could probably get you in.' Murrall smiled. 'I'll drive. I'm not sure you'd make it on foot.'

Bailey followed the lumbering detective towards the car park located at the rear of the building. He didn't want to admit it, but Murrall was probably right. He was running on fumes.

Ash felt her bile rise as she thought about Bailey's wavering loyalty. So what if every cop in town wanted to talk to the guy? She'd risked her life to protect the treacherous Wallace, and Bailey was the one who'd sent him her way. He owed her far more than the answer to a simple question. She couldn't believe she'd conned herself into having feelings for Wallace. He'd betrayed her, just like everyone did if she gave them enough time.

She got to her feet and reached into the bag Reeves had brought for a pair of low-heeled slingbacks, which she popped on her tender feet before leaving the office. As she stepped into the open-plan area, Miller stood up, eyeing Romero.

'Hey, Chris,' he said a little too casually. 'You need anything?'

'A walk,' Ash replied coolly.

Miller shook his head slowly. 'Harrell asked us to keep you here. Where we can be sure you're safe. That's not a problem, is it?'

Ash smiled. 'No,' she replied, backing up. She wasn't buying the line about keeping her safe. They could sense the change in her, and they were afraid. She no longer fit their pre-packaged, cookie-cutter preconceptions, and that made them uncomfortable. 'I'll just pace my cell,' she added sourly, noting that Miller and Romero weren't sure whether or not to smile.

Let them feel uncertain and uncomfortable. When the time came, it would give her the edge.

Murrall flashed his warrant card at the uniformed officers outside the private room and was nodded through. Bailey followed him inside to find Mayfield lying on his back, his right wrist handcuffed to the metal frame of the bed. The room was on the third floor of the building with a window that overlooked a narrow well separating the wards. It had a terrible view of stained brickwork, drains and frosted windows, but in Bailey's opinion it was still too good for its occupant.

'Come to gloat, detective?' Mayfield asked sarcastically. 'Because I wouldn't want you to make a fool of yourself. I won't serve a single day.'

'Don't be so sure,' Murrall interjected. 'The Box is hanging you out to dry. MI5 really doesn't like double agents.'

'MI5?' Mayfield snorted. 'The Foundation will make sure I never see the inside of a cell. One way or another.'

'Then you've got nothing to lose,' Bailey observed. 'If you think they've already marked you for death, you might as well cooperate. Which is why I'm here. I need to know about Archangel.'

Mayfield grinned like a Cheshire Cat. 'You think they're going to kill me? The Foundation doesn't work like that. We're brothers in arms. No man gets left behind. They'll come for me.'

'Sure,' Bailey countered, but he was shaken by Mayfield's certainty. 'And they won't punish you for everything you've already told us. All the stuff you gave the paper.'

Mayfield hesitated, but there was no discomfort in the pause, he was relishing the moment. 'What? Telling the people of the world they can't trust their own governments? That they shouldn't have any faith in their law enforcement agencies? You might find a few of us, but you'll never find us all, and in the meantime you'll have sowed the seeds of suspicion and paranoia, destroying the trust that you take for granted. It's another crack in a system that we're going to destroy. How do you know *he*'s not a member of the Foundation?' Mayfield indicated Murrall, who bridled at the accusation. 'You want to know about Archangel? I couldn't tell you. Like I said, no one knows the whole picture. Sounds exciting though. Archangel.'

Murrall approached the bed menacingly.

'Do whatever you want to me. I don't know anything about Archangel. But what I do know is that today is the day everything changes. That's what we've been told. All of us. Today marks the end of your world and the start of ours.'

★

Ash answered the phone on the first ring and breathed into the receiver, unwilling to give anything of herself away.

'Chris?' Bailey tried.

'Yeah,' she replied reluctantly.

'I spoke to "M". He doesn't know anything about Archangel, but he did say that something big is happening today,' Bailey revealed. 'Something that will change the world.'

'OK,' Ash responded.

'How's John?' Bailey asked urgently.

'Check the news,' Ash suggested, before hanging up.

Bailey had been a bust, but if something big was happening today, there was one man who might be able to figure out what it was. She brought her PC to life, ignoring the rows of unopened emails, and checked her contact folder for Pavel Kosinsky's number. The call rang through to his voicemail.

'Kos, it's Chris,' she said, trying to remember how she used to sound. Friendly? Alluring? Definitely weak. 'Give me a call when you get this.'

82

The sun was starting to set, but even though the light was fading, the park was alive with excitable children freed from school, and as he looked around, Wallace regretted his suggestion that they meet here. He tried to gauge whether any of the myriad dog walkers were in fact FBI agents and eyed the rush-hour traffic with suspicion, watching for the lingering gaze of any passing commuters. The lean coach who barked orders at the athletics team as they warmed up on the track had glanced in the direction of Steven's van a couple of times, but his familiarity with the children was too natural for him to be a plant.

They were parked near the intersection of Driggs Avenue and 12th Street, opposite a grand orthodox church with a bulbous dome. They had a clear view in every direction and Wallace had suggested the location because it was one of the few public places he and Pavel were both familiar with that he didn't have to refer to by name. When he'd finally convinced the security specialist to meet, all he'd had to say was, 'the park we went to'.

Persuading Pavel had been surprisingly simple. Wallace had been on the FBI's Most Wanted list the very first time they'd met, so it was a status Pavel was accustomed to and it didn't deter him. His main concern had been the fact that Wallace's face was now all over the news, making it dangerous for them to be spotted together. Wallace had assured him he'd take precautions, but had been careful not to mention that he'd be bringing Steven Byrne to the meeting.

They'd driven to Brooklyn in a GMC Savana which had been parked in a garage behind the house on Belmont Avenue. As they'd travelled across the city, Steven had explained that the old place was one of a number of safe houses he'd set up around New York after he'd got involved with the Foundation. The back of the grey van was packed with large black Peli cases, bigger versions of the ones Wallace used to transport his camera equipment.

They'd arrived half an hour early and had circled the park a couple of times, checking for any signs of surveillance. When they'd parked opposite the church, Steven had climbed into the back and produced a radio frequency scanner from one of the flight cases. The portable device automatically searched the airwaves for radio signals. So far, all they'd heard were cab drivers, police dispatchers and local DJs – nothing that suggested anyone was staking out the location.

Wallace recognised the Chevrolet Express as it approached them from the south. The van trailed a slow line of traffic crawling towards the intersection. Sunlight glared off the windshield, making it impossible to identify the driver until the vehicle had reached the lights.

'That's him,' Wallace said, nodding towards the idling van.

Pavel didn't see them until he was almost level with the GMC, and his eyes widened as he registered Steven in the driver's seat. Wallace and Steven stepped out of the van and crossed the street, picking their way through passing traffic, while Pavel found a spot and parked.

'Thanks for coming,' Wallace said as he opened the passenger door and climbed inside.

Grim-faced, Pavel stared directly ahead and failed to acknowledge the two men who slid into his van.

'Pavel Kosinsky,' Steven tried as he shut the door. 'I've heard of you. I'm Steven—'

'I know who you are, and I'm doing my best not to have a factor five freak-out,' Pavel replied. 'Like, part of me is geeking out because you're Steven Byrne. And the other part of me is screaming "danger, danger", because you're super-hot right now.'

'Sorry to spring this on you,' Wallace said, 'but we need help.'

'We need you to identify a user,' Steven added. 'The Foundation is planning something big.'

'The Foundation? I thought *you* were the Foundation,' Pavel responded.

'Don't believe everything you hear,' Steven countered. 'I've made some mistakes. I'm trying to put them right.'

Pavel nodded. 'What user?' He moved into the back of the van.

'Someone on SideVox . . .' Steven began.

'Does anyone still use that?' Pavel asked as he booted up one of the terminals. 'Solid state,' he nodded at the machine proudly, before glancing at Wallace, slightly embarrassed.

Wallace got the impression that meeting Steven was the geek equivalent of having face time with Dave Grohl.

'They still do,' Steven replied. 'Username is Gozer the Gozerian.'

'Ghostbusters,' Pavel noted.

Steven nodded. 'And the post mentions the Foundation and something called Freefall. It looks like a boast.'

Pavel started the adjacent terminal, and switched on a couple of devices located under the counter. 'So, you guys have got a choice. You can either face forward or you can step outside,' he told them.

Wallace's puzzlement must have showed because Pavel added, 'Yes, meeting one of my heroes is a big excitement, but when that hero owns one of the world's largest digital security companies, it's perhaps better if he doesn't see my methods.'

Steven nodded and faced the road, and Wallace did likewise.

'People say digital is dangerous,' Pavel observed as he worked. 'They say it can be manipulated. Sure, I can hack CNN and change an article so the news you think happened never did, but do you have any idea how difficult it is to really change things? To be invisible? To change history? Well, you probably do, Mr Byrne, but this guy, he won't know. It's hard, John. Someone's always keeping tabs. Somewhere there's a machine tracking your IP address, logging your machine ID, storing records of everything you do, everywhere you go. To truly rid the world of all your binary, well, that takes genius, and we're few and far between. Most people leave a trail of crumbs. You just have to know where to look.'

Pavel hesitated.

'Gozer the Gozerian is a woman. She's been criticised on the boards before, guys saying she's not bona fide because she's a woman. Maybe the knuckle draggers are why she bragged,' he continued. 'So if we get into the machine code . . . and take a look here . . . Interesting.'

The sound of the high-powered computer fans almost drowned out the noise of the passing traffic. Wondering how long they had to sit there, Wallace glanced at Steven, who shrugged.

'No peeking,' Pavel cautioned, before adding, 'Just kidding. You can look. I'm done.'

Wallace and Steven turned around to see one screen displaying the Kosinsky Data Services logo, while the other showed the identity card and personnel file of a young woman who worked for a company called Zadkiel Consulting.

'Shit. Zadkiel,' Steven observed.

'What?' Wallace asked. 'Who are they?'

'They develop transaction software and settlement systems. Real specialist stuff,' Steven replied. 'The company takes its name from Zadkiel, one of the seven Archangels.'

Wallace felt his stomach flip.

'Her name is Whitney Potts,' Pavel revealed. 'She's a senior programmer. Been there six months, she's been assigned as the team lead on the new Federal Reserve Settlement System.'

Wallace's puzzlement must have showed because Pavel continued, 'It's a centralised clearing system that links every bank in America to the Federal Reserve. Thanks to the Blake-Castillo bill, after tomorrow, every financial transaction will go through this settlement system. Whether it's you transferring ten bucks, or this guy buying a company for a billion,' Pavel nodded at Steven. 'Not that mine's for sale,' he added with a smile.

'That's what Smokie's going after – money,' Steven announced in frustration. 'Ending anonymity, making the internet a safer place, the rest of it was just cover. This is the real reason he wanted to make sure the bill passed into law. Can you check their corporate filings?' he asked.

Pavel got to work immediately, pulling up Zadkiel's Delaware records. After a few moments, he nodded. 'Yes. Here. A majority acquisition by Donal Funds LLC, a subsidiary—'

'Of the Erimax Corporation,' Steven finished his sentence. 'It's an investment firm that was started by my grandfather. That means Smokie's already got control of at least part of my business. That's why he wanted me out of the way. But how? How'd he . . .' He trailed off, aghast, then collected himself. 'Where's she based?'

'She's working on Liberty Street,' Pavel replied. 'The main hub.'

'What hub?' Wallace asked.

'Twenty-three Liberty Street, opposite the Federal Reserve. It's the main hub for the new central settlement system. It's secure and it has great data connections to all the major banks,' Steven responded, but he was distracted, as though the principal parts of his mind were elsewhere, trying to figure out another problem.

'The system is supposed to go live at midnight,' Pavel observed. 'It's been all over the news. We should call the Feds,' he suggested. 'Where's Chris? I heard she'd been found. You guys normally work together, right?'

Wallace lowered his gaze, devastated by the last memory he had of Ash. 'She's with the Bureau,' he said flatly.

'If we call them, there's a chance the complaint gets intercepted by someone loyal to the Foundation, putting everyone who knows about it in danger,' Steven told Pavel. 'We can't trust anyone. We need to stop this.'

'What do you want me to do?' Pavel asked.

'Stay by the phone. If you haven't heard from us by eleven, then we'll have to take the risk – call the Bureau,' Steven replied. 'But don't tell anyone about this before then.'

He opened the passenger door and stepped out, leaving Wallace to contemplate the nagging feeling that he should stay with Pavel.

'Coming?' Steven asked, hovering by the open door.

Wallace looked at the man's haunted face, and reminded himself that he had to do whatever he could to set things right.

'Yeah,' he replied, exiting the vehicle. He followed Steven towards the grey GMC, gulping down deep lungfuls of the chill evening air in an effort to bring his nerves under control.

83

They parked on the corner of Liberty and William on the south side of the street, opposite the Federal Reserve. Wallace watched as Steven placed an FBI parking notice on the dash before climbing into the back of the van where he pulled a small, holstered pistol from one of the flight cases. He unzipped his trousers and strapped the holster to his inner thigh, concealing the gun by his groin.

'Just in case,' he observed, before exiting through the rear doors.

Wallace stepped on to the sidewalk and took a deep breath, then slammed the door and followed Steven west, along Liberty Street. A uniformed police officer stood on the stone steps outside the main entrance of the Federal Reserve, a heavily fortified stone building with barred windows and a parking exclusion zone that covered nearly the whole of the north side of the street. The man's auburn hair showed beneath a peaked cap and he scanned both directions, watching passing pedestrians as they came and went. A liveried Federal Reserve police car was parked directly ahead of him, and behind it was a short line of vehicles that displayed placards similar to the one Steven had put on the dash of the GMC. When he looked up, Wallace saw security cameras pinned to the corners of the building, and wondered what other, unseen defensive measures were employed to protect this key strategic location.

The building next to them was a modern skyscraper which loomed over its shorter, more prestigious neighbour. Wallace heard voices above him and saw people walking along a mezzanine promenade that ran the length of the street. When they reached the corner of Liberty and Nassau, they climbed a flight of steps that took them on to a flagstone courtyard that joined the promenade. Most of the traffic coming through the building's glass doors was outbound. They'd arrived a little before seven, and the skyscraper's occupants were heading home.

They stepped into a gleaming white double-height lobby and approached the security guard sitting behind an expansive reception desk.

'We're here for Whitney Potts, Zadkiel Consulting,' Steven told him.

'What are your names?' he asked, slowly reaching for the phone.

'Steven Byrne. I'm her boss,' Steven replied. 'And this is Craig Weathers,' he added, glancing at Wallace, who was surprised to hear him use Smokie's real name.

While the guard placed the call, Wallace studied the roster of companies located in the building: banks, law firms, technology companies, and divisions of the Federal Reserve that had overflowed from the building across the street.

'Place your index finger on the scanner, please,' the guard said as he hung up. 'And face the camera,' he added as he manipulated a web camera into position.

Steven complied and Wallace did likewise, earning chipped visitor passes in return.

'Thirty-ninth floor,' the guard told them. 'Take the fourth elevator. You need to swipe the reader to make it go.'

As they approached the security gates that guarded access to the elevators, they were ushered towards a full body metal detector by another uniformed guard.

'Any phones in the plastic tray, please,' the man said sombrely.

Wallace had lost his phone at the warehouse, so he simply stepped through the machine, which remained dormant. He was struck by anxiety as he thought about the pistol strapped to Steven's thigh, but was surprised when the tech entrepreneur followed him through the scanner without incident.

Their passes got them through to the elevators and the two of them stepped into a mirrored car. Steven swiped his visitor's card over a reader and pressed '39'.

'How did you get through the scanner?' Wallace asked as the doors slid shut.

'Ceramic,' Steven replied. 'Even the bullets.'

Wallace marvelled at his companion's resourcefulness, but his relief was short-lived, and as the elevator rose, his nerves started getting the better of him. He couldn't help but feel that whatever waited for them on the thirty-ninth floor would not be good.

The car drew to a halt and the doors slid open to reveal an opulent, wood-panelled lobby. A receptionist sat behind a high counter that bore the Federal Reserve logo. Wallace followed Steven out of the elevator, and sensed movement as he drew level with the doors. Steven bucked to his right, and something flashed to his left, an arm, a gloved hand, and something hard and plastic. Wallace felt a terrible, stabbing pain, and realised that he and Steven had both been hit by stun guns. As his body shuddered and his legs gave way, he was greeted by a ghastly sight. Three men in the horrifyingly familiar Pendulum uniforms stepped forward, their heavy boots dominating his fading vision as his head hit the floor.

84

The sound of her phone brought her back from darkness, and Ash opened her eyes to find herself slumped over her desk. The office lights were on and daylight had died. She looked through the open door and saw Miller and Romero still at their desks, both on their phones. They'd added their voices to a growing chorus of people who suggested she needed to be hospitalised. Harrell had started talking about a psych evaluation, but Ash had reiterated in the most forceful terms that she was not going anywhere until she knew she was safe. He'd backed out of her office like the frightened bureaucrat he was and she heard no further talk of mutiny.

Ash answered the phone but said nothing.

'Chris?' Pavel's accent was unmistakable.

'Yeah,' she replied, running her hand over the stubble that covered her head. The contact points were still tender, but she liked the sensation of the sharp little spikes digging into her soft palm.

'Where have you been? I got your message. I've wrestled with this, but I've got to tell you, I was with your friend John Wallace,' Pavel revealed. 'They told me not to let you know, but I'm worried they're going to bite off something that's too big for them.'

'You were right to call,' Ash told him, suddenly alive and alert. 'What is it?'

'They've got a lead on a hacker who might be part of the Foundation. Her name's Whitney Potts. She works for Zadkiel Consulting. They seemed to think it was important that Zadkiel was an Archangel.'

Ash smiled inwardly. She knew this was bigger than an assassination plot.

'They're helping build the new Federal Settlement System,' Pavel continued. 'Whitney is based in the Federal Reserve data hub, twenty-three Liberty Street. Byrne thinks the Foundation are going after the system. He's going to try to stop them. I couldn't just sit on it.'

'No, you couldn't,' Ash assured him, hanging up.

Don't be afraid, baby.

The thought rose unbidden, and she felt a flush of anger as it forced its way into her mind. *I'm not afraid*, she told herself as she got to her feet. She'd already figured out how she would slip her guards and leave the office.

'Hey,' she said to Miller as she approached the doorway. 'You think you could grab me a sandwich? I'm starving.'

She threw him a friendly smile.

'Sure,' he replied, rising. 'What d'you want?'

'I don't care. Whatever they've got.'

Ash watched Miller cross the open-plan office, heading towards the elevators. She smiled at Romero, who briefly looked up from her computer.

Ash retreated into her office and opened the bottom drawer of her desk to retrieve a Glock 26 and the two clips she kept as back-up. She thrust the tiny handgun into the waistband of her trousers before picking up a billfold that was stashed at the back of the drawer. She slipped the money into her pocket, swapping it for the cell phone she'd found at the warehouse. She turned her back on the door and placed a call.

'Federal Bureau of Investigation,' an operator answered.

'The Foundation has placed a bomb in your building. It will detonate in five minutes,' Ash said, before hanging up.

'You OK?'

Ash turned to discover Romero hovering by the door. Had she heard anything?

'Yeah,' Ash responded, concealing the phone behind her back.

'Miller's on the line. He wants to know if you'd like a soda,' Romero said.

Ash shook her head.

'Listen, I know everyone's been on your case tellin' you to go home, but it's because we're worried about you,' Romero confessed. 'You've been through a lot.'

Ash couldn't care less about Romero's pathetic attempt to connect with her. It was just another ploy to get her to do what they wanted. Go home. Rest. Recover. Forget about what happened. Roll over. Play ball. Be a good little doggy. She was done with that.

'I just don't want you thinking that—'

Romero was interrupted by a klaxon, and the sound of a distorted voice being relayed on the building's public address system: 'Evacuate the building. All personnel are to proceed to their evacuation points immediately. This is not a drill.'

The message was repeated continuously over the insistent sound of the klaxon.

'Come on,' Romero said. 'We'd better go.'

Ash followed her out of the office, and they joined a crowd of agents and administrators who were heading for the nearest fire exit. The stairwell was already packed, but they made quick progress through the building, moving down in a nervous, unnaturally quiet throng. When they spilled out of the Duane Street exit, Ash seized her chance. Donna and Angela, two of the administrators on their floor, cut between Ash and Romero, creating all the distance she needed. She skipped through the crowd before Romero realised what was happening, and by the time Ash heard her name being called, there was a tide of bobbing heads between them.

She ran on to Broadway, where the traffic was slowing as drivers gawked at a skyscraper shedding its occupants. She flagged a cab heading south and jumped in the back. As it moved off, she glanced over her shoulder to see Romero push her way to the edge of the crowd and scan her surroundings in desperation.

85

'Wake up!'
        'Hey!'
'Please!'

A chorus of urgent voices bounced around Wallace's head and for a moment he was unsure whether they were real or imagined. As his heavy eyelids rolled open and he came to his senses, he realised that the cries were coming from nearby. The world drifted into focus and he saw the tiny squares of a metal grate. He was on some kind of gantry, which straddled a utility duct that stretched far beneath him, running the full height of the building. Judging by the background noise, he was in some kind of service area or plant room. He tried to move his hands, but they were bound. He'd been hog-tied, his hands and feet strapped together behind his back. He rolled on to his side and saw a low metal lip that marked the edge of the gantry. Beyond it was some kind of motor, which was about six feet wide and four high, and was encased in a shiny black enamel housing. Next to it was a wide platform where a dozen people stood. A mix of men and women, they were all calling to him urgently. They were animated but immobile, and when Wallace saw their hands, he realised why. They'd all been handcuffed to a steel rail that delineated the perimeter of the platform.

'You gotta help us, mister!' a rosy-cheeked, plump woman pleaded, her voice full of panic.

Wallace struggled against his bonds, but they only seemed to grow tighter. His body ached with the effort, and his shoulders felt as though they might pop from their sockets, but he kept at it.

'Use the floor!' one of the men yelled.

Wallace couldn't see who'd made the suggestion, but he realised that the lip that edged the gantry might just be thin enough to act as a blade.

He manoeuvred himself into position and rolled on to his back, so that the lower half of his body hung out over the edge of the gantry, beneath a metal guard rail. His insides were thrown into turmoil as he suddenly realised that overbalancing would send him tumbling off the edge, plummeting into the duct below. His arms and legs screamed as though they were close to breaking, but he could feel the line of rope that connected them, and pressed his body against it. He swayed from side to side, rubbing the rope against the top of the lip.

Hewn from rough metal, about a quarter of an inch wide, the lip soon started to fray his clothing and he could feel it biting into his skin. He ignored the pain, telling himself that if it was cutting flesh, it would also be severing the rope. The discomfort matured into real pain, and Wallace thought he could feel the lip deep in his body, heading for a kidney. *You're just scared*, he told himself, willing his body on. He almost overbalanced, but recovered his position by throwing his head back against the grate, causing a mighty clang to echo around the plant room. His skull rang with ripples of pain, but once the smoky tendrils of unconsciousness had passed, he continued his task.

His arms and legs suddenly jerked free as the rope snapped, and the movement sent him toppling over the edge of the gantry. For a moment he felt weightless, before gravity kicked in and yanked him down. Sheer instinctive reflex forced his arms apart, and the rope that had bound them slipped away, allowing him to bring his hands up and round his body to grab hold of the guard rail, just as his head slid beneath it. He hung for a moment, the rope falling away from his legs, tumbling dozens of floors into the dark depths of the duct, leaving his legs free to kick at the insubstantial air.

Wallace heaved himself up, pulling his body back on to the gantry, before getting to his feet.

'Yes!'

He heard a woman cry with relief, and ran to the platform where the group had begun to chatter excitedly.

'Keep it down,' a black man in a bloodstained white shirt said urgently. 'We don't want them to hear.'

Everyone fell silent as Wallace approached. There were eight men and four women of various ethnicities, all in their thirties or forties, all dressed in the business casual attire common to mid-level office workers. The man in the bloodstained shirt stood about six-three, looked whippet-thin enough to run a marathon, and had the demeanour of a leader. His face was caked in drying blood and his nose had been broken.

'My name's Miracle Oyewole,' he said.

'What happened? Where are we?' Wallace asked, looking round.

They were definitely in a plant room, and he guessed it was somewhere near the top of the building. To his left was a row of air-conditioning units, power transformers, cable boxes and unfamiliar heavy machinery. To his right, beyond the gantry, was a steel access door.

'I'm a systems team leader with the Fed,' Miracle replied. 'They came at six, after most people had gone home. Whitney and her team let them in. They rounded us up and put us here. I don't know who you are, but you pissed them off. We thought they were going to kill you.'

Miracle's colleagues murmured their agreement.

'How long have I been out?' Wallace asked.

'No idea. But they brought you in here around an hour ago,' Miracle revealed. 'They were pretty rough with you.'

That explained the soreness, Wallace thought. 'What are they doing?' he asked.

'We don't know, and we don't really care. We've got a more urgent problem,' Miracle said, nodding his head towards the back of the black enamel housing Wallace had seen when he first came round.

Fixed to the shiny surface were four grey blocks, each one marked 'C4 High Explosive Demolition Charge'. They sat beneath a detonator that had no timer. Instead there was a radio receiver and a green LED that blinked every five seconds.

Wallace sighed deeply, filling his lungs with smoky, oil-infused air.

'There are more over there,' Miracle nodded towards the machinery, 'and we saw them planting some in the offices before we left.'

'Do any of you have a phone?' Wallace asked.

'No,' Miracle replied, while his colleagues shook their heads. 'They took them.'

Wallace backed away, heading for the gantry.

'Where are you going?' the rosy-cheeked woman asked fearfully.

'To find a phone and get help,' he replied. 'Or tools . . . something I can use to get you out of here.'

He jogged across the gantry but slowed as he approached the steel access door. When he put his head against it, the metal felt cold and soothing, but the hum of the surrounding machinery made it impossible to hear what was on the other side. He grabbed hold of the flat handle, took a series of deep breaths, counted to three and opened the door.

★

The man in the Pendulum mask seemed almost as shocked as Wallace. He stood in a concrete corridor, across from the access door, casually holding a sub-machine gun. Nervous adrenalin gave Wallace the edge, and he launched himself at the man as he raised the gun. Momentum moved them both, and Wallace felt the satisfying impact of the man hitting the wall, his head cracking against the unyielding concrete. Wallace grabbed the man's face and smashed his head against the wall – once – twice – after the second time, the gun clattered to the floor, but the man's survival instincts kicked in and he swung a gloved fist, which connected with Wallace's cheek and sent him reeling.

Wallace staggered back, but saw the masked man reaching for his weapon and forced himself forward. He brought his knee up into his opponent's face, knocking him backwards, but the man was equally determined, and grappled Wallace, charging forward, pushing them both through the plant room door. Wallace couldn't keep pace, and his feet collided with each other, tripping him, sending him tumbling near the spot where he'd regained consciousness. He landed heavily, and felt the breath rush from his body. His attacker didn't hesitate, and followed up with a kick to Wallace's ribs that was so powerful the world seemed to lose all its colour. Wallace screamed. He knew another one of those would permanently disable him, so he rolled towards his assailant and stood up.

It was a simple, ugly, awkward move, but there was nowhere for his opponent to go, and the man was pushed against the steel guard rail. Remembering his teenage Aikido training, Wallace turned and grabbed the man's left hand and, using his body as leverage, executed a kote gaeshi throw, sending him tumbling over the edge of the gantry. The man flailed wildly until he'd fallen from view, his scream echoing around the duct until a distant impact silenced it.

Wallace looked at the Fed employees, most of whom were in

shock. Miracle's eyes were wide with disbelief, but after a moment he nodded his head slowly. Wallace couldn't believe what he'd just done, but if he hadn't thrown the man, there was no doubt that he'd now be dead. He staggered across the gantry, stepped through the access door and crossed the concrete corridor to pick up the discarded sub-machine gun.

86

The cab came to a halt on the corner of Nassau and Liberty and Ash thrust a twenty at the driver before jumping out and running up the steps. As she crossed the stone courtyard and headed towards the skyscraper, she saw a couple of security guards through the atrium window, one sitting behind a counter, rocking back in his chair, the other manhandling a metal detector as he stood beside a full body scanner. They were laughing about something, and their spontaneous display of emotion rankled Ash. Confident and assured, their uniforms conferring status and giving them purpose, they'd never truly experienced life. They thought it was a steady wage, a few beers at the weekend, and hours passed trading sexist jokes while making a half-assed effort to do their jobs. She wondered how either man would have coped strapped to that chair in that basement. They deserved it, not her. They needed their minds broadened. She was already familiar with all the darkness in the world. They were the ones who needed those easy smiles wiped off their faces.

By the time she walked through the revolving door, she was fuming, and she knew her anger was showing on her face because the two men stiffened and looked at her as though she was a potential menace. The old her, the woman who'd died the day they shaved her head, would have tried to understand why she was so angry, to contextualise it and explain it away as the product of a damaged childhood. But she knew better now. Anger unsettled people, and when they were thrown off balance they became vulnerable.

'Can I help you?' the tubby one behind the desk asked.

'Whitney Potts,' Ash replied, trying not to growl.

He glanced at his colleague, who rolled his eyes. Tubby shifted ever so slightly, but his body language signalled what was coming next. They'd judged her. The shaven head, the scarring on her skull, the cuts and bruises, the erratic, inexplicable movements of her limbs, the blistering rage emanating from every pore. They thought she was a hazard, but they hadn't seen beyond the surface. If they had, they'd have realised just how dangerous she really was.

'Building's closed,' Tubby replied. 'You can wait outside, or you can come back tomorrow.'

'Yeah, tomorrow,' Manhandler chimed in. 'During the day, when it ain't our shift.'

'OK,' Ash conceded, moving towards the sniggering guard. 'You got me. I'm crazy. Cuff me. Keep me down. Kick me out.'

When she was a couple of paces from the man, she drew her Glock and aimed it at his head. His smile fell away and he froze instantly.

'And you!' Ash yelled at Tubby. 'Put your hands up right now!'

He complied immediately, but Ash couldn't be certain he hadn't already hit the panic button she was sure would be concealed at his station. She couldn't take any chances and she would have to work fast.

'Move! Both of you!' she commanded, gesturing towards the security gates.

Wallace followed the service corridor, which doglegged left and led to a heavy fire door. He pushed the handle and swung his body against the door, forcing it open while gripping the gun with both hands. A quiet, carpeted corridor lay on the other side, and Wallace could see a number of empty offices leading off it. He ran into the nearest one, noted the Federal Reserve logo on all the paperwork that was stacked on the desk, and lifted the phone. The out-of-service tone droned in his ear, and he quickly hung up, searching the drawers for a discarded cell phone. He found nothing and quickly ran to the neighbouring room where he repeated the process and got the same result. The phones were out.

The corridor was eerily quiet, and Wallace only had the low hum of the air-conditioning system to keep him company as he crept on. He came to a sharp right turn, which he took slowly, craning his head round the corner to ensure there were no nasty surprises. His heart sank when he saw an opaque security door blocking his path. There was a card reader next to it, but if his captor had one, it would currently be at the bottom of the service duct, lost in one hell of a mess. Wallace was about to return the way he'd come, when he noticed that the LED on the card reader was green. Worth a try, he thought to himself as he sidled up to the door and grabbed the handle.

He was surprised when the door gave at his touch and pulled it open. Hearing the sound of distant voices, he stepped into a cold corridor and carefully shut the door behind him. The walls, floor and ceiling were covered by thick fabric panels, which deadened sound and made the space seem even more claustrophobic than it was. The air was cold, but Wallace hardly noticed the chill. His heart started racing as he moved forward.

'You were meant to be sittin' in jail right now.' Smokie's low, menacing voice was unmistakable. 'Instead, you're gonna take the fall for this. Dead, of course.'

Wallace slid against the right wall as he approached an intersection. To his left was an open double door that led into a huge server room, where row after row of servers hummed, the noise accentuated by hard floor tiles. Wallace peered through a duplicate doorway to his right and saw a smaller room full of computer workstations. He recognised Whitney Potts from her personnel file, but she seemed much smaller in person, her five feet four inches almost lost behind the workstation she was seated at. Of the other fourteen stations, only three were occupied. All of the operators were male; one was black, one was white and the third looked Middle-Eastern. Like Whitney, all three of them were lost in deep concentration, and didn't seem to be listening to Smokie, who stood next to Steven Byrne, training an AR-15 assault rifle on him. Smokie wore Pendulum body armour, but unlike the other three men who were walking around the room with their guns at the ready, he'd removed his mask. It rested on a chair adjacent to the one in which Steven Byrne sat. The blood and bruises on Steven's face were a testament to the beating he'd endured, and he looked groggy and defeated. Smokie had his back to Wallace, but Steven was looking directly at the doorway and gave a flicker of recognition when he caught Wallace's eye.

'I think we're done,' Whitney said, and Smokie turned around and approached her terminal.

Wallace withdrew and pressed his back against the wall, unwilling to risk being seen.

'So this was all about money?' Steven asked, his voice distorted by his injuries. 'A grand robbery.'

'Robbery?' Smokie replied, his voice rising an octave. 'You still don't get it. I started the Foundation because I know what it's like to have nothing. To be starving, cold and broke. Not having enough money to pay to heat your house, or make the rent. A child having to watch his mother turn tricks so she can buy food. And all the time there are rich motherfuckers with more than they know what to do with, spending money on diamond-encrusted steering wheels, bigger yachts, more bling, more shit while children around the world are dying because they can't get clean water. This ain't a robbery, it's justice.'

'So you take money from a few rich people?' Steven pressed.

'Ain't a few. We're taking all of it from every rich son of a bitch.' Wallace registered the glee in Smokie's voice. 'You were an easy mark, Steve. You wanted to make your kids' deaths mean something. Internet anonymity! That ain't what the Foundation's about. It was started to level the field and that's exactly what we're going to do. The settlement system that's supposed to set a new standard in financial security has connected us to every bank in America. Any account with more than fifty thousand dollars in it is gonna get drained and that money is gonna get shared out to anyone who has a balance of less than five hundred bucks.'

'They'll just roll it back,' Steven objected.

'You might understand all this tech. You might know what Blockchain means, how a transaction audit trail is built, but most of the politicians approving this stuff don't know how it works. This is a new world. Control the people writing the code and you can do whatever you want,' Smokie responded.

'We can post fake ledger entries backdating the transactions for up to two years. And when this place goes up, there will be no record of what we've done,' Whitney put in. 'People might have paper statements, but we're talking about money from fifteen million high value accounts being redistributed to sixty million low ones. Even if people can prove what happened, by the time they do, the money will probably be long gone. Freefall, baby,' she smiled at Smokie. 'The whole system is going down.'

'And you're gonna pin this on me?' Steven asked.

'On your corpse,' Smokie said. 'Billionaire driven crazy by grief tries to fulfil the political agenda of his dead son. See, Max was the one with the record for political activism.'

'He took the fall for you,' Steven objected.

'And you're going to do the same thing,' Smokie responded.

'The story writes itself. Even with this witch hunt they won't find every Foundation member. We'll lay low for a while, until there's more work to be done.'

Wallace peered around the corner and saw Smokie standing over Whitney, studying her terminal.

'It just needs a "run" command prompt to execute the program,' she told him. 'I thought you might want the honour.'

'Whitney, you guys have done a great job,' Smokie said.

The gunshot startled Wallace, and he backed against the wall as Whitney's body fell from her chair. He heard screams that were quickly silenced by three other shots, and when he finally summoned the courage to snatch a glance into the room, he saw that all four programmers lay dead on the floor, murdered by Smokie and his men.

'OK!' Smokie exclaimed, returning to Whitney's workstation, raising his hands to the keyboard to type the command.

Wallace acted without thinking. He stepped into the doorway and started firing, aiming at the two men furthest from Steven. Bullets tore into their body armour and sent them falling back. He felt burning pain in his upper right thigh as one of Smokie's bullets struck home. Wallace dropped to his knee but kept shooting, spraying a third man with bullets. He saw that Steven was on his feet and that he'd produced his concealed pistol.

Steven moved fast like an old lion suddenly filled with one last burst of youthful energy. He shot the three men Wallace had hit, drilling rounds through their masks. Wallace was shocked by the speed and ferocity of Steven's assault, then dismayed when a bullet caught Steven in the chest and sent him spinning backwards. The gun went flying from his hand and clattered against the floor.

'I'm gonna fuckin' kill you!' Smokie yelled, closing on him.

Wallace forced himself to his feet and took aim, trying to avoid Steven, who had collapsed to his knees. He pulled the trigger and heard the satisfying staccato of gunfire, as the sub-machine gun spat bullets that thudded into Smokie's body armour. Smokie flew forward and collapsed face down, crashing into the hard white tiles.

He rolled over and tried to target Wallace, but Steven fell on him and wrestled the gun from his grasp. Enraged, Smokie punched Steven, driving his fist home again and again, until Steven was utterly senseless.

'Stop or I'll shoot!' Wallace yelled.

Smokie ignored the command, and when Wallace pulled the trigger, the gun clicked empty.

The sound had more of an effect on Smokie than any instruction, and he turned and scanned the room for a weapon. He and Wallace spotted Steven's discarded pistol at the same time and both moved as quickly as their wounded bodies would allow. Wallace willed himself to ignore the pain radiating from his bloody leg and limped forward. Smokie staggered towards the gun, and for a moment Wallace thought the gangster would get to the weapon first, but he made a final effort and collapsed within reach of the pistol, which he grabbed and brought swinging round into Smokie's face. The blow caught Smokie on the cheek and sent him reeling. As Wallace got to his feet, Smokie rifled in his pocket and produced a remote detonator. He flipped the protective housing that covered the trigger, and smiled.

'None of you understand. I just want to see it all burn,' he wheezed, a trail of blood running from the corner of his mouth.

'Don't do it,' Wallace implored him, but Smokie's finger began to descend. Wallace pulled the trigger.

Nothing happened, and Wallace registered the muffled click of a misfire.

Smokie laughed. 'See you on the other side,' he cackled.

The gunshot reverberated around the room, and the bullet drilled a hole in Smokie's shoulder. The detonator went flying clear and tumbled to a halt beside Whitney's motionless feet.

'You fucking bitch,' Smokie rasped as he collapsed.

Wallace turned towards the door to see Ash aiming a small black pistol at Smokie, her eyes full of murderous intent.

'Put it down, Chris,' Wallace said gently. 'Let's bring him in. He can identify every member of the Foundation.'

'I should've killed you,' Smokie snarled.

'You were the one who did this to me,' Ash remarked, touching her shaved head. 'I recognise your voice.'

Smokie smiled. 'You're better now, ain't you? You're like me. I see it in your eyes.'

Wallace could see nothing but pain and conflict. He could sense her anguish and desperately wanted to make it better. 'Chris,' he began.

Ash fired without warning, shooting Smokie twice in the skull, killing him instantly. She watched his body fall, and then, to Wallace's horror, she turned the gun on him. Her eyes were wild and devoid of compassion.

'Chris?' he tried. 'It's me.'

She wavered, but kept the gun on him.

'I'm sorry,' Wallace said. 'I should have been there for you. I should have done better. Please believe me.'

Ash lowered the weapon and strode into the room. She ignored Wallace and marched up to Steven, who was lying dazed and prone. She raised the compact pistol, aiming it at his face, and steeled herself to pull the trigger.

'Don't, Chris,' Wallace pleaded. 'He's not with them. Put your gun down.'

Her face flashed with emotion and tears welled in her eyes as her arm trembled with the weight of what she was about to do. Bloody and wounded, Steven gazed up at her, resigned to his fate.

'I'm ready,' Steven whispered.

Wallace recalled what Steven had said about having decided on a way out. He'd resolved to make Ash his exit.

'Do it,' Steven urged.

'Chris, don't,' Wallace tried. 'For me. For everything we've been through.'

Ash wavered and glanced at him. He didn't see any warmth, but noted a shift in her demeanour, as though she was performing a calculation. Finally, she lowered the gun, and Wallace exhaled deep relief.

'Steven Byrne,' she said, her speech harsh and fast, 'I'm arresting you for conspiracy and attempted murder. You have the right to remain silent, but anything you say may be used against you in a court of law. You have the right to consult an attorney, and if you cannot afford an attorney, one will be appointed for you.'

As the adrenalin ebbed away, Wallace felt nothing but sadness. Whatever had once existed between them was dead. She continued to ignore him as she took a seat on a nearby chair. Her eyes never met his. Instead she kept them and her gun trained on Steven, and listened to the sound of approaching sirens.

Epilogue

The blinds sliced the sunlight into slivers of gold. Ash sat in an Eames chair and studied the face of the woman seated opposite her. She was gentle and her every movement spoke to that quality. Even the slow way she swept a strand of long black hair off her ivory skin suggested someone seeking to exist in harmony with others. Her gestures were small and soft, her voice low, as though she was trying to seduce the entire world, her eyes wide with optimism, undimmed by the steady train of misery that ran through her office.

Six weeks ago, Ash had been freed from captivity and her world had changed. She'd arrested Steven Byrne, who'd confessed to financing the Foundation's operations, and was now in Rikers awaiting trial. Ash's longstanding opposition to Pendulum and the Foundation had established her as one of the few agents whose loyalty was beyond question. Her trustworthiness and achievements had been recognised. She'd been promoted to Supervisory Special Agent, and given the job of leading the taskforce responsible for hunting down members of the Foundation. It was an issue of national importance, and the whole country, from the citizen on Main Street to the President, longed to know that every traitor had been rooted out and brought to justice. With Smokie dead, no one knew the true extent of the Foundation's reach. Her official estimates put it at between five and six hundred members worldwide, but privately she knew that the figure could be much higher.

Her professional life wasn't the only source of change. Harrell had insisted she go into therapy to deal with any residual effects of the kidnapping and torture, and so each week Ash walked six blocks south of Federal Plaza to visit the office of Dr Lana Hilden, a specialist in post-traumatic stress. They spoke of Ash's childhood, her time with Wallace, the stresses of work, and the glaring nothingness that stood in place of her love life. Ash played along, sharing and caring, smiling and nodding, pretending to lap up the doctor's advice. She felt better, but it was nothing to do with the hours spent in this bright, modern office. Nor was it the result of the exercises Dr Hilden had given her. Ash felt better because her father no longer visited her dreams. Like a ghost with one final task, she believed he'd been set free because she'd finally learned what he'd been trying to teach her all those years ago.

People were weak. She saw it all around her. Her superiors all eyed each other with suspicion, wondering who was truly loyal to the Foundation. Her colleagues suffered from the same paranoia. Every day she woke to a world filled with betrayal, infidelity, abuse, violence and corruption, and nearly all of it stemmed from human weakness. Allow people too close, and that weakness became a threat, a destructive force that would consume everything in its path. She'd let Wallace get too close, and had almost died because of him. Her father had been a monolith, standing alone, placing himself above all others, and even when he'd murdered someone, he'd walked free, because he'd never allowed anyone to get too close, and had always protected himself against the possibility of betrayal.

Ash was in the middle of a course of cosmetic treatment on the scar that encircled her neck, mainly to keep Harrell happy and give him no reason to suspect that her experiences had changed her. All that was left was a faint line. The cosmetic

surgeon had said it was similar to an old C-section scar, and Ash had smiled inwardly at the fact she now had a permanent reminder of the twisted birth of her new self.

Her hair had started to grow back, but she liked to think that beneath her short crop the burns still marked her skull, a permanent legacy of the lesson that had been seared into her head: Trust no one.

'Have you spoken to him since?'

Dr Hilden's voice intruded on her thoughts.

'John Wallace,' she clarified. 'Have you talked?'

She crossed her legs and straightened her grey pencil skirt.

'No,' Ash replied.

'And how do you feel about him?'

'The same,' Ash lied. 'I'm busy, and he kinda disappeared. I don't know where.' *And I don't care*, she thought, but knew better than to articulate.

If she suspected the deception, Dr Hilden said nothing. Maybe she was playing a game, too?

'Why don't we leave it there, Christine?' she suggested. 'We'll pick this up next week.'

Ash smiled broadly, her mask conveying warmth and friendliness, while inside she felt nothing but rage towards this patronising quack.

'Thank you, Doctor Hilden.' She got to her feet.

'Please, call me Lana,' Dr Hilden suggested, returning the smile.

You need a friend, do you, Doctor? Ash thought to herself as she left the woman's office and headed back to work.

Bailey's back prickled with mid-morning heat and he regretted his decision to wear a dark suit, but didn't see that he had much choice. Anything else would have looked out of place in a cemetery, and as he walked along the path, flanked by the rows

of gravestones set on Highgate Hill, he reminded himself that there were worse things than a little sweat. He'd worked hard to stop himself from going to the Dark Side, and always tried to be grateful for life's little blessings, in an attempt to ensure that he never again lost himself to depression and anxiety. All those nights wasted on booze and pills, those terrifying panic attacks, they were all symptoms of post-traumatic stress which he'd avoided treating.

Once he'd recovered from his injuries, he'd returned to Jean Davis and her tiny office on Edgware Road. He'd apologised for deceiving her and had asked for her help. They'd been talking for the past four weeks and he felt better than he had in years. His work bringing Mayfield to justice had earned a promotion to Chief Inspector, and he was assigned the job of identifying the Foundation's blackmail victims, many of whom had been too embarrassed to come forward.

His first arrest had been Diana Fleming, the British negotiator who'd sent him and Melissa to Mayfield. She'd been distraught and full of contrition, and Bailey had discovered that she'd been trying to protect her husband. His company specialised in machine tools and the Foundation had proof that it had broken sanctions against North Korea. Bailey had almost felt sorry for Fleming when she'd been charged, until he'd reminded himself that she'd been prepared to send him and Melissa to their deaths.

The Blake-Castillo bill was in the process of being repealed, the idea of regulating the internet tarnished by Smokie's criminality and the Foundation's blackmail. As the full extent of the conspiracy had become known, support for the initiative had dissipated faster than mist in a hurricane.

Bailey's duties had meant regular contact with Christine Ash, who was leading the Bureau's investigation into the Foundation, but their easy rapport was gone. Maybe he'd said or done something during a booze-fuelled bender that had driven her

away from him? She was courteous and professional, but guarded. Bailey got the sense that she'd been through a lot, but she never wanted to talk about it, and he hadn't found the opportunity to have a real conversation with her. He'd read the Bureau report, and knew that there were big questions over her escape. The Bureau hadn't been able to identify her rescuers, and Ash had suffered memory loss, meaning there was no official explanation of how the four men had died in the nightclub where she'd been held captive.

No one had heard from John Wallace, and he wasn't responding to any emails. He'd spent two weeks in FBI custody getting medical treatment and being debriefed, but had vanished the moment he'd been released. Maybe he'd returned to Afghanistan? Or maybe he was drifting the American continent, keeping himself hidden from the remnants of the Foundation? Beyond vengeance, they had no ostensible reason to want him dead, but Bailey could imagine how paranoid Wallace's experiences must have made him. He didn't blame him for wanting to stay off the grid.

Bailey was sad to have lost touch with Wallace, but he had other things to be grateful for. Frank and Jimmy had recovered from their wounds, which had made Salamander happy. They'd slipped back into an 'ask no questions' relationship, but Bailey knew that their shared ordeal had brought them closer than ever.

When he'd heard how Terry had died in his son's arms, Bailey had almost wept. Salamander had wanted to kill the man responsible, but Mayfield was proving to be a valuable source of information, and the Met was working with the Security Services and the FBI to link his cell to the wider Foundation network. Danny had cried like a newborn at Terry's funeral, and on the few subsequent occasions Bailey had seen the young villain, he'd seemed more subdued.

Bailey could see a small group gathered beside a grave, and

recognised the two children, each holding one of their father's hands. Connor Greene acknowledged Bailey as he joined the small gathering of friends and family who'd come to honour Sylvia Greene's stone setting. Francis Albright and Melissa Rathlin stood nearby and both nodded greetings in Bailey's direction. Connor's sister, Marcella, stood with her two boys and a man Bailey presumed was her husband.

The vicar gave a reading and said some prayers, and everyone, including Bailey, cried for the memory of a good woman who'd made one mistake which had put her life in jeopardy. Mayfield had shared the information they'd used to try to blackmail Sylvia. Early in her career, Jack Diggs, a crooked policeman who'd died a few years back, had pressured her into dropping an investigation into a paedophile who was later convicted of murdering two young boys. Sylvia had hidden her shame from everyone, but the corrupt Erimax internet security software had enabled the Foundation to find the old evidence in a secret file concealed on her hard drive.

Her bravery and the sacrifice she'd made were unparalleled. She'd forgone a life with her husband and two boys in the hope that Bailey would be smart enough to piece together the puzzle of her death in a way that wouldn't put her family at risk. She'd sacrificed everything to protect those she loved, and it was the knowledge of her altruism that made Hector and Joe's tears particularly painful to witness.

When the service was over and the mourners were milling around, wondering how to return to their normal lives, Connor approached Bailey and offered his hand.

'Thanks for coming,' he said, his eyes red raw. 'I just wanted to know how much we appreciate what you did. I knew she'd never choose to leave us . . .'

Connor collapsed against Bailey and the two men stood in an emotional embrace for what seemed like an age. Finally, when he felt able to bear the weight of his grief alone, Connor stepped back. His mouth opened and closed a couple of times, but no words would come, so he simply nodded at Bailey and hurried away to join his boys.

'I wish we could bring her back,' Melissa said as she drew alongside Bailey and took his left hand, which just gave the faintest twinge. Apart from the occasional dull ache, his bones had fully healed.

'So do I,' he responded.

Melissa had been crying and her make-up had run, but it didn't make her any less beautiful. She was another blessing he had to give thanks for. They'd spent a lot of time together analysing the information Mayfield had given the *London Record*, and one night Bailey had plucked up the courage to ask her out.

As they stood in silence, watching Connor and his sons shuffle slowly down the path towards the road, Bailey put his arm around Melissa's shoulder and pulled her close, grateful to be alive.

The visitors' room was exactly as he remembered it. The guard led him to one of the many white PVC stools and he sat on the hard plastic. He touched the peaked tip of his baseball cap, pulling it down over his face. With over 1,500 visitors per day, it was unlikely anyone would even notice him, but he'd still gone to some lengths to disguise his presence, wearing a cap to hide his face and giving a fake ID at check-in. He'd first had the idea almost six weeks ago while still in Bureau custody, when he'd heard the rumours that the Blake-Castillo bill was going to be repealed. All those pointless deaths, all that needless pain: nothing had changed.

He hadn't done anything about the nagging thought but had sat with it, churning it around in his mind to see whether it stuck. He couldn't shake it, the idea that he had to make amends for what he'd done. That he had to make all the suffering mean something. The lives that had been damaged and lost created a debt that needed to be repaid. There was only one man who could help him.

Visitors and inmates were using the intercom system to trade words across the reinforced glass divide, and as he looked around, he could see that some of the conversations were heavy and sad, while others were alive with anger, but none could possibly be like the one he was about to have.

Steven Byrne shuffled towards the stool on the other side of the partition, and his face betrayed surprise as he took his seat. He'd recovered from his wounds, but looked tired and drawn, as though Rikers was slowly draining the life from him.

The media overflowed with stories and conjecture about the disgraced billionaire, but one tale that seemed true was that Steven had been betrayed by his lawyer Alan Cook. The bald man Wallace had seen sitting alongside Steven in the Senate Committee hearing had been blackmailed by Smokie into forging papers that had given the violent gangster control of some of Steven's empire. Cook had committed suicide rather than face the ignominy of arrest. Another betrayal. Another casualty.

Wallace lifted his receiver as Steven did likewise.

'John, what are you doing here?' he asked.

That's exactly how this begins, Wallace thought. He'd spent weeks imagining this conversation, and whenever he'd played it out in his head, those had been Steven's opening words.

'I want to make amends,' Wallace replied. He could never bring Erin or Max back, but he could prevent their father's life from ending in such abject failure. 'You told me that you wanted to do one good thing. One good thing to honour your children's memories before you leave this world.'

Steven nodded, his face sombre.

Wallace knew exactly how he felt. In his darker moments, he

thought about joining Connie, taking the easy way out and ending it all. But she deserved better. She deserved meaning, and Wallace was determined that something good would come out of all the destruction. He'd lost everyone who'd ever meant anything, including Christine Ash. He choked whenever he pictured her face looking up at him, her eyes blazing with boundless hatred. It pained him to think of the anguish he'd caused someone he loved so much. She was the last person who might have been able to redeem him, his only meaningful connection to the world. With her gone, and after everything that had happened, he knew that he could never have a normal life.

'It's not too late, Steven,' Wallace assured him. 'It's not too late for us both. We can do something good together. We can change things and make sure that what's happened to us – the pain, the people we've lost – we can stop that from happening to anyone else.'

Deeply moved, Steven stared into Wallace's eyes.

'I'm offering you my help,' Wallace told him. 'We can do one good thing before we leave this world.'

Acknowledgements

I'd like to thank my wife, Amy, for being nothing short of amazing. My three children, Maya, Elliot and Thomas, deserve medals for being so gracious about the amount of time I spend locked in the office with my imaginary friends.

My editor, Vicki Mellor, gets a special mention for all her valuable insight and for trusting her instincts and gambling on a story that would unfold over three books.

My thanks also go to her successor, Jen Doyle, for the hard work and inspiration that has helped shape *Freefall*.

Thanks also to Sarah Bance for copy-editing *Freefall* so thoroughly.

To Hannah Sheppard, my literary agent, for being such a delight to work with, and for a steady stream of beach photographs that remind me what the outside world looks like. Thanks also to Christine Glover, my wonderful screen agent, who ensured that *Pendulum* found a great home.

Jo Liddiard, Katie Brown and Helen Arnold did sterling work marketing, publicising and selling *Pendulum*, and have earned my eternal gratitude for helping it reach so many readers. I'd like to thank the entire team at Headline for making the publication of *Pendulum* and *Freefall* such wonderful experiences. I'd also like to thank the teams at Hachette Australia and Hachette New Zealand. I'm grateful for all your efforts.

I'd like to express my gratitude to Jason Bartholomew, Nathaniel Marunas, Amelia Iuvino, Elyse Gregov, and the whole team at my North American publisher, Quercus, for their sterling work. The first reviews of *Pendulum* came from Kate Moloney of Bibliophile Book Club, Liz Barnsley of Liz Loves Books, Jackie Law of Never Imitate, and Christine Marson of Northern Crime. As the first *Pendulum* reviews, these four will always be special, but I'd also like to thank everyone who takes the time to share their thoughts on my work. After spending months labouring over a book, it's encouraging to know that the effort is appreciated.

I'd like to thank my family and friends for all their kind encouragement and support. Janet and Jeff Ford, Paula and James McLellan, Shirley McLellan, Jonathan and Sheena Forrest, Sarah-Jane and Ralph Rogers, Jane and A.J. Johnson, Simon and Nessa Crown, Arvinder Mangat and Amanda Fong, J.B. and Clare Berty, Roy and Jane Hughes, Bryan Oxby, Maurice Leyland, Jane and Richard Sellman, Stephen and Belinda Bayfield, Neil and Kate Williams, Penny and Philippe LeToquin, Matt Hubbard, Phil Bland, Rachael Cahalin, Susan Hayes, Steve and Jane Ellsmoor, Lucy Cudden and Ifan Meredith, and so many others to whom I owe my sincere appreciation.

Winklewuss! You know who you are.

To all the crime and thriller authors who have been so friendly and welcoming: Anna Mazzola, James Law, Kate Rhodes, Mary Torjussen, Jenny Blackhurst, Roz Watkins, Felicia Yap and Kimberley Howe, among many others. I'd also like to offer special thanks to James Patterson for his kind words about *Pendulum*.

A special shout of appreciation goes to Dean Baker, Tom Coan and Tallulah Fairfax for helping me see *Pendulum* in a different light.

I'd like to thank my manager, Pat Nelson, for being a stalwart champion of my work. Also Adam Sydney, my author pen pal, who sends words of wisdom from his home halfway up a volcano, and Jenny Rowe for all her research and insight.

Graham and Hilary Sedgley and family deserve a special mention. If you ever fancy a second career, Graham, you might want to consider becoming a bookseller . . .

Thanks to Joe Haddow and Simon Mayo for making the BBC Radio 2 Book Club such a memorable experience, and I extend my appreciation to everyone who was involved in the selection process.

David Headley, Daniel Gedeon, Harry Illingworth, Emily Glenister and the entire Goldsboro Books team deserve special thanks for championing *Pendulum*.

Thanks also to Steve and Denise Lawson of the Nantwich Bookshop for supporting *Pendulum* and making me feel so welcome.

A nod of gratitude goes to Josh Sedgley for my author photograph, and I'd like to thank Ann Fisher and the Fisher family for making us feel so welcome at Oakley Hall.

To all the bloggers, reviewers and booksellers who helped spread the word about *Pendulum*, your enthusiasm is very much appreciated.

I finished *Pendulum* by thanking everyone who took the time to read the book. I'd like to reiterate my heartfelt gratitude. The world is full of wonderful books, so you have my thanks for choosing *Freefall* and taking the time to read it. I hope you enjoyed the experience.

Did you miss the explosive prequel to
FREEFALL?

You wake. Confused. Disorientated.

A noose is round your neck.

All you can focus on is the man in the mask tightening the rope.

You are about to die.

John Wallace has no idea why he has been targeted. No idea who his attacker is. No idea how he will prevent the inevitable.

Then the pendulum of fate swings in his favour.

He has one chance to escape, find the truth and halt his destruction.

But with a killer on his tail, everything can change with one swing of this deadly pendulum . . .

THRILLINGLY GOOD BOOKS FROM CRIMINALLY GOOD WRITERS

CRIME FILES BRINGS YOU THE LATEST RELEASES FROM TOP CRIME AND THRILLER AUTHORS.

SIGN UP ONLINE FOR OUR MONTHLY NEWSLETTER AND BE THE FIRST TO KNOW ABOUT OUR COMPETITIONS, NEW BOOKS AND MORE.